Children of the Master

Also by Andrew Marr

FICTION
Head of State

NON-FICTION
The Battle for Scotland
The Day Britain Died
Ruling Britannia
My Trade: A Short History of British Journalism
A History of Modern Britain
The Making of Modern Britain
Diamond Queen
A History of the World
A Short Book About Drawing
We British: The Poetry of a People

Andrew Marr

Children of the Master

FOURTH ESTATE·*London*

First published in Great Britain in 2015 by
Fourth Estate
An imprint of HarperCollins*Publishers*
1 London Bridge Street
London SE1 9GF
www.4thestate.co.uk

A catalogue record for this book is available from the British Library.

ISBN 978 0 00 759645 4 (hardback)
ISBN 978 0 00 759647 8 (trade paperback)

Typeset in Perpetua Std by Palimpsest Book Production Limited,
Falkirk, Stirlingshire

Printed and bound in Great Britain by Clays Ltd, St Ives plc

MIX
Paper from
responsible sources
FSC® C007454

For Isabel Claire

                        Kung walked

        by the dynastic temple
and into the cedar grove,

        and then out by the lower river,
And with him Khieu, Tchi,

        And Tian the low speaking
And, 'we are unknown,' said Kung,
'You will take up charioteering?

        'Then you will become known,
'Or perhaps I should take up charioteering, or archery?
'Or the practice of public speaking?'
And Tseu-lou said, 'I would put the defences in order,'
And Khieu said, 'if I were lord of a province
I would put it in better order than this is.'

And Kung said, and wrote on the bo leaves:
        If a man have not order within him
He can not spread order about him;
And if a man have not order within him
His family will not act with due order;

        And if the prince have not order within him
he cannot put order in his dominions.

And he said
        'Anyone can run to excesses,
It is easy to shoot past the mark,
'It is hard to stand firm in the middle.'

And they said: If a man commit murder
        Should his father protect him, and hide him?
And Kung said:
        He should hide him.

From Ezra Pound, 'Canto XIII'

Prologue
Photographs

A good politician seizes the moment; and if the moment resists,
she knocks the bugger against a hard surface until it gives up.

The Master

There are special days. Not so many. Far more often
come the amiable days when we dress, shower, eat and work,
when we laugh at one another and we pass on secrets, and
we eat moist chicken and drink cold beer . . . and none of it
really touches our inner selves. Most days we slip through,
the snow creaking, barely touching the sides. As in a symphony,
not every moment – not every day – can be intense. And
there are also the days whose smells, music and colours burn
themselves into us so that we are changed for good. On such
days, speckles of dirt on a kettle lid can be beautiful, and a
song whistled in the street can sit inside our skulls forever-
more.

Caro Phillips, who was a good person, believed that today
would be a special day. She pulled open the curtains and a
cold, pre-dawn light filled her bedroom.

She had acted ruthlessly. Because she had acted, everything

had changed. She saw the orange and green rug under her bare feet properly, for the first time. She'd bought it years before. Beautiful, just beautiful. She saw her dressing gown flopping from its hook on the door, a dollop of shadow beside it, and felt love for its soft familiarity. She saw her own shadow, quivering, and reached out to touch it. She didn't glance in the direction of the bedroom mirror, saving that until she reached the bathroom.

The face, as she'd hoped, was both familiar and, this morning, strange. It was a good face. Laughter lines; there had been a lot of laughter. A slight caramel tan, the residue of life-changing days in Rome. She smiled at herself: teeth tamed in adolescence by train tracks, a slightly overlong top lip, summer-sky-blue eyes. Ever since she could remember, she'd been able to knock people backwards, almost literally, with her smile – men and, yes, absolutely, women too.

And because she was a good person, all her life strangers had brought her good things. She looked harder into the mirror. No, not a sign of dangerous redness or a broken vein. Self-control, an early renunciation of delicious tobacco, and caution with alcohol. And then she looked at herself properly: the eyes were looking at the eyes, complete self-consciousness. This was the face of the king's first minister of the treasury, the most powerful face in the United Kingdom, the face of Nefertiti or Gloriana.

Now Caroline noticed its coldness. This was the face of a woman who had done something terrible – not murder, but something like murder. She felt she could smell her own electricity. She thought of poor Angela, poor sweet Angela, who smelled not of that, but of the coast, and of honeysuckle, and who was at this very moment in a cramped prison cell, perhaps bereft, feeling that her life was over. Caro washed, peed, showered, towelled and began to dress.

She could imagine the prison cell vividly. The walls would be painted to a height of about four feet in a medicinal green; and above that in white. They would be covered with little raised bumps, which would break and flake if you pressed them. There would be small messages, not many, scratched into the paint or written in pencil, not all misspelled.

Back in Caro's bedroom there was a large black-and-white photograph of Angela in a silver frame, given to her on a previous anniversary. Under the Master's direction, she had allowed a journalist from *The Times* to take that picture away with him after an interview; the paper had used it on the front page. It had done Caro a lot of good. Angela was staring with her dark, intense look, her wiry black hair blowing across her face like seaweed, her collar shining like a bone. The picture had been taken down at Pebbleton in Devon in the good days. Caro remembered taking it, and she noted that it was well composed: the stubby tower of the church, beside which they lived, was clearly visible over Angela's black-shirted left shoulder.

Behind Angela's picture, but larger than it, was a more recent photograph: the unmistakable, world-famous face of the Master. Caro had a lot to confess to him. He would talk as he always did about keeping it simple, about honesty and clarity and her brand. 'One lover, heaven; two lovers, hell.' That was one of his. But somehow, she felt, he probably already knew what had happened. He knew everything. Well, not everything; she would surprise him later.

Walking down the narrow stairs towards breakfast, Caro noted a great dark blaze of sunrise, a bruise-coloured mountain rolling fast across east London. Today was without doubt going to be special.

Then, on the bottom step, Caro saw the interloper. Wearing the familiar pink cheesecloth nightie, one bare foot tucked over the other to keep it warm, she was looking up at Caro with a solemn expression. It was the girl. Caro did not believe that her house was haunted, nor that, in any conventional sense, she had a guardian angel. But at important times, on days that mattered, she was accustomed to meeting herself, her earlier self, aged eight or nine; and talking. Caroline could see her ribs moving under the nightie, and her cold toes wriggling. She stopped. She could go no further, neither around nor through this . . . inconvenient moment, this folded, unavoidable interruption.

'Why the long face? I would have thought that today, of all days, you might want to celebrate with me. It's not as if I've killed anybody.'

The girl replied in a calm, clear voice. *But I used to have a lisp*, Caro thought. 'Caroline, you are not stupid. You know perfectly well that you can end a person's life without actually killing them. You can starve them of the future, and then they . . . waste away.

'Why are you doing this? You didn't used to be cruel. We were tough, you and me, but we were never cruel . . . I haven't killed Angela, not in any way, you silly little thing. She's destroyed herself. She was always weak, and you can't just hold up the weak forever. We have always been a good

4

person, and we still are. But now we have the courage to act, and make the world a better place.' For 7.30 a.m., and before breakfast, it was a long speech.

Caro's younger self seemed, if not satisfied, at least disinclined to continue the argument; so Caro walked through her, filled the kettle, popped on two pieces of toast and turned on Radio 4.

There was a lot to do today – media, the PLP, perhaps the Palace – and Caro couldn't afford to daydream or dawdle. As she sipped and munched, however, she allowed herself some quiet reminiscing. The soft side of Angela's breast; her tight tummy muscles; pushing her down onto a bed. Flushing slightly, Caro concentrated on John Humphrys, who was interrogating her Tory opposite number about the speech she'd given yesterday in the House of Commons. The poor chap couldn't decide whether he was for it or against it; whether it was an outrageous betrayal or a moral stand. Humphrys was having gentle fun with him, batting him around like a cat whose claws were still sheathed.

'Wa- wa- well, John,' went the south London MP, 'we've given Miss Caroline Phillips the benefit of the doubt, haven't we . . . We have to ask what she's wa- wa- wa- up to, don't we?'

'Yes, Mr Porter, we do, and that's why we asked you to come on the programme this morning, and that's why I have to press you for a clear answer.'

'Wa- wa- *wight*. Absolutely *wight*, John . . .'

'Have you any idea what you think, Mr Porter? Or perhaps, you haven't been told what to think yet?'

This was all too easy: the old Welshman wasn't even trying. Perhaps things were going to be all right after all.

Caro leafed through the *Guardian*. There was a poll showing the Labour lead down to five points. She scanned the news pages, but there was no mention of her. She knew she needed to get a move on, but still she lingered. She flicked over from *Today* to Radio 3, and struck lucky: a Mozart piano sonata, one of the B-flat majors; almost certainly Uchida. Yes, today would be a good day.

Before she left the kitchen table, Caro flicked her laptop open to check Twitter, her alerts, and Buzzfeed. Lots of below-the-line chatter from the usual racists, homophobes and sad-sacks; but from the party, nothing but bland approval.

The pre-agreed statement by the outgoing prime minister, Alwyn Grimaldi, was still running, unchanged.

The Rome conference, apparently, was still grinding on. The Mail Online had a picture of David there, looking lean and dashing in a white suit, with the vice president of the United States. They were speaking from behind lecterns set up in a conference room of the hotel, with their national flags behind them. The usual old bollocks, no doubt.

Rome had been . . . transformational. But that was not something Caro could allow herself to think about this morning. She put Rome into a small mother-of-pearl box to be opened later on, when there was quietness.

Caroline went downstairs, still listening to the radio: she'd had speakers positioned up and down the narrow townhouse so that she could follow a radio interview or, more often, music, from room to room. Then her train of thought was rudely derailed by the phone. That wasn't unusual at 7.32, but it was the house phone, not either of her mobiles. Who had that number? She couldn't bear to speak to her parents yet – the anxious bleating, tinged with disapproval. Still, curious, she picked up the receiver.

'That was magnificent. *Magnificent*. I told the editor. He wasn't sure. But I told him. Magnificent, I said. Absolutely magnificent. Speaking for the common people. Giving us all, in the Westminster bubble, a bit of a lesson, bit of a kicking. Magnificent. I'm saying so in my column today, and I've got them to put it on the front. They do what I say. I wanted you to hear it first.' Caro automatically moved the receiver just a little further away from her ear.

It was Peter Quint. Whenever she spoke to Quint, she had the sensation of being just a little dirtied; already she felt that there was greasy plug of something in her ear.

'Peter! How lovely to hear your voice. But I'm a little surprised, so early in the morning. We haven't spoken for a while. I thought you were very much a David Petrie man. Didn't you call him "the future of socialism" only last week?'

'Yes, yes, mock away. Now I'm calling you "the future of Britain", which I think trumps that, doesn't it?'

There was definitely something in her ear. Itchy.

'Peter, it's early. I'm heading off for a busy day. How can I help you?'

'Not just a busy day. This is a momentous day, Caroline – I can still call you Caroline, I hope – and I just wanted to know exactly how momentous. We're bidding for the first proper interview after you've moved into Number 10. I'd talk to your press people, but I wanted to give you a heads-up myself.'

'I'll get somebody to call you later, Peter, I promise. I'm all at sea myself, as I'm sure you'll understand.'

'Have you spoken to Angela? In your position, with all the resources of the Home Office, you must . . .'

'Goodbye, Peter.'

Loathsome man. But if Peter Quint was fawning on her to that extent, she must be home free.

The house phone began to warble again. Caro glanced at the number, and let it ring. She allowed herself to think properly about David Petrie, his Scottish joking and his dark, long-lashed, girlish eyes. Gay men, she knew, tended to like him. In all truth, before the past twenty-four hours he had hardly even looked at her, and had probably hated her on principle. But he'd made her heart race, long before they'd spoken properly, because of his naked, contemptuous and threatening ambition. Well, that was another unopenable door safely closed. And, after all, neither of them was free. He was married, and untainted by scandal. And she was famous for the other thing. No, it was completely impossible at every level. It couldn't be happening.

As she opened the front door, Caro drained the last of her coffee, and smiled briefly to herself. She would need David Petrie in the months ahead. That last little undefined crack of possibility kept her cheerful. The car was waiting. The office had sent the Rover, she hoped with Paul inside.

There was just one photographer outside on the pavement. She couldn't see any camera crews. Good. Fixing her face into a smile, she walked through the door and into the midst of half a dozen men who'd presumably been crouching behind the low brick front wall, and who now leapt into the air like a ragged rugby lineout. She reeled back slightly to avoid being hit in the face by a camera, and closed her ears to the sudden hubbub of questions, spittle-flecked lobs of sound – 'Oi, wha' say, Caroline?' – 'Arter a job?' – 'Oo's ya boss?' – 'Yah-yah-yah?'

She remembered what the Master always advised: 'Whatever they say, keep smiling. Wave at them. Smile, smile, smile. They're looking for a guilty or an angry face – that's what sells a photo to the picture desk. Smiles are small change.'

So that was what she did, not even flinching when one snapper, scurrying to get the best angle, banged against the wing mirror of the waiting car and knocked it off.

All the paps had their own personal tricks: one of them specialised in walking backwards in front of his target, and then appearing to trip and fall. The innocent victim would automatically reach forward, with a look of concern or shock, to catch him; and that was the picture the snapper had been waiting for – that grimace, that moment of shock. The snapper snapped fast, even as he was going down. More Westminster careers had started to slide downwards, the Master had told her, after a distorted face appeared in the papers, than had ever been destroyed by parliamentary inquiries.

Once she was inside the car, buckling up, Caro held her smile. Paul was driving. As the car pulled off, with hands banging on the roof, she closed her eyes and tried to remember her last peaceful moment that morning.

Leaving the house, she had passed a wall of pictures and

photos. There were snaps of Devon, of Angela, the boys. A Peter Brookes cartoon from *The Times* that showed her in a pulpit. A pin board just inside the front door was covered with scraps torn from newspapers, and other mementoes. Prominent among them was a stained, creased cardboard invitation, engraved with gold leaf and signed by the Master himself. He'd given it to her, and told her to keep it safe: 'That's where it all began.'

Absolutely No Partners

For the politician, every party, every social engagement, is a puzzle, a crossword to be solved. There are hidden clues, connections to be made, information to be passed on. You solve the puzzle. And then you leave.

The Master

Ten years earlier, when the new century was still a kid, that invitation had been new, stiff and with a thin line of gold leaf around its edges – just one of several hundred dropping that morning into letterboxes around London, Edinburgh, the Cotswolds. Each had the name of the recipient handwritten at the top in faultless italic, clearly by an expensive fountain pen held by an expensively educated hand. Then came swirls of black, embossed Gothic print. 'Neil Savage invites you to his All Hallows Party. Formal wear. Absolutely no partners. Refusals only.'

The party had been held at Worcestershire Hall, in Worcester Square, Mayfair. One of the last grand Edwardian houses still in private hands in central London, the address underlined the lavish nature of the invitation, and refusals had been few.

Neil Savage – more properly, Lord Lupin – was not, in any case, a man accustomed to being refused. Private banker, art collector, philanthropist, crossbench peer, he was known for his foul temper and his brilliant wit. 'Often disliked, never ignored,' he said of himself, with intense satisfaction.

And that Halloween, as the black German limousines nudged one another around the dark and windy square, the party had begun with a certain style. Young men, their gold-sprayed torsos bare despite the cold, stood at intervals along the front of Worcestershire Hall holding blazing torches, so the arrivals had to squint against the billows of smoke, and brush small embers off their clothes. Straggling up the Portland stone stairs and into the house, they were greeted by servants in white tie and tails offering cocktails with squid ink and peppers, vodka and absinthe. Champagne was available for the weak-stomached.

Lord Lupin himself, dressed all in black with a red bow tie, whiskers painted onto his chalky face, gave a passable imitation of Mephistopheles as he greeted the guests one by one. In they flowed: one former prime minister – no, two former prime ministers; half a dozen other senior politicians from each party; once-feared newspaper editors; minor royals, portly and inclined to be affable; radical playwrights with long, well-cut grey hair; radical establishment artists who made large plastic eggs for the Chinese market; gelded rock musicians; celebrated lawyers; notorious bankers . . . plus, of course, the shadowy PR men who kept the country moving – in the wrong direction. By 7.30 p.m. it was already clear that this was a party like no other; not a single face here, not one, was anything other than exceedingly famous.

In those days Worcestershire Hall had not yet been gutted; but it was dilapidated. Chilly, underlit rooms, with dusty curtains and dirty Dutch pictures, led off from one another in endless confusion. 'No Old Masters here, I'm afraid. Just Old Pupils. The family . . .' Lupin said. Dark little staircases spiralled up and down, apparently pointlessly. Only when the guests reached the old ballroom, laid out for a feast and glittering with hundreds of wax candles, was there any real glow of welcome. At one end, a small Baroque orchestra was playing melancholy and haunting music, a tripping gavotte, a dying fall. In front of the orchestra, exquisite young men and women dressed as satyrs and fauns were performing some old, complicated dance, as if in a Peter Greenaway film.

The guests gathered in knots, broke up again and re-formed as they circulated around the house. In even the most neglected rooms there was always a candelabra and a sofa, where a journalist or a photographer might be placed. The flashes of photography ricocheted through the house like perpetual lesser lightning. And there was plenty to photograph – all those seamed, creased, famous faces: the curving eyebrows and drawn, tortured, gathered-up and stitched flesh of actresses better known for who they had bedded than for their talent; the pendulous, hairy jowls and stained-toothed smiles of public servants. There a law officer, here a criminal; and here the two together, a hand resting lightly on a shoulder. Swarming through the dark honeycomb of the house, human crocodiles, human lampreys, human prairie dogs, all jostling and snapping when they spoke.

And, just as there was plenty to capture, so there was plenty to speak about, so many old friends to discover. Stories of old political battles, long-forgotten legal suits and complicated love tangles were being rehearsed as the drink disappeared. Good old Burgundies, flinty unoaked and vintage Chardonnays circulated on the silver trays – sweet, succulent southern sunshine for gaping, dusty northern gullets. For those who preferred, the best Islay malts and vintage brandies were there to scald and burn on the way down. The massive mahogany table at one end of the ballroom was expertly stripped by the beautiful staff, who brought round plates of bloody grouse, like the aftermath of a Balkan massacre, and slivers of white halibut, and dishes of oysters.

All was going swimmingly until, about an hour into the party, something strange began to happen.

It was like a quiet but irresistible wind. The susurration started at the downstairs bar, worked its way up the main staircase, arrived in the ballroom, and then pushed outwards into numerous smaller rooms and crowded corridors. As it shouldered its way through the guests, the disturbance gained strength. Gasps spread with the speed of an epidemic; mutters grew to the volume of a waterfall. Everywhere there was a shaking of the atmosphere, a shared shock you could touch and watch move from group to group. 'It' was nothing but comprehension, Lupin's boldest artwork taking shape. It was an awakening, the more real the more the guests looked around.

Almost every single person there, they realised, was not just famous, but infamous – disgraced. There in one corner were those who had lied while taking Britain towards damaging and dishonourable conflicts. Opposite them was a clutch of politicians who had been caught hiring themselves out like common prostitutes – and look, the men who had hired them – and observing it all from the other end of the room were the prominent, well-paid journalists who had ignored it because they were too busy bribing officers of the law in order to destroy decent people. Eating their canapés were NHS bosses who had tried to conceal deaths caused by incompetence and cruelty. Swilling down their wine were bankers who had destroyed their own banks and scurried off with barrowloads of money to roll in after they were stripped of their knighthoods. Loud laughter came from popular entertainers accused of raping young fans, and ex-DJs whose paedophile obsessions had become public. All evening Neil Savage, Lord Lupin, had been waiting, wondering when the penny would drop.

The very few who hadn't already been disgraced looked as guilty as if they expected it at any time. There, for instance, nursing a whisky, was the Conservative peer Lord Auchinleck, with a face like a swollen, furious baby's and pouchy eyes, his little pot belly squeezed into tartan trews of his own design.

Hardly anybody had been invited to Neil Savage's most lavish party who had not been publicly exposed for their greed, lust or overweening ambition. But mostly greed. Almost without exception, every person there had once been on the front page of a newspaper, looking ashamed – or shocked, as a photographer tripped over in front of them.

What kind of honour was this? What species of revelry? The wind of panic grew stronger. Within minutes, people were uneasily shuffling towards the front door, only to be confronted by another row of cameras. At Worcestershire Hall that night there was no hiding place.

It was a one-time lord chancellor, who'd lost his job because of his addiction to rent boys and cocaine, who confronted the host. 'What the fuck? *What the fuck?*' he spluttered as his large purple forefinger jabbed Savage.

Lord Lupin smiled coolly back. 'Fanny, Fanny, we're all friends here. What's the problem? Don't like the food? Don't like the music? You clearly do like the booze. So maybe it's the company?'

'This is some kind of sick trial by media, you ghastly little shit. Some kind of joke, and we are all the punchline,' replied the elderly man. 'I feel like making *you* my punchline, actually.'

'Calm down, Fanny.' By now there was quite a circle of equally upset men – and a few women – crowding around the banker-philanthropist host. 'Yes, all right, I am making a point this evening,' said Lord Lupin. 'You are the people *they* would like to disappear. You are the people *they* would like, for their own paltry peace of mind, to think are villains, rare creatures who break the rules. But you are not – none of you – anything more or less than ordinary human beings, with your appetites and your competitive instincts and – forgive me – your swollen cocks. And you are still here. I am still here. So laugh at disgrace, I say. Mock the smug hypocrisy of the herbivores and dreary midgets who pretend to judge you. Raise your glasses, drink deep and – *Welcome to the Underworld.*'

Lord Lupin regretted the party when he awoke around mid-morning the following day. After a lifetime of political interference, he'd learned that some of his best jokes had unexpected consequences. It was Lupin, back then simply Neil Savage, the aspiring rock guitarist, who had dissuaded the young Tony Blair from a career at the bar and pointed out to him that the then-failing Labour Party provided the smoothest route into Parliament and onto a front bench. It was he who, as a young man, had turned Boris Johnson away from his youthful Eurocommunism and towards the Bullingdon Club. Neither of these pranks had turned out exactly as he had expected.

And now there had been a death. It was most unfortunate. The ex-lord chancellor had followed Lupin's speech with a bellow, a flailing fist, and a heart attack. Central London roadworks ensured that the ambulance arrived late, and the overweight grandee expired. On the night for dead souls, there was now one more to remember.

After the Funeral

First, you know nothing — but they like you. Then, second, you know stuff, but they hate your guts. Between popular uselessness and loathed effectiveness, you have — how long? About a weekend.

The Master

The funeral had been a long one, in a polychromatic Anglican church so high that the streets for half a mile around smelled of incense. It had, apparently, been the ex-lord chancellor's wish to inflict on all his atheist friends the full rigour of a proper funeral service. A wit and a man of faith, as well as pederast, he had long abhorred services with Beatles music and heart-tugging slide shows of the deceased as a young child. Ritual was the best sedative for sorrow — common wisdom which had been forgotten. So all of those milk-and-water agnostics and politically-correct pew-dodgers had had to sit through endless readings from the penitential Psalms, from Corinthians and Revelation from the St James Bible, to kneel for prayers, shuffle forward for the Eucharist, and sit again for a socking long sermon that made disapproving reference to the All Hallows party.

After the Funeral

The ex-prime minister, universally known as the Master, who was in his way a serious believer, had read one of the lessons. After the service, with the coffin taken away for burial, half a dozen members of his former cabinets had stood around stretching their backs and rubbing their buttocks and wondering about lunch. The Master had a brace of limousines waiting, and he took them half a mile away, beyond the reach of the paparazzi, to a quiet public house, The Moon in Her Glory.

A back room, once reserved for 'the ladies'. A battered round deal table, half a dozen Victorian chairs, and a hatch for the beer.

'White-wine spritzers, everyone?' asked the former prime minister, slapping his hands together.

'A wee spritzer?' spluttered Murdoch White, the former foreign secretary and defence secretary. 'Hell's bells. You always were a degenerate metropolitan ponce. A small whisky and a half of IPA for me.'

'Murdoch, Murdoch. So predictable. You're an incorrigible dinosaur. You're like a bigoted, scaly old sea monster that only comes up once a decade to roll your eyes at us. Anyway, that was what we always drank.'

'Aye, when you were sodding prime minister it was. We'd have drunk cabbage water if you'd told us to. Now you're not.'

One by one the others — Margaret Miller, former home secretary; Sally Johnson, former party chair; Alex Brod~ industry and then briefly chancellor; the sly, Machiave figure of Leslie Khan, the party fixer and Northern Ir secretary – ordered their drinks. None of them asked for a spritzer.

The Master recovered quickly. 'Well, it may not be a proper oak table, but here we are assembled, the Knights of the Grail, together again for the first time since my esteemed former chancellor broke the enchantment and cast us out . . . Yeah, yeah, I'm joking guys, come on . . . But it's kind of good to be together again, isn't it?'

'Bloody sad too, though,' said Murdoch in a gravelly Ayrshire growl.

'Yes. Poor old Simon. What a way to go. He had many more years in him, I'd have thought,' said the ex-prime minister.

'No, no, I didn't mean that,' said Murdoch. 'Though it's a pity the poor bastard died with the anger on him. No, I meant it's a bloody pity we're all here, out in the cold, fuck-all use to anybody. Just – *sad.*'

Miller and Johnson, the two gatekeeper women who had supported the PM to the last, and beyond, broke in, protesting. Their leader, the Master, was doing good work in the Middle East, and raising large sums for Africa with his speeches. They both spoke at some length, and the Master had the grace to look faintly embarrassed. When they'd finished he shook his head, rapped the table as if calling for silence, and began to talk in that familiar tone of unctuous, confiding seriousness.

'No, Maggie, no, Sally. Murdoch makes a very good point. Yes, of course, we all do what we can. Public service runs through us; it's in our DNA. But where it counts most, here at home, we've become completely voiceless. New Labour has vanished back into the Labour Party – with, I have to say, entirely predictable results. The Tories have ripped us out of Europe. The Scots are off – partly, I confess, my fault. It's back to a choice, apparently, between permanent class war or heartless free-market fundamentalism, fairness or efficiency – but never both. Exactly the choice we devoted our lives to eliminating. I've never been as depressed about this country as I am now. We have capitalism, but we have no social democracy. It's a bloody waste . . .'

'And the worst of it is,' Leslie Khan interjected, 'we're all actually at the height of our powers. I know things I learned the hard way as a minister, and I've learned new things in business since. I know how to make a government department work, and I know how to rally public opinion. But I can't get a hearing. The newspapers, for what they're worth, won't commission articles from any of us. They don't even pick up on our blogs or tweets. That little shit who made fools of us all at his damned party had a point, perhaps. We are the politically undead. We live in limbo. We've always been frank with ourselves, so let's be frank now. This is a convocation of fucking zombies.'

'Agreed,' said the Master. 'Lurid language, but not so far from the truth. It might be a limbo of air-conditioned offices and first-class flights, with the occasional television studio thrown in, but it's a limbo nevertheless. Whenever I think I'm going to be let back into the conversation – when there's the right *Newsnight* moment, or whatever – I do my bloody best, but it's all "Yadda-yadda-yadda, Iraq, illegal war, liar, blah, blah, blah."'

'Fucking cunts,' interjected Murdoch. 'Hypocritical little shits. God, I hate the fucking *Guardian*.'

That got everybody, even Leslie Khan, who had once worked there, nodding their heads and grunting.

'It goes back to my old paradox' – the Master again. 'When you first arrive in power, you have maximum authority. You are the people's choice. You have momentum. The wind at your back. But you don't know how to *do* anything. By the time you've learned the lessons, worked out where the levers are and how to use them, sucked up all the tricks of survival, then ten to one your authority has gone. You've become discredited, disgraced, or merely boring. It's all over. You can have either wisdom or power, but never both at the same time. So my question is this: under such an arrangement, how can a serious democracy ever be properly run?'

There was a silence. The chips and the sandwiches arrived. Even they looked sad.

The former prime minister continued. 'You end up with the next lot of innocents, perhaps not making exactly the same mistakes, but lots of new mistakes of their own. Miliband. Grimaldi. And by the time they've learned from them, again, it's too late and they're out. For the past few years I've worked on the assumption that there's nothing that can be done about this. Our faces are no longer welcome. Nobody listens to us any more, and they never will. So all that accumulated understanding, from a little wisdom to a lot of gamesmanship, is just going to go to waste. But recently I've been wondering – Leslie, Murdoch, girls – *need it be so?* If our faces are too old, let's find some new faces. If we can't use what we know for ourselves, why can't we use it for others? When the left, the unions, don't like the way the party's going, they don't just sit back. They organise, as we know to our cost, and they try to take the power back. Is there any reason we can't do the same?'

Khan was brushing his little beard with tapering fingers. A little smile of delight appeared on his face. 'Oh Master, you're not suggesting we run *moles*, are you?'

'Entryists? Like a bunch of Trots?' barked White.

'No, not as such. But if we could identify just a few bright, talented, potential new leaders, and help them up the ladder, we could control the party by proxy. Fresh skins, sleepers – call them what you will. But sleepers for common sense, moles for the American alliance, entryists for a sensible European future – all that.'

'Manchurian candidates?'

'Well,' said the former prime minister, 'we don't need to go as far as brainwashing, still less assassination, do we? Just a little help here and there. A team. And we give the party a new leader, a better leader. A leader we have shaped, and who we control. Once we thought the future was ours. Let us dare to think it again.'

The Early Life of David Petrie

If you want to survive in politics, you need to have deep roots.
And if you don't, you have to pretend to.

The Master

For a small country, Scotland is geographically complicated. Parts of Ayrshire, for instance, look like the Highlands, particularly when the cloud is low. Shaggy, dun-coloured moorlands are populated by shaggy, shitty-bottomed sheep, crowding across roads that weren't resurfaced during the long reign of Queen Elizabeth. Just as in the Highlands you drive past grey, harled, barrack-like settlements of 1960s council housing, their desolate gardens fenced in with wire, and defeated Co-op stores, and scowling public houses with wired windows. But when the clouds lift, the absence of soaring mountains becomes apparent. Instead, weak riffs of sunlight show giant A's of steel and collections of industrial buildings. For this was once mining country, with conical bings like the burial mounds of ancient Strathclyde kings – and even now, years after Margaret Thatcher's death, the rusting steel sheds and the pervasive layer of coal dust haven't gone.

The Early Life of David Petrie

So this is a country where it's easy to answer the question: why do folk get involved in politics? If you relied on the papers, you'd think it was pure greed, with a pinch of vanity; and you'd be wrong. In David Petrie's Ayrshire, being Labour was like going to Mass, like learning to drink half-and-halfs, like supporting Kilmarnock, and like not hitting your women. It was what a proper, decent, grown man did. The folk memory of the miners' strike, the poll tax, the closure of Ravenscraig, was transmitted almost wordlessly, father to son, mother to daughter. And if a man needed any more explanation, the pudgy, braying faces on television — though Blair, mind you, was as bad as a Tory — rammed the lesson home. There were *sides*. Us, and them. Them, us. Chrissakes, pal, what more did you need to know?

It wasn't like that now, though. The Labour folk had been split and scattered by the 2014 independence referendum. These days, the Nats were better organised, strutting through the streets, 'Yes' badges all over the place, cocky as you like. A Saltire flew over the council chambers. But it wasn't always so. Back then, being Labour was bleeding obvious. The system, the whole bloody world, was set up to screw the working classes. The working classes had no choice but to fight back. Only the odd funny-looking Tory, in tartan trews maybe, or Presbyterian minister, or some kind of Orangeman, didn't get it. Davie Petrie had known this all his life.

Later on, when he was famous, everybody got Petrie's story subtly wrong. Wikipedia, the BBC website, profiles in both the *Spectator* and the *New Statesman* and a hurriedly-written biography by a rising young journalist, all missed what really mattered. Yet nobody would ever be able to say that Davie himself had lied about his own background. The public story, the official story, was all boot-strappy and hard graft: David Petrie had grown up in a working-class family in a village south of Glasgow, joining the trade union movement early and working his way up through scholarships to create his own building company, paying top-dollar wages to his boys, handing over chunks of his profits to local causes. It was a story of Catholic self-improvement, of the importance of family, the story of a clean-limbed hero. No university drinking clubs; no wealthy, behind-the-scenes patrons; just a simple, passionate, moderate, justice-loving man of the streets.

And a lot of that was true; but it was a sunny painting without shadows or dark corners – so much so, that the truth was a lie. There had been little that was decent or working-class about David Petrie's early life. He had been born in a privately owned bungalow in an Ayrshire village to an alcoholic local builder, a formidable bully, and his long-suffering, though in fact highly intelligent, wife.

Later on, David Petrie would be famous as a kind of survivor, like the sole cavalryman making it back from the Khyber Pass, all his comrades lying slaughtered in pools of their own blood. That is, he was a rare Scottish Labour MP after the Nationalists had poured down the mountainsides in 2015. Somehow, like a burr, he'd clung on. As Scottish voices had begun to disappear from London public life, Petrie's Ayrshire tones were still being heard in Parliament and on the BBC, an almost reassuring reminder of times that had gone. 'I feel like a dinosaur, to be honest, woken up to find the mammals have taken over,' he'd once said on *Breakfast News*. But like the dinosaurs, there was something unshakeably tough, almost stony, about the man.

David's first memories were of fear and pain. His father's head was out of focus, a blur of grey and red; but his hands and feet were close. Knuckles, the signet ring, the smell of shoe polish, a boot in the arse, a giant hand scrunching his jumper and lifting him up. Bellow, skelp. Sometimes, when the gate slammed and he heard Da's feet come up the steps, he filled his pants and trousers with hot pee. Then he was disgusted with himself, and almost welcomed the belting. It was an old, weathered black belt with a metal buckle. The boy David was also smacked, punched, left out in the garden in all weathers, and subject as he grew up to all the torments a self-pitying builder could devise. A Christmas holiday full of unlikely winks and vague, enticing promises would be followed by a Christmas morning, silent and present-less – Da oot, Maw locked in her bedroom.

Da oot, mind you, was a damn sight better than Da in.

'Come awa, son. It's time you came down to the fitba. Dinnae look so bloody scared. We're going to have a good time, you and me.' And sometimes, good things followed. A chip butty, a can of icy Irn Bru; being taught how to take a drag, deep and fragrant and blue.

But Da's moods were as changeable as scudding clouds. One can too many. A missed scoring opportunity. Cheek from the visitors' terrace. Then he'd feel a sudden poke on the nape of his neck.

'See ma boy? A wee Jessie I've got, is all. Doesn't understand a bloody thing about the game. Don't know why I bother bringing you, do I, Dolores?'

Even Da's mates thought he went too far. 'Dolores, big man? Where the fuck's that come from?'

'Well, look at the wee girl, with her big dark eyes. Disnae need mascara. Did you ever see sic a sight?'

And his Da was always right, of course; the tears stung their way down the side of his nose, and mixed with snot, and hung on his lip. He'd have his grey woollen jersey on, bought from the Co-op, and he'd wipe himself with the sleeve. And then his Da would whack him across the side of his face, and his Da's friends would go *Chrissake, Boabie,* but mebbe laugh. And the boys on the field would win or lose, but it didn't matter much. He wasn't a great boy for the football.

And then back at home, the belt. Thick, black leather, with wee yellow lines where it was cracking and with the metal thistle buckle at the business end. Beer and the belt. They went together like love and marriage.

Many years later, the adult David Petrie was told while being examined after a skiing accident that he had broken no fewer than four ribs as a child. He remembered the sleepless nights, all right. At the time there was no question of hospital. But a few deep white scars, like chalk marks, still remained on his back and legs.

The adult David Petrie was known as a snappy dresser – flash suits. The truth was, he bought suits with braces. He never wore belts. The adult Davie Petrie enjoyed a drink – a beer, a glass of wine, a gin and tonic. But the very faintest smell of Scotland's national drink, the sick-sweet scent from his father's open mouth, brought an instant queasiness. He simply couldn't stand the stuff.

His dad, Bob Petrie, was a very popular man. David only realised this much later: Da was liked. Other men wanted Da to be their friend. Out of the house, he told jokes. People laughed at them. Big Bob was a good workman and a relaxed boss. He liked a drink, everyone knew that, and where's the harm there? The bungalow was on the very outskirts of the village, surrounded by its own hedge. In space, enough space, a wee bit lawn around a wee bit house, no one can hear you scream.

Big Bob's big laugh, though, was well known in the pub. A low staccato series of growly grunts — *heuch, heuch, heuch* — building up to a full-throated *har, har, har.* There was a lot of laughing. His business grew fast, swollen by contracts from the local council. This was Labour territory, Labour people, Labour laughing. Bob was friends with the councillors, and actually a Labour Party member himself, although he never turned up at ward meetings — 'Nae time for blethering, no offence boys, I got a business to run.'

Only later on would Davie understand the kickbacks, the backhanders, the no-nothing-for-nothing; those raucous sessions in the bar were always about business first. *Heuch, heuch; har, har.* Big Bob sweated easily as he grew ever larger, but he was not a man to waste energy or time.

Neither David nor his mother Eileen were seen much in the village. They felt as they looked — at the edge of things. Sunday school, the Scouts, even lining up to jeer the idiot Orangemen, all passed them by. Bob was careful not to hit his wife on the face or arms — one of those tricks of civilised life passed down from some fathers to some sons. As David grew older and bigger, Bob's weekly beltings were replaced by the more painful methods of verbal terrorism. Jibes about his voice, mockery of his changing body. A hot, moist, whiskery, whiskied mouth at a bright red ear, a finger and thumb pulling him up by his sideburn. *Big girl's blouse, ya*. Once, just once, when he was changing for football at school, a teacher, Miss Leckie, had seen fresh welts on his legs. A social worker had come round to the house. David could still remember the tense little quartet of them sitting in the best room, his father forcing smiles and 'joshing'. *Heuch, heuch, har, har*. Like one of those plays from the telly. There was never the slightest chance of David being taken into care. Nobody wanted that. Bob's connections made it completely impossible; anyway, Davie would have hated leaving his mother alone in that overheated but cheerless house.

Mere misery doesn't kill you, not in Scotland. Davie grew up to be a silent, handsome, self-possessed young man. Layer over layer. Skin on thickening skin. And life got better. He found schoolwork ridiculously easy. The school library was small enough, but he read his way through it, the whole damned room. Maths, encyclopaedias, cowboy stories, it didn't matter. His second great escape as a teenager was discovering a natural talent for, of all things, football. He made the school team a year early. Bob, the big man, found this very hard to deal with: for years it had been an important part of his story that his son was a 'Jessie'. Yet here he was, big long legs, scoring goals and coming home covered in mud and bruises week after week. Grudgingly, Bob made his way to the touchline once or twice. Laddie worth something after all? Maybe he and David would finally have a real conversation – a Scottish one, of course, elliptical and self-mocking, more silence than words, but ending in grunts of assent and a feeling not unlike warmth.

They never made it. When Davie was seventeen, Bob was hit by a car as he was coming out of the pub. He was killed instantly, blood all over the pavement. Eileen laughed when Councillor Daley and the polis came round to break the news, which was put down to shock ('The puir soul, she can't accept it.' 'Aye, puir Eileen, what's she going to do wi'oot Boab?'). But David watched as her smile failed to disappear, remaining almost constantly on her lips for a full week afterwards. It was the most shocking thing he'd ever seen, but the truth was, he felt better too. When he came home from school in the afternoons Eileen had sometimes put the television on and was sitting boldly in the best room, eating ginger snaps.

Bob's funeral was a big affair in the village. The sun shone. The fields around, brimming with rasps and the dancing shaws of tatties – King Eddies and Désirées mostly – glinted and waved in the sunlight. There was a holiday air. By now many of the fields had been filled in by the spreading housing estate – nice houses, big windows, decent-sized rooms – Bob did good work – so that the boundary between town and village had almost closed up. Councillors and local bigwigs were all there, and the crowd from the pub, and a dozen relatives from Glasgow, so the RC chapel was packed. The local MP, a tall, pale, droning man, gave the eulogy, talking of how many houses for ordinary decent Labour folk Bob Petrie's men had built, what a supporter he had been of good causes – 'aye a haund in his pocket' – and how missed he would be as a father and husband. At this he poked the air, almost animatedly, as if he was looking to be contradicted. Davie, a man today, almost bursting out of his new suit, looked straight ahead with a solemn expression. His mother caused a flutter in the pews behind her by audibly snorting. She raised her chin, smiled slightly, and looked straight at the priest, a ferrety, pockmarked little Irishman, who avoided her gaze.

Bob's death had brought calm, even a kind of peace, to the bungalow. He didn't leave much behind him in the way of clutter. Eileen took his golf clubs and the porcelain model of Robert Burns he'd once given her down to the Oxfam shop along with his clothes.

But David Petrie's hopes for university were over. He'd been offered places at Glasgow, sixty miles north, and further away still, at St Andrews. Everybody said he was very smart. One teacher had used the word 'preternatural', which he and his mother had had to look up, and had a good laugh about. He had hoped to study engineering, or maybe even history. But the foreman, one of the few of his father's friends David had liked, had come to him and Eileen and made it clear that the business would vanish if there was no one to succeed.

A plan was agreed. Uncle Markie, a prosperous lawyer from Airdrie, would step in as boss for a year or two while David learned the ropes. Then, if it still existed, the business would be his.

Nursing a pint in the railwaymen's social club, Uncle Markie spoke about Davie to some of the lads from Petrie's Builders: 'He's a big, braw boy. Good stubble on his chin. No' as cheery, like, as the old man. Keeps himsel' to himsel'.

But bright, they say, a good head on him. And there's naebody else, Bob always telt me, ready to tak the wheel. So gie the lad a chaunce, eh?'

And indeed, Davie did have an old head on young shoulders. He quickly understood that without the right political connections, the company's work would dry up almost immediately. So he too joined the party, not bothering with the Young Socialists or any of 'that militant rubbish', and found he could speak well at meetings to creasy, crumpled, half-cut older men. He wrote cheques. He turned up for the quiet one-to-ones in back rooms. He picked up the council minutes before they'd been typed. He played 'a round or two', well enough, with lawyers and surveyors. As for the lads themselves, he learned the forenames and the nicknames and the kids' names. He could tell Bluey from Ham, Sparks from Gerry-Antrim. He learned who lived with his mother and who was the bright-eyed woman in the office with two men at home, not one.

He turned up at the ward meetings, and the branch meetings, and sat patiently while lonely men rehearsed the history of the party and the mistakes of the current leadership. He was sent to the constituency general management committee, and with only a year under his belt was chosen as a delegate to the national party conference. It was there that the drug of politics first entered his bloodstream, and he realised that perhaps there was more to this game than simply protecting contracts.

Home again, and the arguments were vicious, as they were all around Britain at the time. The so-called 'super colliery' had closed in the next constituency; there was still open-cast, but in the dark-grey pit villages around Glaikit the mood was bitter, though too mournful to be revolutionary. David Petrie defended his party leader with a passion and fluency he hadn't realised he had. It didn't make him popular, at least to start with; but it did get him listened to. By his early twenties he was almost as big a figure in the town as his father had been in the village. But he didn't stand for the council. He could either use his connections and reputation to build the business, and keep his mother secure, or he could renounce all of that – and for what? Ayrshire, Scotland, and the Labour Party could manage well enough without him.

So every day he came into work, as Petrie's vans pulled up outside the unfinished Keir Hardie Close or James Maxton Way; as the number of 'girls' in the office doubled, then doubled again; as the smarmy wee Prod at the Clydesdale agreed a much bigger loan; as he bought out a local scaffolding company and leased a dozen new cement mixers, young Davie Petrie would smile to himself and think, 'Fuck you, Big Bob. Aye – *you*, you second-rate cunt.'

So Petrie sat out the fag end of the Blair and Brown years, making money and growing thicker, and growing the company too. He married up, an Edinburgh graduate who had been to a posh school in St Andrews and whose father farmed a big estate. He built his own house, using stone from a new quarry north of Glasgow, and built a new bungalow for his mother next door to it. He fathered two children, and was a notably gentle and loving father to them. His PA noted that for the first time he was leaving work before 9 p.m., and told the office, 'It'll be the making of him.'

These were the years of the Scottish National Party's triumphant hegemony. Labour folk in Scotland sucked sour plums, kept themselves to themselves. Petrie didn't waver in his allegiance, but he made sure to get on well with his local MSP, and even to oil up to the housing minister in Edinburgh. He was old enough – just about – by now to play both sides.

From the outside, there was no doubt: Davie Petrie had survived, and more. Inside, it wasn't so easy. He struggled with his wife; he was slow to express affection. He hated being touched. At times, triggered by the most meaningless, trivial things – one of his sons laughing on the telephone, losing some paperwork – he would be overwhelmed by a black rage that had him shaking, his fists balling, his teeth clenched. This scared him, and he learned to deal with it, turning his back and walking away, using breathing exercises he'd been taught at a gym class. He kept himself fit. He liked to walk up the braes behind the village, where there was a little birch wood and a burn running down. He'd squat down and stare at the magic of the colourless water running over green stones, and rub his fingers on the moss and smell the wild garlic. He loved the view that spread out in the distance – wobbly blue lines of Ayrshire hills, with Glaikit and the colliery hidden in the foreground. Good times.

Well, mostly. Even then, some days, there was a blankness from the moment he awoke, a wall of white vapour, a background drone. He felt almost outside himself. Some other dim creature, it seemed, a badly-put-together, ungainly homunculus, was acting the part of David Petrie. Away from Glaikit, they might have called it depression. There were occasions, in the pub or at Tesco's, when he bumped into loutish young men he'd known as boys at school. In their presence, he felt himself shrinking: the wounds weren't yet quite healed.

By the time David Cameron and his snooty coalition were in office, David Petrie was being asked to speak to Labour conferences on behalf of 'small business'. Not *that* small, by now. He had money in his pocket. He had become a past master at the art of influence-peddling: money flowed out of Petrie Associates into the pockets of Labour councillors and council officials; more money flowed out of the council coffers into Petrie building projects. He had a *Mastermind* brain, right enough: special subject? Aye – planning permission.

Davie chose to distribute a little of his wealth to his party during the Miliband years. Largely because of a long-standing feud with the local Scottish National Party, he helped fund the 'Better Together' campaign against independence in 2014. Close call, but. His Nationalist minister friend from Edinburgh rang him at home and warned him that he was making a big mistake: a new Scottish state would be looking at major house-building projects, and would remember its friends. David told him where to go – 'Aye, right, and awa' to Kelty with *you*, Minister.' (They used to say, and not so long ago, that when the devil had finished building Hell, he used the rubble for Kelty, in Fife.)

For Davie and his kind, the referendum marked a complete change. It started with comments in the pub about the Labour Party being shoulder to shoulder with the Tories. Then there was some nasty business. A woman put up a 'No' poster in her window, and her neighbour, whom she'd known since they were girls, came round chapping at the door.

'Planning on staying long, Elsie?'

'Whit d'ye mean, Sally Catherine? All my life.'

'Aye, but your kind willnae be welcome round here after the eighteenth. Just a gentle word.'

Or so the story went. Davie never met 'Elsie', and no one could say exactly where she lived.

More worrying were the 'question time' sessions in the school, heaving with yes supporters, and the spread of 'Scotland, Be Brave' posters in shop windows, a daft, sexy girl in a kilt, wi' red hair; and a general feeling in the coffee shops and pubs of the town that it was nobler to be Yes than No. Was he still even on the right side? Once upon a time, no Catholic would have dreamed of going anywhere near the damned Nationalists, but that sleekit Alex Salmond seemed to have won the archbishop round somehow. These days, if you boasted a season ticket at Celtic Park, you were almost certainly a 'Yes' man. So Davie's moral and political planet began to crumble at its little green edges.

There was even talk that the SNP would take the constituency from Labour for the first time ever. They were certainly digging in up north in Glasgow, though hereabouts there was a strong local party, still with the old inherited NUM discipline. Lanky Boswell, Davie's second cousin, who'd gone on to uni in Dundee, and come back as a primary teacher and raving Nat, would seek him out some nights in the pub after work and give him gyp.

'See here Petrie, you're a good guy. You just haven't been paying notice, and you find yourself on the wrong side. Folk around here don't like you playing footsie with the Tories. They just want – no bedroom tax, keep the health service going, dinnae grind the faces of the folk on welfare – all the things you want too, I know, Davie. Whit's the problem?

'The London Labour Party's corrupt, just pale-blue Tories. It's not too late to come over. We're a broad church and we're friendly folk; you ken most of us already.'

Davie would respond with his old lecture on the 'Tartan Tories' and the importance of solidarity, and of building social democracy right across the United Kingdom; but he found himself almost wearying of his own arguments. The truth was, the 'Yes' folk had made some bloody good points. Quite a few local party members had defected. Inside, Petrie was still angry and bored, but when it came to politics, it was all too obvious that time was short. If he was a Labour man, it was time either to do the necessary or to get off the pot.

A Perfect Girl

I don't know what charisma is. Nobody does. But it comes from God, and it makes power tolerable.

The Master

Caroline Elizabeth Phillips's seemingly effortless success in life had been based on two things. The most important was her irresistible likeability. Whenever she walked into a room, whether it be the lounge bar of a pub or, later on, a dreary, low-ceilinged political meeting room, the temperature rose. People who had been down in the dumps found themselves smiling; misery-gutses discovered they just wanted to be liked. This, apparently, was charisma. She'd had it since she was a toddler. She was the kind of small child whose hair every adult wanted to ruffle. She smiled, they smiled back. Easy. Sometimes she almost glowed. Yet her father, Thomas Phillips, was a dourly forgettable man of business. People struggled to remember his name even if they were closely related to him. Her mother, Simone, was sharp-tongued and energetic, but, like her husband, essentially bland – bland with lemon sauce. Between them they had produced a source of light. It was as surprising as if two affable Burgundian peasants had given birth to a saint, complete with spangled wings, or as if a pair of Brummie shopkeepers had spawned a multi-coloured dragon. Of course you'd have to know the family to understand just how extraordinary it was. In photographs, Caro looked pretty enough, but not remarkable. In the flesh, her oat-coloured radiance entranced everyone lucky enough to come across her.

Caro disapproved of the word 'lesbian'. 'For one thing, it denotes an islander, it's inappropriately geographical . . . And beyond that, people make assumptions,' she had told her mother (who certainly did). 'They think they know what music I like, my political opinions, how I decorate my house. They think lesbians are driven by sex, and have "pashes". Lesbians wear lesbian clothes, and eat lesbian food, and watch gloomy Nordic lesbian films about gloomy Nordic lesbians. Well, if even part of that's true, then I'm not a lesbian. I'm an old-fashioned, friendly, meat-eating, Christian woman who happens to love other women. Not even that. *An* other woman.'

That other woman, Angela, had been known as 'Pep' when Caro first met her – tall, dark, and only just a teenager. Pep stood for pepperoni, which stood for pizza, which stood for pizza-face. Angela had suffered from relatively mild acne. That was the kind of humour their school specialised in.

To a visitor, this school looked warm, even cosy. Based around a 1930s country house in Sussex, originally constructed for a shipbuilding tycoon, it had many acres of games pitches, and modern outbuildings. Queen Eleanor's prepared the daughters of wealthy commuters for Russell Group universities. From the outside, it might have been a spa resort or an affluent golf club. The main building had a pleasantly arts-and-crafts feel to it; with its long, sloped roofs, high chimneys and cream pebbledash, it spoke of a conservative-minded, late-in-the-day architectural admirer of Ruskin and Morris. 'Pleasant' was a word that was often used of it. Just like Sussex itself, Queen Eleanor's was . . . pleasant.

But behind the fresh cream paint and the well-kept hedges, the school was not what it appeared. Its pupils were mostly sturdy, normal, healthy-looking girls with their hair in clasps, their gleaming metal orthodontics and their knees the colour of turnips. But there is nothing on this small green planet as dangerous and terrifying as English schoolgirls in packs. On the surface, serge and cheesecloth. Below it, claws and fangs, the splash of blood and the muffled squeal. Girls left this lovely school prepared to throw themselves into abusive relationships or starve themselves to death, or if they'd done pretty well, settled for decades of dogged, surreptitious alcoholism. A girl might come to Queen Eleanor's with a straight back and a clear eye; she would be lucky to leave without slouching – hating herself, curled up, sarcastic. Emotional survival in this pleasant – so, so pleasant – place, with its choir which did Purcell, and its glossy, neatly-lettered rolls of honour, was harder than in the drab council estates of Ayrshire.

What about the families? Powerful men who knew about the world – barristers, accountants, company directors – sent their daughters there. In due course, later on, they would idly wonder why little Sarah, Penelope or Tessa had become so sullen, so thin and so uncommunicative on the family's annual skiing holiday to Val-d'Isère. What had happened to the once-easy conversations around the breakfast table? Once in a while, a particularly bold father might clear his throat and ask Julietta or Tamara whether she was happy. In response he'd be confronted by a face as white as a sealed envelope, or a shrug of skeletal shoulders. He would rarely press the point: Queen Eleanor's sent its platoons of damaged young women to Oxford, Cambridge and the cream of foreign universities. It attracted the offspring of television celebrities, and it was the most successful sporting girls' school in the Home Counties: its hockey team thrashed the London day schools, and it had one of the best girls' football teams in England. It was a school parents boasted of; but to thrive there, you needed not only to be pretty, but to have a poisonous tongue and a hide like an armoured personnel carrier. Suicide attempts were not unknown, though none had recently been successful when Caroline Phillips, long-limbed and handsome, glowing with self-confidence, had been dropped off by her nervous parents and left with two large suitcases to unpack.

She, and they, had expected a dormitory, but by that time the girls got their own bedrooms, although bathrooms were shared. Trying to forget the empty feeling in her tummy as the family Audi turned and headed back down the school driveway, Caro had just begun laying out the lilac-striped shirts, the blue skirts and endless pairs of white socks when suddenly her door was shoved open by a pack of hunting girls, smelling of tobacco and peppermint. She was shoved down onto the bed, her cases upended on the floor, and she was subjected to an hour of relentless questioning – boys; fit brothers; bleeding yet? Did she do herself? Ciggies; pills; any spare cash?

Humiliated but dry-eyed, she survived. Before they'd left she had handed over the £60 her father had said should last her the whole term, and a small box containing a pair of earrings, just given to her by her mother as a starting-school present.

'We are the bitches, we are the witches. Make us rich and never snitch, or we'll cut your throat, no hitches,' Farola Ponsonby and Africa Crewe chanted as they left her.

Caro wondered whether her looks and her ability on the hockey pitch might not, after all, be enough to protect her. She carefully refolded her clothes and put them away. She pulled out the framed photographs of her parents and her brother. And she put them away too.

It was several days later, while playing table tennis, that Caro first noticed Pep. Pep was very tall, very thin, freckled, with intense dark eyes and cascades of black hair. And yes, there was some acne. The thinness was not unusual at Queen Eleanor's – even the teachers joked that each year was divided into A and B streams, anorexia or bulimia. But the intensity of Pep's stare was extraordinary. The moment their eyes met, Pep looked away again, but Caro felt an instant, completely unfamiliar shudder.

The two girls soon struck up a friendship based on reading, cheerfully incompetent hockey and music. They hung around together. In year four, Caroline put an arm around Pep's bony back. In year five, Pep returned her kiss; her mouth smelled of peppermint, and their tongues touched. By then they were leaders in the school Christian Union, and were an admired, deferred-to couple. At Queen Eleanor's this was hardly exceptional. The school had a long-established Sapphic reputation, and at a time in British history when lesbianism was going mainstream, this caused barely a ripple among the parents. To have a gay daughter was, for a dull executive on the London commute, chic.

As for the staff, they had plenty of other things to worry about. Caroline and Pep were among the girls who had developed to a fine art the communal destruction of teachers. One of them might begin to hum, in a high tone, in the middle of a lesson. Another would pick up the hum, and it would spread around the class. As soon as the teacher pounced in one direction, the noise billowed up from another. Group punishments had no effect. There is nothing half as frightening and destructive as a group of middle-class English girls intent on mischief, and Queen Eleanor's was not alone in being unable to cope.

The high mistress, the chief uncoper, was a large-bosomed, horse-faced woman whose greatest talent was her inability to see what was going on in front of her nose. Everything about the school was *marvellous*. Her girls were *marvellous*. She was lucky in her *marvellous* staff. She had surrendered long ago. She walked the corridors with a glassy, painted grin, in a bubble of invincible optimism. It so chanced that idiot optimism, an inability to see looming disaster on every side, was a considerable skill in the Britain of her time. She could have run anything – a lousy, malodorous hospital; a violent, drug-infested prison; a tax-squandering, inept government department. In each case her smile would have been as bright, her self-confidence as intact, and her calmness hugely reassuring to all who worked for her. Everything would have been splendid.

So there was, as far as the high mistress was concerned, no 'mucking around' at Queen Eleanor's. Once, and once only, she had been persuaded by a newspaper article of the need to give the girls a lecture. But all her glossy circumlocutions had made this entirely pointless: the younger girls had no idea what she meant by 'skulking in dark corners', and the older ones had simply tittered. Anyway, the teaching staff were almost unanimous that the alternative – insanitary, dangerous and occasionally life-wrecking 'messing about' with boys – was worse. As the deputy head once remarked, 'I'm so old I can remember when the girls who kneeled were the pious ones.'

By the time they were in the upper sixth, of course, Caro and Pep had fallen out, and were barely speaking. Caroline's charisma meant that she was constantly surrounded by admirers – sporty girls, musical girls, oddball girls. Pep, meanwhile, embracing her frizzy, black-eyed eccentricity, had plunged into darker places, cutting and 'restricting' and reading far too deeply.

The day came when Caroline's parents were called in for the 'What next?' conversation with the headmistress.

'Caroline is exceptionally talented. She will do exceedingly well. She has done marvellously here and we have done marvellously with her. But we cannot quite decide, just at this moment, at what, exactly, dear Caroline will excel.'

Her mother asked what sort of careers Queen Eleanor's girls tended to pursue.

'In the old days, it was all public service – the Foreign Office, the army, and so on. But . . .' Her voice faded away. This was a hard one. In the *Queen Eleanor's Chronicle* she had become a past headmistress of the art of euphemism. Patti Vidal, undoubtedly the stupidest girl the school had ever known, had become a glamour model, largely famous for her hindquarters. Few of Patti's films could be referred to by name, never mind seen, by decent people. 'Actress', the head-mistress had written firmly. 'Royal Shakespeare Company, etc.' Amy Brewer and Madelyn Strindberg, from the following year, were currently serving time in a Singaporean prison after a few exciting months as drugs mules. 'Working in international pharmaceuticals' appeared against their names. Lorraine Gatto, who had been a senior prefect, had apparently now opened a dungeon off Sloane Square, complete with whipping bench, nipple clamps, a suspendable cage and other useful gadgets. The headmistress had thought long and hard about Lorraine – such an obliging girl – before writing the single word 'Rehabilitation'.

But, faced with these transparently pleasant and intelligent parents, she hesitated. 'Many of our girls these days go into entertainment – film, television, music, that kind of thing – and others do charity work. But Caroline is especially gifted. Everybody wants to be her friend, you see. She sings like a bullfrog and dances like a cow, but she lights up a room.'

'You're not suggesting she just waits around to find some chap to marry, I hope,' her mother said.

'Absolutely not. With the spread of pre-nups and so forth, we no longer recommend marriage. No. The extraordinary thing about Caroline is that people *believe* her. I think she needs to do something quite big, perhaps something in public life.'

'Politics? She says she'd like to read politics at Edinburgh.'

'You know, I was thinking more of banking. I think she's too nice, too straightforward, for politics,' said the headmistress.

She had rarely ever said anything as nice about any girl to her parents; but on this occasion she was dead wrong. Caroline was perfect for politics.

Pep's parents, who had adopted her as a young child, never actually turned up to see the headmistress. There was no need. Their girl was utterly determined on a religious vocation. Her mum and dad joked that she'd become a nun. They were spared that. Angela studied theology at Sheffield, and after a year travelling in South America, she returned determined for ordination as a priest in the Church of England. Since they had left Queen Eleanor's, Caroline and Angela had completely lost touch.

A Terrible Story

They think we are cynics. But if you don't come into politics to make the world a better place, you'll quickly find it a desolate trade.

The Master

There was literally nobody in Glaikit who David Petrie would have considered less likely to recruit him into a real political career than Tony Moretti. They'd known one another since school. Tony had been a couple of years ahead of Davie, and he was the same stoop-shouldered, lank-haired malcontent now that he had been back then. He'd been a Yesser, of course. The son of the local chip-shop owner, he was now a journalist – what else? – working for the Scottish Socialist newsletter, which at least kept him virtuously poor. He'd regularly denounced Davie's father and the Labour clique in the council, which rather put him up in Davie's estimation. Years of serving in a fog of cooking fat had given him a red, slightly pockmarked face, and his politics were appropriately rancorous; he seemed somewhere to the left of Galloway and Sheridan. So when Davie opened his door one evening to see Tony sternly staring back at him through his thick glasses, he had been unwelcoming – polite, but unwelcoming.

'Weel, Moretti. This *is* a surprise. Come to see how the "embourgeoisificationists" are doing?'

'Naw, Mr Petrie. Here with a story. Need your help.'

Eyebrows raised, Davie had let him in, helped him off with the scruffy, revolutionary-badged leather coat, and made him a cup of tea. It turned out that Moretti had one hell of a story; one that would change Davie's life.

It all went back to the Forlaw massacre, he explained. A deranged gunman, a loner called Tom Hooper, had killed fourteen schoolchildren getting off a Scouts bus, as well as the driver and a passing policewoman. He'd then turned the gun on himself, but had succeeded only in blowing off part of his jaw. Patched up, convicted, voiceless and despised, he was now one of Scotland's most heavily protected prisoners, at HMP Grampian. It turned out that Hooper had been involved in anarchist as well as survivalist groups, and Moretti had been working on a theory that somehow he'd been drugged before the attack, as part of a conspiracy against the far left. To Petrie's surprise, Moretti told him that he'd been allowed to visit Hooper in jail. That was why he needed his help.

'Seems a bloody mad conspiracy theory to me, Tony. I hope that's not why you're here.'

'Naw, Mr Petrie, that was a'ways daft. It's what he told me efter that made my hair curl.'

'Looks straight enough to me, Tony. And less of the "Mister". Fire away then.'

'Weel, Petrie, it wis a sore long bloody trek to get to see

the man at all. His lawyers didn't want me to go. This guy's so hated they don't want another word written about him – ever. Time and memory loss; they say that's his best hope. Mebbe so. But, see, I didn't understand why anything mattered to that guy any more, a man who'd been political, after all. Family don't visit, naebody visits. Naebody asks what he knows. So I said I was writing a book. A lot of hassle with the prison service, right, but at last I get permission to contact the guy directly. He writes back: Okey-dokey, come over. The prison's south of Peterhead. New, like. Train to Aiberdeen, then the bus. Guys like him are kept on their own corridor, bottom floor. They didnae want me wi' the other visitors – with a' the neds, I guess, he's had a few beatings already – so we meet in his cell, wi' the screw standing by. With me so far? Right.

'I asks Hooper to tell me about his political views. He just shakes his heid. I tell you, Mr Petrie, he's a terrible sight. Nothing much on the wan side beneath his cheek, just a great hanging sack of purple, and lang white scars. He's got a wee mouth left on the other side. He can suck up food through a straw, but he cannae speak.'

Davie felt queasy. Tony Moretti was not what he'd expected. He was composed, direct and unembarrassed. He seemed to have human sympathy for this man who Scotland was trying to forget. 'That's terrible. I thought these days – you know, reconstructive surgery?'

'Naw, not for the likes of him. Anyway, I ask him ma questions. But he's no' interested in a' that tripe. He just writes some notes of his own.' Moretti delved into a scuffed shoulder-bag. 'I brought them.'

There were a few short notes written on torn pieces of lined paper, in pencil and in awkward capital letters – not the writing of an educated man.

<u>WRONG</u> I HAD <u>GUN</u> AT ALL
POLIS SAID I COULD NOT
TOLD GO STUFF THEMSELVES
<u>MINISTER</u>/NOS WHAT I CAN SAY
NO. BODY BELEEFS ME

'Not sure I can make head or tail of these, Tony. What's he saying?'

'Well, I asked him, of course, and he can nod and shake his head. Turns out the local police tried to get his gun licence revoked. He'd always been a weird one – reputation for hanging round schools, that sort of thing. And he did have pretty wild views. But the police recommendation was squashed, over-ruled, whatever, higher up the chain.'

'Who by?'

'Good question. I tracked down the chief copper from back then. First off, he didnae want to talk to me – "troublemaker" and all that – but I wore him down. Turns out that quite a lot of Hooper's story is true: the copper did try to get Hooper's firearms licence removed, he told me, but the chief constable intervened. My man didnae argue. Nae point. Pension, and a'. Efter we were finished he started greeting. Man o' seventy years, but.'

'What about the chief constable? Did you go to see him?'

'He's dead now. But wan step further up the ladder, the

guy Hooper says was behind it all is very much alive and kicking. Lord Auchinleck these days, Tory minister at the Home Office at the time. Freemason, I'm thinking. Big golfer, and – you guessed it – best pal of the dear departed chief constable.'

One step at a time, Davie thought to himself, and you could end up taking a very weird journey. 'I think that's what they call circumstantial. Why would Lord Auchinleck concern himself with the gun licence of an obscure saddo and – forgive me, Tony – political nutter, living in a small town in Scotland?'

Moretti smiled a slow, sad smile, and his dark eyes caught Davie's.

'Bingo! Right damn question again, Mr Petrie. You could make a useful legman for the newsletter yet.'

He paused, and his voice became slower, deeper. 'Have you heard of the Cricklewood Boys' Home affair? No? Well, this is where it gets verra interesting. It wasn't a proper home, apparently, more a kind of haulfway hoose for lads coming out of young offenders' institutions and council care. Lots of skinny, fucked-up, scared wee boys living there in the 1980s and 1990s. You ken where I'm going?'

'I'm afraid so.'

'Well, so I am. It was a wee paradise for paedos. Early days of the internet. Harder back then. Nods and winks. Men came from all over. Tom Hooper, for one. Politicians as well.'

'A certain chief constable? A certain Lord Auchinleck?'

'Aye. And *aye*. So they couldn't have wee Tommy Hooper shooting his mouth off, could they?'

'Not the most felicitous expression, Moretti, and still circumstantial. But – sweet *Jesus*. A sex ring cover-up that led to the Forlaw massacre. That's fucking dynamite.' David Petrie exhaled. He felt sullied, as if he needed to take a shower. He felt himself shaking with anger as well. He thought of his two boys, and those waifs in a north London hellhole. It was like something out of Dickens. No. It was worse than that.

'So why'd you bring this to me, Tony? It's the biggest story of your career.'

'Well, I guess that's it – the career. I've got strong principles, Mr Petrie, the kind I'm afraid you and your like will never understand. But that makes me suspect in the eyes o' the wider world. There's a huge effing cover-up gone on. It isn't just Auchinleck – there's a whole bunch of them. I wouldn't be surprised Labour as well as Tories, Liberals too. We go big on this in the newsletter and they'll just stamp on us a'. Bring in the high-heidyin lawyers, criminal libel, you name it . . . Just some kind of left-wing conspiracy mania. But you – you're different. The chancy wee footballer, son of the big man, wha's dribbled and dodged his way intae the Premier League. You've spoken at national conferences. You've met the likes of Miliband and Straw, and that top shite Murdoch White. Wan of them speaks out on this in public, and the balloon goes up. It a' goes sky high. It'll help Labour in the next election – and Christ knows, you're going to need some help under that bampot Grimaldi. It'll help you too, because you'll get the praise for bringing the story out. And it'll help me, because you fucking well credit me for this or I'll tear your balls off, Mr Petrie, no offence. We'll get it into the nationals. And then we'll get the bastardy bastards, and give those poor wee boys the justice they've been denied.'

David Petrie realised two things. First, that he'd badly under-estimated Tony Moretti. Second, that he had no choice. Politics, if it was about anything, was about justice. Boyhood should be sacred. His job now was to take this story and rub the faces of a few men in the shit until they cried for mercy. To his surprise he found himself feeling elated. Energetic. He wasn't bored any longer.

On an Island

Always, the politician must inspire people; but not in a ridiculous way, obviously. Not too much . . .

The Master

When, a few weeks later, the former foreign secretary Murdoch White, himself an Ayrshire man, who had retired to the Isle of Arran after the Egyptian war, called him up and asked him to come for a visit, and to stay the weekend, Davie Petrie was ready.

Most of Labour's leading figures from Scotland, back in the day, seemed to have died early, or faded away from politics: Smithy himself, big Donald and wee Cookie all went far too early, while Derry, Brian Wilson up in the Highlands and John Reid, now running Celtic, had absented themselves from political life. Murdoch White, however, was still a player in his seventies, a tall, gangling, balding man with a hangdog face, he had kept the flag flying against the SNP and was a regular on the Scottish edition of *Newsnight* – variously known as *Wee Newsnight* and *Newsnicht*. He had retired to play golf and fish, but found that he missed the excitement of Westminster.

The converted manse he had bought looked more like a small baronial pile, white-harled and spacious. Ostensibly, he had lured Davie there to talk about building a glass-fronted extension looking out over the Atlantic breakers. The two men spent most of the weekend walking together and staring at the view, or sitting over a chunky glass – malt for White, gin and tonic for Davie – and, as Davie put it to Mary later, 'Just blethering.'

Not just. Murdoch needed to know whether Petrie was 'sensible'. By this he meant, was he basically pro-American, sound on Israel and pro-business?

'A long time ago, Davie, when you were just a bairn, the Labour Party made itself unelectable with basically communist views. The Master, with quite a few of us helping him, changed all that. He showed that we can have social justice and prosperity at the same time; if we don't shoot for the moon and if we accept the realities of the world, we can make life better for folk, and they'll trust us. So not too much of the teenage Trotskyism, eh Davie? Another glass?'

'Small one, Mr White. You can rely on me. I'm solid working-class, and I won't sell my people out. But you know I'm a businessman first and foremost. I deal in balance sheets. Hiring and firing. Foreign markets don't concern me – yet – but I was born with a good hard head on me. I'm not very keen on the Yanks, but who else do we have these days? The fucking Palestinians don't make *me* weep.' He rapped his forehead with his knuckles. 'Hard heid.'

'Europe?'

'Ach, it's a corrupt old bunfight, but there's too much

money there. By hook or by crook, we have to get back in. No' the euro though.'

'As for yourself, what do *you* want, Petrie?'

'You won't be expecting this, Mr White, but the real answer is justice. There's a guy I want to bring down, and I'm going to bring him down if it's the last thing I do.'

White raised his eyebrows but said nothing as Davie – he couldn't help himself – spilled out the story of the Forlaw massacre, the child sex ring, and Lord Auchinleck.

When Davie had finished, Murdoch White puckered his mouth. 'It's a horrible story. On the other hand, Auchinleck was always a horrible man. Known him for years. Thank God he's not one of ours. Well, once you're an MP – *if* you become an MP – you can certainly take him down. Parliamentary privilege is a fearsome weapon in the right hands.'

'You say if I become an MP?'

'The selection's the thing. Nicola Sturgeon and Alex Salmond – slippy wee fishes – have almost wiped us out. After 2015, our game's all about survival. Hold on to the redoubts. Don't let the bastards through. Fix bayonets. Ireland rations. All that. One day, seat by seat, we'll fight our way back. But even now there's a few wee places the bastard Nationalists haven't got. Glaikit's wan. So get selected, and you'll be elected as an MP. Can't help it, really. The old guy's retiring – we've helped him along a little, and in any case, it's the kindest thing for him. His ticker's shot. But getting selected isn't a formality. It's a plum constituency, so all the busy little bees – the sleekit Oxbridge boys and girls, never done a hand's turn – will be up from London buzzing around.

Crusade will have their union candidate too, and he – or she – will be formidable.'

Davie had worked all of that out long ago. 'Aye, but it's hardly impossible. I'll be the local candidate, unless they line up the council leader. And I've got a lot of friends in the party.'

Murdoch White snorted. 'No, you dinnae. There are no friends in our trade, laddie. You can't control what Crusade do, so you'll have to stitch up all the branch parties early on. Hard graft, no help for it.' He bent over and vigorously rubbed his face with both palms, as if massaging himself awake. 'It's an illusion to think the local candidate has an advantage. That's what the newspaper writers will tell you, but they know nothing. The truth is, most folk – our side, Tories, Scotland, England, anywhere – are looking for somebody they can project their hopes and ideals onto. They know fine well they're going to get fooled again, but they want to *believe* – somebody fresh, bit of glamour, clean sheet of paper. They don't necessarily want Davie Petrie, that guy who's been hanging around Glaikit half their lives. Go into this thinking you're ahead and you'll fall flat on that bonny face of yours.'

Petrie shrugged, and raised his eyebrows.

'You need two things, my young friend. You need a story – something to inspire folk. I can help you with that. And you need to show some steel. That bit's up to you.'

Davie was uncharacteristically quiet over lunch on the Sunday. He handed across the drawings for White's extension that he'd brought with him, along with several pages of cost- ings. He'd brought two sets. The one he passed over had a 20 per cent mark-up on them; the other 10 per cent. White wanted him, quite clearly; he might at least turn a little profit from that. Neither man was feeling like small talk. By the time a local taxi arrived to take him to the ferry, Davie's mind was whirring over the task ahead. Murdoch White was quite right. Born politicians proved it first at the local level.

The constituency of Glaikit covered the small town itself, once known for its weaving, and now for having one of the lowest levels of life expectancy in the UK. There were two former mining villages on the outskirts, one of them Davie's, which had long since been swallowed up by the town. There was a skirt of rich farmland. Glaikit had returned a Labour Member almost since the days of Keir Hardie.

Once he had informed his branch party – a small gathering in the back of the pub, all of them well known to him – Davie had leaflets printed announcing his candidature. Labour here was intertwined with the Catholic Church, and many of the families bore Irish names, so he was badly shaken to learn that Crusade's candidate was a bus driver called Patrick Connelly – the brother of priests, and well known in the local party. The second piece of bad news was the quality of the blow-ins from London: a popular former government minister who'd lost his seat at the last election, and a senior adviser to the current leader, who'd been profiled in the *Guardian*, amongst them. Murdoch White had been right. This was going to be a tough fight.

Davie was undressing for bed, tugging off a sock. Mary was already under the duvet. She was pretending to check his Twitter feed, but he could see she was barely concentrating.

'So. What then?'

'I don't like it, love. You've built up such a lot here. I just don't want you to get hurt.'

'You mean you don't think I'll win?'

'I'm no' saying that . . . Well, not quite. It'll be hard, obviously. Those guys from London . . . I'm just saying . . . What about the kids? You're barely ever home at the moment, and when you are, you're like a great big grumbly bear with a sore head. This . . . this is all numbers and tactics . . . doing folk down . . . putting the best face on. Is that how you want to live your life? Do you actually want a family, big man?'

Davie grunted. This could go either way. Mary's temperature was rising, and he could see a full-blown row blowing in his direction. He was too damned tired for that. 'Hey, darling. Wheesht. I know I've been an annoying bugger recently. Aye, a bear. It's been a hard pounding, you know, down the road. I've got more than a hundred employees dependent upon me' – he stabbed his chest with a squat finger. 'That's a lot of families, a lot of bread on a lot of tables. And it's harder getting the contracts in than it used to be. There's less and less money coming through the council. Everybody's squeezed by the banks. Bloody taxman's on my back too, emails every week. So aye, I know I look like I'm not noticing, not listening. And sweetheart, I'm sorry. But see here, if I get a new start, in politics, all of that'll be off my shoulders. The boys in the office are well capable of dealing with it.

'I know politics is a mad business, but look at it this way.' (I'm making a bloody speech, he thought. Good tactics? Bad tactics? Hell, but it has to be said.) 'The kids carry on here, nothing changes, except that they get regular stays in London

– and that can't be bad for them. I go down there and I work my arse off, we don't have any scratchy moments, and then I'm home at the weekends and we can enjoy ourselves. The old days again. Play our cards right, and we'll end up living down there at least some of the time. A whole new life.'

As he'd been talking, Mary had started to comb out her hair, never a good sign. 'You mean you'll be down there having the time of your life, dandering about – gadding – up to all sorts. I'll be left up here alone with the ironing. Where's *my* company? Where's *my* life? What about our marriage?'

'You've got Mum – you like her. And you never see me during the week anyway. Not properly. You spend all your time thinking about the boys. All you'll do is swap a grumpy, distracted builder for a rising young politician, spreading his wings.'

'As long as it's only your wings. And by the way, do bears have wings?' He could see that she wasn't entirely convinced, but at least there was now a half-smile on her face. Storm ducked. Davie yanked down his boxers and slid under the covers. After a few moments of tense waiting, he moved his arm across and began to stroke Mary's left breast through her nightie. She groaned, exhaled and turned towards him . . .

'Brace yourself, Janet.' The old joke. But just at that moment a loud musical clang echoed up the stairs.

'Jesus Christ almighty. Who's that at this hour?'

'Well I'm not bloody going,' said Mary. 'Your dressing gown's hanging in the bathroom.'

Pulling it around him as he hopped down the hallway, Davie

saw a tall silhouette in the frosted glass of the front door. He had a nasty suspicion that he recognised it.

'Ah – Mr White. This is a bit of a surprise. Er, late, and all . . .'

'I've never come across a politician who sneaks off to bed at this hour, Mr Petrie. Take it I'm welcome?' Murdoch White pushed his way into the house, pulled off his wet overcoat and made himself at home in the front room. '*Newsnight*'s still on, man. A small one would do fine.'

Davie gave in without even trying to fight. He went upstairs to pull some clothes back on. Mary was lying under the duvet, and didn't respond when he explained. She just lay there, pretending to be asleep.

Downstairs, White had given up on the telly and turned the sound down. He drained his whisky, and turned to Petrie. 'Things all right upstairs?'

'Oh, yes. We tend to turn in early.'

'Well that's going to stop, I can promise you. But I mean, things all right – you know – in the bedroom department?'

'Mr White!'

'Oh, I know, not my business. But you see, Mr Petrie, it is now. In a way, that's why I'm here. On paper, and at first impression, you seem to me to be an absolutely ideal candidate, a man who can help revive our party and bring it back to power. We have faith in you. Some important people know your name. Now, that's a big thing I'm saying.'

'Aye, and you know I'm grateful, Mr White . . .'

'But if we're going to put in the time, and the energy, and who knows, the money as well, to help your career, David

Petrie, we need to be sure that you can go the distance. Being in politics is a lot like being a top-flight sportsman. We can't have any distractions. If it turns out that you're a secret homo, or you bash yourself off to kiddie porn, I need to know now. Even if you and your wife are fighting all the time – that'll weaken you for what's ahead.

'You need to be a good sleeper. You don't have to have a clear conscience, but you do have to be able to put it to one side. You need to eat well, and to have no more than one or two drinks a day. You need energy, strength, oomph. Forgive me, but you need to be able to crap regularly. More politicians have been pulled down by irregular bowel habits and poor sleeping patterns, just being a bit pasty and weary, than by all the clever ploys of their enemies. So I need to know you inside out. Are you clean, man? Are you strong? What's behind that shiny pink young face?'

And I thought *I* made speeches, Davie thought. 'Jesus, Mr White, you make it sound like I'm joining the SAS or MI6. I thought I was just trying to be a Labour candidate.'

'Oh, you can be a Labour candidate without our help, if you're tough enough and wily enough. You can probably become a Labour MP without our help. You might even rise to be a junior minister one day – you've got what that takes. But I thought I'd made it clear to you that I'm talking about something different. Something a bit more interesting. I want you to be able to go all the way. And that's not like the SAS, it's like running a marathon every week of the year. As far as MI6 is concerned, then sure, you're going to need a brilliant memory and a talent for skulduggery, and always to be the best observer in the room. The shrewdest. The most attentive. Does all that put you off? Does it frighten you, Petrie?'

Davie realised that he was sitting on the edge of his own sofa, his back upright, while Murdoch White sprawled; he seemed to himself like a little boy at an interview. So he went over to the sideboard and poured himself a glass of wine, forcing himself not to offer the older man a top-up.

'No, Mr White, it doesn't frighten me. I'm happily married. No skeletons. I've got a pair of good kids – too old for ADHD, too young for drugs. I have the odd glass, but no problems there. As to fit, well, I don't go to the gym or anything like that, but if you've ever tried to run a building company, you'll know you need to be a pretty tough physical specimen. I think I am. Tough. Pay attention. If I remember rightly, you won your first by-election with a majority of just 2,224.'

Murdoch White, for the first time, shifted slightly in his seat. 'I did. But what's that got to do . . .'

'Which you increased to 6,550 at the general election two years later. Memory. Or at least a head for numbers. No, I think you and your friends – about whom I'm increasingly curious, by the way – have put your chips down in the right place.'

The two men sat silently, staring at each other, neither smiling.

Petrie stood up again. Where was Mr White staying tonight, he asked politely.

'Where? Here, I hope. You've got a spare room, surely, in a big house like this?'

There was a beat. The clock ticked.

'OK, sure. Just as long as you're not going to monitor my visits to the lavatory.'

Murdoch White laughed. Davie showed him to a small room next to the two boys'. After climbing into the narrow bed he lit a cigarette, strictly forbidden by Mary Petrie, before going to sleep.

As Davie returned to bed he thought, 'The man sleeping in my spare room was once one of the most powerful men in the country. George W. Bush knew him by name. He's addressed the United Nations. And now he's in my house. Am I ready for this?'

David the Ruthless

Study weakness, particularly in your friends.

The Master

Mary certainly wasn't ready. The following morning she listened to her husband's explanation of their unexpected guest's presence with an expressionless face. She made breakfast for Mr White, with the minimum of words and a few tight smiles. Fergus was hammering a football up and down the corridor, a tiny freckled fury in a Celtic shirt, while Callum sat at the kitchen table, swinging his feet and eyeing their visitor.

'What's your name?'

'My name is Mr Murdoch White. I'm a friend of your daddy's.'

'That's a silly name. And no you're no'. Why are you staying in the spare room?'

'I'm in the Labour Party, like your daddy. And we're going to make your daddy a very important man. Would you like that, Callum?'

'My daddy's already got a heid the size o' an elephant's arse.

66

That's what Mr Smedley says. Mr Smedley's a teacher. And he's a coon . . . a coon . . . a . . .'

'A councillor, Callum,' said Mary Petrie, without the ghost of a smile.

But Callum was now in full flow. 'Mr Smedley's my teacher and he's a coonsollar, and he disnae like Daddy. We call him Mr Smelly.'

'That's a bit rude, young man,' said Murdoch White.

'Well, he is smelly. He's got a smelly bum. He says everybody's got a smelly bum. But they don't.'

Suddenly concentrating, White pushed his plate away. 'This Mr Smedley. Does he ever — touch you, Callum?'

'For goodness' sake, Mr White, let the boy alone,' said Mary, her face crimson.

'No, he's just smelly. But he rubs his thing. He doesn't think we can see, but we can. He sits behind his desk and he rubs his thing.'

Mary gaped. Murdoch White smiled, and took out a small notebook from his jacket pocket. At this point a bleary Davie arrived in the kitchen. He had a list longer than his arm of people to see, but he had to get down to the office first, and check that everything was moving forward. There were still houses to be built.

White turned to him. 'So. Councillor Smedley. The teacher. A Labour man, of course — couldn't be anything else, around here.'

'Aye, Wally Smedley. Smelly Smedley, the kids call him. Been around for years. No friend of mine, but.'

'Oh, I think you'll find he's going to be a great supporter.'

'Wally Smedley? With respect, Mr White, you don't have the local knowledge. I'm telling you, he's not one of ours.'

'With *respect*, Mr Petrie, I think you'll find that I do, and that he is. Just ask your most observant son here.' He left to go upstairs, ruffling Callum's hair as he went.

'I don't like your new friend, Dad.'

Davie arrived at the newly built two-storey office behind the superstore where his business was now based. Waiting for him on his desk were the minutes of the last meeting of the planning committee, with half a dozen paragraphs highlighted in bright-green marker pen. His secretary had left a few 'must read' emails on his screen. The timber suppliers in Alloa hadn't been paid, again. The local bank had closed and there was now a useless head office up in Glasgow, but Davie had a private number, and spent a stressful but useful few minutes on the phone. A foreman had phoned in sick. One of the bungalows in James Murphy Close was taking in water after the heavy rain.

It took him an hour to escape. A routine morning. Success was delegation, he reminded himself – delegation with just a whiff of fear behind it.

Back at the house, Murdoch White had returned downstairs, established that the boys had left for school, and asked for another round of toast. After he'd scraped his plate and she'd made a second pot of tea, Mary finally asked him, with impeccable good manners, how long he hoped to be staying with them.

'Well, I've got a life of my own, Mrs Petrie. I wanted to get back to Arran, but I think I'll stop here for as long as Davie needs me. I have to keep an eye on things, don't I? Just so long as the contest's hanging in the balance. Say – a month?'

Mary Petrie was quite a woman. She had taken nervous horses over high stone walls. She'd played on in a hockey match for half an hour with a cracked shinbone. She'd won an essay prize at university by not sleeping for a week. She'd shut her ears to the protests of her distraught parents so she could marry a hairy-arsed builder from the grotty little town she now lived in. She'd given birth twice without an epidural – not even gas and air. But in all her long life Mary Petrie would never do anything as remarkable as she did now. What she did was – nothing. She didn't reply. Nor did she gasp, goggle, throw the teapot or scream. She just gently replaced a carton of milk in the fridge, and began to rub away the marks around the sink. Then – 'A month it is, Mr White,' she said. 'If you can stand us, you will eat with the family. But no more smoking in this house, if you please.'

Taking her measure, the former foreign secretary stood and nodded. 'Here's my proposition, then,' he said. 'I will stay until your husband has been selected as the prospective parliamentary candidate for Glaikit. On the evening of the general election I will come back and accept a glass of whisky, and light one small cigarette. Agreed?'

'Agreed,' said Mary. 'And while you're here, you can help the boys with their homework, too.'

'Your boys, Mrs Petrie, are very vigorous, and seem quite intelligent. But I'm afraid they are beyond help.'

When Davie returned to the house, he put his iPad on the kitchen table.

'Mr White, I've made a kind of wee spreadsheet. All the party members in the five branches who really matter. Here are the ones who I know will back me whatever happens. Here are the ones we need to win over. In the last column there are just a few notes. Nothing much.'

'Well, we're off and running then,' said White. 'I'm going to go down to the council building and sniff around a bit. You can find me at the Wallace Bar at lunchtime.'

'The Wallace? That's a bit rough for the likes of you, Mr White.'

'It's where the union boys drink. At least it was ten years ago, the last time I passed through this godforsaken hole. And I'm a Crusade man myself. Fully paid up. Happened when the bastards gobbled up the draughtsmen's union. Buy you a pint of 80 Shillings if you happen to stop by.'

'No, I don't think so, Mr White. I wouldn't be welcome there. But I thought the idea was that you were going to come around with me.'

'You need to be seen by yourself. Make some good, strong, one-to-one contacts. If I show up in somebody's front room, I'll be the centre of attention. That's no good. So you go off and do your thing, Mr Petrie. Unless I'm badly mistaken, you'll do it very well. And then come down to the Wallace and have a pie and a pint, and tell me all about it, and meet the boys. I'll have warmed them up nicely for you. Promise.'

And indeed, Petrie had been around long enough to know the drill. When a politician enters a house looking for support, what's the first thing he doesn't do? He doesn't talk about politics.

He began with a retired couple, long-standing party members and well respected in the city centre branch, where he had least support. 'No point trying to pull the wool over your eyes; you know why I'm here,' he told them at the doorstep. After he'd been invited in, his eyes flicked desperately around the living room for the photographs. Yes, there they were. A middle-aged couple in the sunshine, somewhere abroad — could be Australia, could be South Africa — but not dressed for a holiday. And another picture, of a grinning boy and girl with dirty knees, in the sweatshirts of the local school. So, one grown-up child overseas. Don't see them enough. Cost of air travel. Prestwick. And another one who still lived nearby, hence the grandkids. The local school — that was the way in.

'Those two look a bit older than my Callum, but he loves it there. Whose are they?'

'They're our youngest, Katy's. They're a wild pair, but they're lovely kids. They come around every weekend. The swings. A kickabout in the park. Poor George is going to give himself a heart attack with those kids one day. But you wouldn't have it any other way, would you George?' George looked uncertain, but nodded dutifully.

'And didn't I hear that your older girl went off abroad and made something of herself?' said Davie, guessing wildly.

'Aye, she married a computer whiz-kid from Dundee, and they're off in San Francisco, living the high life. No kids. She Skypes us every week, and that's great, but we hardly ever see her.'

'Skype, eh? Didn't have you down as a computer guru, George.'

George raised his mottled, hound-dog face. 'I'm no guru, Mr Petrie. But even though I'm retired, I haven't got all day. Let's cut to the bloody chase, shall we? You want to be our candidate?' With that, he began to cough uncontrollably.

'Aye, I do. Because the local hospital's bloody useless, George, and you know it as well as I do,' said Davie, revelling in his own quickness.

A quarter of an hour later, after consuming some home-made gingerbread and a mug of tea, David Petrie felt he had them in his pocket. There was always the danger that some big figure from London might arrive and blow them over, but they seemed too prickly and too proud of the town for that.

The second home visit was rather harder. Elspeth Cook, stern matriarch, was something of a legend in the local party. Her angry divorce years back had split two branches in bits. She lived in one of the few harled prefabs from the 1940s that were left on the outskirts of Glaikit. The veteran of many Labour conference speeches, she had the uncompromising face of a class-war fighter who felt more sure of herself the more she was defeated. Davie felt nervous as he knocked on her door. He barely knew her, and he was all too conscious that he didn't have a plan.

The snarl of a terrier – a Westie called Rosa, with a nasty nip – greeted him as the door opened.

'Aye, aye,' said Mrs Cook. 'Thought you'd be round. Fancy yourself as a politician now, do you, wee Davie?'

The pictures in her crammed, overheated front room told a very different story from those in the house he had just left. An anti-apartheid poster from the 1960s; a framed appeal for support for miners' wives and children from 1982; and a tinted portrait of Keir Hardie – probably worth a bit. The only personal photograph Davie could see showed an unappealing young woman, her face as expressionless as a bar of soap, wearing steel spectacles. This would be the daughter, Bunty. She was, as they said round here, affection-ately enough, 'a big daftie' – not necessarily educationally subnormal, but profoundly dim. Not much scope for idle banter there.

But Elspeth Cook turned out to be not quite what Davie had expected. 'Right now, you'll sit down there. You and me have to have a good talk. I've got a new batch of potato scones, and a big boiling of tea. So park your arse and prepare your-self for fearsome Granny Stalin.' She grinned broadly.

A few minutes later, after they had polished off some warm scones dripping with butter, she got down to business. 'See, Mr Petrie, I'm one for the workers. That's the basis of my socialism. Two sides: us and them. You may think that's a wee bit simplistic, but the more I look around, the more it makes sense. I'm no communist, and I'm certainly no Trot. I know change takes time. But what I can't quite get my head around is why, though you're a nice-looking boy, right enough, I should vote for a boss as our next candidate, rather than young Pat Connelly, who's a worker after all. One of us.'

'Well, I'm scarcely a boss. I started laying bricks for my dad. There isn't a job – electrics, plumbing, joinery, plastering – that I can't do better than most of the lads on the sites. All I've done is work hard and give work to local men and women who need it. I've always been on the side of the underdog. What's so wrong with that?'

'Come on, son. The way I hear it, you've been sucking up to the councillors and officials for years, just like your dad, and cornering a nice wee profit all round this town. You pay your men the minimum wage, but no' much more. It's a great big new hoose you've built for yourself. No' objecting, mind. But you're hardly a proletarian, darling, are you?'

Davie put his case again, with all the eloquence he had. He made a lot of eye contact, and they had some good laughs, but at the end the redoubtable Elspeth seemed unmoved.

'I'll be honest, pet, I like you more than I thought I would. But I'm voting for Pat Connelly, and I'll be telling the rest of the comrades to do the same.'

Davie walked back up the road – he'd deliberately taken the bus rather than driving – and reflected on the size of this blow. Granny Stalin was much loved hereabouts. She was a real character, a good woman. There must be a way in.

As he stared idly through the bus's grimy windows at the familiar chip shops, charity outlets and a derelict-looking estate agent's, Davie remembered something Murdoch White had said the previous evening. 'See, the simplistic view of politics is that it's all about blackmail and arm-twisting – find a fellow's weak point, scare the living daylights out of him, and you've got him for life. Well, in my experience that's sometimes true, but it's only part of the story. Friendship and guilt work even more strongly. Do a guy a favour, and you've got him for a year. Make *him* do *you* a favour, and you've got him for ten. A branch party isn't just a collection of individuals. It's a family, a tiny tribe. And like any family it has its feuds and its leaders. All you need to do is understand the feuds, and make your mark with the tribal leader.'

Elspeth Cook was certainly the tribal leader. He couldn't let her go. So when he got off at the stop by the council chambers, instead of heading straight to the Wallace, he went in.

Bunty. She wasn't handicapped, just good, old-fashioned, stupid. He knew she had a job, of a kind, at the council. Works? Administration? He'd often seen her pale, round moon of a face, with two expressionless currant eyes and a limp, wet mouth that never closed, behind her formidable mother at branch meetings, at the GMC, even at conference.

'Can I do this? Can I really go this far?' he asked himself. But he had no choice.

He found her quickly enough, sitting behind a Formica desk, staring dully at a computer screen.

'Hello, Bunty. Remember me?'

Bunty stuck a fat white forefinger into her mouth, licked it slowly, then took it out and drew it across her jumper. A little lump of goo sat at the edge of her mouth.

'Aye. You're Mr Petrie, right enough. Or you were yesterday. I'm no' stupid, you know.'

'I know that, Bunty. Now, I need to ask you something. It's possible that in a little while I may become an MP and go down to London. If I do, I'm going to need a personal assistant. More than a secretary, somebody to look after the constituency work and keep an eye out for me. I'd like it to be you.'

'Would I live in London?'

'Aye, Bunty, you would.'

'And would I live in a flat? By myself?'

'Aye, Bunty, you would.'

'And would I have money to spend – on food and stuff? And go about?'

'Aye, Bunty. Not a lot. But aye.'

'And Mr Petrie, would the work be difficult? And would you get cross at me?' She coloured.

'No, Bunty, it wouldn't be hard. And I wouldn't get cross with you.'

'OK, then.'

They shook hands, and he turned to leave, satisfied with his brilliant stroke.

Bunty spoke again. 'Mr Petrie, my mum will be dead happy I've got a chance at last.'

'I'm sure she will, Bunty, I'm sure she will.'

'Mr Petrie, are you doing this just to get my mum to vote for you?'

'Certainly not, Bunty. I'll just need someone I can trust down there.'

He didn't suppose that Elspeth Cook would be fooled for a moment, but the strongest binding force on the planet is a mother's love, and she might just go for it. But one further touch was needed. He dialled Elspeth's number, told her what he'd done, and insisted that it shouldn't affect her decision to vote for Patrick Connelly.

'I'll vote for who I bloody want to, you cheeky young man,' she replied. 'And as I've told you, that's Pat Connelly, right enough.'

So Davie had lumbered himself with Bunty Cook. If he did ever get elected he'd have to look at her every day, possibly for years. The sacrifices he made . . .

But although Elspeth Cook continued to proudly speak up for the bus driver Connelly, what she said to her friends about Davie Petrie won him votes across the local party. Later, he would reflect that she had probably won him the nomination.

The Wallace was a proper bar. There was a television – only for the football – and although smoking had been banned for years, the walls and ceiling were still stained a dirty yellow-brown, a memorial to the lungs of generations of long-dead drinkers. The barman was young and truculent, a Nationalist who made himself deliberately offensive to the overwhelmingly Labour-supporting customers. They, however, approved of his rudeness – a proper man should never hide his views. The Wallace had been the favoured haunt of the railwaymen's union and the Transport & General long before it was inherited by Crusade, whose small offices were only a street away. The district organiser, Douglas McGuinness, a tall, white-bearded Irishman who claimed to be a direct descendant of Wolfe Tone, was drinking with Murdoch White. He looked up as Petrie entered.

'So, this is your laddie?'

'Not my laddie, Douglas,' said White. 'Davie Petrie here belongs to nobody. It's just that I can spot a winner. I know Pat Connelly's one of the boys, but you might think about a little side bet, just in case.'

The days of the union block vote being wielded like trumps had passed during the long Ed Miliband rumpus. And indeed, as the former leader had hoped at the time, many individual trade unionists had joined the Labour Party in their own right. But in Glaikit, as in many constituencies, the habit of union solidarity died hard. Shop stewards and ordinary paid-up members would come into the Wallace and scan the union paper to find out what the leadership thought. Crusade had an authority in the town rivalling that of the Kirk itself. Who was their boy? What did Douglas McGuinness want to happen?

Murdoch White had used the past hour well. Luckily, Davie had always encouraged union membership among his employees – one eye to the future – and had spoken up in the past against New Labour in ways they appreciated hereabouts. Most of the Crusade members, when it came to the general management committee, would vote for Connelly first; but it would be closer than predicted, and many would happily switch to Petrie.

And so the first days passed. White and Petrie had drawn up their lists, and went around the town ticking off addresses. Lines and arrows connected one member with another. Sometimes White told Petrie to 'cast a wee bit of bread'. So Davie would tell the church minister who took the minutes for a particular branch that, for instance, he'd once been on holiday with Douglas Alexander. Then they would monitor where the story appeared. Who was talking to whom? Another arrow would be drawn on the chart. Eventually they ended up with a swirling, dynamic and relatively accurate picture of the secret life of Glaikit – the rivalries, the alliances, the drinking buddies and the unofficially extended families. Davie found it all infinitely more interesting than the mundane business of fixing councillors and knowing who'd take a backhander. Though those furtive little felonies also helped to bind in a few who prided themselves on their independence.

A fortnight before the final selection meeting, Davie was beginning to allow himself to hope. He had given up drink – apart from the occasional obligatory pint with potential supporters – and was eating less, and all the pounding of the streets had made him fitter than he had been for years. But there were two big problems left. First, Labour rules insisted that at least one woman should appear on the short-list. And second, the London carpetbaggers were pretty damn impressive.

Murdoch White had clear views about how to deal with the woman problem. 'In effect, we need to run a couple of our own people. Good enough to be plausible, but not good enough to win on the night.' So they talked up a primary-school head teacher with a good party record whose whining, nasal voice and invincible self-belief were simply intolerable. And among the candidates from outside the constituency there was one outstanding woman. She was, in a small way, a celebrity cook, and quite well known from the television. A handsome mother of two, she had worked publicly for the Labour cause for years before declaring her hand. To Petrie's surprise, White was very keen to get her through the nomination process.

'But she's damn good,' Petrie protested. 'I'd vote for her myself.'

'No you wouldn't, don't worry.'

White drove over to her house himself, right across Scotland to East Lothian. He introduced himself, and told her not to worry about the black spot on her record – that she had sent her children to a private school, even though there was an excellent comprehensive on her doorstep.

'The party's changing, and fast. We just want the best possible candidates. So the main thing is, be honest. Tell the whole truth. They'll respect you for it.'

And so, on the night of the open meeting, when she was asked the traditional last question – 'Is there anything in your past that would embarrass the Labour Party if it became known?' – she did tell the truth. All of it. And the pile of ballot papers with crosses against her name was embarrassingly small.

On paper, two good women had very nearly been chosen for Glaikit. In reality, neither had ever had a chance. That left the southerners, and Connelly.

There was one last incident before David Petrie's coronation. Murdoch White had had a brief conversation with the schoolteacher 'Smelly' Smedley.

'Just a wee word in your ear about what young Callum Petrie's been saying. And I'm afraid he's not the only one. It's not a big problem, Mr Smedley. It's just one of those silly things. This could get right out of control if the head teacher had to be told. We don't want to make any trouble. We just want Davie to get his chance.'

Walter Smedley was in his early sixties, and lived with his elderly mother. Divorced with a daughter long gone, no one knew where, Wally had let himself go, if only on the outside. He was an intellectual. That was no problem. The problem was, he looked like one. His clothes were always slightly stained. His shaving had become erratic, giving his great head, an object that seemed crudely carved from sandstone, like Samuel Johnson's, an awesome ruggedness. His almost super-natural talent for teaching now flickered only intermittently. Living with his books, he spent sleepless nights and long days caring for an angry, half-blind old woman who no longer knew who he was. The private truth was that Walter Smedley was almost a saint.

To Murdoch White, with his famous face, Smedley said nothing – merely nodded his long head. But the following day he visited the Petries' house after school. With his mother by his side, Callum was asked to repeat what he'd said about the teacher, 'to my face, boy'. The boy flushed, began to whimper, and tearing himself from his mother, ran upstairs.

Wally Smedley turned to Mary. 'I wish, Mrs Petrie, that I had not had to put you through this unpleasant experience. And even more, I wish that your husband was here. What I have to say I would have preferred to say to him. But I'm not going to demean myself by chasing around town, trying to find that –' He stopped himself.

He didn't look well, but he continued. 'You may know that

Mr Murdoch White, who I gather is working for your husband, and indeed living in this house, has approached me with a very unpleasant story about myself. I don't blame Callum, or any of the boys – they are only boys, after all – but Mr White has threatened me that he will spread a disgusting and slanderous untruth.'

Mary held up a hand to protest.

'No, Mrs Petrie, it is worse than that. Please give me a moment. Mr White has implied that unless I back your husband as our parliamentary candidate, he will go to my headmistress, who is a kind but foolish woman. He appears to think that I have rather more pull in the local Labour Party than I do. If he does spread this horrible story, then I'm sure it must be clear to you that whatever the truth of it, my life will be ruined. I have my mother to think of. You're an educated woman: you may know your Yeats, Mrs Petrie. He famously lamented that the best lack all conviction, while the worst are full of passionate intensity. Good men, weak; bad men, strong, you see. Callum is welcome in my class at any time. He is a clever boy, and I will do my level best by him. But my message to your husband is that I will not, under any circumstances, support him. He didn't even have the courage to blackmail me to my face, like a man. Tell him, *I* am my own man still. I have nothing to apologise for. Gossip – and be damned.' And Mr Smedley, his balding head still streaked with the rain, belted up his mackintosh, turned on his heel, and left the house.

Mary, shaken and impressed, called David to tell him what had happened. He had just been addressing some local Fabians with Murdoch, who said tersely, 'Well, we must act.' They went together to the school. As they were waiting for the headmistress to see them, they shared that day's *Guardian* quick crossword.

Wally Smedley had, it turned out, the most beautiful copperplate handwriting.

I could not leave her, you see. But thanks to Mr White, I had to. How could I have stayed? It's all too disgusting, too humiliating — and all completely untrue. Walter Smedley.

He had killed his mother with a shovel, a single blow to the back of the head. Then he must have written his note and left it on the open bureau, before walking into his garage and hanging himself with a length of hosepipe.

The local press treated it as a tragic mystery, and speculated that Smedley had been driven to the edge by the long years of caring. A policeman interviewed Murdoch White, and concluded that the note meant nothing.

Mary and Davie had glanced briefly at one another and tacitly agreed that this was too deep, too dark, to talk about. Later, in the kitchen, Murdoch addressed what had happened. 'No man ever led other men without doing harsh things. What happened was nobody's fault; and I for one believe your son.'

In bed upstairs, Callum told his dinosaur, 'I just made it up, I don't know why.' He was quiet for a while, but soon pushed the whole matter behind him, and was once again the cheeky, happy little boy he'd been before.

*

The selection meeting was perhaps the most exciting few hours of Davie Petrie's life so far. Coached by Murdoch, he made a belter of a speech. Nothing against any of the folk who had made the journey up north, he told the crowded and overheated room, 'but is this the kind of town so thin in local talent we have to hire outsiders? Folk who've never known how cold it is on Glaikit Glen playing a wee bit fitba. Folk who've never been bawled out for backsliding by our own Granny Stalin. Folk who, for whatever reason, couldn't get chosen in their own backyards, so they've come up here to our backyard.'

For each of the incomers he had a carefully prepared line of attack, the result of many hours spent in front of a computer screen over the past weeks. The man from the leader's office had once written a column for the *New Statesman* in which he'd said that if he'd been a Scot he'd have voted for independence in 2014. Davie read out the whole paragraph, and was gratified by the hissing. 'He's no' even a Scot, mind, yet he's a Scottish Nationalist!' Another, now working for a trade union in London, turned out to have been briefly a member of the Federation of Conservative Students. Two down. As to Patrick Connelly, the depressed-looking bus driver who was his main local rival, Petrie offered the hand of friendship. 'You all know Pat Connelly. He's carried you up and down this constituency – aye, and your kids too – and I stand here and I tell you that we may be opponents, but that he is a reliable and a decent man. He's no' the most cheerful fellow, perhaps, but we could do a lot worse.'

As Murdoch White had predicted, Petrie's praise finally sank Connelly. Any candidate who could afford to be so confident and large-spirited clearly had no fear of the former front-runner.

In fact, Petrie nearly overdid it. He needed Connelly to come first in the opening round of voting, preferably ahead of the guy from the leader's office. But after Davie had spoken, the London blow-in spent the next ten minutes saying that while Pat Connelly might be a good bus driver and a decent councillor in a quiet week, he didn't have the oomph necessary to make his mark at Westminster. Then an increasingly upset Connelly savaged the London man back – a jumped-up metropolitan hack from Chelsea or somewhere, where a two-bed flat cost more than the entire housing stock of Glaikit, while Petrie stood at the back of the room handing out mugs of instant coffee and waiting.

Still, as planned he came third in the first ballot; and as White had predicted, those who just found Connelly a bit depressing, and those who couldn't stick the idea of a toff parachuted in from London, switched, and on the second ballot Davie came through triumphantly. He had abused nobody, except in jest. He had committed himself to very little. He had held out the hand of friendship to a man he'd thown. Poor Pat Connelly didn't know what had hit him; he seemed dazed, and about half the size he'd been at the beginning of the meeting. 'Welcome to politics,' said Murdoch White.

'Local Boy Chosen', crowed the *Glaikit Post*. At the subsequent election, Davie's campaign literature would show the Petrie family standing together with the slogan 'He's built half of Glaikit. Now let him build a better Britain.'

Funny Farm

The good politician understands that there are no chance meetings, only unexpected chances.

The Master

The collection of brick buildings didn't make immediate sense. They were too scattered for a farm, too well-maintained for cheap housing, and not substantial enough for a hotel. A riding club, perhaps? And in the late-afternoon sunshine there were indeed a couple of young women on ponies crossing the lawn that backed onto a minor road.

In their path stood a middle-aged man who appeared to have a swarm of insects inside his clothes. He scratched feverishly at his armpits and midriff. He windmilled his arms and stamped his feet in a dance of exasperation. He clawed at his longish hair and shouted, then threw himself onto his knees and rubbed his face in the dampness of the grass.

'Poor Stephen,' said one of the young women.

'Yah. Poor Stephen. Stephen's fine. He'll be fine tomorrow,' the other replied. Both girls were expensively well spoken and gaunt.

Watching all of this from the window of her minicab was Angela. She leaned over, paid the driver for the ride from the station and opened the door, lugging a small suitcase.

'Thanks. I'll be fine from here on.'

At St Peter's Asset Management, Caroline Phillips had been immensely popular. She couldn't help it. Everybody loved this frantically hard-working and ambitious student of currency swaps; at the heart of the City, the steel and limestone palazzo of Damazer House almost overflowed with laughter as Caro and her new friends bought, sold, crunched the numbers and sold again. All through that first year, from April until early October, the sun seemed to splash through the windows and paddle gold fingers through the hair of the chosen. Caro's mere presence had lightened St Peter's, and her manager recommended her for promotion a mere eight months after she joined.

She should have been very happy, and mostly she was. Young Caro had all the joys and sweetmeats that London life could bring in the twenty-first century. She had admiration, a challenging and interesting job which hadn't even existed a few decades earlier, a colourful collection of international friends, enough money, and a status unthinkable for earlier generations of young, non-royal women. She had, in short, everything . . . except purpose. For even then, Caroline was too clever, and perhaps too moral, to believe that making money was a purpose.

So when, at a C of E seminar for City employees, held at a Blitz-battered and restored Wren church, she bumped into Angela, her first emotion was jealousy. Caroline had been drifting – working hard as she drifted, admirably, lucratively, pleasantly. Angela, however, had a vocation. Just as when they'd first met at school, Angela had an intensity, a sense of urgency that beautiful Caroline lacked. Caroline's world was full of promise, stretching out in the sunshine. But Angela's world was more interesting; it had shadows and meaning, and it wouldn't go on forever.

Angela suited the priesthood. Caroline wore black suits by Dolce & Gabbana. Angela wore black suits by Wippell's of Exeter; and she wore them better. With the bare minimum of make-up, and in a well-tailored jacket, she had become very striking – almost beautiful. She still burned with moral force. Addressing the seminar on the subject of how little it would take for everyone there to make a difference to the lives of bright teenage girls in Ghana, she used her hands like magic wands, and spoke with the self-confidence of a poet, a born preacher.

Afterwards, when Caro went up to her, feeling oddly nervous, Angela was surrounded by a trio of admiring executives from Goldman Sachs. She seemed barely to remember Caro from their school days at all. She merely shook her by the hand and gave her a bland smile. Caroline left the room feeling wretched.

She had just picked up a copy of the *Evening Standard*, and was about to plunge into the tube at Bank station when she was almost knocked off her feet. Two firm hands grabbed her head and covered her eyes. She gasped and spun around, thrusting off her attacker; and there was Angela, shaking with laughter.

'Got you! You should have seen your face!' Then Angela put both her arms around her waist, pulled her towards her and kissed her very firmly and insistently on the mouth.

'You can't do that, Pep,' Caro spluttered. 'People will see. This is where I work . . .'

'I can do anything I like,' Angela replied, licking her lips. 'I am an ordained minister, with the great good luck to be living in twenty-first-century Britain. You haven't come out? Not my fault, sugar.'

'Well, I'm not really . . . You see, it's complicated . . . That is . . .'

'I know, hon. You're not actually a lesbian, blah, blah, blah. But you can't deny that you liked that kiss. You were squirming like a fish.'

'I know. Yes, I did.' And then Caroline said something impulsive, although she was naturally cautious about these things. She turned her back on the man dishing out free copies of the *Guardian* and said, firmly and clearly, 'Whatever I am – and I don't know – what I do know is that I'm in love with you. I always have been.'

Over the next few years, life changed very fast for both of them. Caroline discovered that behind Angela's self-confident exterior and success as a priest, her life had been the reverse of simple. Back at school Caro had known, of course, that Angela had been adopted, didn't know her birth mother and had an awkward relationship with the admirable but strait-laced couple who had adopted her. Perhaps it was the urge to create a family she could rely on that had led her into a very early and ill-advised marriage which ended after eighteen months, its residue being at least a dozen epic rows, one mortgage and two young boys.

These she had brought up with the help of her adoptive mother, who had dropped everything to come and live with her in her vicarage in Devon, but who could not stand Caroline's arrival on the scene, and left shortly after it. For a while, at least, Caroline's large City salary, with a cheering annual bonus, allowed the two women to buy in enough help for both of their careers to continue. Angela preached, visited, and quietly skedaddled east to London most Wednesdays. Caro skedaddled west each weekend. At times they seemed to be living on the A303. There are worse fates. They got through a lot of Bach. In London, they had parties. They had a civil partnership party, crammed with Caro's friends from the bank – everyone came – and later on they had a wedding, not in a church but with lots of vicars and laughter. Caro, despite her principles, toasted David Cameron.

But it didn't take Caroline long to realise that in the years before their unexpected reunion, Angela had developed a new and dangerous, if extremely common, vice. She was drinking well over a litre of white wine a day. Well-made golden joy juice was freely available everywhere; in ever larger glasses it took the edge off a scratchy day, erased disappointment, uncorked conversation. The two of them would share a decent Chardonnay or Pinot, curled up on the sofa, and drank with friends all across London. There was something inside Caroline, some biochemical brake disc, which meant that she never went beyond half a bottle. Angela lacked this. One bottle, then two a day; the 6 p.m. freshener became the lunchtime tonic. Caroline raised the subject with her from time to time, but it never seemed worth a full-on argument; and as Angela pointed out, she had to cope with two demanding and puppyish boys as well as her work. She needed some help. Apart from Caro, nobody ever noticed. Angela began to fall asleep earlier each evening. Just occasionally, she embarrassed them at a dinner party. Just occasionally, she threw up into her handbag in the taxi taking them home. Caro remonstrated. Angela swiped back. The joy juice wasn't making them happier any more. Finally, after several years, it had led them to Melody Farm, an expensive but reputedly effective rehab clinic – that scatter of red-brick buildings which wasn't quite a hotel.

Angela had discarded her clerical collar and the dark suit she usually wore. In jeans and a zip-up top she looked fit and vigorous; but her eyes were red, and her face was sallow and puffy. Walking with self-conscious care, she made towards the main building, passing a small white-painted sign which read simply 'Melody, Ltd'. She ignored the man on the lawn, who had now stood up and was thrusting his arms in her direction, calling out, 'Oh – OH – *ooohhh*.' She also ignored the two riders; and they her. After checking in, she was shown to her expensively booked quarters in the former stables, which had a luxurious, high, old-fashioned bed, and a kitchenette with kettle and toaster. She unpacked, flung an Andrew O'Hagan and the selected poems of George Herbert onto the bed, then made her way to the communal area, which was housed in another brick building. Purple sofas were arranged in a giant U-shape; sprawling on them were a couple of well-dressed Arabs, a suspicious-looking woman in an expensive jacket who Angela thought looked somehow familiar, and a grizzled old man with heavily tattooed arms. His head was shaven, and there were more tattoos crawling up his neck.

Angela introduced herself. Only the woman in the jacket replied, with a single word: 'Sadie.' The rest stared off into the middle distance. Behind Angela, the two riders entered the room. Away from their horses, they were tiny.

Angela had been in places like this before, and made a quick assessment. She guessed that she was halfway down the pecking order. The Arabs would be there for drug addiction, probably cocaine and pills, possibly smack. They, and the poor soul doing cold turkey out on the lawn, were by common consent at the top of the pile. Then came the alcoholics. That was Sadie and her, and there were surely others around too. The eating disorders, who included the two riders, came last. Alpha, beta, gamma. In theory this was a democracy of the damaged, in which everybody helped everybody else out – made sure they kept hydrated, helped them up when they fell over, shared stories to bolster their straining willpower. In practice, the druggies were too self-absorbed most of the time to pay attention to anyone else. And when they were coming off, by God they swanked about it. The alcoholics, on the other hand – her team – were the biggest liars. Angela had called in at the M&S by the railway station and bought herself a bottle of white wine and a carton of apple juice. She'd poured the juice down a drain and filled

the carton with wine. At this moment it was sitting inno-
cently in her kitchenette. She thought she'd invite Sadie over
for a quick one. She looked like fun.

Sadie made meaningful eye contact. She understood the
casual invitation to 'have a look at the stables'. Probably she
had her own stash hidden somewhere as well.

As they idled across the lawn back to Angela's room, Sadie
said, 'I can tell you think you recognise me. Let's not have
one of those tedious conversations where you ask whether I
was at school with you, or if I'm on telly. I'm the prime
minister's wife – I mean the former prime minister's wife, of
course. And before you start, I'm nothing like the woman
you've read about in the newspapers. Nothing.'

'Is that a good thing? I don't read the papers very much.'

'Good and bad. They have me down as a greedy, conniving
bitch. Well, I dispute the conniving part. They think I'm
amoral, with no sense of humour. In fact I'm a practising
Christian, and I've got the biggest fund of dirty jokes in central
London. They think I'm addicted to money and handbags. I'm
not; as you've probably worked out already, I'm addicted to
nothing worse than wine. And I love my husband very much.
He knows I'm here; he's a bold man, and he may even come
and visit. Now, you?'

'Oh well, nothing very much to say. I'm an alcoholic lesbian
vicar, and my congregation think I'm on pilgrimage in
Jerusalem.'

A burly man in a white T-shirt, with a close-cropped beard,
came around the corner towards them as they arrived at the
stable block. He was carrying something in his right hand. 'But

I don't, dear. I know you're here. And I know why, too.' He waved a now empty apple-juice carton at her. 'Naughty girl.'

'Oh, fuck. And fuck you, too. Don't be so bloody patronising. I'm sorry, Sadie, it seems the cavalry have headed us off at the pass.'

'Never mind. Better for both of us, probably. But what's with the language? Are you really a vicar?'

'Ah well, the good old Church of England. There's the mark of a cross in the sunburn between my boobs. Shall we try the hot tub before the light goes?'

And so it was that Caroline Elizabeth Phillips, loyally visiting her girlfriend in her weeks of need, first came to meet the Master. Saturday was visiting day. Caro arrived by Saab. The Master arrived in a helicopter. By then his wife and Angela were firm friends. They shared a sense of humour, which had kept them going through some tough days – no sneaking off to the local pub, so far – and an embattled belief in the relevance of the Gospel. Angela didn't care much for politics, but she talked a lot about Caro, who had at last decided to 'do something' and join the Labour Party. Sadie saw in Angela a tough, troubled woman who seemed to her the nearest thing she would find there to a reliable confidante, who wouldn't go running off to the press. Angela, who immediately after their first encounter had avidly Googled her new friend, found a much-misunderstood and underestimated woman, with a fund of wonderful stories and a sincere devotion to the supposedly troubled former prime minister.

It was no surprise, then, that over a picnic provided by the rehabilitation centre, the Master and Caro found it easy and entertaining to talk.

Later, calling Sadie from a hotel room in Boston, the Master said, 'Your boozy new friend, the Sapphic lady who wants to be an MP – she's quite something, isn't she? She's got the magic dust.'

'It's her partner you mean; she's the one who caught your eye. The boozer is the vicar. But the girlfriend has something, I agree. You might look out for her.'

And later still, when Angela was back at Pebbleton, dashing out the parish newsletter and answering her sons' homework questions, she paused to say to Caro: 'He's quite something, isn't he? The Master. I could tell he really liked you. Not like that.'

'Yes, I think he did,' Caro replied. 'Not like that, but yes.'

Over the next few months, the two couples came to know one another better. Sadie greatly admired Angela, who was now moving in the Christian–business circles which occasionally hosted the Master. He and Caro exchanged emails. At a Christian socialist conference he had agreed to address, he gently corrected her misapprehensions about the current Labour Party leadership, and from time to time he suggested phrases that might help her as she gingerly embarked on her first public appearances as a would-be politician. She in turn rallied him with encouraging jokes when he felt particularly beleaguered by a hostile and unforgiving media. The more he saw of her, the more the Master found common cause. Caro was passionate about educational opportunity, about getting people back to work, and about the environment. She was Europhile, but also an admirer of Washington – she followed American politics, and baseball, as a hobby. She never mocked the Master for his religious seriousness. So when, one day, he suggested that it was time for him to do something concrete to help her to put it all into practice, to get into the House of Commons and become a proper politician, it wasn't entirely unexpected.

Caro Gets Selected

Any fool can get elected, and most of them do; but it takes real
ruthlessness to get selected in the first place.

Yes, him again

Angela was unimpressed by the news. 'But you're not
tough enough, darling. You're not manipulative. And the Labour
Party hardly exists down here in Pebbleton. You're going to
have to move. You're going to have to move out. Just when
we're so happy. Politics – it's a horrible world – look in the
newspapers. They'll have you for breakfast.' She was doing
the washing up, and scrubbed the plates as if they were guilty.
Then she came over and kissed Caroline lightly. 'I just don't
want you to get hurt.'

'You mean you don't want me to bugger off up to London
when I'm so useful down here, looking after the boys.' Caroline
was cleaning the table, but was so distracted that she was
simply sweeping crumbs onto the floor.

'You've only just given up that ridiculous City job of yours.
You're beginning to enjoy life a bit. Why make yourself miserable?' Angela was gripping her wine glass so hard that it broke.

She checked her hand for blood, then threw the glass away, saying nothing.

Caroline certainly looked miserable. But she straightened up and forced a smile. 'Because we're all put on this planet to do something. You've always said it. I've always known it. And I think this is what I can do.'

Thanks, no doubt, to the Master, Caro had been put on the national candidates list. She made several stabs by phone and email for various seats whose local parties clearly had no interest in her. One morning, after several months poring over the *Guardian* for news about sitting MPs dying or retiring, she had jumped into her Saab and headed for Northamptonshire. The constituency of Barker needed a new candidate to replace Leonard Lomax, a former miner who was retiring before the next election, at the age of seventy-eight. She stayed at the only hotel in Barker, a Travelodge, and in the two days she spent there she met enough constituency workers and officials to think that, lesbian or not, she was in with a chance. There were lots of women in the local party who were aching to give the old male establishment a smack in the face, she told Angela.

But as they walked together up the steep hill that overlooked Pebbleton church, listening to the faint distress of sheep on the other side of the valley, Angela ran through the other candidates.

'Sweetie, they're a formidable lot, you have to admit it. There's the guy who used to be the environment minister. Everyone in the party loves him. There's the one who wrote all the speeches for the two Eds; he's had a lot of telly exposure, and the media are always gushing about him because he used to be in the army. And there's that woman who lost her seat at the last election, and who's supposed to be in the running for mayor of London. Caro, you are sweet and you are pretty and you are clever, but you're not in their league.'

They were standing in the lee of a beech coppice, hidden from the rest of the world. Angela leaned over and cupped Caro's face, and began kissing her gently.

But Caro pulled back. 'You haven't seen me in action, vicar. You haven't seen me really try. I love you, and I love all of this, I really do; but politics is something I know I can do well. Every week you preach about helping the less fortunate. Every week, more money from the collection than the church can afford goes off to Syria, or Burundi, or wherever. I know you mean what you say. But you have to let me do my bit as well . . .'

Angela cut in. 'Off in the world. Away from this little hidden valley. I thought this was *paradise* when I first saw it; and when you came here to join me, I knew it was. And now you're off – Northamptonshire, then London, then who knows where. I do respect what you want, Caro, but with this, little by little, you're leaving me. I think you only get one chance at happiness in this life. You only get one paradise. And if you walk out of it, you can't walk back in again. So – I'm sorry, darling Caro, but no, I can't do this.'

Caro said no more, but pulled Angela's face towards hers. She saw again the intense, freckled little face of the girl she had first met all those years ago, and she thrust her tongue into her mouth. They fell onto a carpet of leaf and moss, and made love. Stained with moisture and mud, they were noticed as they walked back through the village. But nobody said anything. They liked their vicar, and in Pebbleton they still believed in the oldest, most sacred law of English life: live and let live.

There had always been comments, of course. Angela was the first female vicar in the area, and when Caroline started arriving down from London most weekends, the obvious conclusions were drawn. Lady Broderick, the nearest thing Pebbleton had to a squire, had spoken to Angela one night after evensong.

'Now, vicar, you know I'm a traditional soul. I'm thrilled that you've brought back the King James and the Book of Common Prayer, and some of the good old hymns – which, trust me, is why fewer of the pews are empty. No incense, yet, and I approve of that as well. So please believe that I'm also speaking for others when I say that, while I'm a modern woman, I regard – er – unnatural practices as a sin. Forgive me for speaking so plainly.'

Angela, scarlet, replied, 'Lady Broderick, we are married. You are speaking to a married woman.'

'Not as far as I'm concerned, young lady.'

'The law ...'

Lady Broderick's jaw tightened: 'The Church ...'

Angela had stood very still, scarcely breathing. 'But ours is a God of love, Lady Broderick, and a God of infinite mercy. He made us as we are.'

'He did indeed, vicar, He did indeed. But that doesn't stop us from trying to live according to His instructions. Unnatural practices trouble me. But what I was going to say – and we're much less narrow-minded around here than you might think – is that as far as I'm concerned, so long as we don't have rainbow flags hanging from the rafters and kissing in the pulpit, your life is your own.'

There were of course gossips in the village. The old men who hung around outside the hairdressers every morning waiting for the daily arrival of the newspapers had a lot to say.

'What is it that lizzies actually do?'

'Hah, that's the question.'

'Fiddling around, I shouldn't wonder. Fingers and suchlike.'

'Turns your stomach.'

'All right for you, Mac. Worse for me.'

'Why's that?'

'My own poor dear wife is called Lizzie. Always has been. Can't look at her in the same way now.'

'Better go and get some advice from the vicar.'

A noise somewhere between 'catarrgh' and a filthy laugh greeted the arrival of the small mobile shop, laden with tabloids, full-fat milk and cigarettes.

Not long after their walk on the hill above the church, Caroline returned to Northamptonshire for the final selection meeting. In Pebbleton, it was a long, grey wait.

The following evening, Angela had just fed the boys their supper and packed them off upstairs to do some homework. Still no word. Oddly, nothing on Twitter. She had a meeting with the community policeman ahead of her, and was feeling lonely and scratchy. She was just about to pour herself a fortifying glass of wine when Caro burst in. As usual, she was like a warm wave of sunshine on a February morning. The vicarage immediately seemed to glow a little brighter.

'Well!'

'Well?'

'Good news and bad news.'

'Bad news first.'

'The bad news is, I'm not going to be around here quite so much, because' – Caroline imitated blowing a trumpet – 'I've got it.'

'You saw them off?' Angela was excited and pleased despite herself.

'I know. Impossible, but I did it.'

'Stop right there,' said Angela. 'This calls for a drink.' She brought a bottle of Suffolk gin, some tonic water which had lost its fizz, and a small bottle of bitters to the kitchen table. They sat for a moment in silence, drinking and listening to the sound of the wind in the Douglas firs behind the vicarage.

'Anyway,' began Caro, 'I had a stroke of luck to start with. You remember that the guy who used to write the Eds' speeches called me and suggested we travel up by train from London together. When I got to the station the others were there too – the old environment minister, who looks just like he does on the telly, very smart; and the woman who was going to run for mayor of London.

'So we got one of those arrangements with a table and four

seats, and we talked all the way up there. It was pretty obvious that they saw me as the innocent. They wanted to know what I was going to say, of course. Well, you know me. All that time in the City, busily researching away. Always prepared. So I had it ready. Lomax, I said.'

'The MP who's retiring?'

'That's the one. Lennie Lomax, I told them, was the very model of a good old-fashioned Labour MP. Started life down the mine, strong union man, collected the subs, strong as an ox, and a bastion of good sense in Parliament. Way back, he supported Kinnock against the militants. Didn't like Blair's Iraq war, but served as a whip nevertheless. Leonard was a rock. Leonard was everything the constituency needed. I told them I was just going to say how great Leonard was, and promise to do my best to be just the same kind of MP. And they all nodded at me and pretended not to take much notice. When we got there, we were picked up and whisked straight into the selection meeting. I chose to speak last. And they did it, one by one, the complete idiots. They got up on the stage and picked up the microphone and promised to be exactly like Leonard Lomax. First the clever journalist who wrote the Eds' speeches said he wanted to be like Leonard Lomax. Then the environment minister said that, as a long-time admirer, he wanted to be like Leonard Lomax. Then the woman who isn't going to run as mayor of London said she knew Leonard Lomax very well, and she wanted to be just like Leonard Lomax.'

'They stole your speech? The sods.' Angela was genuinely outraged on Caroline's behalf.

'Up to a point, dear heart. What was Lennie Lomax? He was a drunk, he was idle and he was an idiot. He treated the general management committee like shit. He was a complete embarrassment for years. Everyone in the local party hated him. So while those three were praising him, I could see the faces in the room getting longer and longer, and I could feel the temperature dropping like a stone.

'When my turn comes, the first thing I say is, "I don't think we need a microphone in this room, do we? We're all friends here." Then I go and sit down at the front of the stage, so I'm almost in the audience, rather than talking at them. And then I say, "Well, poor old Lennie Lomax. I understand a bit of sentiment, but frankly he wasn't a good representative for this seat. He didn't work hard enough, and he didn't treat his constituents with sufficient respect. I'm afraid I'm sitting in front of you today because I *don't* want to be Leonard Lomax." And there was this huge cheer, and they started to clap. And then I made a few jokes, and I said that I was a Christian and a gay woman, and that if they were bothered by either of those things, now was the time to say so. But they were just so pleased I wasn't drunk, brutish old Lennie Lomax that I won by a mile.'

Caro was so pleased by her own cleverness that she hadn't noticed Angela's return to the early-evening gin and tonic. And Angela was so blown away by Caro's story that she'd poured herself a second one.

'You . . . are . . . quite something. Maybe you were born to be a politician after all. I'm going to miss you horribly. I'm going to miss you so much it hurts me inside, as if I'd swallowed broken glass. But I'm going to be with you every step of the way. After you're elected I'll take time off mid-week and train it to London. And you, madam, will find ways to get down here. We will do this together.'

As the sun went down and the smell of the wood-burning stove began to percolate through the old vicarage, the two women snuggled together on the sofa and talked about the new, very difficult but not impossible, and exciting life ahead.

Politics Today

I tell you what, things would be a lot better today if the bastards hadn't kicked me out.

The Master (not on top form)

The first Conservative administration of the post-EU era had proclaimed itself a 'national government', on the basis that a handful of Eurosceptic Labour MPs had crossed the floor to support it, as did the eight Ukip Members. But the euphoria of victory had carried it for only a few months before exhaustion set in.

Political theatre is like actual theatre. It exposes frailties and it accelerates fate. Rivalries which, in civilian life, might have taken eighty years to fully emerge, gape in politics after a few months. Small flaws of character, which in the life of a dentist or a gardener might be merely irritating eccentricities, will tear a cabinet minister to pieces in less than a year. And so it had happened to the Conservatives' national government. Relatively decent people had been transmuted into gurning gargoyles and grotesque puppets, and set against one another, until the stage was mottled and sticky with blood. There was no brave new world. In parliamentary politics, there never is.

How, meanwhile, had the country fared? Formerly, Britain had been a divided, frenetic little archipelago, buzzing away thanks to high levels of immigration and the fickle favours of international capital. Freed to be herself, she began to fall back. Immigration almost ceased; the unions reasserted their power. The right-wing agenda proved less popular in practice than it had seemed during the election campaign. The abolition of comprehensive schools, and the introduction of fees for hospitals, had seemed like clarion calls in the manifesto; the reality in the streets of many cities was disgruntled and confused. Scotland's socialist upsurge became unstoppable.

A few of the City institutions that had threatened to leave the country in the event of Britain's departure from the EU, and relocate their headquarters to Paris and Frankfurt, had carried out their threat. Things hadn't been quite as catastrophic as the Europhiles had predicted, but house prices in London and the south-east tumbled. Bankers, having been the villains of previous decades, were rather missed once so many of them had gone – or rather, their free spending was missed by the smaller businesses that had depended upon it. Britain's proudly independent Treasury, no longer having to pay vast subventions to Brussels, found that the numbers still didn't add up. Three cabinet ministers were filmed frolicking happily on a bed by the seven-year-old daughter of one of them; the footage was posted on Facebook, and went viral. In other words, politics continued too much as usual.

It was in these circumstances that Alwyn Grimaldi rose to become leader of the Labour opposition. He'd been a fixture on the political bores' circuits for years – a regular speaker at Fabian conferences, always present at political book launches, a reviewer of newspapers on television programmes. His dandified clothing, Mediterranean colouring and exotic name led many people to write him off. But he was not only phenomenally well-organised and a reasonably sharp performer in the House; he had fashioned what the commentators call a 'narrative'. What this meant was that he spoke well and clearly about the mortal battle going on between global corporate power – mostly still centred in America, but increasingly in China as well – and the power of old-fashioned, elected democracies. Only politics, he argued, could redress the unfairnesses and evils of the relentlessly inventive and ever-young energy of capitalism. 'We are the civilisers,' he said, 'and we live in a country that still badly needs civilising.'

He had, in short, a story. He sounded like a latter-day Karl Marx, shorn of the simplistic political extremism that had caused so much mayhem during the twentieth century. The fact that he'd worked in corporate PR helped. Other Labour figures were more handsome, or prettier. They had more sensible names. They had better-cut suits. Like him, they had turned their backs on the Master and the legacy of New Labour. But somehow none of them matched the edgy, mildly paranoid mood of the time as well as did Alwyn Grimaldi.

Meanwhile, one small pebble at a time, the government's authority slipped away. A jolly, genial law officer who'd thought he'd be promoted to home secretary discovered the hard way that he wouldn't be. Behind his florid, Falstaffian mask he was a lean and angry man. Rather than accepting his demotion, he attacked the prime minister in highly personal terms and resigned his seat. The Conservatives threw everything at the by-election, and lost it. Under pressure, the PM mustered a cross-party majority to suspend David Cameron's five-year-Parliament rule. One stone . . .

Then the PM's old enemies in the 1922 Committee put it about that he'd become depressed, and there would have to be a leadership challenge. Foolishly, he denounced the anony-mous voices as 'fruitcakes and no-hopers', only to discover that a well-spoken and well-regarded female committee chairman was prepared to appear on the *Today* programme and announce that she would take him on. Two stones . . .

Still, no further landslide would have taken place had it not been for an entirely random accident on the slopes of Val d'Isère. The chief whip, pursuing a son skiing too fast down a black run, lost control, hit a pine tree, and was killed. The prime minister lost his closest political friend, and the only man who had a grip on the party. That by-election too was lost, this time to Alwyn Grimaldi's Labour Party. None of the commentators had expected this. So they were cross. As a result all of them, led by Peter Quint, who had been mocking Grimaldi as Labour's worst leader since Michael Foot, promptly reversed their positions and found glints of greatness in him.

Tory backbenchers, not knowing what to think – because no one was now telling them – grew uneasy. The party was at this time in bad-tempered coalition with the remaining rump of the UK Independence Party, which despite having lost its *raison d'être* after Britain's withdrawal from the EU,

struggled on in a mood of bloody-minded euphoria. Its fundamental position was that the Tory Party wasn't grumpy enough.
Certainly its own MPs, a colourful collection of chain-smoking,
shouty people, seemed furious about absolutely everything,
all of the time. One morning, in a spasm of pure fury after
reading a *Daily Mail* diary item about his exuberant bow tie,
its leader, Roger de Coverley, announced that he was withdrawing support from the coalition 'forthwith'.

In politics, 'forthwith' is a satisfying word. Forthwith! The
rumble of individual stones quickly became a deafening
avalanche, and the prime minister, bowing to what seemed
inevitable, went to the king and asked permission to dissolve
the House of Commons for a general election. The king, who'd
never much liked him in the first place, cheerfully agreed –
even though there was no obvious reason for an election.

If there's one thing the British people hate, it's an unnecessary general election. It gets in the way of the television
schedules, and greatly increases the number of irritating people
knocking on your door. But the die was cast.

In Barker, Caroline Phillips had Leonard Lomax's majority of
several thousand to defend. The constituency wasn't entirely
'safe' – it had gone Tory during the Thatcher years, and Ukip's
Paul Lambert was still haunting the countryside. Caro, therefore, fought like a tiger. She rose at five, and didn't return to
her room at the Travelodge until after midnight. She drank
no alcohol, lived on coffee and fruit, and spoke herself hoarse.
She had to begin to shake constituents' hands with her left
hand, because of the bruising on her right one. She was, at

least, known. Her sexuality and her beauty had ensured that she was one of the new candidates who was featured in the national media websites.

Perhaps, in the circles around Alwyn Grimaldi, word had already gone out that she was favoured by the Master. At any rate, neither the leader of the Labour Party nor any prominent shadow cabinet figures ever came to Barker to support her during the campaign. Nor did the Master himself. But his wife came; and a cluster of once-famous New Labour figures; and dozens of bright young things from London, whose work in obscure political consultancies apparently allowed them the time and freedom to help Barker choose its new Member of Parliament. Their old-fashioned canvassing, street by street, house by house, revealed that Caro's early lead was narrowing. The Muslim areas of the constituency were divided between radicals who supported the newly formed Islamic British Front, and those who remained loyal to the Labour Party. Luckily, the latter tended to be older, and more likely actually to vote.

Caro's Conservative opponent was a lean, elderly and supercilious grandee called James A. James, who had served as a minister under David Cameron. He had lost two constituencies so far, which only increased his bottomless contempt for the British electorate; but his rasping voice and eye for an opponent's weak spots made him dangerous. He pecked away at Caroline, portraying her as a cynical, wealthy, metropolitan blow-in who knew nothing about either Barker or the real world of profit and loss. 'The young girl', he called her. When they met face to face for debates in the constituency, he seemed completely impervious to her charm. Caro, who'd never experienced rejection like it, found herself spooked.

Then, a fortnight into the campaign, a Scottish journalist called Tony Moretti turned up. He said he was there to discuss a story about some skulduggery or other in the local council, but when they met, he urgently suggested that she ask James A. James whether he had ever visited a certain address in Cricklewood. The next evening, in front of a large audience at a local school, she did. The air seemed to go out of him. He had been two Jameses before; now he was barely a Jim. He didn't even turn up at the count to observe Caro winning the seat with an increased majority of 10,000. And when it was all over, she got a personal call of congratulations from the new prime minister elect, Alwyn Grimaldi.

In Glaikit, David Petrie had a far easier ride. The Scottish Nationalists had, bafflingly, chosen a former Tory, a baker called Fisher-Donaldson, to fight him. On Murdoch White's instructions, Davie said nothing about the Forlaw case or Lord Auchinleck; the Master, after consulting with his wife, had decided to pass the information about the sex ring cover-up to Alwyn Grimaldi, as it would have the maximum political impact coming from the party leader. And so it proved: it knocked the stuffing out of the Conservatives, and it also put Grimaldi, warily and uneasily, in the Master's debt. (Had Tony Moretti and his comrades at the Scottish Socialist newsletter known that all their hard work would result in a substantial boost for the Master, whom they despised from the soles of their boots to the tops of their skulls, they would probably have done away with themselves.)

David Petrie had no need to get in on that act. Compared to the struggle for the nomination, the election itself was almost an anticlimax.

And so, on Friday, 21 September 2018, the Earl of Dimbleby, chairing the BBC's election coverage, was able to announce that the barely known Alwyn Grimaldi was the country's new prime minister. 'It is customary on these occasions,' said Lord Dimbleby, with the merest hint of a sardonic smile, 'to describe the result as historic, and to suggest that nothing will ever be the same. But I rather think we've gone beyond that, haven't we?' And he winked.

At his recently-bought country house on the South Downs, the Master held what he called a kitchen supper, though a more accurate description would have been council of war. Sadie, sober now for more than a year, was an immaculate hostess, far more amusing than she had ever been in the old days of power. Leslie Khan, Margaret Miller, Murdoch White – all the old warriors were there.

'Well everybody,' the Master said, 'stage one is complete. The Tories are out. We do have the tiny, tiny little problem of that fool Grimaldi, but our people are in place, enough of them to give us a real choice when the time comes. We have some spectacularly talented and driven new MPs. Now, as we all know, it's our job to make sure they don't put a foot wrong, that they climb the ladder so fast it's almost impossible to concentrate on their rise. So keep them close. Make them your friends. If they give you any kind of trouble, bring them to me.'

There was a delicious scent of shepherd's pie, and a couple of bottles of decent Burgundy had been opened, but the Master led his guests outside before eating. To general bemusement, a stocky farmer was waiting for them with no fewer than four shotguns under one vast arm.

'I've taken up clay pigeons, everyone,' said the Master with boyish glee. 'You must all have a go. It's the most relaxing thing. I find it helps me to think.'

Only the former home secretary Margaret Miller and Murdoch White accepted a weapon.

Leslie Khan was laughing. 'Oh dear me. Oh dear, dear, dear me. Oh dearie, *dearie* me. This must never get out. Imagine the papers. Imagine the cartoons. Master dearest, this is just too funny for words.'

Murdoch disagreed. 'It's not funny. It's not funny at all. It's bloody dangerous. What are the rest of us going to say the next time some halfwit jumps up and says, "Oooh, he's just a Tory"?'

'Tories shoot birds,' said the Master. 'I just shoot imaginary enemies. Pull!'

Like a little pink plate, the clay disc soared across the horizon. The Master failed to bring it down with his first barrel, but shattered it with his second.

Peter Quint

All journalists are bastards. They just are; I don't know why.
The Master

Caroline was having a lovely time. The Master's wife had taken a personal interest. An Italian leather-goods company apparently wanted a British politician as a non-executive director – this was completely within parliamentary rules, as long as she declared it. The income allowed her to take a lease on a flat in north London, which Angela helped turn into a cosy nest. Caro found magazines and websites queuing up to interview her, concentrating on her supposedly pious background. Her unabashed use of the term 'Christian socialism' intrigued cynical, secular journalists. She charmed her way through media encounters, and was soon a favourite Labour backbench interviewee. Labour women whom she dismissed as 'the sisterhood' and the Master himself called 'the coven' tended to shun her, but as a lesbian she had a trump card. Her first campaigns were well-chosen: in support of persecuted Christians in the Middle East, and for the setting up of refuges for street children in British cities. The first won her the support of Conservative-minded newspapers. The second involved fundraising in the City. She exploited her connections with St Peter's Asset Management, and soon had a network of friendly supporters in what remained of plutocratic London.

So life was good. She was that rare thing, a popular politician. The trolls went for her, but as Caroline had learned never to peer under stones, she barely noticed. Angela had promised to move east from Devon. Every day brought a new challenge, an interesting test. At last Caro knew that she was doing something substantial with her life.

Not that everything worked perfectly. She wasn't much impressed with the actual House of Commons. The *Palace of Westminster* is an ancient ship beached on a mudbank. In its bowels there are tangles of pipes and metal ladders, old boilers and dank stinks. It has its staterooms, floridly decorated with historical scenes by Victorian painters. It has its galleys and its restaurants, their staffs more or less permanently aboard. Its decks overlooking the Thames, and its world-famous grotesque superstructure, the unlikely towers and the huge funnels from which smoke no longer billows. Its voyages typically last for five years, during which time the huge crew learn the shortcuts through its maze of corridors, and the rhythm of its days. They form firm friendships, and they make lifelong hatreds. They all fall in love, but only a few with other people. What most unites them, however, is their distance from land. From the *Palace*, England, Scotland, Wales and Northern Ireland seem very far away. Beyond the encrusted hull there can be found whirlpools, jagged rocks and far-off counties inhabited by those dangerous, incomprehensible creatures, the voters.

And on this voyage, Caroline Phillips found herself seasick. It was a real feeling, a non-metaphorical nausea brought on by the bearpit of the Commons chamber, the vile food, the stale air, and above all the affected sympathy of her colleagues. On bad days, she felt she was walking around wearing a T-shirt that read *Lezzie Christian Nutter*. Was there really a place for her in the modern Labour Party?

When she had taken her troubles to the Master, he'd pointed out that those who fitted in easily also became indistinguishable. That wasn't exactly Caro's problem during her first few months, but she still found things harder than she'd expected. She'd prepared a good maiden speech, and it had been listened to respectfully by the couple of dozen MPs who were in the chamber at the time. She'd got herself onto a committee – a small one, but still. She dutifully issued press releases, and the press dutifully ignored them. She'd been invited onto a panel on a Radio 4 women's programme, but it had clearly been designed to undermine the new prime minister, and in defending him she had come across as prim and humourless. So for all her efforts she still found herself, as she told Angela, 'big in Barker', but nowhere else.

As time went on, the Angela problem became a tougher one. Caro's only options were either to skimp on her constituency work, or to leave London on Thursday evenings, drive down to Pebbleton, spend Friday there, and then head up to Barker for the weekend, getting back to town by mid-morning on Monday. That was what she did, covering thousands of miles every month. But she was soon exhausted. Even maintaining a pretence of interest in Angela's boys was becoming beyond her. She needed her energy for politics.

Every morning, as she rolled over in bed in her north London den, Caro checked her phone for messages; every morning there'd be some she'd slept through. Once, it was the Master himself. 'Time to reach a new level, Ms Phillips. I want you to win Peter Quint over. Regard it as a kind of test.'

Peter Quint was a famous figure. Caro set out to woo him. She had been given two tickets to a dinner at the American ambassador's residence, at which the guests would be serenaded by a great Motown star. Angela wasn't available, so she invited Quint as her other half.

'If I were anybody else, Mr Q, this might be thought rather forward of me. But we both understand it's business; I am no danger to your reputation, nor you to mine. This is just a chance to get acquainted.'

Quint wasn't stupid. 'We both know who's behind this. But it's a good idea.'

The US ambassador lives in a grand house tucked inside the north-west corner of Regent's Park, guarded and secluded. And it was indeed an extraordinary evening. There was a full orchestra for the singer, excellent Southern food – the ambassador was from Mississippi – and a sprinkling of the most interesting people in London.

Over dinner, Caroline fixed Peter Quint with her gaze, and tried to project her most intense warmth upon him. To her surprise, he merely blinked and looked back.

'You're not interested in me, are you?' she asked. She

wasn't offended, just intrigued: this had hardly ever happened to her before.

'Why would I be?' he asked. 'You're being pushed up the tree by a mutual friend. But you don't seem to stand for much. You've got no power. You're clearly not a gossip. Why would I be interested in you?'

'Most men are.'

'Well, you are pretty, I give you that. But you're not interested in men, are you?'

'Not in that way. But that's hardly the point, is it?'

'I'm sorry,' said Quint, swallowing a yawn, 'but what other way is there?'

'Most men aren't that interested in sex,' said Caroline. 'Well, they are a bit, but what they want most of all is to be admired. They want women with big eyes who ask them questions and pretend to listen to the answers, and tell them how *fascinating* they are. You're mostly just big babies who want your tummies tickled.'

This was uncomfortably close to the truth. Peter Quint had recently been kicked out by his girlfriend. And her departure had left, he had to concede, a mirror-shaped absence.

His rented flat off the Bayswater Road had been hurriedly reconverted into the office which hid all his professional secrets. Pinned to a large, framed corkboard that covered one wall were the recent columns of his so-called rivals, with every simile or half-interesting fact circled in green ink. Scraps of information were neatly filed on the desk – things that had been said by long-dead politicians, jaw-dropping statistics filched from Wikipedia, biographies and books of political analysis, marked and annotated. And, of course, all his own previous columns, neatly pasted into large black-covered books. For Peter Quint was not averse to quoting himself. Once a year or so had passed, nobody remembered what had been in any newspaper; thinking up new things to write was a waste of effort. These days, Peter Quint's prodigious output was at least 80 per cent plagiarism. The remaining fifth was based on a remarkable contacts book, and a talent for social occasions.

As Caroline had already noticed, Quint had a thing he did with his eyes. He would put them slightly out of focus while people were talking to him, and then he would look beyond them. His glance would graze his interlocutor's shoulder, then bounce over it. He'd start with the faces closest to him, then move over their shoulders too, to the rest of the room. Once he'd worked out who was the most important person present, he saw nobody else. Like a blind ball of ambition he'd wobble against the people around him, and keep moving, and keep wobbling, until he'd wobbled up to the important person. Then, suddenly, his eyes would come back into focus, and brim with gleeful interest. And he'd stand there, chubby and immovable, wibbling and agreeing with whatever the important person said. This did not make him popular at parties – and he spent much of his life at parties – but it was, in a way, his job.

Caroline had found Quint mysterious. In truth, his story was fairly straightforward. Quint had risen slickly through a provincial grammar school, York University and the BBC trainee scheme before landing his first political column at the ripe old age of twenty-three with the *Mercury*. He became the last of the old-school columnists. He had the face for it. A broad brow, lustrous grey hair brushed back over it, an aquiline nose and a strong jaw gave him a vaguely classical look. His byline photograph was magnificent – intimidating, imperial, impossible to fault. 'Why, you look like a Roman emperor, my dear,' his adoring mother had told him when it had first appeared in the *Observer*. 'Y-e-e-e-s . . . But Nero, or Caligula?' his more knowing girlfriend had asked. Quint, however, had armoured himself long ago against the nay-sayers. He was perfectly capable of sitting silently, gazing at his newspaper photograph with a smirk of admiration, for an hour at a time.

The Master had taken Quint under his wing because he was *not* untalented. He could produce a thousand words of literate, biting and often amusing copy in well under an hour, on any topic, and from almost any viewpoint that was required. He understood the dilemma of the political columnist: how to keep being read.

Interlude
How to be a Political Columnist

There are two gambits, Peter Quint would say. **Here's** the problem: if you write what you believe, and stay consistent, your readers will quickly get sick of you. They'll know what you're going to say before you've said it. Why should they read on? One answer was to keep on saying it, only ever more vividly. But that meant saying it more extremely. Trouble was, you ended up ranting, stuck in fourth gear with your extreme viewpoint, and unable to reverse neatly back into common sense. This he called Liddling.

The alternative was to change your view regularly, and pick subjects the readers didn't expect. Keep moving. Zigzag. The danger then was becoming a professional, and therefore wearisome, contrarian. Everyone thought the Russian president a dangerous lunatic? Then your job was to warmly defend him. Popular opinion was turning against Alwyn Grimaldi? As one of his most long-standing critics, you leapt to his defence. This also had a limited shelf-life, though longer than the alternative. It was more interesting. Quint called it the Jenkins gambit.

During his salad years, Peter Quint had tried both. He had swung back and forth in his defence of Labour and the

Interlude: How to be a Political Columnist

Tories – never predictable, but never taken quite seriously either. He had snarled, spat and confected anger. He could be quite good. But the truth was that he was too comfortable, too thoroughly pleased with himself, to be convincingly angry. So he learned to oil. Again, the boy was good. He had buttery, palm-oily skin. His hair was oily. He became a sucker, a climbing vine. Extreme left-wingers and staunch conservatives felt his slick attentiveness coil itself around them, and assumed he was a genuine admirer. Sometimes he was. His columns were full of gossip he picked up from hanging around beside people at parties. For that reason, they were worth reading. Anyone on the up, or who held a position of power or influence – a senior civil servant, a flavour-of-the-month broadcaster, all ministers and shadow ministers – would be slobberingly flattered. But everybody else – those who were beginning to fall from favour, those who clearly would never make it right to the top, the averagely intelligent backbenchers – would feel the lash of Quint's contempt.

For Peter Quint was an admirer of power, not of politics. Increasingly he felt that anybody who had gone to all the tedious trouble of getting him or herself elected was self-evidently a moron. A well-paid journalist, who'd never been elected, who'd never tried to steer anything bigger than a moderately-sized lawnmower, had, he felt, the right – the duty – to look down on MPs from a great height. And looking down was what Peter did second best. He hung on the system like a growth, oiling up . . . and pissing down.

The Master was Peter's oldest, and still most influential, source. These days he rarely got to speak to him directly, but the Master had plenty of excellent go-betweens, from former ministers like Murdoch White to sexy, intriguing Ella James. It was absolutely clear to Peter that Ella and the Master were more than colleagues, although it was equally clear that this was in a category of information never to be relayed to his readers. But the Master had been making Peter Quint's life hard over the past few months.

For reasons Peter had not yet got to the bottom of, the Master was constantly promoting rising Labour MPs Peter had never heard of, but was now obliged to praise in his columns. Ella would make a call: 'You might take a look at the new Member for Neath. We'd be ever so grateful.' The problem was, they rarely lasted long. First there had been Facey Romford, a fresh-faced farming socialist. Interesting: he was handsome, he spoke well; but, it later turned out, he had a penchant for bondage and sadomasochism. Photographs were produced. No more Facey Romford. Then there had been the reformed Islamist Abu al-Britani, a bright and compelling spokesman for community tolerance and moderation. He'd even spoken out against the veil. Al-Britani, however, turned out to have been working for IS all along: he was apprehended at a royal garden party with a bomb inserted in his back passage. He, and it, were removed to a safe part of Green Park and ignited. Some well-bred trees were damaged.

Then there was Annie Baldwin, a feisty girl – but then came 'Zebra-gate', and the animal-rights people made sure that Annie returned to obscurity. Soon the Peter Quint column was being mocked each fortnight by *Private Eye* for its promotion of brilliant new Labour MPs who then mysteriously imploded (except for those who exploded). *Private Eye* called it 'the curse of Quint' – but 'Quint' wasn't the word the magazine used; it had childishly renamed him.

Peter hated all this. He hated it so much that he affected to regard it as simply a bit of light-hearted fun, and even went along to a *Private Eye* lunch to show what a good sport he was. The lunch was held in a former reform school for wayward girls in Greek Street, Soho, where the food was excellent, and only the shifty and dishevelled nature of the diners hinted at what was really going on. Unfortunately, Ian Hislop, the then editor, announced Peter to the assembled gathering as 'our good friend Peter Cunt'. Shunning a tempting-looking salmon soufflé, Peter stormed out.

Had he been a bolder soul, he might have cut his connections with the Master there and then. But Ella had been flattering and persuasive, and the Master's wife had condescended to have lunch with him. It was at around this time that he got the story about Alwyn Grimaldi's sister.

Now Peter found himself boosting the career of a young and determined new Scottish MP called David Petrie. And this time, it seemed, the Master was on the money. Petrie had barely put a foot wrong, and was already widely tipped to be heading for better things.

It occurred to Peter that his column would be stronger if it had a villain as well as a hero. Well before her invitation to the US ambassador, he had wondered whether that uppity lesbian Caroline Phillips was getting much too easy a ride elsewhere in the media. Their evening together strengthened his dislike. She was arrogant, self-assured, and she thought a

free evening out would win him, Peter Quint, over. So the
next morning he began to go for her, just the odd phrase and
sentence to start with. Quint was far too intelligent and astute
to attack Caro's sexuality or her apparently strong religious
views, but he did make it clear that he suspected her growing
reputation was based on the pathetic susceptibilities of the
male politicians around her – a weakness that Mr Peter Quint,
for one, did not share. Though he did like his tummy to be
tickled, that was true.

In the Rose Garden

Beware your constituents. The friendlier they are, the more cautious you should be.

The Master

Winter was ending. The government of Alwyn Grimaldi ground on. That talented, exotic and untrustworthy man had scored a few early big hits. Relations with Edinburgh had calmed down. Almost everything had been devolved: Grimaldi now agreed to devolve the Post Office and the weather. His greatest victory had been the transformational security deal with the Middle Eastern caliphate. In late 2018, Caliph Abdülmecid III had been welcomed to London. Almost all the old countries of the European Union had by now banned the veil and imposed a moratorium on the building of new mosques. Grimaldi saw his opportunity.

The bones of the Westminster Concordat promised that there would be no British interference in the affairs of the caliphate, and guaranteed freedom of worship for Muslims in Britain. In return, the caliph had signed a wide-ranging security pact; since his religious police were now working with the British security services, there had not been a single further attack. From now on, disaffected young Wahhabis and Deobandis from Birmingham or Cardiff were simply encouraged to return to former Iraq or Syria and do good works rebuilding shattered cities, offering aid to the displaced, and protecting the new rulers.

There had been outrage on the right of politics, and among some disillusioned mullahs, but the overwhelming reaction from British voters was one of relief. Grimaldi, who until then had been regarded as a likeable but ineffectual creature, found himself popular. He seemed to have put on two inches in height. He carried himself differently. The cartoonists, who had focused on his nose and compared him to Pinocchio, laid off a little bit. In the Commons, where his wafer-thin majority depended upon a couple of flaky, borderline-certifiable backbenchers, he began to exude something like authority. The newspapers, with Quint and Rawnsley to the fore, revised their assumption that his government would last no longer than a few months.

And yet, in his moment of triumph, Grimaldi had made some lethal enemies. Washington was livid – the president included Great Britain in his 'axis of appeasement'. Closer to home, the Master and his cronies, some of whom had been prepared to give Grimaldi the benefit of their many doubts, now saw him as a traitor – and worse, popular with it.

The plan remained unchanged. The Master, however, intimated that Grimaldi had to be terminated sooner rather than later. Peter Quint's paper obediently ran a big investigation into the sources of funding for the large new mosques that were being built along the British coast, from Southwold to

Aberdeen. Saudi money had dried up, dampening the London property boom of the early years of the century. But now new gentlemen, bearded and wearing flowing white robes, arrived by plane from Damascus and Aleppo with huge wealth at their fingertips. Pure the caliph himself might be, but the caliphate contained as many traders and middlemen as before.

Not all the new Muslim money went into the restoration of the sacred sites. Quite a bit of it purchased country houses around Sunningdale, or went to the direction and beautification of mosques. In one of his most pungent columns, Peter Quint asked what had happened to Britain's money-laundering regulations, and to the planning system, which seemed oddly relaxed where the mosques were concerned. He revealed that Alwyn Grimaldi's sister was working for a Middle East construction company, and that several key cabinet ministers were living a lifestyle which appeared to be incompatible with their salaries. All of this information – some of which was true – had come via Ella. Alwyn Grimaldi's reputation took its first serious knock.

None of this would have mattered very much, except that something strange seemed to have happened to British politics. Westminster was completely losing its grip on the country's imagination. The newspapers might praise, then chastise, the government – but who read the newspapers? The websites, and the generations that fed on them, were interested only in entertainment and celebrity murders.

After the intellectual man of ideas, Ed Miliband, and his irate nemesis Michael Gove, hardly any politicians were recognised by the general public at all. It began to look as if the entire democratic system was nothing more than a conjuror's trick: it depended on the public paying attention, and as soon as they stopped, the colourfully-painted pieces of pasteboard lay inert and useless on the table. The Grimaldi government spoke: and was not heard. Schools got on with teaching extreme religious views, or nothing very much at all, just as they liked. The failing privatised rail companies were now failing in public ownership. The collapse of parts of the National Health Service had meant a return to private doctors charging what they could get away with. The cheapest and most popular ran their clinics as wholly-owned subsidiaries of pharmaceutical companies. Relentlessly, year by year, the number of people who bothered to vote continued to decline.

Alwyn Grimaldi, who understood that elected power was in a final and desperate struggle to survive against the power of the market, did not merely sit back and do nothing. He struggled to repeat the success of the Westminster Concordat. National work centres were established to provide compulsory literacy training. The mayor of London, Lady Penny, had been allowed to establish a new free-floating currency to be used inside the M25 only, and the so-called 'red penny' was now worth almost as much as a regular pound sterling. But the government found itself virtually ignored by what remained of the printed media, and by television and internet bulletins. There is something worse in politics than abuse. The Labour government of Alwyn Grimaldi found itself boasting to a nation of turned backs.

As Caro enjoyed the early-spring sunshine in Regent's Park, it did not seem to her that all was lost. Peter Quint's attacks on her in the press may have been an irritation, but Caroline was a buoyant girl. She was a cork. There was life, and growth, and hope. She passed the rosebeds.

'*Remember me*' . . . '*Peace*' . . . '*Perception*' . . . she read as she walked. Hardly any of the rose blooms were visible yet – just an occasional splash of yellow or deep blood-red – but the very names seemed colourful and promising. Remember me, who I was. Perception. Light trails of scent. Caro thought: I am changing, this is a time of change for me.

'*Sheila's Perfume*' . . . '*Deep Secret*' . . . '*Thinking of You*' . . . '*Octavia Hill*' . . . On she walked.

'Queen Mary's Gardens, Regent's Park,' had been the last words the cultured, neatly painted and silk-scarfed woman had said the day before, in the central lobby of the House of Commons. Before their meeting, going on what she'd picked up from the local newspaper, which described Leila Umar as 'outspoken', Caro had expected to be confronted by an angry-looking woman in a burqa. Or was it a niqab? She could never remember the difference. But this particular constituent, a dentist from the outlying part of Barker known as Springtown – a tough and down-at-heel suburb despite its name – confounded Caro's expectations. Mrs Umar was dressed in an M&S suit, and appeared poised and relaxed among the passing MPs and journalists, half-amused and, from the very first, eloquent.

Leila Umar was observant enough to notice the new MP's surprise. 'Not your average Paki?' she'd teased Caro. 'You all need to do a lot of rethinking about our community, Mrs Phillips. I know your Mother of Parliaments very well indeed.

We are not all village girls. But I want to talk to you properly. Not just as my Member of Parliament, but as, I hope, a friend. So let's meet somewhere quieter and easier tomorrow. At last, at last, spring is coming.' And Leila had suggested this fragrant, leaf-green oasis with its beds of roses just to the north of the choked, honking chaos of the Marylebone Road.

There was a flash of sun, a flush, a fleshy warmth here. And there was colour – not just the apple of the grass and the emerald of the newly budding trees, but the turquoise and scarlet of saris, and the gold and black of an Arab woman in a chador, with an elaborately patterned scarf.

Caro reflected on the apparent distaste shown by the English for their own public parks. Here there were Chinese and Indian families, Japanese tourists and French voices; but the only white English flesh was that of the occasional passing runner. She found herself wondering if the British, as they grew ever more slovenly and frantic, had lost the habit of simply standing back, sniffing the air and enjoying the moment. She felt she had a talent for the big questions. (Tart Angela had said, 'Less so for the big answers, dear.') Or was it simply that in London there was little time for sniffing the roses and noting the changing seasons? This was a frantic city, no longer really part of England, where everyone seemed skittering and scurrying, clawing themselves up invisible walls, teetering on wobbly ladders, buffeted by the high winds of ridiculous ambition.

The wind was cold, and she hugged her coat tightly to herself. Silly place to meet after all, at this time of year – not even a coffee shop anywhere about. Caro was about to leave when she saw Mrs Umar waving at her from a bench. She seemed very small by comparison with the two green-uniformed gardeners who were noisily spreading muck on a rosebed from the back of a trailer, and who might regard her with contempt. Just my imagination, probably, Caro thought; but she felt herself warming to Leila Umar nonetheless.

Leila stood, and they shook hands rather formally, then walked together towards the ornate little bridge across a small pond.

'You did not expect to be approached by . . . our community so early?'

'I'm in Parliament to help everybody in the constituency, of course.'

'Yes, of course you are. And of course I'm here for help. But also to speak to you as a friend, who knows the town of Barker very well. All my life I have lived in Springtown. My papa came over from Pakistan in the 1960s. My husband is also from Barker. He is an electrician and, by-the-grace-of-Allah-the-merciful-the-wise, a good man, a kind man.'

'I'm glad to hear it. Why did you think I wouldn't expect to be approached by constituents who happen to be Muslim, though?'

'Ah, I thought that like most of your people, you would be bigoted and against us.'

'Well, I'm not. But to be candid, Mrs Umar, I'd been worried that I wouldn't be very popular with you. There were a group of Muslims in the audience on the evening of my selection as candidate who, if you remember, made much of my private life.'

'Many people are old-fashioned. Even I, perhaps, am a little old-fashioned, Mrs Phillips. And by the way, may I ask, where does the "Mrs" come from?'

Caroline had long expected the question, though not today: 'Well, I'm married, and I . . . I feel more comfortable with it. It's just my choice.'

'Everything is your choice, sister. That is England.'

'But Muslims are particularly harsh on gay people.'

'Ah, little sister' – though surely Mrs Umar, with her wrinkle-free skin, huge dark eyes and soft hair tumbling out from below her scarf, was younger than Caroline? – 'all people of religion, everywhere in the world, believe in limits of that kind. The noble Quran is modest and restrained on these subjects. As compared, for instance, to your own Bible. I have read that you are a Christian.'

Caroline stiffened. She wanted this conversation to be over. 'Mine is a God of love, not of prohibitions.'

Mrs Umar stopped, tightened her green and yellow scarf, and then declaimed like a Victorian actress, waving her gloved hand under Caroline's nose: 'Let those who find not the where-withal for marriage, keep themselves chaste, until Allah gives them means out of his grace.' That's *chaste*, not *chased*, sister. The noble Quran. 24.33, I think you'll find. It sounds reason-able to me. Good Muslims have never had to deal with the dirty-minded prying and prohibiting of your own St Paul.'

'Very well, Mrs Umar. I am who I am, and whatever our differences, I'm of course at your service. I want to be the Member of Parliament for everybody in Barker, irrespective of their personal views.'

'That is indeed very liberal of you. What a liberal country this is,' said Mrs Umar drily. 'My thanks. Shall we turn to the matter in hand?'

Ahead on the path, a dishevelled man was running towards them. He didn't look like a runner kind of runner – he was wearing jeans and a thick jersey. Instinctively, Caroline drew to one side to let him pass. But as he did, he turned and spat at Mrs Umar – a long yellow stream of frothy gob landed on her sleeve. Caroline was briefly paralysed with shock. The man took a few further steps, then turned and spat again. This time he hit Mrs Umar's face. The spit dribbled down her cheek. She looked back at him, expressionless. He turned and ran on.

Caroline half-shouted after him, then stopped and automatically reached up to brush her constituent's face. But Leila flinched away and used her scarf to clean herself. 'Well, that was well-timed.'

'I'm terribly sorry. How horrible for you. I should have done something. I didn't know . . .'

'That's all right. What could you have done? Brute. But at least now you see. For us, in this liberal country, this kind of thing happens all the time. You never know who will be next, where will be next. Now, we – the community, that is – followed the election campaign, of course. We noticed that defending women's rights was something you talked about. Rather a lot. You gave that interview to the *Mail*. So we have discussed this, and we have decided to trust you with our most precious plan and hope.'

'Can I be clear,' Caroline asked, 'about just who "the community" are?'

'My dear, nothing sinister, I assure you. We are simply the ordinary, mainstream Muslim people of Springtown. No terrorists, no extremists. Just hard-working British shop-keepers and tradespeople, mothers and grannies and children – all looking to you.'

'You are very eloquent, Mrs Umar. What exactly do you want me to do?'

Mrs Umar walked in silence for a moment or two before replying. 'The Jews. The Jews have it. In north London. Hendon, Golders Green, up that way. An *eruv*, they call it.'

'Yes . . .' Caroline vaguely remembered something about Hasidic Jews and the erection of poles and wires.

'Well, in Barker we want much the same thing. If it's good enough for the Jews, it's good enough for law-abiding Muslims. We want an area – not a very big area, just a few streets in each direction around the mosque – where we will be allowed to live in peace under God's laws.'

'You want a special . . . Sharia . . . area? In the middle of my constituency?'

'Exactly. Where our women don't have to be frightened because they are dressed modestly. Where our men, Mrs Phillips, don't have semi-naked flesh rubbed in their noses, and the stink of alcohol from shops and pubs. We have our own ways of dealing with people who misbehave, and flout God's law. We just want to be left alone to govern ourselves in peace – modesty and peace – without extremists marching through our streets. We cause nobody any harm. And if the government is worried about hot-headed young boys taking up violent *jihad*, then frankly their best bet is to help us reinforce the authority of our own elders and our mullah.'

This was not what Caro had expected when she'd taken the short taxi ride to Regent's Park. She could see the dangers. There was already a campaign in Barker and the neighbouring towns against the building of a third, and larger, mosque. Supporting Mrs Umar's proposal wouldn't make her popular with her white constituents. On the other hand, she'd just seen for herself the kind of abuse Muslim women had to put up with; and if something similar had been allowed for the Jews of north London, what really was the case against giving it to Muslims in the Midlands? She needed time to think.

'I need time to think.'

'So you're not turning us down flat. This is good news. I told them before I came down here that you were a good woman. You see, you are not all the same. That's what I said.'

At that moment a figure in a full black burqa waved at them across the pond and whooped in a broad Barker accent, 'Eeh, Leila! That you, swee'haa?'

'Oh my goodness, Mrs Phillips, there's Fatima. What a coincidence. She lives just around the corner from me. She's studying international diplomacy at London University.'

Fatima bustled over. The two Barker women exchanged kisses and hugs, and Mrs Umar introduced Caro.

'An MP? Well, we aa moving in posh circles. Teck a phoatie?'

'Yes, of course. You don't mind, do you, Mrs Phillips? And then perhaps one of the three of us, all girls together?'

And so, as Caro and Mrs Umar grinned bravely in the cold, the picture was taken on Fatima's mobile phone by a helpful passer-by. Fatima was smiling too, a smile of contempt, but you couldn't see that under her burqa.

Once Caro had left, Mrs Umar met the runner around the back of a rhododendron bush, thanked him – 'That was well done' – and handed him a slim envelope.

David Petrie, MP

In politics, you are never alone; in politics, you are always alone.

The Master

The House of Commons chamber was smaller than David Petrie had thought it would be. It was dimly lit, and smelled of leather and dust. The corridors around it were populated mainly by statues of half-forgotten statesmen, a convocation of icy, silent, sneering marble. Attendants drowsed, and the smell of stew rolled up from underground. David's office, manned by Bunty, was shared with a man from Wales who seemed to be conducting half a dozen different affairs, although he had a wife back in Swansea. He was the first man David had ever met who had his hair 'done' rather than cut. He kept photographs of himself on his desk. Davie had taken against him from the start.

The fat wodge of constituency work that arrived by mail and email every morning he found easy enough to cope with, despite Bunty. Occasionally, when some piece of paper went missing, Bunty would explain, 'Ah elbow-filed it.'

'What?'

'Ken, like this,' she'd said, nudging a pile of paper with her elbow straight into the wastepaper bin beside her desk. 'Ye dinnae really need it.'

And the strange thing was, she was almost always right.

The work wasn't too hard – running the workmen at home, keeping on top of balance sheets and cash flow, had been tougher. But out in the corridors at Westminster, waiting in committee meeting rooms, queuing for his coffee and sandwiches, Petrie felt out of place and lonely. He kept yawning. Nobody seemed to know who he was. Sometimes he imagined his father's questioning face: 'Big man, eh?'

No, he knew himself better than that. He was a medium-sized, uncomfortable man, just pretending to be confident. He became adept at using his tablet and his mobile to make it look as if he was working, when really, most of the time he was just waiting for someone to come and talk to him.

Davie found, to his surprise, that he was a bit older than the average new MP. They all seemed so bouncy, desperately ambitious and glossy with self-confidence. There was no anger in them. He had anger; the swift defenestration of Lord Auchinleck, after a devastating little column by Peter Quint, had been too fast, almost too painless to stop him feeling angry. He made a couple of friends, Scottish Labour men he'd known back home from conferences and TV discussions. But he didn't feel he'd joined a club worth joining.

There were a lot of women around – 'making eyes', as Mary would have put it. Researchers, more than MPs. Journalists, too. After a while, there was one girl in particular. He assumed she worked for some regional TV station or other, and she always seemed to be popping up – bumping into him, smiling, catching his eye, smiling. But she had a tight, professional face; hardly any lips.

One evening he was in the Pugin Room waiting for a guy from *The Times* who was doing a feature on the bright new MPs to watch. (Why had they chosen *him*? The Master's team? Of course.) He liked the Pugin Room – the wallpaper with gold on it and the plush chairs and all the dark wood corresponded better to his idea of what Parliament should be like than the functional cafés over in Portcullis House, or the dreary communality of the Strangers' Dining Room. The Girl Who Smiled came up to his table and asked if she could join him. She sat down without waiting for an answer, waved at the waiter as if he was a friend, and ordered a round of sandwiches and a gin and tonic. She was pretty, he thought: a shrewdly clever face, dark-brown eyes that held your attention and didn't let go. A friendly lass and all. Some kind of English accent – not London – which Petrie couldn't place. He enjoyed telling her about Ayrshire, and the business he'd built up. He found that, without meaning to, he was making the firm sound bigger and grander than it really was. She went on about how great it was to find a Labour MP who'd actually done something in the real world. He showed her the palms of his hands, still slightly callused from proper work. They had a laugh. Enough of a laugh so that when the *Times* guy arrived he was wearing his eyebrows halfway up his damned forehead. As soon as he came, she upped and left; gave Davie her card. But she was discreet enough not to even peck him on the cheek.

Not a peck. Not that he was tempted. Lonely; not tempted.

He went back each night to a flat in Dolphin Square, rented from an ex-MP who had lost his seat at the last election, and let his mind wander. He didn't think about Mary, but he thought about sex. Sex, Murdoch White had warned him, was a distraction he couldn't afford. To feed the anger inside him, the only thing was power. Nothing could get in the way of that. So he would pour himself a drink and call home and talk to Mary for at least half an hour, sometimes longer. The boys were in bed by then, of course, but he'd often call again at breakfast time, and get a few cheerfully garbled sentences back.

The London flat was posher than he was used to, with deep leather sofas and a huge flat-screen TV, and was walking distance from the Commons. It made things easy. To start with, Davie didn't have much ambition to see London. He'd never been one for the theatre, or opera, or any of that shite. He went out a few times to the pictures, or as they called them here the 'fillums', but it wasn't much fun sitting by yourself with a bag of popcorn. The London boozers were anonymous and expensive; if he wanted a few pints, the Members' Bar, or even the Pugin Room, were cheaper and easier. Anyway, in those first few months he was determined to put his shoulder to the wheel and show folk what he was made of. Thanks to the Master, he was the first of his intake to get onto a select committee – the best one by far, the Public Accounts Committee – and he worked hard in the Commons library boning up before its sessions.

To his surprise, all sorts of invitations arrived within the first few months – offers to meet journalists, invitations to the Irish embassy, suggestions that he might join the cross-party group on pelagic fishing, or coastal defences (Glaikit was hardly a coastal constituency, but one village and a small strand of oily pebbles apparently counted), or the Anglo-Russian group, or the Scotch whisky group . . . and so on. With all of that, and meetings of the Parliamentary Labour Party, and the constituency work, it was perfectly possible to stay in the Commons until ten or eleven at night without ever being at a loss for something to do. So the weeks rolled glibly by.

As with every new MP, Davie carried an uncomfortable burden inside him – the maiden speech: the first outing, the public dive into the fishbowl. It had to be done, and done well; it had to be seriously received and widely noticed. Only once he'd taken that plunge could he really relax.

(Taken from Hansard: the maiden speech of the Honourable Member for Glaikit:

Mr Speaker sir, I am grateful to you for allowing me to catch your eye.

The people of Glaikit are, like people everywhere, a mixter-maxter sort of folk. Historians tell us they were among the ancient Caledonians, and also the first Scots who arrived on our shores from Ireland, plus of course the odd ravaging Norseman and – I say this with a slightly heavy heart – many English incomers, welcome as they are. We are sophisticated people. We have an Italian café. The Glaikit Temperance Hotel has a Thai curry night. (Laughter) In its long history, Glaikit has been a royal burgh and a manufacturing centre. It was burned by William Wallace, and was a great Covenanting centre in what we still call the bloody times. But, Mr Speaker, and here is the point (cries of 'Hear, hear' and 'At last') — the people of Glaikit have always been entirely consistent and solid in one respect: they have, ever since the founding of the Scottish Labour Party in 1888, elected Labour Members to represent them in this House. (Interruption) It may offend some of my Scottish Nationalist friends to say so, but the people of Glaikit have always had their heads screwed on. (Interruption) The Honourable Member for Glasgow Deep South is entirely wrong. Yes, there was a Member for Glaikit who represented the Unionist cause in the 1950s, but he was not elected as a Conservative and Unionist Party candidate: he got into money troubles and he left his wife and he left his honour and he left his party behind; and the people of Glaikit duly turfed him out at the next election. The unlamented Tim Walker does not count.

I was born in the village of Smeddum, just outside Glaikit, the son of a local builder, and I am proud to say that I am a builder too. I have built many decent homes, paid for with public money, and private; and my company has managed a proper provision for our people without losing too many ordinary folks' homes to Maggie Thatcher's quite pernicious 'right to buy' legislation. I was brought up in a warm, loving, working-class family, a church-going family, and when I am asked what I hope to do in this place, my answer is always the same: I am a builder. I am here to build. I am proud of our new government, under our young, vigorous and determined new leader. (Interruption) I have to say to the Honourable Members opposite that their contempt for him is born of fear, as they know very well. I, however, am here to build — like all of my colleagues on this side of the House — a fairer Britain.

David Petrie, MP

Perhaps I should say 'rebuild', because we find ourselves now amidst the rubble of earlier mistakes. We are cut off from our European markets, and we have lost much of our once-mighty financial power. Well, Mr Speaker, I regard that as in some respects a good thing. For too long, the interests of international capital and of the City of London dominated Britain. For too long, an overvalued pound made it nearly impossible for manufacturers, offering decent jobs for decent wages, to survive. But we are not daunted. We stand on the threshold of a new country and new possibilities, which will enable us to rebuild our industrial base. (Interruption) Yes, yes, that does mean regional subsidies and help from central government. I sit on this side of the House because I believe in the power of government. But it means, more than that, all of us pulling together, using all the talents of our bright, well-educated people, relearning the confidence to build new businesses across Scotland, through the north and the Midlands of England, and yes, even in the soft south too. To do this, we need people in this House who have dirty hands. Once upon a time, this chamber was full of former mineworkers, and sheet-metal workers, and road-menders, who had come up through the trade union movement. On the opposite side, there were businessmen – hard-faced, no doubt – but men who had built real businesses before they went into politics. And then we went through the long years when politics was dominated by spivs and children, by spotty-faced youths who had been parliamentary researchers, or junior officials, before arriving here knowing absolutely nothing.

Well, Mr Speaker, we have all learned, up and down the country, the consequences of a Parliament of empty heads and soft hands. Here, Mr Speaker, are my hands. They are not pretty hands. They have a fair few scars and calluses on them. My nails are thick, and they have been broken. But they are, Mr Speaker, the hands of a builder, who knows what life is like out there. And they are hands that are ready to keep building, at the service of this new Labour government.)

Sitting in the shadows high above the chamber were Murdoch White and Alex Brodie, the one-time chancellor of the exchequer; the Master had felt it would draw unnecessary attention if he were to attend in person. White and Brodie could not see, of course, the thin white scars across Petrie's back and legs, but they could hear an unusual passion in his voice – something unexpected, unexplained and interesting, a raw and angry double bass. From down below in the chamber itself, they heard the rumble of approval. They heard the shout of 'Gissa job!' from the Tory benches which meant that Petrie sat down to deflating laughter.

Brodie scratched his ear. 'Not bad.'

'Better than not bad,' said White. 'Passion. A couple of jokes. A bit of history. No, the boy has made his mark, even though that stuff about his hands was badly judged.'

'Yes, left him open. And it wasn't a great speech, Murdoch. There wasn't enough about our place in the world. Where was the fucking politics? There wasn't the faintest hint of a challenge to that fool Grimaldi. If we're going to grow him, he needs to be known as a lot more than Bob the Builder from Scotland.'

'There's time enough.'

'Not that much.'

A Lesson at a Dinner

In politics, there is only one safe appetite: the appetite for power.
The Master

Gradually, David Petrie got to know his fellow back-benchers better – the good-looking idle dossers, the mediocre but frantically ambitious, the left-wing posers who'd been to public school and owned half a dozen flats for rent, and a few who, he reluctantly admitted to himself, were genuinely decent.

Murdoch White had called in to his office to find out how things were going. 'Need to introduce you to some people, Davie. Useful folk . . .'

And the great Alex Brodie, now out of Parliament and working full-time for an international consultancy, duly asked him for dinner. Alex Brodie . . .

Davie turned up at a tiny, white-stuccoed townhouse, like a dolls' house made of icing sugar. The one next door was painted pink, and the one beside that mint-green. They didn't seem to Davie like houses for serious people. Back home, he calculated, they would have been worth a hundred thousand pounds or so, tops. Here, in Mayfair, they must have cost many millions. So that's what former Labour ministers earned for themselves, he thought, impressed.

Davie intended to enter the sugarhouse with a sneer, but when the door was opened by Brodie himself, he found his expression had lapsed into an ingratiating gape. 'Quite a place you've got here,' he blurted out. 'Cosy, mind. I guess it's all hedge-fund managers and bankers as neighbours?'

'Well, yes. And consultants, and a few embassies. Technically it's not mine, of course. It's leased by the company. We're based offshore. Don't approve, myself. I used to be in charge of taxation, remember. Gave the accountants a piece of my mind. They just laughed; these days, it's that or go out of business. Come in, Mr Petrie, it's just a small party. We've been hearing great things about you.'

In the living room there were the smells of real wood-smoke, varnish and candle-wax – prosperous, comforting smells – low lighting, and a man dressed like a doorman carrying a tray of drinks. Standing in clusters here and there, murmuring, were two or three other MPs Davie knew by name: the irritating Welshman who shared his office, that uppity moral-majority Christian dyke from Barker, and a couple of frontbench spokesmen. Holding court in one corner was Sir Leslie Khan, the former party fixer – as close as Davie had been to Labour Party royalty – with his neatly clipped Elizabethan beard, tired, knowing eyes and long, Armani-draped, insect-like limbs. Davie remembered what a former leader had said about Khan: 'Our indispensable Machiavelli, but not as naïve as the original. Nor as nice.'

Khan turned and stared at him. It was a very odd feeling. Davie felt ten or eleven years old. His face was flushing. Entirely against his will, his blood temperature was rising. How *did* the man do that?

Khan walked over to Davie just as his host was handing him a glass of wine. 'Mr Petrie. We've heard some good things about you. But the question is this: why hasn't anybody else?'

'I'm sorry?' Davie downed his glass, and reached nervously for a top-up.

Khan wasn't finished. He pointed a long white finger in Davie's direction. 'Working hard. Busy little beaver. Milk monitor before you know it. Wagging your little tail. Wig-wag, wag-wig.' His finger moved like that of a disapproving Frenchman. 'But no profile, as such, for all that scurrying about. Not like the delectable Mrs Phillips over there.'

Davie felt irritated. He'd got here on his own merits. He'd built a decent business with his own hands. 'I think I'll take care of my profile myself, Mr Khan. That woman gets on my tits. Anyway, your own reputation isn't so great these days, is it? And there was that piece about me in *The Times*. We may be simple folk in Glaikit, by your standards, but it went down well enough where it counts. My party chairman is purring.' Damn. He was gabbling. He hadn't meant to say so much. He hadn't meant to be so rude. The rest of the room had fallen silent. The dyke woman was smiling at him. Probably she was laughing at him. She did have a lovely smile.

But Khan held his eyes, and said in a soft, emollient voice, 'Very good, Mr Petrie. A man who knows his own worth. Quite right. And right, too, about my own poor standing in this unforgiving world. I do my best to spread a little truth and light, and what does it profit me? Scoffers and cynics all around. Never mind. The piece in *The Times* was fine. Something we arranged, Mr Petrie – a little welcome present. But for goodness' sake, it wasn't aimed at your general management committee away up in Scotland. They don't matter a damn. Any Labour MP who's worth his salt is hated by his local party chairman. What matters is what people down here, your colleagues in the party, the gentlemen of the press and the pollsters, make of you. And the truth is, in your case, they make nothing. They haven't the faintest idea who you are. And meanwhile we have the problem of certain journalists who are not impressed by you, Mr Petrie.'

'Who? And by the way, am I the only one here without a drink? And how do you know all this anyway, Mr Khan?'

'It's a bore to say so, but it's actually *Sir* Leslie these days. There's a nasty little gossip columnist trailing about. He was going to do a story last week about your drinking problem. Well, we killed that. What *is* a drinking problem, anyway? For most people, it's wanting a drink in the morning; or as they used to say, drinking more than your doctor. But for a politician, a drinking problem happens as soon as somebody says the words, forms the thought. So be careful, Mr Precious Commodity. Even we can't kill everything.'

Petrie flushed. He knew it was true about the drink. Back home, the nauseating memory of his father's boozer's breath, and the cloying atmosphere of deal-making and backscratching among the local power brokers, had kept him well away from Scotland's most obvious and traditional temptation. But here in London, things were different. With the prospect of only the empty flat ahead of him, he was conscious that a few times he'd been the last man out of the Members' Bar. Then in Dolphin Square, after the call to Mary, he'd been polishing off half a bottle of vodka more nights than not.

He was still, he felt, in control. There had only been two moments that worried him. Once, he'd been in the flat. It was late. There was some music on. He'd been trying, but failing, to have a wank. Then he heard a noise behind him. He'd spun round, and there was his father, Big Bob Petrie, standing there and leering at him. Davie had shouted an obscenity, dropped his glass, then gone to the kitchen and downed several pints of water before he calmed down. Well, the meaning of that was obvious enough; no need to ask a shrink about it.

The second incident, unfortunately, had been in public. He'd been drinking at the Sports and Social Club bar in the bowels of the Commons when he'd thought a fat Tory fucker was laughing at his accent. The man was like a giant haemorrhoid, bulging and pink. Voice like a marching band. 'Don't mind me, Jock,' he'd said. Davie had raised his fist. 'Wouldn't do that, if I were you,' a heavily built Tory in a military tie had said. 'Bunter here was in the SAS.' Davie had cursed, and thrust his face nearer to the haemorrhoid's. But he didn't want a broken nose, and had allowed himself to be gently man-handled away by a Labour whip. Remembering it now, he felt a hot flush of humiliation. That was what the journalist must have heard about.

For the rest of the evening Davie was uncharacteristically

quiet. They sat down to a supper that must have been cooked and brought in from outside, fragrant, creamy and immaculately served. Posh girls in long skirts brought three delicious courses – little segments of pink and green and yellow in sauces that were tart and sweet at the same time, and like nothing he'd ever tasted before. The wines had intimidating labels – swirly letters, drawings of castles – and Davie was self-consciously careful to take only a little. The conversation, despite his earlier embarrassment, was excellent. The reputations of most of the current Labour leadership were shredded. Grimaldi, according to some slanderous whisperers, had family money hidden offshore, and was looking for a way out. And there had been an affair with the editor of a women's magazine. She'd lost her job, and might be prepared to talk. Fascinating insider information about who was going to be offered some of the still-vacant junior ministerial posts was idly dropped.

Khan leaned back and told some wonderful, indiscreet stories against both himself and the Master. These days they were both running international consultancies in competition with each other; their alliance wasn't quite as firm as it had once been. An indiscreet email from a would-be lover, leaked to the *Guardian*, of all places, had described the Master as having a particularly firm 'butt'; Khan told the table he had been the first to spot this, many, many years before: 'I have been following those two particular hard-boiled eggs all my political life.' What was the Master really up to? Stories circulated around the table, as the laughter grew louder and the evening more relaxed.

A Lesson at a Dinner

When the wine was finished and (to Davie's disappointment) whisky, not brandy, had arrived, Davie was led off by his host to a pair of armchairs. He was inclined to treat Alex Brodie, with his chiselled face and thick mop of white hair, more seriously than he took Sir Leslie Khan. It was Brodie who had taken some of the early, brutal decisions which had mitigated the first effects of the disastrous financial crash. Famously pessimistic, he had blotted his copybook briefly by accurately describing the looming world financial disaster, and the change in the political atmosphere it would mean. These days, perhaps to his own surprise, he was looked upon as an elder statesman, a wise counsellor on all things financial. Brodie had stood by the Master from the beginning; of all that group of centrist revolutionaries, he was the only one whose reputation stood higher now than it had in the 1990s. He was a fervent pro-European who had, it seemed, dedicated his later years to campaigning for Britain's re-entry. Petrie felt this was a doomed cause, but he admired the man nevertheless.

Having declined the whisky, Davie was sipping a glass of water. Brodie gestured at it. 'Good move. Khan's a vicious sod, but he's right about that. I should know. It's so damned easy in this trade – all those dinners and suppers, and all those long nights. All that stress. But everyone notices. Everyone's watching. I remember' – and he named a former party leader – 'used to make a big deal about how he only drank half-glasses of wine. Yes, but two dozen of them in a sitting. I once counted. You're going to have to get used to spending whole balls-aching evenings nursing just one glass. If you don't, you're finished, believe me.'

'Aye well, Mr Brodie, you've got me there. He didn't need to say it right out in public like that, mind, but I'll tak' tent, as we say at home.'

'Good man, Petrie. Good man. You can take a friendly word of criticism. That matters. So let me risk your ill favour just a little further. Murdoch tells me you're an ambitious man. Right?'

'I suppose so.'

'Right, then you need to get marching. Committee posts aren't enough. We need to get you onto the front bench.'

'The front bench? Chrissakes, I'm barely in the door.'

'Somebody has to be first. Might as well be you. As I say, we have great hopes for you. But you waited a long time before your maiden.'

'Yes. I thought it better to make the right speech later than the wrong speech sooner.'

'Agreed. Jolly good it was, too. But, forgive me, a chap in your position has to go further. You've got to make people sit up and pay attention, by telling the House something they *don't* expect from you. They've got you down as a local man of a certain eloquence, who'll probably eventually become a competent junior minister. Well, that's not enough for us, and it shouldn't be enough for you. You need to get back into the chamber and intervene on something. In politics, every day that you don't make people think about you is a wasted day. Nine-tenths of MPs never realise that. So get back in there, and shake them up. Make the right people angry.'

'Hmph. That's simple enough, then. Any ideas?'

'Trident. What do you know about Trident, Mr Petrie?'

'Four submarines. Fucking expensive. The Nats want to kick them out of the Holy Loch. So do most of the Scottish people. They're controlled by the Americans anyway, really. The real threats these days are from religious nutters and climate change – and a great big bugger of a submarine with great big buggers of nuclear missiles on it is bugger-all use against any of that. So, aye, Trident then. I'm agin it. Spend the money on hospitals and pre-school education. There's no such thing as a strong power with a weak economy. So that's my theme, then? It's no' very obvious material for comedy, Mr Brodie.'

'Not quite, Mr Petrie. That's exactly what I would have expected you to say. You've said it pithily and with some passion, but it's what everyone would assume a newly-elected Labour MP from Ayrshire was going to spout. That's Bob the Builder's speech. No, the speech you're going to make is in *favour* of Trident, calling on the government to bring forward its modernisation schedule and making the case for a new submarine to replace the oldest one.'

'You must be mad.' Petrie had a vision of Granny Stalin in full flow at his GMC, calling for his resignation.

'No, I've just been around for a while. Think about it. Trident keeps Britain at the international top table. Who cares about that? Fair point. But it brings huge numbers of jobs to Scotland. *Your* Scotland. It means we maintain a level of engineering and technical expertise we wouldn't have without it. That point you were making about rebuilding our industrial economy? Now the Iranians and the Saudis are in the nuclear club, you can never tell what we'll need it for. But deterrence means more these days, not less. And above all, Mr Petrie, it'll get you noticed. Not just here, but in Washington.'

'Washington?'

'Washington. No successful British prime minister since the Second World War has operated without the approval of Washington. Look what happened to Wilson. In pure party terms, remember Neil Kinnock.'

'They'll bloody lynch me. The comrades, I mean.'

'So that's how you start your speech. You talk about how nervous you were before your maiden speech, how long and hard you thought about the right subject. And then you say something like this: "Unfortunately for me, Mr Speaker, today I seem to have chosen a subject which will – probably literally – result in me being ripped limb from limb by the time I have finished. My leader, the prime minister, is not exactly known for physical violence – cue knowing laughter – but there's always a first time. If there are any doctors in the House, can I crave your permission, Mr Speaker, to have them on standby for the next twenty minutes?" That kind of thing. You'll get them listening, and at least half of them will be on your side.

'Then you carry on, talking about your constituency. There used to be engineering up your way, didn't there? Bus fabricators, marine engines. So talk about Scotland's great tradition as a nation of engineers and inventors, shipwrights and designers. A local builder's not quite in the same league, you admit. But you hold up your hands again, and talk about all those years of hammering, sawing, wiring and plastering. You've already reminded all those soft creatures around you that you come from the real world, and that you have a strong sense of history.

'By now they aren't laughing. They're beginning to listen to you closely. So you talk about the Israeli nuclear programme – the Labour left hates that more than anything else in this wicked world. And then you talk about the Iranians, the Saudis, the North Koreans, and so on. Then you pause. A dramatic silence, just long enough to get the speaker staring at you and the Tories wondering if you've lost it. You tell them you have new information to share with the House. By now they're on the edge of their seats. The Commons *never* gets to hear anything first. Palm of your hand.

'So you tell them that the new Egyptian government has accepted an offer of nuclear advisers and limited quantities of enriched uranium from Saudi Arabia. You can't disclose your sources, but you're sure the foreign secretary will confirm the gist of this to the House in due course. Up in the press gallery, a couple of them have already dashed out to phone their desks. You conclude your speech by saying that in a dangerous world it's not right to allow our skills, built up over many decades, to rot away; and it's not right to send the message that Britain is turning away from her allies. That will be taken as a direct attack on Grimaldi, of course. But you don't mention him. The words "the prime minister" never pass your lips. Mention Tory leaders instead – Neville Chamberlain, Stanley Baldwin – and the complacent decay of the British military during the 1930s. Then swing around and launch a full-frontal attack on the coalition and the Conservatives for underfunding defence. Paint our side as the patriotic side. Pretend, at least, to get really angry. You'll make a splash, I promise you.'

'Jesus. That's not bad.'

'It's bloody good. A veritable warrior of a speech. An Amazon to follow the maiden.'

'But what about that stuff about Egypt? I've never heard of that.'

'A little gift from us. It's absolutely true. The Egyptians are gearing up. They're way behind, but they're starting. Making it public, and in the House of Commons of all places, will greatly embarrass the Foreign Office. They've known for months, but they're keeping it quiet. Twitter will go bonkers. Your name will be everywhere.'

'And when am I supposed to do this?'

'There's the defence estimates debate next week. If you get in an early request to the speaker, he can hardly refuse you; your maiden went well.'

'I'm no' a bad word-spinner, but Jesus, Mr Brodie, I wish I'd taken notes. I've mebbe had a glass too many.'

'No need for that, Mr Petrie. Call me Alex – and I'll call you David, by the way. Here –' and the cadaverous former chancellor handed over a dozen or so immaculately typed pages.

'Everything you need. Word for word.'

'But who . . .?'

'We. Us.'

'The debate's just a few days away. Shouldn't we get some press interest going?' said Davie, struggling to get some of the initiative back.

'Don't worry about that. Parts of your speech have already been released, with an embargo of course, to the PA. I'm afraid it will be interpreted as a direct attack on the woeful Grimaldi. We haven't released the bit about Egypt. Let's save that for the day itself, shall we?'

Staggering out into the cool night air, David Petrie considered a taxi. He had only the dimmest idea of how to get from Kensington back to Pimlico, but his head was buzzing so insistently that he decided he needed to walk. At this time of night, although the roads were still busy, the pavements were almost empty. Even so, it took him nearly an hour. His knees and ankles had turned to rubber, and Mary was asleep when he phoned her.

'Evening. Sorry. Sorry.'

She groaned, and put the phone down on him.

Pebbleton

The political life is a life of sacrifice, mostly by those who love us most.

The Master

Damn. Sheer vanity. Angela should have pulled on wellies for her rendezvous with the village shop – with, not at, because the village shop was a battered white van that made its way to Pebbleton each morning from Drake, Easter Saltley and Waterthorpe. Instead, she was wearing her Edwardian-style lace-up boots, in a soft yellow leather she particularly loved. Well, she was paying for it now. The water gurgling off the fields through the village had penetrated to her feet. There would forever be little white tidal marks from the boots' toes to their ankles, and however much she scraped and polished, they would never go away. The boots were ruined. Bought many years ago in a small shop in the York Shambles, she'd never be able to replace them. Damn. Damn the rain. Damn Caroline.

But as she walked down the hill from the vicarage to the main street, Angela found it impossible to maintain her ill-humour.

There was something glorious about knowing such a lovely place so well. The matching estate cottages, with their neat brick patterning, built by an improving landlord before the First World War, didn't have a single occupant Angela didn't know, or at least know about: tough farm labourers now long-retired; the district nurse; the local historian, who'd once been a big shot on the council. She knew about their failures, their lost children and brutally truncated careers; and she knew about their successes, the chief of which, she always thought, was the daily bravery of simply keeping buggering on.

Sometimes Angela feared that her religion was intermittent, but this morning she felt a breath of love for the lives going on behind the brick and pebble-dashed walls, these good people. God's love; God reminding her. And, slowly but surely, she was bringing them back to the church, whose echoing stone nave had been so sparsely filled in her first months here. The intimidating Lady Broderick had become a friend; and she had followed Lady Broderick's advice. Good old hymns with good old music. The Book of Common Prayer. The King James Bible. Short sermons with a few jokes in them and a strong moral point. She hadn't got Caro's way with words, but she worked hard on those sermons, and found it a pleasurable task. It was hardly a miracle cure, but it had worked. And the more people who came to church – at first shyly, gathering in the pews towards the back, but then coming out of themselves – the more she came to know and understand this community. She began to feel she was rooted here, like a strong tooth in a jaw. One of her boys was at the local school. The other was, at this moment, getting off the bus in the nearest big town, Exchester, where he had made new friends. Was this 'home'? It was beginning to feel that way. Every lane, every field, every smell, every passing conversation carried a message.

So, as she contemplated the pinkish water gurgling at the edge of the pavement on its way down to the river, and caught the scent of clay, she remembered a worried conversation with the man who had taken over the big farm at Easterly. We all live off topsoil. That was his point. For tens of thousands of years, mankind had survived because of the rich, slowly cooking chemical soup of ground stone, worms, decaying vegetable matter, microbes and water which covered, like a thin blanket, the underlying geology. Bronze Age tribes had grown rough barley and fed their shaggy cattle on this very soil; and the estate workers from the Roman villa had introduced onions, chickens, rabbits and leeks, fancy stuff from the south, to this soil. Alfred's Saxons had lived off it, fighting the Norsemen for it. The very same pink soil had produced the farms and wealth carefully noted down by the Norman robbers in their Domesday Book; it had nourished the families of the sea dogs Raleigh and Drake; and the doomed, desperate yeomen who had marched to Sedgefield; and, much later, it had grown the grub that kept the British Expeditionary Force fighting in Flanders. In short, said the philosophical farmer of Easterly, no topsoil, no us.

It was very thin, mostly not more than the depth of a human leg. And yet – the young farmer had pointed out to sea – look what we're doing. And Angela saw the band of bright-red water extending several hundred yards out to sea from the bottom of the cliffs and the rocky shoreline. That was the soil, the very stuff this county, with its rich farmland, fat cattle and glossy green woodland, was made of. In the twenty-first century, heavier winter rains, and new farming methods with fewer hedgerows and less rotation, were steadily driving the soil into ditches, then streams, then down tarmac, and into the rivers and finally the sea. Pebbleton, like all the villages around, had once had an intense, wary and knowing relationship with the soil. That was going. How many of her parishioners, the farmer wondered, could any longer identify the plants all around them?

It was, she'd told Caro on one of her increasingly rare flying visits from Westminster, a slow-motion catastrophe. It was a failure of imagination, really, more serious than anything being debated in the House of Commons. 'You think we're somehow behind the curve, out here in the sticks, chewing our bits of grass. But this is the real world. Just as real as any housing estate in Barker, or any row about public spending in London. My eyes are more open to the future and what's happening around us, sitting in my little study overlooking the Pebbleton graveyard, than yours are in Parliament.'

Splashing past the pub and the hairdressers, noting a growing flush of light blue towards the west, Angela couldn't remember how that conversation had ended. Probably not well; not well was how things had been going since she'd become the partner of Caroline Phillips MP. She was, as she'd predicted, lonely. But she was angry as well. She felt torn in two directions. On the one hand there was this wonderful new life, where she could make a real difference and dig herself in properly. God, surely, wanted her to be here, consoling and cheering up these admirable, slowly-spoken people. She loved everything about this place. Dawn breaking over Pebbleton Hill, with its oaks and conifers, could move her almost to tears when she pulled the bedroom curtains aside. The splinters of spring sunlight, gouging their way through fields bright with winter barley, set her heart fluttering. For the first time in her life she noticed the arrival in spring of the white hawthorns, and inhaled with delight the banks of wild garlic, twisting up among primroses and bluebells. At times she felt she was actually living inside a gospel, illuminated by wise-fingered monks, whose greens were greener, its golds brighter, than in the humdrum England of the early twenty-first century.

But then, pulling her in the other direction, there was Caro. This too, she felt, was God's love being offered to her. Those cornflower-blue eyes, candid and challenging, could make her almost sick with delight. Caro's slightly imperfect mouth, with its fractionally too-prominent upper lip, was, Angela felt, the single most beautiful thing in the universe. Caro was her soul-sister, her real mother, her confessor as well as her lover. When they were apart, Angela simply felt a little deader, and, at night, as if there were an agonising open wound along her side – as if she were a tree split open by lightning.

There was the shop, a 1964 Bedford, pulling in outside the hairdressers. The usual half-dozen local men, the old salts, were waiting for their newspapers, cigarettes and milk with immemorial patience. Gray's 'Elegy' (Miss Symonds and the lower fifth). Well, Angela had a verger – unpaid, sold postcards, a demon with the electric polisher, arms like a gorilla's — who had tolled a few parting knells in his day; and yes, there was ivy on the clock tower, and yew trees in the graveyard, even if there were no more elms. Hear me now, Miss Symonds.

But, dear Lord, she was going to have to choose . . .

Angela didn't usually read the papers. She found them distracting and irritating. Why fill your mind at the start of a fresh, God-given day with human misery, anger and failure? Normally she would put on Radio 3, and when the boys had gone she would read some poetry — Herbert, Traherne or Crashaw. But this morning she'd been woken by a text from Caroline. Early for her. It had read: 'Front page of the *Mail*. We need to talk.' During the few minutes it had taken Angela to dress and walk to meet the van, she had managed to push the anxiety down. It would not be, it could not be, that Caroline had been caught out having an affair. She was not that person. And Angela would die if it were so; thus, it could not be so. But the sense of having to make some kind of brutal and imminent choice had been bubbling through her mind nevertheless.

In front of her in the queue for the hatch of the van was a notorious local gossip, rare in disliking Angela. He had a gentle, baby face with a little watery smile. Angela believed in charity, but she found it hard in his case. If Caroline was on the front page of the *Mail* snogging some London woman, and she bought a copy, he would see it all.

'Good morning, vicar. Early for you to be up. Don't tell me you're back on the cigarettes? Or is it a lady's purchase?'

'Oh, Mr Walker, I'm always up with the early birds.'

'So I've heard, vicar. Playing ducks and drakes and all sorts. If you're going to be staying long in these parts, you might want a pair of rubber boots.'

'I just want a paper or two. For my sermon.'

After he had been served, Mr Walker hung around the hatch so he could see what Angela picked up. She chose *a Daily Telegraph*, big enough to wrap around the *Mail*, which she folded inside it. But the gossip was too quick for her.

'The *Telegraph* and the *Mail*, vicar? King-and-country choice. I don't think your socialist girlie-friend would approve of that. Or maybe she's blotted her copybook already?'

'Keep your tongue from evil and your lips from deceit, Mr Walker.'

'Vicar?'

'Psalm 34, Mr Walker. It's the text for this Sunday's sermon. I'm just doing a little research for it. I look forward to seeing you joining us. Such an enthusiastic member of our little community.'

Mr Walker gave Angela an insolent wink.

Back in the vicarage, having kicked off her ruined boots and turned on the electric fire, Angela spread the papers out on the table. Ignoring the *Telegraph*, she hurriedly scanned the front page of the *Mail*. To her intense relief there was no picture of Caro, nor, so far as she could tell, any mention of her. The story was headed 'Sharia Shame Splits Labour'.

Under the byline 'Peter Roth, political editor', the article claimed that a 'shocking new plan to legalise female mutilation and savage Islamic punishments in the heart of England' was causing 'civil war' among Labour MPs. Somebody called David

Petrie was quoted talking about 'the suicide of our moderate and humane Christian culture', and 'political correctness gone completely insane'. It was only when she turned to page two and the rest of the story that Angela saw Caroline's face grinning back at her. She was flanked by an Asian-looking woman in a headscarf, and a rotund figure in a burqa. Angela's first reaction was to laugh. This couldn't be right. Caroline was a level-headed Christian feminist, about as far from endorsing the brutalities of FGM as anyone she could imagine. But something had happened. The article made her seem a dupe and a fool. Angela found herself growing angrier and angrier on Caro's behalf.

Her girl needed her help. Once, long before, she and Caro had been walking in north London and had passed a yoga outfit that called itself Fierce Grace. Caro had turned and said to her, 'That's you. You have grace, but you're a bloody flame-thrower when you need to be. You are my Fierce Grace.' Now Angela really felt that she was. She had to choose. She'd known it all morning. So she chose.

Now, Angela did two things. She put in a call to Caro in London, leaving a message on her answerphone. Caro spent most mornings, so far as Angela could tell, in committees. Next, she went to the Church of England website and searched for vacant ministries in the Midlands.

None of the first few she saw appealed instantly. There was a country church looking for 'a prayerful priest in the Catholic tradition', which rather ruled out women. There was a bene-fice looking for a rector but making much of the 'evangelical and enthusiastic nature of our church', which didn't sound like Angela's bag either. No King James Bible there. But then, on the outskirts of Barker itself, there was a vacancy for a priest who could demonstrate 'Christlikeness' and an enthusiasm for 'reaching out to unchurched communities'. That sounded intimidating, but at least it was in the right area, and it might just be somewhere that an experienced woman vicar would be welcome. Feeling hellish, before she could stop herself or allow herself to succumb to second thoughts, Angela had emailed a Mrs Droop, PA to the archdeacon.

No answer yet from Caro. But Angela, in her mood of Fierce Grace, did not pause. She clambered into her battered Hyundai and drove the five twisting miles to Pebbleton Hall in search of Lady Broderick. She found her half a mile from the house with a pair of shears, dealing severely with an insolent, ill-behaved hedge.

'This is a private road, vicar. The council won't send its machine along. Terrible bore, though I do find a certain relish in *snipping*. Sometimes I have unruly thoughts. So you're planning to leave us, are you?'

Angela reddened. How had she possibly guessed?

Lady Broderick calmly stowed the shears in a shoulderbag she was carrying, full of withies. She rotated her lower jaw, showing a line of sharp yellow teeth. 'This is going to be a bit of a chinwag, vicar, isn't it? I'd better hop in. We can have a little something up at the house.'

Ten minutes later, the two women were standing in front of an open fire. It had been lit first thing in the morning. A dispiriting, sulphurous smell and a thin trickle of black smoke were all the evidence. The logs appeared untouched. No warmth of any kind reached them.

'Cosy here, vicar, isn't it? Now, let me say straight off that this is most unfortunate, and extremely inconvenient. When your name came forward, I wasn't at all sure. We're simple people here in the West Country, and not quite up with things. So it took a little bit of time for us to get used to you. But we've become quite fond of you, Angela – can I call you Angela? And I've become *very* fond of you. I like the tone of your services. A nice religious feel, but not too much. Between ourselves, I've always felt that our Redeemer can sometimes be a little . . .'

'Preachy?'

'Yes. In the wrong hands, you see. A bit . . . strident. Our Saviour *means* well, of course, vicar. We all understand that. Heart of gold. And he's got a heck of a task. But he's very hard-line. And in my experience it's never a good idea to . . .'

'Push things too far?'

'Exactly so, vicar. Exactly so, Angela. That's why you and I have always got on so well.'

Angela held her tongue. Then, unbidden, some lines came to her. Thank you, Lord. She intoned:

'A fine aspect in fit array
Neither too mean nor yet too gay
Shows who is best.'

'I beg your pardon, vicar?'

'George Herbert, Lady Broderick. A good Church of England man. He wrote a poem about it all – "The British

Church". We're in the middle, not too much one thing or the other, not extreme. Not . . .'

'Too much?'

'Exactly.'

Lady Broderick had brought out two small, slightly dirty glasses, which she now filled with a musty brown liquid. Angela sniffed hers cautiously.

'Madeira, m'dear. Like the song. Just the thing at this time of day, I find. Now, back to business. I will take onto these bony old shoulders the task of finding ourselves another vicar to replace you. It's a pretty living, and we've never had too much difficulty, though you'll be hard to replace. I could ask about your calling and what happened to it, and whether you find us either too wicked or too dull for your continued attention, but I expect I'd be wasting my time.'

'It's nothing like that, Lady Broderick.'

'No. I gather it's more about your – I hate the word, but your *partner*. She's in a spot of political trouble, isn't she?'

'How did you know?'

'Oh, that sweet Mr Walker popped by earlier. So I did a bit of Googling. It's a very odd proposition Mrs Phillips is supporting. We can't have Muslim enclaves in a Christian country. Mind you, in the great days of Devon, when my ancestors meted out punishments far from the nearest court of assizes, there was the odd hand lopped off, and a bit of branding and so on. But things have moved on. I don't understand about this female genital mutilation business.'

'Well . . .'

'And I don't want to hear a word about it, or read another

word about it. Too horrid. So quite what your Mrs Phillips is up to . . .'

'Well, that's what I have to find out. But . . .'

'But vicar, this is really about your priorities, isn't it? If you're going to make your life with this Mrs Phillips — who I have always rather liked; she has a certain something — it can't be with you down here, and her up there. I hope you liked us here, and that you will carry a little bit of Pebbleton in your heart always. But sex first, sentiment second, I always say.'

'Do you, Lady Broderick?'

'Rarely. It just came to me. And I know there's more to it and so forth, but what I mean to say is that I understand.'

'Do you, Lady Broderick? How wonderful. I've loved it here. I've loved the church, and the people. I thought I was going to live here always . . .'

'Steady on, vicar. Don't let's push things. I'll see to it that someone keeps an eye on your two boys while you make your new arrangements.'

Angela was making effusive thanks and backing towards the door when she remembered she hadn't drunk any of her Madeira.

'Don't worry,' said Lady Broderick. 'It's really not very nice. Like many of our traditions. Go, as you'd say . . .'

'In peace. Thank you, Lady Broderick.'

Driving back along the lane towards the coast road, Angela's Hyundai hit a large pothole. A spray of chocolate-coloured water splashed across the windscreen. She put on the wipers. The topsoil would have to wait.

A Warning from Bunty

And watch your bloody back.

The Master

David Petrie had a very sore back. He'd have to get them to change the chair in his Commons office. After leaving Moncrieff's Bar the previous evening he'd been in a pretty bad way. But he was still a fit guy. Bounced up again at 7 a.m., cool shower, and then back to work. He was determined to improve the next speech Murdoch White had given him, to show the buggers. His 'Strident Trident' speech, as *The Times* had called it, had made him half-famous, and earned a dirty look from the PM's PPS. Now the Master's men had been back in touch, telling him to go on the attack. They'd handed him two neat pages of vicious political assassination. It was horrible, but it was beautifully done. He'd been sitting at his desk for hour after hour, trying to find even one slipshod phrase.

There were none. This was even better than the defence speech, and that had been a belter. The extraordinary thing was that, yet again, it sounded exactly like him. Who *were* these people? They were taking words out of his mouth before he'd had time to think them. He almost felt sorry for the poor woman. They'd passed at the barrier coming in that morning. She was obviously an early starter too. She'd given him a smile, but it was rather a blank one. Luckily, they'd never pretended to be friends. She wouldn't know what had hit her. But his bloody back was bloody sore. He wanted one of those fancy chairs with lots of levers, like the one in the office back at home in Glaikit. But would that come out of expenses? Probably. Then the local paper would run a story about how the new MP had spent a thousand quid on a chair, and that would be another lot of voters who'd never turn to him again. Sod it. Thanks to the business, he still had enough money in the bank to buy it himself. He groaned slightly. Bunty, sitting opposite him, looked up.

'Mr Petrie, man. You're sounding awful. Do you want a throatie?'

Davie had a sudden horrible vision of Bunty offering him oral sex. He answered rather sharply. 'No. A bit of a bad back, that's all. Can a man have no privacy?'

'It was only a cough sweet. Mental.'

'What?'

'Menthol.'

'Oh, I see. No, it's just that I've been sitting in this chair for too long, working on the big speech I'm giving tonight.'

'I forgot to say, Mr Petrie. Nasty Neill from the whips' office was on the phone for you. He wanted to know what you're going to say in your speech, and was it the same as all the shite you said in the *Daily Mail*?'

'And what did you tell Mr Neill?'

'I telt him that as far as I could tell, you were gonnae make a speech about black ladies' bits. I said it seemed a bit rude, but it was OK because you hadnae written it yourself.'

'Bloody hell, Bunty. Why did you say that? The whips' office hate me enough already. Anyway, I write my own bloody speeches. I do my own heavy lifting.'

'Sorry, Mr Petrie, but it just looked to me as if that speech had been all neatly typed out by somebody else. You've been sitting there for hours pretending to work on it, but you're not doing anything, really, are you Mr Petrie? I don't think you're very interested in black ladies' bits.'

'This is about cruelty and civilisation, Bunty. Not that I'd expect you to understand.'

Bunty sniffed and helped herself to another throatie. Petrie had noticed that she had settled in to her new role in a far more relaxed way than he'd expected. She didn't seem intimidated, or much impressed, by anything at the Palace of Westminster. Now she resumed the conversation he was finding so irritating.

'Shall I tell you what I think, Mr Petrie?'

'Go on, Bunty.'

'I think it's not about cruelty and civilisation. I think it's about shafting that Mrs Phillips. I think you've been – what do they say? – put up to it, Mr Petrie. Am I no' right?'

Petrie flushed. What was it with this girl? Had he made a terrible mistake in bringing her down here? She certainly wasn't stupid.

'This has nothing to do with shafting Mrs Phillips, Bunty,

except in so far as she has put her name to a ridiculous and damaging idea which I am determined to shoot down. I'm quite capable, thank you very much, of making my own decisions and writing my own speeches. Perhaps you wouldn't mind explaining to me why you don't think I am?'

This wasn't, he reflected, the kind of conversation he had ever envisaged having with his PA. But Bunty kept going.

'Oh, I know you're a very clever man, Mr Petrie. My ma told me that. She said I had to keep a good eye on you. But see, that piece in the newspaper was really all about that Mrs Phillips. And the girls down in the Portcullis café – I say girls, but it's blokes too, all the young folk who work for the MPs – we get together, you see, and we have a wee blether, and everybody says, Mr Petrie, that you could be going right to the top. But so could Mrs Phillips. The party's goan to have tae choose. So the girls think, and the boys think, that it's either her or you. I think it's going to be you, Mr Petrie. Because I think the powers that be are on your side.' She pushed the sweet round her mouth, making first one cheek bulge, and then the other. 'Somebody else wrote that speech. I'm no' completely dumb. And by the way, that girl you fancy's been asking around after you. She wants to see you again.'

'I don't know who you mean.'

'That girl you thought was a TV researcher, Mr Petrie. You liked her well enough to buy her a drink the other night. She said you were looking at her bosoms. But she doesnae work on the telly. She works for the old prime minister – the one they cry the Master. She's really nice. She's called . . .'

'Yes, well, I'm sure she's a very nice girl. And yes, I may

have committed the major sin of buying her a drink. But I'm a married man, and whoever she works for, she doesn't work for me. In any way.'

'Oh, well that's good news anyway, Mr Petrie. My ma was getting a bit worried. For Mary, like.'

'You mean to say, Bunty, that you've been passing gossip about my private affairs back to your mother in Glaikit?'

'Oh, aye, sure thing. Ma said she knew you were trying to butter her up like a hot scone – getting me this job and all. But she said it didnae matter, because we talk every day. And she said if you started to misbehave, the constituency would get to know about it straight away, and she'd have you by the short and hairies.'

'Short and curlies, Bunty. Short and curlies.'

'Aye, well. Them too.'

Public Servants

The good politician, presented with a pair of somebody else's shoes, will grow his feet.

The Master

In the days after he kissed hands with the king and accepted the premiership of Britain, the new prime minister had had dozens of meetings. He had met the chiefs of the Defence Staff, the chairman of the Joint Intelligence Committee, his new chancellor, the governor of the Bank of England and the American ambassador. Oh yes, and he had had his photograph taken by the government's official photographer, an image that would be on file and would be used all around the world. Alwyn Grimaldi, in his trademark cream suit and scarlet tie, seemed to stand a little awkwardly in front of the cream marble pillars in the Downing Street drawing room. His Welsh-Italian heritage was made flesh in a narrow skull with darkish skin and prominent, bushy-black eyebrows. He was smiling, but not happily.

Over in the government whips' office in the House of Commons, they had loyally framed and mounted Alwyn Grimaldi.

'Clown,' said the chief whip.

'It runs in the family,' said his deputy.

A schedule of emergency spending cuts, presented by the chancellor earlier in the week, was now in the hands of the whips. It would be part of their job to force these revised estimates through a House of Commons in which they had almost no majority. Since the election results had been declared, the chief whip had been reading his way through the memoirs and histories of the Callaghan Labour government of the late 1970s to see how it had been done then. He was not reassured. A litany of brutal threats, blatant bribery and outright deceit had only just kept that government going. Dying MPs had been stretchered into the House so they could be recorded through the Aye lobby; road bridges, power stations and pipelines had been promised to buy off wavering MPs. And in the end, of course, the whole rickety structure had crashed down anyway, leaving Margaret Thatcher to stride through the wreckage to her first devastating victory.

The chief whip had been reciting some of this ancient history to his deputy. 'Someone wrote a play about us, you know. Back in the early 2010s. It was on at the National Theatre. The whips – it made us out to be heroes, despite everything.'

'Well, that's something. It's a bloody impossible job, but at least if you get a bit of recognition . . .'

'Trouble is, back then the whips were saving big people – Callaghan, Healey, Shirley Williams, even Tony Benn. We've got a cabinet of midgets by comparison. Think of them. They're all thirty-somethings straight out of think tanks, or they've worked as researchers or whatever. No real jobs, no real grasp of the country around them.'

It was a familiar moan, but the deputy chief whip felt it was spot on. 'And the troubles we're facing now are just as bad as they were in the 1970s. Maybe worse. There's the deficit. The pound weak as fuck. Now we're out of the EU, the Americans are calling the shots more than ever. And the country's just . . . grumpy. Even the weather's against us – the floods, the coastal battering, the summer droughts. How long before extreme weather produces extreme politics?'

'At least there's one thing we don't have to worry about so much right now. The party's more united than it used to be. The Tories and the Lib Dems are knackered after all those years of power and feuding. We'll get our majorities – most of the time. Grimaldi's new. The boys and girls will give him a chance.'

'I'm not so sure.' The chief whip gestured at the photograph. 'There's something brittle, something thin about him. That ridiculous suit, that scared-looking smirk. You know how things are. We build them up and then we knock them down, cut them off at the knees. I don't think our great leader has a very long career ahead of him.'

'Well, he has to stand up to the Yanks. That's the first thing. They want this new defence, trade and intelligence agreement. If Grimaldi told them to get stuffed, the party would back him every inch of the way.'

'If?'

'Oh, I know. He's a clown, basically. But we have to give him a chance.'

*

The same photograph of Alwyn Grimaldi was on prominent display at 35, rue du Faubourg Saint-Honoré in Paris, the palatial eighteenth-century home of Napoleon's sister Pauline, otherwise known as the Princess Borghese. Grabbed from the Bonapartes by the Duke of Wellington, for more than two centuries it had been the British embassy. Its Yellow Room, its Blue Room and its splendid Red Room, with Pauline Borghese's grand golden bed, retained a sense of Napoleonic splendour, tucked away and under the control of the old enemy, in the heart of Paris. The current ambassador, Sir Anthony Bevins, enjoyed everything about the posting that his predecessors had loved so much – the view overlooking the little private lawn, the wonderful parties, the invitations to the opera, and the many splendid restaurants nearby.

But Sir Anthony was a worried man. There was a cloud in the sky, growing steadily more menacing, that had not confronted previous ambassadors. Now that Britain had left the EU, the British rated less here. At the Elysée Palace down the road, questions had been asked about whether such a modest little nation, no longer in the Union, really needed quite such a splendid embassy.

'It's all a little . . . *1945*, don't you think, Ambassador?' the French president's press secretary had muttered to Bevins at the cocktail party he'd thrown to celebrate the king's birthday. 'All this . . . *grandeur Britannique*.' The Brazilians and the South Koreans were both looking for new accommodation.

That wouldn't have worried Sir Anthony, had not similar noises been coming from the Foreign and Commonwealth Office in London – itself housed in a grand enough building.

It couldn't be denied that the Paris embassy was exceedingly expensive. Now that so much of Britain's relations with Europe were conducted via Brussels, was it really a good investment any more? The British newspapers had withdrawn from Paris; the BBC had retreated too. The embassy felt embattled. During his last visit to London, Bevins had deflected the suggestion of downsizing with an airy wave at the gigantic staircases, huge paintings and echoing corridors of the FCO. Something very similar, he pointed out, could be said about that place. But very soon he'd need a more serious response. These days, the real work was done by Number 10 and the Secret Services. The Grimaldi government was pushing through new cuts all round. The permanent secretary had summoned him back to London for a face-to-face. It was all, undoubtedly, ominous.

So Sir Anthony, uneasily aware that he needed all the friends he could get, had been delighted when the former prime minister whose friends called him, perhaps partly in jest, simply 'the Master', had said he needed a discreet base where he would not be bothered or spotted. He had asked to use the embassy – unofficially, of course. Since the Master and his old coterie often stayed in the Borghese Palace when they were passing through Paris, nothing could be easier.

On a brisk March morning, then, the Master stood, almost like an eighteenth-century monarch, greeting his loyal lieges. There was Sir Leslie Khan, beautifully dressed in a blue alpaca coat. With his nineteenth-century beard, the Master thought, he suited Paris. There was Alex Brodie, the rumpled, rather grey-looking former chancellor; foul-mouthed Murdoch White, down from his island, grumbling about his complicated journey; and Sally Johnson, the former party chair. In the old days she'd been dressed by Marks & Spencer's. Today it was Givenchy.

Sir Anthony ushered them in, ordered coffee and cakes bought in from Fauchon, had a few words with the Master about the threat to the embassy and was encouraged by his exclamation of shock; and left them to it, as he was expected to do.

The Master, far from being diminished by his long years out of power, seemed fitter than ever – lean, tanned, with a full head of grey hair – and brimming with energy and confidence. All that money had lacquered him, like a honeyed gloss. He was wearing jeans. Worse still, they had been freshly ironed.

'Guys! Hey! Thanks for coming. You've all got a bed made up here, and I've booked us a table at the Bristol this evening. Now then! London, guys! We have half a dozen people in place, all of them good, all of them new. I'm afraid the government itself is despised. They're all kids. They mean well, but no . . . intelligent observer . . . thinks they're up to it. Alwyn – well, you probably remember Alwyn from his days as a researcher in Number 10. Nice kid back then. But he still is. Thanks to you – you in particular, Murdoch, and you, Leslie – we have a couple of excellent contenders. Guys! Our problem is that it's still too early for them. We have to hothouse them' – the former leader palpated his fingers as if he were trying to cast a spell – 'and force their political growth, so they'll be ready.'

Sally Johnson, always famous for her ability to prick the Master's exuberant optimism, swallowed the last of an immaculate vanilla macaroon, licked her lips like a cat, and interrupted. 'Small problem. I mean literally a small problem – he's only just over five foot high. But there's, already, as it were, a prime minister. And much as it may amaze us all here, the man won an election.'

The Master appeared not to have heard her. He got gently to his feet and walked to the window. He looked out at a cluttered private courtyard, making it seem as if he were gazing at a Glorious Future. Being in Paris helped, but he was good at that kind of thing.

'We are back. *I* am back. That is the point, and we must never lose sight of it. When we choose to bring Alwyn's splendid service to his country to a suitable conclusion, he will be ready to go. And we will be ready. And at least one of our young protégés will be ready. I am relying on you to make sure of that. Take courage, and look around. There is more real political talent in this room than in the whole of Westminster.'

And then he turned tetchily on Sally: 'I can't be expected to think of everything myself.'

Leslie Khan had been playing with a small cigar. He had pulled it out of his breast pocket, taken off the cellophane, spent quite a long time biting off one end, and was now rolling it between his fingers and sniffing it. Smoking was strictly forbidden in the embassy, as it was in every public building across Europe, and the others were fascinated by what he would do next. Leslie had had no intention of lighting the thing, however; it was just a way of getting attention before he spoke. A little trick. A tiny little trick.

'Master, colleagues. We must not lose sight of the bigger picture. None of us are here to further our own careers; we all know that politics without principle and a clear line forward is an empty game. This is about the future of Britain. After all our sterling work back in the 1980s and 1990s, Britain is again alone, cut adrift from the main currents of the modern world. We could have given up. We have villas on the Côte d'Azur, and comfortable yachts – or we have good friends who have those things. But we have all chosen the harder path. So, I repeat, let us not lose sight of the bigger picture.'

The Master, listening intently, nevertheless felt it was time for him to pick up the thought. He smoothed his upper lip as if there were a moustache on it, and patted Sir Leslie on the sleeve.

'The bigger picture. The harder path. Exactly, Leslie. I think we all feel a calling. I know I do. How often have I looked upwards, enjoying a meal or a holiday, and said, "Lord, take this cup away from me. Hey! C'mon, Big Man, bother somebody else." But will He listen?'

Alex Brodie was covertly rolling his eyes and making little revolving gestures against his temple with his forefinger. The faintest smile hovered above Sir Leslie Khan's beard. The rest of them kept their faces straight.

'I know that, perhaps satirically, people call me the Master. They would be better to call me the Servant. Are we not all servants, after all – even you impious hoodlums, sniggering behind your hands – the servants at least of your country and your own political destinies? But, guys, the Americans, I'm afraid, have muffed it rather. I said as much to Hillary recently.

By linking the new World Bank loan to a fresh agreement on military and intelligence cooperation, they have contrived to look like the bullies of Britain, rather than our natural and closest allies. Ever the optimist, I always thought that Alwyn Grimaldi and the rest of the . . . socialist kindergarten . . . would fold. But it looks as if they won't. So we have to ensure that our people start to get things back on track, first with the Americans and then with our friends in Europe. If not, our host's understandable anxiety about his pleasant surroundings here will be the least of it.'

The Master shook his head. 'The ambassador is an awful old fool, guys, I'm afraid. If I had my way I'd close this place down myself. He is the old Britain we were trying to get away from. It's useful, of course, that he's such an old softy. Now, as to the Americans and all that. We have to choose our time well. Grimaldi's government can't survive many months with such a tiny majority, but we need to inherit a government that's worth inheriting. In the short term, we need to prop it up. Leslie, Alex – use your excellent contacts with the Liberals and the pro-European Tory rump to make sure things don't collapse too quickly. We'll get our people into junior jobs. Then we'll need a resignation or two. Then the PM himself. Lots to do.' He rubbed his hands together. 'Lots to do.'

But before that, the former cabinet colleagues enjoyed a leisurely day in Paris. They strolled in the Tuileries, tolerating the odd stare from British tourists. The Master took Murdoch White, who had a good collection of Scottish paintings, into the Orangerie to see Monet's *Nymphéas* – 'The only good paintings of time actually passing in the world.' (The Master was full of surprises.) Leslie Khan, for his part, had always wanted to bed Sally Johnson. Today, thinking of her expensive underwear and her exquisite little room at the embassy, she acquiesced with a cheerful smile. Later, they all went for supper at the Bristol. They ate sea urchins from cold Norwegian waters, and the hindquarters of hares from the Pyrenees. Life, even in 2019, even for exiled British leaders, could occasionally be tolerable.

Back at 35, rue du Faubourg Saint-Honoré, the ambassador was sitting at his ornate desk in his ornate room, wearing a pair of utilitarian plastic headphones. He was pausing, then playing again, a recording on his private laptop. Sir Anthony Bevins smiled his thin smile. Perhaps, after all, there was a way of demonstrating to those in power that the British embassy in Paris remained a useful asset. 'Awful old fool though I may be.'

A Table for Three

The good politician is never picky about his allies. Because no ally is permanent.

The Master

The Poule au Pot in Pimlico was as much an outpost of French civilisation in London as the embassy was of British grandeur in Paris. With its crowded tables, predictable menu, professionally surly waiters and fat green two-litre carafes of house wine, it offered the political classes a private and boozy mimicry of French regional hospitality. Ever since it was first discovered by Elinor Goodman, the then political editor of Channel 4 News (though the credit was as bitterly disputed as the discovery of the source of the Nile), the Poule had been the scene of verbal treachery and unlikely alliances straddling politics. A formidable number of partridges, pheasants and poussins had been stuffed in its kitchens; an even greater number of secretaries of state, ministers and senior civil servants had been stuffed across its tables. Its candles gave off a sickly glow and dropped wax on the tables. So did many of its ageing customers.

It was here that Caroline had arranged to meet Angela, after her urgent message from Devon. She was still shaking with shock and anger about the *Daily Mail* – the sheer treachery of that vile man Petrie – and she was worried about how she would deal with the debate. She had been a fool. She had been taken for a ride by Mrs Umar. That much was clear. But there was nothing that could be done about it now. She needed help. She had called a number given her by the Master, but all that had come back was a text message: 'You need your friends. Talk to Angela.'

It seemed spectacularly unhelpful. Nevertheless, when Angela called from Devon, sounding odd, Caro had cancelled lunch with a fellow backbencher and booked a table here.

A contemptuous-looking French boy, fingering the crotch of his too-tight jeans, greeted her at the door.

'Yes? We are full.'

'I've booked a table. Name of Phillips.'

'Oh, *oui*. Follow me.' Shrugging sadly, he led her to a corner table, set for three.

'No, there are just the two of us.'

'*Non, madame. Sree.* You eat for *sree.* You pay for *sree.* It is enough. I have not an *ars'ole.*' And he looked at her as if she were decaying vegetable matter, and left her.

There was a carafe on the table, two litres of house white. Caro, a little confused, poured herself a glass. She was staring at the menu when she heard an unexpected voice, huskier than Angela's.

'Me too, darling.'

She looked up. The Master's wife, dressed in an expensive tweed jacket, was looking down at her.

'How are you, Caroline?'

Caroline smiled her best smile. With most people this had the effect of a blast of ultraviolet light. But Sadie merely smiled politely back as she sat down. 'I'm joining you. That's why it's a table for three. It's all right, Angela knows. And so does my husband. He's in Paris, rallying the troops like the king over the water.'

When Angela arrived soon afterwards, however, she didn't seem entirely pleased to see Sadie. Nevertheless, the three of them ordered and began to talk. Caroline outlined the night-marish position she found herself in — apparently supporting Sharia law for Northamptonshire, apparently a fellow traveller for FGM. She could deny it all, explain that she'd been set up, but that would make her the laughing stock of the House of Commons, and the enemy of all the Muslims in Barker, of whom there were many. Furthermore, if Leila Umar came out against her, who would be believed? Leila Umar was an impressive and plausible woman.

Sadie listened quietly. Finally she said, 'I've spoken to my husband. But I already knew what he'd say. "Think like a poli-tician. For a politician, every threat, every looming disaster, is an opportunity. Embrace risk. It's the only way forward." So you're to apologise, to eat humble pie when you're attacked by that Scottish man who's jumped on the bandwagon. You need to surprise them.'

Caroline was unimpressed. 'How? By turning up in a niqab?'

'No. Remember why you first softened towards Mrs Umar.

These people are being attacked. The rest of us are complacent. You don't support all aspects of Sharia law. Of course you don't. You were speaking out against FGM long before David Petrie left his building sites. Today, you're known for two things. You're known for your sexual preference, and you're known as a woman of faith. Accentuate it. Talk about the God of love. Talk about mutual respect and decency. Talk about areas for women who happen to be Muslim, where they can feel safe.'

Angela drained her glass and joined in the conversation for the first time. 'That's all very well, but I don't think it will wash. Not compared to what they'll be throwing at Caro.'

'Quite right,' said Sadie. 'So we have to go further. Suppose the Muslim community in Springtown are attacked, just as Mrs Umar was in the park? Suppose there's an angry, extreme Christian leader in the area who picks up Petrie's comments and leads a mob there?'

'Well, of course that would change things,' said Caro. 'But "suppose, suppose, suppose . . ."'

Angela, confronted by a small plate of casserole, suddenly looked queasy. 'Sadie, that isn't why I've just been approached by Titus Croke, is it?'

'Yes, well, Angela, you know what Titus Croke stands for, I'm sure. Against women priests. Against the Catholic menace. But above all, against Islam in Britain – what he calls the march of the Heathen.'

Caroline stabbed a rabbit. 'He is foul. Titus Croke represents everything in the Church, in fact everything in religious life, that I most detest. He's a man who knows only how to hate.

God forbid we ever see the likes of Titus Croke stirring things up in Barker.'

Sadie had barely touched the food on her plate, but now she dabbed her lips, picked up her handbag and rose from her chair.

'God's a little late, I'm afraid. Titus Croke is already on the march. Someone's tipped him the wink. He seems to have got some money from somewhere. We know nothing about any of that. But if you want a cudgel with which to hit back at our smug Mr Petrie, here it is.' She pulled a small piece of crudely printed paper from her handbag. On one side of it was a photocopy of the *Mail* article, with David Petrie's words highlighted. On the other was a call to arms. English people, Christian people, were summoned to meet and march in Caroline's constituency. The stencilled headline read 'Spires, not Minarets!'

'I must go,' said Sadie, 'and leave you, Angela, to drop your little bombshell in privacy.'

Angela, appearing dumbfounded, made a shrug of incomprehension in Caroline's direction. Once Sadie had left the restaurant, she took a hefty swig from her wine glass and began to talk, and talk fast. 'What the hell was all that about? I got a call from someone I've never heard of saying that Sadie was going to be joining us here. Did you invite her? I thought not. So how the hell did she know where we were meeting? And all that about Titus Croke — it was as if she knew in advance what your problem was, and had somehow fixed a solution . . .'

Caroline broke in: 'Because of course it is a solution. If I can make it seem that David Petrie is somehow connected to an extremist mob, then I can show why some kind of protection for Muslims, even if it isn't Mrs Umar's pet scheme, is urgently necessary. He'll look like a thug, and I'll be able to speak for moderation – live and let live. I can remind the Commons about my record, our situation. This is my way out. God, but it's clever.'

'But don't you see?' said Angela. 'Sadie and her husband must be in collusion with Titus Croke. Just this morning he sent me the most vile email. He said that I was doing Satan's work, and that you and I were in, and I quote, "an abominable union". He said lesbians should be excommunicated from the Church, that we were the witches of the modern age.'

'He said that?'

'He said that.'

'Marvellous!'

'Marvellous?'

'Yes, marvellous. If I quote that in the Commons, there's hardly a Member on either side who won't back me, just to show their contempt for that kind of medieval bigotry. In the most bizarre way, this is getting better and better.'

By now, however, Angela seemed livid. 'You really don't get it, do you? Titus Croke has been put up to this by the very people you seem to be working for. The whole thing's a cynical game. It might help you tomorrow night, but what about those poor people in Barker? Somebody could well get hurt. If Titus Croke is involved, frankly it's almost certain.'

'Well, Angela, I can stop that. If I blow the whistle in time, the police will have to step in. Leila Umar and her community will have no choice but to see me as their protector. After that, I'll be able to dictate how far and how fast we go in changing the law for Springtown. And as for you, it's all very well haranguing me about Barker, but it's a complicated place. It's not like your little idyll in a valley in Devon.'

'That's what I wanted to talk to you about. That's the "little bombshell" that Sadie knows about somehow. Caro, darling, we may be having an argument, but I love you more than life itself. So I've come to a decision. I'm leaving Pebbleton. I'm coming up to Northamptonshire. I've already applied for a living there. No more week after week apart. No more of you criss-crossing the country for a few snatched hours. No more of me, angry and lonely by myself, thinking of you. We're going to be a proper couple from now on. I'm going to be your eyes and ears in Barker. I'm going to work with all the communities there, and you're going to have the kind of support you need if you're going to do everything that you can in politics. We are one. We should start behaving that way.'

Angela's speech had been delivered calmly enough. Nobody looked around from the other tables, near though they were. But by the end of it her cheeks were wet with tears, and Caroline was crying too. They dried one another's faces, kissed lightly, and held hands under the table.

After they had left, another of the waiters came up behind the one who had ushered Caro to the table. He put his hand on his bottom and squeezed lightly.

'Funny women.'

'*Oui*. All those uteruses around one table.'

And they both shuddered.

The Sports and Social

I'm not a Tory. But they're more amusing than we are.

The Master

Stale air: the heavy scent of old food left out in black plastic bin bags just beyond the door, and the thicker, sweeter, even more nauseating smell of political disappointment inside. Once, the smell of failure in the Sports and Social Bar of the House of Commons, deep in the hold of the ship, had been masked by cigarette smoke. To still be here at midnight, calling for pints of Courage bitter from Gawain, the green-waistcoated barman, meant one of two things: utterly hopeless alcoholism, perhaps combined with a marriage falling apart; or lowlife backbench fodder, kept back to sit through a late-night debate in the chamber. That was a whips' punishment for minor infractions. You could work your way back into favour by turning up at unsocial hours to nod at a government minister defending the provision of bus services in Derbyshire, or to ask hostile questions of an opposition MP making an impertinent speech about the chancellor of the exchequer that he had researched among the trolls of the internet.

The Sports and Social

Tonight, two Labour MPs, Sarah Harris and Eric Baxter, were sharing beer and whisky with a heavily-built veteran Conservative universally known as 'Quite Concur'. Sarah had written an article for the *New Statesman* which had been regarded by the prime minister as unhelpful; Eric had returned late from a family holiday, and missed a tight vote. Both were now working their way through the salt mines. Quite Concur had a face as round and knobbly as a Jerusalem artichoke, but less expressive. Nobody was entirely sure whether he was a shrewd observer, ever alert to the shifting fortunes of his more senior colleagues, or a drifting dirigible of flannel and oxygen, a right honourable vegetable. But he was a friendly soul, who always stood his round. All three were abuzz with that rare thing, a late-night vote on a backbench motion which had been bitterly contested and would make the news the following morning.

'I am frankly disappointed,' Sarah Harris said. 'I can't for the life of me understand why Caroline Phillips, of all people, would spout such politically-correct drivel. I mean, we've all got Muslims' – she made it sound like a social disease. 'I had her marked down as a possible future leader. Damned if I still do, after that.'

'Small one?' asked Eric Baxter.

'Sharpener,' said Sarah. Quite Concur raised his eyebrows.

'Something to refresh,' said Eric.

'Tincture,' said Sarah.

'Tincturissimo?'

'Quite concur,' said Quite Concur.

'But Sarah, young Mr Petrie fell flat on his face, didn't he?'

'Yes. Caroline was saved by that religious nutter and his threat of a pogrom. Doesn't mean she was right.'

'But the vote went with her. I'd never have believed that possible a few days ago,' said Eric, on his way to the bar.

'Quite concur,' said Quite Concur.

Eric returned with three triple whiskies. 'Just cooking whisky, boys and girls. Have to tighten our belts. Gawain doesn't know how long he's got a job. Bottoms up.'

'I don't really get Petrie,' continued Sarah. 'He looks and sounds like a working-class left-winger, but if you listen to him, he's curiously right-wing. He's in favour of Trident, NATO and the Americans. But there he was tonight, suddenly championing the cause of mutilated Muslim girls. Why might that be, do you suppose?'

'Touch of Islamophobia? Give him a few years and a few rungs up the ladder, and he'll be marching us into some hot and dusty foreign country for another fruitless crusade,' suggested Eric, who had made his name by voting and speaking eloquently against the Iraq war in the Blair years.

'But one day you'll back him for leader, won't you, Eric?'

'Well, do you know, Sarah, perhaps I might. He isn't soppy. Full head of hair on him. And he isn't a twat, either. He took a terrific belting this evening from your Mrs Phillips. Looked white as a sheet. But he'll bob up again, mark my words.'

'There are rumours that he's close to the Master.'

'Quite,' said Quite Concur, who was becoming less voluble as the whiskies took effect.

The two Labour MPs, feeling that they had cracked a mystery, got up and prepared to head, a little unsteadily, towards the Members' taxi rank. Tomorrow, they wouldn't recall a single word that had been said.

After they'd gone, Quite Concur sat up a little more confidently, and addressed the by-now completely empty bar. He soliloquised. 'Alwyn Grimaldi. Knew his father in the squadron. Very clever man, very clever son. Always had a soft spot for young Alwyn. We on our side regard him as a bit of a loon, of course. One of those boys who think the Americans are always in the wrong. The United Fruit Company. Bay of Pigs. Edward Snowden. All that. And now, because our lot are being so beastly, in he comes. Electoral upset. Wham. The king's first minister, no less. Can't last. Every Labour Member is asking himself or herself, who next? Keep my ear to the ground. Not a great reputation for brains. Doesn't matter. In politics, character second to intellect. Gordon Brown. What matters, hmm? What matters is what's happening. Cabinet discredited, no obvious replacement – but Alwyn's going to have to go before the election. Rum business. I don't think Alwyn's that bad. But nobody listens to me. There are a few dark horses; Caroline Phillips and David Petrie are two of them. Now they're set against one another. Kind of cage fight, something like that. Mark my words, somebody's stringing some . . . strings. Pulling them . . .'

Quite Concur got to his feet, and found his office without difficulty. There, he pulled off his jacket and braces, delicately unlaced his shoes, clambered onto a small sofa and slept the sleep of the just and the wise.

In the Master's House

Y'know, it's not as big as people say.

The Master

Oh yes it was. In the Master's house there were, as the saying goes, many mansions. From the outside, it was an expensive but not extraordinary stuccoed north London home – pillars, railings, a modest flight of steps, the bottom floor picked out in arsenic green. Inside, it plunged down into a huge basement, leapt up four floors to a gigantic roof terrace hidden from prying eyes by frosted glass, and writhed back into what had once been a substantial garden, with a clutter of new rooms.

Sadie ruled the upper areas, where she had two wardrobe rooms, her own bathroom and a study, and where the shared bedroom was situated. The Master reigned in the lower depths, where he had a gymnasium, a library, a home cinema and, right at the back and deepest down, what he called his 'war room', and Sadie called the playroom. It wasn't a study in the normal sense. One wall was given over to an enormous white-board, covered with a mind-dazing scatter of words, symbols, arrows, question marks and numbers, often with dollar or Euro signs in front of them, in red, green, black and blue marker pen. If this was the war room, and that was the battle-field, it seemed to be a battle limited to obsessive and greedy mathematical philosophers. The Master understood every square inch of it. He likened it to the plot of an enormously complicated and daring novel, which instead of writing down with the aim of eventual publication, he was choreographing in real time, his characters living, three-dimensional people whose fates he plotted from his basement. The different colours represented different plotlines – the red was about ridding the country and the party of Alwyn Grimaldi; blue and green represented the intertwining trajectories and careers of 'the children' through whom he intended to rule again; and the money, mostly in black marker pen, was money.

'More tripe than Trollope, more dick than Dickens,' had been Sadie's mordant observation. Like most marriages, theirs was a complex collusion of self-interest, love, irritation and shared secrets, and the truth was that Sadie admired her husband's subterranean scriptwriting and plotting. It would only ever harm their enemies, and it kept him away from the corrupt foreign leaders and cynical tycoons who were always trying to inveigle him abroad. Sadie wasn't even particularly concerned about Ella: she regarded her husband's needs in that respect as a pathetic, boyish weakness, rather than a threat to her own position. Ever since they'd first met in a publishing house, where she had been working and he had been applying the finishing touches to the first volume of his autobiography (he'd been twenty-three at the time, and not even elected to

Parliament), she had enjoyed moulding him from an embarrassingly callow, puppyish enthusiast into the wealthy and powerful man he had become, and who he remained today. Nobody knew his flaws better than Sadie; as to his mistakes, they had mostly made them together. Sometimes, she thought, she regarded him more as a wayward son than a husband, but in that spirit she liked the work he did downstairs.

Now she was standing on the stairs, looking down into the playroom, where the Master was sprawled on a low leather sofa, wearing only jogging pants, staring at the whiteboard.

'He's a bit of a cow's arse,' she said.

'I can't bear him. I don't want him anywhere near me. Promise me that,' he said, and groaned.

'He has issues. He has . . . physical problems. Be a little charitable. You don't have to speak to him.'

'They're all cows' arses. Michael, Clive, Paul – the lot of them. Why do we need Peter Quint?'

'Because people listen to him. Don't ask me why. He flips and flops all over the place, but he's sly, and he knows the smell of a news story. When you told him to get behind David Petrie, he wrote a couple of brilliant pieces. He even went up to Scotland for the background. Petrie would never have had the pick-up he's been given by the Tory press and the broadcasters if it hadn't been for our Mr Quint. If you're going to pick a cow's arse, at least pick the one the rest of the herd sniff.'

The Master tugged absent-mindedly at his belly hair, then swivelled in the sofa and looked hard at his wife.

'You really think we should do this? After all this time, you think we should switch horses?'

'Well, darling, we started off with quite a sizeable herd of them, didn't we? And now we're riding just two. If we make the right choice, we'll have the party under the thumb of somebody who understands how the world works again, who's prepared to take unpopular decisions . . . But I needn't tell you all that – it's *your* speech.'

She walked down the stairs and across the room to one of the Master's desks, from which she picked up a carefully folded piece of chamois leather. 'Petrie is, I'm told, a man for the ladies. He's got some good ideas, but he's volatile, flamboyant. I think he's brittle. Caroline Phillips, on the other hand, has the perfect back story for here and now. A gay woman with a stable partnership and a strong religious background. She's going to be our Margaret Thatcher, depend on it. So it's time to simplify the story.' And she walked up to the whiteboard and, before the Master could stop her, swiped out a square metre of squiggles which had prominently included the letters 'DP'.

The Master, however, was Master of his own whiteboard, if not his house. He unfolded himself with the athleticism of the Pilates addict, and reinserted Petrie's name in red ink, albeit with a question mark after it.

'I like him,' he said to himself. 'He's got an inner anger. He's not quite predictable. Anyway, where's the fun in a one-horse race?'

Then he changed colour, to blues and greens, and began to draw arrows and squiggles, and to add further words. They included 'Grand Project!?', 'Rome!' and 'Ella-Leverage?!'. Like all bad writers, the Master suffered from a lifelong addiction to exclamation marks.

Family Life

Sex? Well, that's a problem. Always has been.

The Master

Up in Glaikit, Mary, Callum and Fergus had quickly become used to David's absence. If he'd thought a little more deeply, he might have been worried about that, but in truth he was mainly relieved. He phoned every day, sometimes twice; but as the boys' worlds changed and evolved without him, the conversations grew briefer and less satisfying to both him and them. They acquired friends he'd never met. He lost track of where their schoolwork had got to. Mary was drily helpful for a while, but after a few months she was warning him, 'I'm no' letting you off the hook, Davie Petrie MP. They don't talk about you any more over supper. They're changing every day. If you want to stay their real father, their proper father, you're going to have to find a way of coming back more often.' From time to time she mentioned Davie's cousin Angus, who had taken to coming around, doing small jobs about the house, keeping Mary company. The boys liked him a lot.

Davie tried. Murdoch White had told him that the first

necessity for a successful political career was a strong family background. 'You need to be rooted. You need a place where you're your real self. Kids cut you down to size. And they remind you of how quickly the world is changing. They're not a distraction, not in this mad world; don't let them go.' So when he could dodge around the votes and the endless meetings, Davie schlepped across town for the sleeper train north. Sometimes he jumped into the car and drove without a break for more than four hundred miles, just to spend a night in his own bed with Mary. It was exhausting, and it affected his performance in the House. He talked to colleagues about moving the family south, but they all advised him against it. The cost of a house in London was prohibitive. He'd be taking the boys out of one education system and throwing them into a different one where they might not thrive. Sure, his family would be only a few miles away, but the late-night voting and the evening meals in the Members' dining room wouldn't go away. What they didn't say, but often thought, was that the strange and lonely life of an MP required a bit of something extra, some night-time solace; and the less spouses knew about what went on in London, the better.

Still, Davie wasn't tempted. Or rather, he was tempted, but he coped. Mary was bonnie, and sensible, and better educated than he was; from a distance, he thought that without her, he'd never have climbed so far. She'd kept her looks. She'd fattened up a little, but in a way he liked. Above all, she'd kept her sense of humour. She could make him laugh like nobody else could, and she could take a rise out of him. She made him like himself better. Why would he go running after some skinny bint from London?

At half-term, and for parts of the school holidays, Mary and the boys would come down to London, where they could just about all squeeze into his Dolphin Square flat. It was a kind of camping. They sat in the television room, the boys on the carpet, to eat breakfast. The boys slept in his study, one on the sofa and one on a futon. During the day, if he could get away, Davie took them on adventures around London. They went to the zoo, which Callum and Fergus thought less impressive than Edinburgh's. They went up the Shard, and around Westminster Abbey, where Davie showed the boys the great black tombs of all those old English kings who had gone north to slaughter the Scots – it was a strange thing, but living in London, after years of fighting the Nats at home, had brought out a belligerent Scottish patriotism that Davie hadn't realised he had. So he pointed out where the Stone of Destiny had once stood, and told them the story of that; and he took them to London Bridge, where all the Jacobite gentlemen's heads had stood on pikes like rotten fruit; but he wasn't sure if it was actually that bridge, or another one; and when he took them to the Tower of London, he reminded them that the Honours of Scotland were in Edinburgh Castle.

But mostly it wasn't history lessons, it was just a family holiday. They wandered through the fancy, expensive shopping streets, with fancy grocers and fancy paintings on sale, and fancy watches that cost more than a car, and fancy cars that cost more than most men would earn in ten years. And they'd find a pizza place, or a McDonald's, and maybe see a film.

Later, although it was a small flat, Davie and Mary would make love like in the old days, because it felt exotic and a bit of an adventure being in such a narrow, unfamiliar bed; and those little London holidays were some of the happiest times the family ever had.

On later visits, Davie took them to the villages of London – to Hampstead and Highgate, Dulwich and Greenwich – and told them that London wasn't really just one place, it was a whole lot of places stuck together. And they learned to eat Chinese dumplings off trolleys in Soho, and spicy meat in Brazilian cafés; to eat curried food with their fingers in the East End, and cold cherry soup and duck like the Hungarians. He told them that London wasn't an English place really, not in the way that Glasgow, and even Edinburgh in a way, were Scottish places. London belonged to all the world. Hundreds of different languages were spoken there. So being in London was like going on holiday all around the world. Callum was more grown-up now, but Fergus said London smelled of poo; and Mary said that yes, it did, but you didn't say poo, you said drains. And that night Fergus said he needed to go drains, and they all laughed. But by then, when they went to bed Mary and Davie would lie beside each other all stiff and formal, like those early English kings and queens in Westminster Abbey; for something had happened, but they were both too scared to talk about it.

The something that had happened was the obvious thing, the thing that always happened when a man and his wife were apart for so long. Davie wasn't tempted by the skinny girl who worked for the Master. She was nothing on his Mary. But then, he wasn't quite *not* tempted, either.

Ella James, who Davie had originally thought worked for some TV station or other, was actually what the Master called 'my eyes and ears', or sometimes 'my girl Friday'. As the months went by, Davie found himself getting ever more help and hints from Murdoch White, Leslie Khan and Alex Brodie. They would summon him to one of their houses, or sometimes for a meal in a discreet restaurant south of the river. They picked him up when he was down – most notably after that terrible trouncing in the House by Caroline Phillips – and taught him which journalists to cultivate, how to spread gossip without being fingered, even how to dress. Davie had always fancied himself as quite dapper, but Leslie Khan, with his neatly trimmed beard and handmade shoes, told him he looked like an IFA, an independent financial adviser, which was apparently a bad thing. He sent him to a tailor in Savile Row, who measured his shoulders and arms, his chest and inner leg; and cut out big pieces of brown paper and pinned them together; and later on fitted him with a suit covered with little chalk marks for small alterations; and charged him nearly £5,000. But after this, Davie felt different. He just looked more self-confident. Whether it was really the suit, or just the morale-boosting effect of spending so much money, it did make a difference.

Khan in particular was full of small, obscure rules. Don't wear brown shoes within two miles of Westminster between Monday morning and Friday lunchtime. Never eat while walking out of doors – you might be photographed, and you'll look like a lout. Never wear plum-coloured corduroy trousers – infallible sign of a rascal. Never use Velcro, for any purpose whatever. Never be seen in public reading the *Sun*, the *Mirror* or *Private Eye*. Don't read *Prospect*, the *TLS* or the *New York Review of Books*, but do buy them, and be seen carrying them. The occasional Virginia cigarette if you must; Turkish are for poseurs, cigars are for Tories and Russians only. Don't say too much, particularly in political arguments. To wait silently, and then speak briskly and clearly at the end, is always more effective than simply piling in. And much more besides.

Neither Leslie Khan nor Alex Brodie, who tended to advise Davie about public speaking, ever mentioned sex at all. Perhaps they took it for granted that he and Mary were safe. Perhaps the subject embarrassed them. Perhaps there was some other reason. At any rate, neither of them tried to warn him off Ella as she became more and more part of his life.

That was easy enough, because Ella served as the Master's representative on earth. The Master himself was very rarely available. His current life frequently took him around the world, to China mainly, and South America. His charitable foundation had offices in Portland Square, and if he ever appeared anywhere, it was there, without fanfare or prior warning. The offices were like those of a hedge fund or a private bank, smelling of fresh white paint and cut flowers. Smartly dressed men and women, quiet, polite and with trans-atlantic accidents, held murmured meetings and passed around files of creamy, expensive paper to be signed or initialled. Telephones gently coughed – never rang, never trilled. The carpets were blonde and several inches deep. So were the blondes. Every so often Ella would ring Davie and ask him to come in to the office. Each time, she half-hinted that the Master wanted to talk to him in person. Davie felt his heart racing as he approached the square, but the Master was never there. Instead Ella, with her interesting, mobile face and thin-lipped mouth, would talk him through something that was about to happen in the House. She would explain that the whips were going to call on him for a rather dirty late-night operation to talk out a popular but expensive backbench Bill. She would tell him that the junior defence minister was about to offer him a post as his parliamentary private secretary, or 'bag carrier'; that this was an unimportant and unpaid job, and the minister in question was bleakly incompetent, but that he should accept the offer with grace and gratitude. He would make some American friends, who would turn out to be useful. It was even Ella who told him about his first promo-tion to real government office.

By then they had been secret lovers for months. Ella had made her proposition sound more like a sensible career deci-sion than adultery. 'You *will* have an affair sooner or later. It's not your fault. It's certainly not Mary's fault. But in this city, in this trade, every man – and most women too – needs an outlet. Politics is a passionate business. You're a very hand-some man, even if, unfortunately, you seem to know it. I'm not completely hideous, I hope. So take your time, and think this through. Sex in Westminster is a very dangerous thing. Literally no one is safe. Try to make a pass at someone, and you'll find the story's sold to the papers. Kiss a girl in a pub, and you'll be photographed. Like everybody else, Mr David Petrie, you have normal animal passions. But if you act on them, you'll be completely sunk. Or you *would* be sunk, if you didn't have me.'

This conversation was taking place in the highly public surroundings of the Pugin Room. Ella had a deep, slightly raw voice, and she was speaking just too quietly to be overheard by the MPs all around them. She leaned forward and drew her forefinger down Davie's thigh before cupping his crotch. 'Everyone knows who I work for. Everyone knows that he admires you, and that you and I are working together. Half of London thinks I'm having an affair with the Master; the other half "knows for a fact" that I am. So you see, I'm pretty safe. But here's the most important thing. It's something the Master himself told me long ago: "If you're in public life and you're going to have an affair, make sure it's with someone who has more to lose than you do." And although I'm unelected, I'm probably the most powerful woman in the Labour Party. So I've got plenty to lose.' Then she stood up, looked around the room and said loudly, 'We should go.'

They took a black cab from the Members' Entrance to Ella's flat, and there, on an antique French bed, under the glassy gaze of a photograph of the Master, who didn't seem interested, Davie committed adultery for the first time in his life.

Ella was indeed pretty, in a forgettable way – lean, an unnatural blonde, with long legs, strong fingers, and her tight face. She was abandoned and shameless, certainly compared to the girls Davie had known in his youth back in Scotland. But there wasn't much to say. Nothing about the encounter was surprising. It went on for quite a while, they came together, and Davie felt a hot flush of remorse afterwards, which he did not share or discuss with her. Both of them knew it would happen again – and again.

From the first, however, Davie always wanted more. Not more sex – more intimacy. What was truly disconcerting about Ella was her ability to separate what they did together in private from the rest of their lives. About one thing, she was proved right: there was never the faintest suspicion or fragment of gossip. But this came at a price. Her businesslike attitude to Davie in public, whether in the Master's offices or during their meetings at the Commons, stung him. One moment she had her face buried in the hairs of his chest and her arms around him; the next time she saw him she would be instructing him to do this or that political odd job as if he were an anonymous and junior functionary.

There was no true closeness, no sharing of confessions, fantasies or private jokes. He told her about his mother and the village. He told her, late one night, about what his father had done to him, and the hot but hollow feeling inside it had left him with. She tugged his hair, or brushed her fingers against his cheek, or opened another bottle of wine, but said only 'Poor dear.' When he asked her about her past he got only shrugs or fragments – school here, interest in a pony there, 'nice' parents, all related in a cool, neutral tone. It was as if she were describing someone else, whom she didn't know particularly well and wasn't hugely interested in. Whenever he asked her about the Master, a door slammed shut in his face. One day she told him, 'You'll see him soon enough, if you're good enough. The world is too bloody full of bloody fools gossiping about him. Let's not make ourselves yet another pair of them.'

Petrie came to think that for Ella, the sex was no more than business. In bed, there were endearments, nuzzlings. But the light of day was always cold – swift exits, the radio turned up, toneless farewells. He found it was possible to be sexually fulfilled and very lonely at the same time. Later, when they had moved on to the more intimate stage of having arguments, she defended herself: if Davie was looking to give his life some meaning, it had to be through ambition and achievement. If he was lonely, so much the better; he would work harder. He was married, and he wanted to stay married, didn't he? (He supposed he did.) Did he have any idea how hard it was for her to keep the necessary distance?

The next time Mary, Callum and Fergus came down, Davie tried harder than ever to find enticing amusements and surprising places to eat. He hardly stopped talking – about London, about his job, about the exciting things that were going to happen to him. With every syllable, with every look, he was lying to all three of them. The boys said nothing, and behaved as if everything was normal. But Mary looked at him intently, and asked several times if everything was all right. She didn't know a thing. She knew everything. He said nothing. His 'nothing' was everything. For the first time in his life, he had no words. Now strangers, they clutched each other in the darkness like a pair of drowning children.

Barker

Everybody has to come from somewhere. If you don't come from somewhere, find somewhere.

Himself

Caroline's shattering defeat of cocky, disagreeable David Petrie in the debate about Sharia law was, Angela told her, the first great victory of their new life in Barker. 'If we stand together my love, who can resist us?'

The weeks after Angela's decision to leave Pebbleton had been the most extraordinary blur. Angela, unbound, was like an Old Testament angel – tangled hair flying, colourful wings whirring, everywhere at once. Her new parish was just outside Caro's constituency boundary, and it quickly became clear to Angela, after meeting the curate, the verger, and some of the pitifully sparse regular congregation, that this was a community in desperate need of leadership. This part of Barker was mainly composed of narrow, red-brick terraces built in the glory days when the town was world-famous for its shoemakers. Once, Barker's annual fair had been a magnet for traders and performers from across the Midlands. Even

between the wars, Barker had been a thriving centre of manufacturing – typewriters, vacuum cleaners and bicycles – which
had lured Scots and Welsh workers. But, badly hit by the
Luftwaffe in 1941, the town's factories never fully recovered.
The shoes were made more cheaply abroad, first in East
Germany and Poland, and later in China. Typewriters gave
way to personal computers; bicycles arrived by container from
the Far East. Meanwhile, waves of immigration from Pakistan's
Swat Valley and Sylhet in Bangladesh, where foresight about
global manufacturing developments was in short supply, had
brought new communities to Barker. For obvious reasons, they
rarely got on. By the twenty-first century Barker was as well
known for its gangs as it had once been for its fairs. The chapels
built by the Welsh, and the late-Victorian Anglican churches,
had mostly been converted to housing or to mosques.

Angela had arrived early for her interview, and had chosen
not to book into the only hotel in the area – her enquiries
had revealed that it was run by one of the churchwardens –
but found a bed and breakfast. She had walked the streets,
noting how many families still gathered on the front steps of
their terraced houses, and observing the graffiti and the abandoned toys, bikes and prams in the gardens. She had seen how
the Bangladeshi women huddled close to the walls as they
walked along, and shivered in the cold. Pebbleton it wasn't.
But there seemed to be more chip shops and fried-chicken
outlets than curry houses.

As she walked, Angela felt a curious and intense physical
sensation. A hot, prickling feeling began behind her knees
and then ran up the backs of her legs, rushing up her torso

and neck before crackling around her scalp. She gasped, and felt herself flooded by a feeling of delight and peace. 'I am being called by the Lord,' she said to herself. 'This is how it feels.'

There was apparently a shortlist, though Angela never met any of the other candidates. The interview panel met her in the church hall. They were mostly women in their sixties or older, plus a couple of bulky men in suits, the verger, and a younger man who must have been the archdeacon. They seemed tough, weathered people, but friendly enough. After a short prayer imploring God to give them wisdom in their judgements, Angela was asked about her ambitions for Christianity in a town like Barker, and the differences she expected working here, as compared to a small rural living in Devon. She was warned that the 'parsonage' was in reality a two-bedroom brick house next to a general store. (This in itself had put off another of the candidates.) She was asked about her children, and whether they would go to the local school. Perhaps, she answered; she would have to see. As to the parsonage, the panel were aware that her partner was the Member of Parliament for Barker, and she expected that they would buy a house together, big enough to accommodate both her family and her work on pastoral matters. There was a ripple of approval in the room. She wasn't asked about her sexuality, or her views on women bishops; she got the distinct impression that neither mattered here. These people wanted someone who could rally the fainthearted and spread the gospel in these forgotten streets.

She was chosen, as she knew she would be; as she felt she

already had been. Three days later she had had an offer accepted for a four-bedroomed house recently built on land reclaimed from a railway marshalling yard. It had a neat garden, though the new lawn was suspiciously bumpy, and there were already cracks in some of the ceilings. Entirely happy, she called Lady Broderick, who turned out to know the archdeacon – and who had perhaps put in a word for her – and asked her to send the boys up by train. There was a grammar school in the next town, and Angela, still brimming with flaming certainty that the Lord was with her, knew they would be offered places there, and that they'd like it.

Caroline, when she arrived at the new house for the first time, found herself feeling selfishly jealous. Angela had already crammed the few bookshelves with her dusty Thackeray and Dickens paperbacks, and the broken-backed works of radical theology, feminism and Eurocommunism left over from her university days. She had put up a painting of Pebbleton she'd bought for a song at a charity auction; the furniture had been hurriedly purchased from an IKEA outside Milton Keynes, and was still mostly unassembled. Compared to Caro's cosy flat in London, it seemed nothing to do with her life. But, seeing Angela's radiant face, she pushed aside her misgivings and kissed her thanks.

In bed that night Angela lay on top of Caro, her nose burrowed into her sweet-smelling neck as they hugged tightly.

'A new adventure.'

'Together.'

'Against the world.'

'Us.'

Health and Efficiency

The good minister initiates; the bad minister reacts.

The Master

He had a scratch. It ran down the outer side of his right shin. His legs were pleasingly hairless, although freckled, and the red line of his scratching was obvious.

'It's not a scratch, it's an itch,' said his wife, who was reading her emails in bed.

'Do you think I've got something? It's sort of tingly.'

'Yes, my love. You've got a messiah complex.' Sadie glanced over at him. 'But sadly, it isn't fatal. Not for you, anyway.'

'*My* love, you *have* woken in an acid condition . . . Hey, it's all my fault. We don't spend enough time together.'

Sadie rolled away from him, heaving the duvet over her, and groaned.

The Master climbed out of bed. He slept naked. 'There's nothing today that I can't cancel. We could have a walk. We could have lunch together, just the two of us. Talk.'

'You really are the most invincibly vain man I've ever met. Do you think I don't have things to do? People to meet?'

Health and Efficiency

The Master, feeling hurt but discovering no plausible retort, made his way to the bathroom. Sadie listened to the creak of the floorboards under him. 'And don't just stand in there admiring your bottom in the mirror. For a man of your age, it's undignified. Even in private.'

It was true that the Master was well-toned. Well into his sixties, there was barely a finger of loose flesh on him; Sadie sometimes referred to him as Dorian Gray. The muscles on his arms, chest and legs were well-defined. He had escaped varicose veins, precancerous moles and cellulite. He particularly prided himself on his bottom, which he felt was still a work of art. But 'work' was right: he had worked hard for this body. After losing power, years of travelling had been made tolerable by frantic workouts in hotel gyms from Abu Dhabi to Singapore. When he wasn't speaking, he was jogging. There was nothing he could do about his face, which was scored and tautened by decades of stress, public smiling and late-night reading. So far he hadn't been tempted by Botox or a facelift; and anyway, if anything, he looked too young for his age. He quite fancied thicker eyebrows, he sometimes thought. But meanwhile his body, the feeling of it and the look of it, was a completely legitimate pleasure. Sadie was probably jealous; that, he thought, was probably why she was trying to get him to cut Petrie loose. Feminism was all very well in public, but . . .

After the Master had disappeared into the bathroom, Sadie flung the duvet away and hurriedly dressed herself in jogging pants, sports bra and a Juicy top. The bloody man wasn't giving up on his nasty little Scottish boy. She was a heavy woman, but still young-looking. She lit a vanilla-scented candle and tucked herself on the floor for her customary twenty minutes of mindfulness – mindfulness, she said, was yoga without the moaning. But before she began, she reached for her phone and texted every one of her eight children. Voice recognition helped, but each of the eight messages was personal, appropriate and up to date. Only then did she switch off the phone and close her eyes.

The Master returned, clean and shaven, in a pressed blue shirt and smart grey trousers. He watched her for a moment, and coughed. A spasm of irritation passed across her face. He thought about it, then coughed again. This time her eyes opened and she turned around.

'No, you are not ill. You're pathetic. That's not even a real cough. And so, no, it's nothing serious.'

'Sorry, darling, all I wanted to do was talk. Did you hear the debate last night? Caroline and Petrie?'

'Of course I did. I stayed up and watched it on the parliamentary channel. She trounced him, didn't she? I'm actually amazed that you can't see that.'

'Perhaps you're right. But I've been thinking. Inadvertently, perhaps, didn't we give her a lot more help than we gave Mr Petrie?'

'True. But we had to. He went for her ferociously. That wretched newspaper article, and to use FGM against her – that was completely unacceptable. It was inappropriate.'

'Sadie, you're right. But, hey, that was our guys. Sometimes they get a bit *Hunger Games*. Don't blame the runner. And he did make that excellent speech about Trident and Egypt.

I was talking to Don in Washington' — Don was their eldest son — 'and he said it was noticed there. Caroline hasn't done anything quite that bold so far. Sure, she's lovely, but she lacks a bit of inner steel.'

Sadie, realising that mindfulness was off this morning's agenda, unknotted herself. She had come to feel rather proprietorial about Caroline Phillips. 'Caro's more than tough enough, and she's going to come right. We need to get her a government job. You need to call in some favours. In fact, if you're not too distracted by any passing mirrors, you might get to work on it today. I'm going to see her myself later on.'

'Really? Where are you off to?'

'To help train my team. Somewhere White and Khan can't overhear us.'

Cleanliness

Better out than in. Except for office, obviously.

The Master

There was a freshly painted cream door in the brick
wall on a corner off Kensington Church Street. Above it was
a metal sign that read 'Vitality' and 'The In-Town Clinic'. Sadie,
enwrapped in a thick quilted coat, pulled a bell shaped like
an acorn, and was immediately let in.

Beyond a small urban garden, planted with azaleas and
cacti, the clinic was housed in a ruthlessly modernised set
of Victorian cottages. Much of the frontage had been ripped
off and replaced by a long, curving wall of frosted green
glass. Sadie buzzed and was let through. A spectacularly
beautiful African girl in a white uniform looked up from
behind her desk and smiled.

'Ah, Mrs . . .'

'Shhh,' mouthed Sadie.

'Your guest is here. Mrs Phillips is just undressing.'

Sadie went through to a large, warm room with low lighting.
Banquettes covered in thick white towels lined the walls.

On one of them, Caro was sitting in a light white dressing gown. She looked a little nervous, Sadie thought.

'Nothing to worry about, darling. This is going to be our girls' moment, pure pleasure; and you'll feel like a million dollars afterwards.'

'I hope so. It just seems a rather odd way of spending a Tuesday morning. I had to cancel a . . .'

'Well, that's part of the point. Everything can be cancelled. In your life you need to think more about stress and how to fight it. And after more than forty years married to a politician, I can tell you that *this* works.'

The In-Town Clinic had been founded in the 1980s by a friend of Sadie's, Fara Clara Jenkinson, a socialite, Buddhist, professional anorexic and occasional companion of British princes. Underneath the froth, Fara Clara was as tough as a Levantine arms dealer. But despite her elevated social status, she had very little money. Then she noticed that, in California and certain spa resorts of Middle Europe, many stressed, wealthy women had discovered the therapeutic benefits of 'high colonic irrigation', or having warm water squirted up their bottoms. She borrowed some money, and began to show her entrepreneurial qualities. Although the treatment tended to make husbands and lovers snigger, Fara Clara's discreet and expensive service began to make quite a lot of money. *Good Housekeeping*, *Vogue*, *Tatler* and *The Lady* all ran articles about her, in which the euphemisms bloomed like desert flowers; but frank, quiet word-of-mouth was her best advertisement.

By the beginning of the twenty-first century Fara Clara had refined and extended her services. A range of branded Fara

Clara health drinks – nettle juice with beetroot, carrot and caramel frappé, cold olive tea – were followed by 'home treatments'. Plastic buckets of mud, supposedly sourced from the Auvergne and Baden-Baden though in fact from Wolverhampton and Frinton, were mixed with gold leaf, dry rice and black pepper, to be smeared on exhausted faces and sagging bosoms in the privacy of bathrooms from Virginia Water to Chipping Norton. You could buy Fara Clara oils and Fara Clara candles and Fara Clara pampering kits. Their acrid fragrances were unusual and unmistakable.

But the bum-squirting business remained at the heart of the Fara Clara empire, and it was there that her instinct for innovation could be seen at its most ingenious. Relatively early on in the high colonic irrigation movement, the invigorating effect of introducing coffee into the enemas had been realised. Fara Clara took this one stage further. The In-Town Clinic offered organic Ethiopian coffee treatments, rainforest-friendly ones, coffees with cardamom, and coffees whose beans had been hand-picked on obscure mountain ranges. For special clients Fara Clara offered marijuana enemas, enemas incorporating fluoxetine or other antidepressants, and for the artistically inclined, jasmine tea.

It was rumoured that the wife of a Premier League footballer who found it hard to keep her food down had paid Fara Clara to feed her otherwise: entire meals were bought at the best London restaurants, liquidised, and inserted, half-litre by half-litre. It was only after a doctor, writing in the *Times* health pages, had pointed out that bypassing the stomach entirely rather undermined the point of ingesting food, and was in fact dangerous to the heart, that Fara Clara recoiled from this new business model — what she had wanted to call 'fesstaurants'.

Sadie and Caro were ushered through to the treatment room, with low hospital beds and an entire wall of taps, temperature controls, hoses and nozzles — but there was Cherubini playing, and half a dozen cinnamon candles. A powerfully built Thai woman was waiting for them.

'We have Java, Blue Mountain, organic Ethiopian and English Breakfast this morning. Any preferences, ladies?'

Sadie untagged her bathrobe and lay face-down on one of the beds. The Thai woman immediately covered her with an embroidered sheet.

'Oh dear, are we out of the Fortnum & Mason Christmas Blend already? Well, I'll have the Blue Mountain — I'm feeling strong today. And perhaps a teaspoon of the Prozac mix. No sugar, Dolly.'

Caroline felt most uneasy as she edged herself down onto the other bed. 'What if someone comes in?' she whispered to Sadie. 'I mean, if the *Daily Mail* knew where I was right now . . .'

'Don't worry, nobody will come in. We have the place to ourselves. I booked it all. The Master was happy to pay.'

'Oh. Well, what should I have?'

'First time?'

'First time.'

'I'd try the Java. You'll feel transformed.'

The Thai woman intervened: 'It's Fair Trade, modom.'

Caroline succumbed.

'So, Sadie,' she said as the Thai woman busied herself with preparing the infusions, 'I take it we're here for some ulterior reason. It felt more like a summons than an invitation.'

'I'm sorry about that – my PA can sound a little brisk at times. But yes, since you mention it, I thought this would be a good place to talk. Why don't you go first? Just roll over on your side. Try to relax.'

'Knees to your chest, modom. I'm just going to massage your tummy.'

'Ow. Oowww! So what did you want to talk about? Am I wrong in assuming you're here with your husband's blessing?'

'We don't really have that kind of marriage. If anything, it's the other way round. But we do work together on the big things. And the most important thing I have to tell you today is that it's time for you to join the government.'

'Tuck up, tuck right up, modom. Just roll onto your back. Breathe out.'

'Very kind. But that's hardly in your gift, is it? And thanks to shooting my mouth off about the Barker Muslims . . . Ahh. Oww! That really hurts . . . I'm not exactly the most popular girl . . . Aaahhh . . . with the Grimaldi people. It's too hot!'

'Push out, Caroline. It's just a bit of cramping, nothing more. Half the government still looks to my husband. He has hundreds of strings that he can pull in private. And you're obviously one of the most talented people in the parliamentary party. It feels a bit strange at first, but you'll soon get the hang of it. The arrangements have already been made. The water has to travel up a good five feet, you know. You'll be joining Work and Pensions, as the minister for labour.

Not very glamorous, I'm afraid, but solid, serious stuff. Feeling a little bloated?'

'Sore. I want to . . .'

'I know, darling. Just let it go. You're going to feel wonderful. And you're going to *be* wonderful. You've got a really solid base. That's it. Well done. You've got a great constituency. Better now. You've shown your tough side. Everybody loves you. And above all, you have Angela. She's rather your guardian angel, isn't she?'

'She . . . if she could only see me now. How long does this go on for?'

'Just a little longer. Lots of good clean water in and out, and a bit of caffeine to perk you up. The main thing is to make your mark immediately, as a different kind of minister. There's a viewing tube, if you want.'

'A viewing tube? No! But thank you. When you say "a different kind", what do you mean? Frankly, these days nobody notices junior ministers at all, unless they absolutely foul up.'

'Exactly. That's why we're having this little talk. You're going to get lots of help from people who've made a success before. But I've spent enough time with my husband and his colleagues to start you off. Finished?'

'Ooh. I think so. Your turn.'

'My turn. They usually put music on, but I find nothing takes the mind off things like talking. Thank you, Dolly. Just crack on. The bad minister is controlled by the civil servants. The bad minister learns that Whitehall operates on a flow of paper, and the job is to keep the paper, the decisions, flowing. Round and round it goes. The bad minister learns that a day without headlines is a successful day. That an interview on *Newsnight* in which he says nothing interesting or new is a triumph. The bad minister, being a coward, learns that it's his secretary of state who gets to make the headlines. Just perfect, Dolly. Well done. Keep going.

'All of those things are wrong. The good minister controls her civil servants. They won't like it, and they won't like you. They'll snipe, and some of them will leak. And that will make your daily life unpleasant at times. But it doesn't matter. Your job is not to keep the paper moving. Your job is to make things happen. Sometimes that means throwing the paper away. There was one minister, very well-known chap, who was so worried and offended by the stream of busybody, interfering Whitehall decision-taking that he used to take his red boxes home every evening, lock them in the boot of his car, and just leave them there for months, accumulating. His private secretary was livid, and complained to the permanent secretary; but there was nothing they could do, you see. If they didn't have the paper circulating, nothing happened. And so, although they all mocked him, over time he was eventually able to take control for himself. That's an extreme example, but you get my drift. Ouch. And then there's the business of headlines. Your job is to get noticed, to get people thinking and talking. What's the use of going on television for twenty minutes, in front of a couple of million people, unless they think slightly differently afterwards? Every media interview that doesn't generate controversy, that doesn't make somebody, some-where, angry or a little shaken up, is an opportunity lost. So few of them understand that. Ooooo . . . aaaaah . . . Finally, there's your boss. The secretary of state, with the biggest office and the grandest civil servants, is not your superior, still less your God. He's your rival. You are going to take him down. The good minister only looks upwards, never downwards. In your case, of course, you've been lumbered with Norman Hastings, as decent and pleasant a lump of nothingness as the party has seen for years. So it shouldn't be difficult.'

As the lesson and the treatment concluded, the two women were given cotton kimonos. Sadie wrapped hers around herself, stood up a little shakily, and led Caroline to the recovery room. A low table displayed 'Fara Clara's treats', which included sweet-potato jam, grass tea, and kale and snail smoothies. Caro shuddered, although she admitted to herself that she did feel better, somehow perkier. She took a bottle of water for herself, and handed one to Sadie.

'But how do I pick the issue to fight on? And isn't it true, as everybody says, that events, disasters and random mistakes will dominate my life as a minister?'

'As to the issue, there are others who'll be able to help you, but I certainly can't. Really, the best thing is to do your own thinking. Chew it over with Angela. I think I'm half in love with Angela myself. Very clever lady. And as to "events", you're right. But my husband says that the true politician is the one who sees every disaster, every screw-up, as a wonderful opportunity. Always on the front foot, that's the thing. Never relax. Never go backwards.'

Things turned out exactly as Sadie had promised. The call came from the chief whip himself. The reshuffle had been prompted by a very minor scandal – the immigration minister turned out to have employed a cleaner from Thailand who was not in Britain legally. Caroline was summoned to Downing Street, and was well enough prepared to have dressed in her best royal-blue Jaeger suit, with matching orange shoes and handbag.

At first she was unamused to find that David Petrie, of all people, had been promoted into government on the same day, in his case as junior minister for urban planning. But then, she reflected, her job involved people – real people, people without jobs and people scared about their retirement – while his was just about bricks and concrete. And the *Sun*'s caption under the photograph of the two of them striding up Downing Street was, if predictable, reassuring. Caroline was smiling, while Petrie had a workmanlike glower on his face: 'Beauty and the Beast'. In the *Telegraph*, the third leader commented that Alwyn Grimaldi, having acted quickly as a butcher, was gambling by bringing in some of the brightest, but untested and untried, figures from the back benches as new ministers. 'We applaud his optimism, but we wonder how Mrs Phillips and Mr Petrie will get on, given their recent bitter fight in the chamber over Muslim rights. Mr Petrie lost that fight, and his friends say that he remains resentful. Increasingly, the prime minister's handling of his government resembles that old film, *The Hunger Games*. At any rate, he has given us a new national entertainment.'

How to Cure a Columnist

In a properly run country, journalists would have to wear a mark of shame sewn onto their clothing.

                    . . . (but he didn't really mean it)

Sadie had taken on Peter Quint as one of her projects. The Master may have loathed him, but his wife was tougher, and understood how useful a reliable voice in a mainstream newspaper could be. Now Peter had come to her with his agonising personal problem. If anyone could help him, then Sadie, with her contacts in the land of alternative therapies, was surely the girl.

Peter Quint *oozed*. That was the word he used himself, because it was unavoidable. The problem had started not long after he had signed his first half-million-pound contract for a twice-weekly column, and been profiled on Andrew Neil's politics show. He had always had lustrous hair which needed to be vigorously washed every morning; now he found that by lunchtime it was exuding a thick, sebaceous secretion, visible and itchy. His hands had always been sweaty; now a sticky greenish oil, which smelt of cabbage, began to accumulate between his fingers and in his palms. His feet *poured*. He knew that he gave off a ripe scent – he knew it because that was why his girlfriend had left him. At times when he'd been standing in the same spot for a long while, at a party for instance, he felt there was almost a patch of something – could it be slime? – on the floor around him.

Sadie sent him to Harley Street, to a physician specialising in skin complaints who had helped the Master in the past. He professed himself disgusted and baffled; half a dozen bottles of rattling pills left Peter constipated and unable to sleep, but as slimy as ever. Sadie sent him to the In-Town Clinic, for cold saltwater baths and scourging with twigs. This refreshed – and indeed excited – Peter, but did not solve the problem. She had him fitted with lightweight, breathable shirts and suits; Peter wore them out as if they were clingfilm.

Shortly before the ministerial reshuffle, Sadie had ordered Peter to sell David Petrie, and buy Caroline Phillips – an agonisingly difficult transition which he would have agreed to for nobody else. Thus it was that Peter found himself in Barker to do a 'soft' interview with Caroline and Angela.

He was still on uneasy terms with Mrs Phillips. She was, not unnaturally, suspicious. But he found himself almost falling for the sharp-featured, dark-eyed vicar – to such an extent that he couldn't help raising the subject of his miserable complaint.

Angela was undisgusted and forthright. 'It's a spiritual matter, Mr Quint, not a physical one. Nobody in Harley Street or any of the teaching hospitals can help you with this. Let's be straight about it. You ooze. What do you ooze?'

'I'm told it might be a secretion linked to the regulation of body heat.'

'Nonsense. It's slime. What else is slimy, Mr Quint?'

'I don't know. The seashore?'

'I was thinking more of toads. The truth is, Mr Quint, that you are a bit of a slimy toad. I'm sorry to be blunt. I know it's hard to accept.'

Peter looked sadly at the carpet. Already a dark stain was appearing around the stitching of his recently-bought brogues. 'That's a terrible thing to say.'

'It is a terrible thing to be. Have you any idea what causes it?'

Caro was shaking her head and making lip-zipping gestures at Angela, but the conversation had gone too far to be cut off. And oddly, Peter Quint seemed not angry, but dolefully grateful.

'No, I don't.'

'What causes it is self-importance, mingled with hypocrisy. It's a toxic mix, Mr Quint. You have been wallowing in these vices for decades, I suspect.'

'Well, since 1985 at least. That's when I got my first big column. But what can I do about it?'

'You must rid yourself of the illusion that a newspaper columnist in a small country like this one, in the second decade of the twenty-first century, is a person of importance. You are not important. You have never been elected to do anything. You have never created a business. You have never come up with a single fresh idea, and you have never helped your fellow man in any way. Yet you regard yourself as a significant figure.'

'This . . . this . . . is *unacceptably* painful.'

'Most useful therapies are. The second thing is that you must start to say only what you actually mean, and write only what you think is true.'

'That's my career gone, then. You can't ask me to do that. It's not what I've been trained to do.'

'Perhaps not. But there are plenty of *useful* jobs that need doing all around this country. Why don't you come with me into our little church, and get down on your knees and think about it?'

Peter Quint, for the first time in the conversation, straightened his back, puffed out his chest, and began to sound like his usual self. 'I am not a spiritual person, I'm afraid, Angela. I have firmly agnostic views, based on wide reading and a detestation of religious mania.'

'I'm not asking you to prostrate yourself before your Redeemer – though it wouldn't hurt. I'm just asking you to spend twenty minutes on your knees contemplating your life so far. That isn't long. And it won't cost you anything.'

Peter Quint did as he was told. And for the first time in his life, he failed to file his copy. The interview never happened; or rather, it had happened, but the wrong way round.

Bathtime Talk

Everybody is useful somehow. Well, except farmers . . .

The Master

'You have to speak to him.' Angela was soaking in the bath, a new luxury in their Barker home – the house in Pebbleton, though pretty, had only had a shower. She was barely visible under a thick, strangely scented layer of pink foam. 'I don't like this stuff, darling.'

'Sorry. I know it's pretty foul, but my curiosity was aroused. It's Fara Clara's sweet beetroot pampering foam. Why is beetroot suddenly everywhere, Ange?'

'I imagine there's some deeply secret cell of the National Farmers' Union whose job is to surreptitiously promote unlikely vegetables,' replied Angela, who was a deft cook. 'I mean, look at rhubarb. A few years back, after decades of relative obscurity, it was suddenly all over the bloody place, remember? The TV chefs began to drape it over sea bream, oxtails, you name it. Rhubarb soufflés, rhubarb jam . . . Then there was kale. Horrid stuff. Nobody had noticed it since the thirteenth century, but suddenly it was everywhere. No dinner

233

party was complete without a stinking bowl of kale. You could buy kale crisps. Now it's the humble beetroot that's leapt onto the stage, cavorting around in the most inappropriate way. I can't believe this is all down to the hidden hand of the market. Somebody must be pulling the vegetable strings, and making them dance. You should get some of your clever civil servants to investigate.'

There was a long, vegetable-scented silence.

'But as I say, you really need to speak to him. To Petrie. This confected war between the two of you is getting out of hand.'

Caro sighed, and reached for a towel. 'Stand up, and I'll give you a dry-off. Carrots, that's another one.'

'Not really, dear.'

'I don't mean ordinary carrots. I mean silly carrots – yellow carrots, white carrots. Purple carrots. And green tomatoes. Lift your arms up.'

'You're avoiding the subject.'

'No I'm not.' Caroline began to vigorously towel Angela, from her small, schoolgirl's breasts down to her rather large stomach, and the thighs and buttocks that would have struck Peter Paul Rubens dumb with admiration. She'd put on a lot of weight in the last couple of years. 'I just don't like the man. He's coarse, and he's angry. I can't see him getting much further up the government, never mind to the top of it. I don't see why I should go cap in hand to him.'

'Ooh, keep rubbing. Just there. Aah, that's lovely.'

A few years earlier, this would have been an erotic conversation. This evening, however, Angela's bad back was uppermost in her mind. Caroline drove her thumbs, through the towel, into her girlfriend's lower vertebrae. Angela was still gorgeous, freckled and soft; but on the other hand, she did smell strongly and unmistakably of beetroot.

Immorality

Remember what I said about appetites.

The Master

Davie had taken the news of his promotion more calmly than Caroline. As so often, the first hint had come in bed from Ella, who had rolled over and was staring at his face as if she had never seen it before, with a serious expression, her mouth twisted in a way he found erotically exciting. So, forewarned, he had taken the trouble to flatter Alwyn Grimaldi, and had listened patiently to a pep talk from Murdoch White, mainly on the subject of always taking the credit for successes and moving on briskly from failures, which should always be attributed to the civil service or to one's predecessor, or if they were huge, to the situation left behind by the previous government.

Davie wondered whether the unseemly pleasure he took in the trappings of his new position – the magazine profiles, the larger car and its driver, the more intelligent and attentive private secretaries – was some kind of petty revenge on his father, who for all his energy had never moved beyond a smoky open-plan office and the services of the local cab company. Certainly, the higher he climbed, the less intrusive he found his father's memory was. He would have liked to discuss this with Mary, but when they met these days there never seemed to be time to do anything other than deal with family administration. In any case, she didn't seem much interested in his London life.

That life now revolved around the twin poles of his hectic office and Ella's flat. Some weeks he seemed to be at her place more often than his own, but still the secret held. Every fortnight he'd pick up *Private Eye* with an almost pleasurable shiver of unease; but nothing ever appeared.

Ella had thawed a little, but far too slowly to satisfy Davie's gnawing hunger for intimacy. For he was not a cold man: he thought a lot about Fergus and Callum, and quite a lot about Mary. But he had come to regard them as interesting, distant friends. Mary existed up north, but London was not her town, hardly her planet. Different planets, different rules. When he was back in Glaikit, it was as if he'd never been away. Familiar accents, the different smell of the air – muck and brae freshness, coal fires, burning stubble – and the feel of his sons' heads on his lap as they watched telly together . . . All of this washed over him like an out-of-body experience or a pleasurable dream, so he sank into it and thought very little of his office or of Ella.

In London, things were different. His heart, that unruly riot of gristle and tubing which seemed so much more than a mere pump, flailed against his ribcage as he left Ella's flat: '*Got away with it,*' it said. '*Got away with it, gotta way wi' it, gotta, gotta, gotta . . .*'

And, remarkably, so they seemed to have done.

Everybody else got caught. Parliamentary private secretaries and cookery writers; the husbands of ministers and the wives of secretaries of state; researchers and eminent authors . . . The press and the scurrilous websites found, week after week, further proof of the scandalous fact that sex happened, and not always inside marriage. Yet David Petrie, who as a rising minister in an unpopular government would have been a fat and juicy target, and the mysterious Ella James, already connected in the public mind to her employer, the Master, were never photographed together, never recorded. Apparently, they were never even seen.

In part, this was due to what Ella coldly called her 'trade-craft'. They could walk together through the centre of London, but Davie would be on one side of the road and Ella on the other. They made eye contact and exchanged complicit smiles, but always from a distance, unphotographable as a couple, divided by traffic. They chose separate tube carriages, and seats a few rows apart on buses. At parties, they would enter separately and make a point of introducing themselves to each other, competing to see whose false politeness was the more ridiculous.

Davie sometimes wondered whether this no-contact public game pointed to a deeper truth about their relationship. Yet these were the only terms on which it was possible. London in the early years of the twenty-first century was the most public city in the world, and perhaps the hardest to hide in; but even London had its dead spots, its blank triangles. Davie and Ella had become anti-connoisseurs of restaurants and pubs, experienced in finding the about-to-be-closed curry houses with a patina of dirt on the window, the no-longer-fashionable trattorias where only tourists with ten-year-old copies of *Time Out* were ever found, the restaurants which specialised in obscure and unappetising cuisines. In their quest for privacy they had eaten kangaroo and alligator meat, glutinous Mongolian stews of lamb fat, and insect-stuffed Mexican delicacies. Once, they had even found a Belarusian restaurant. No one else was there, nor, by the look of the place, ever had been. They told one another they were paying for their passion not by being exposed to public shame, or poisoned or stabbed by jealous rivals, but by becoming slightly pasty-faced, badly fed and flatulent. Some of this they walked off late at night. From Green Park to Kensington Gardens, the squares of Bloomsbury to the duller stretches of Regent's Park, every one of the stands of sprawling rhododendrons, tangles of holly and yew, and derelict Victorian sheds where wheelbarrows and rollers were locked up, held a memory of their subterranean life together.

Davie understood that he was becoming addicted to Ella. She never gave him enough of herself – it was always mere sex – but their games had a human reality that made the struggles of politics tolerable. Yet he knew that she always had the upper hand. At times, he wondered if she was really his friend. Had he ever mentioned her to Tony Moretti or his SNP cousins back home, it would have been regarded as proof positive that he'd been corrupted by power.

Bunty, certainly, had never liked Ella. Davie had had to adapt to Bunty's implacable outspokenness on the subject. She had learned to say little when anyone else was in the office. But if she and Davie were alone, Bunty would start up.

'Hoo's the hoor?'

'Bunty, that is . . . inappropriate.'

'Well, she is a hoor. She's got her hoory claws into you, and you're making a damnt fule of yourself. A'body knows. It's only a matter of time before it's on the front of the *Sun*.'

'Nobody knows.'

'A'body knows. Well, leastways, *I* know.'

'Is that a threat, Bunty?'

'Naw, Mr Petrie, it's a statement of puir honest Scottish fact. I don't want to be mean, but do you think the hoor wants you for yourself? You're no' exactly what the girls would call an ar-wee-see.'

'Now you're being offensive. And I don't even want to know what RWC stands for. Shall we get down to work?'

'Right Wee Cracker. Nae offence.'

As in so many other areas, bloody Bunty was turning out to be nothing like a fool.

At precisely the moment that this conversation was taking place, the Master was licking the last of the champagne strawberry jam off Ella's impressively concave stomach. His brow was furrowed with concentration as he moved towards her pubic hair.

'Mmm. Fortnum's? Waitrose? I'm losing my touch. But I never weary of the taste. How are you getting on with our Mr Petrie?'

Ella groaned lightly. 'You know I'm your helpless plaything.

I'll do anything you want. But I wish you hadn't given me bloody David Petrie as your project. He is sooo, so boring.'

The Master continued to graze. Ella noticed that the liver spots on his back were becoming more prominent. In between light kisses and snuffles, he murmured, 'Boring in bed?'

'Yes, but that's the least of it. Bed's soon over. No, it's much worse than that. I mean just boring-boring. The man hasn't got a single interesting idea in his head. He's completely self-obsessed. He just goes on and on about his rivals and his childhood and his position in the party. He never says anything about real politics. He doesn't seem to know what that even means. I have no idea, even now, what drives him.'

'Nothing wrong with being self-obsessed. Not a lot wrong with an absence of clear views. Remember, his purpose is for us to mould him and use him. The last thing I want is for him to strike out on his own, or begin to think that he can.'

'More jam?'

'No, I've got to watch the tummy.'

'Too bad. I still think he's boring, and that's the big problem. You've got the photos – I left them in the top drawer of your desk – so you've got David Petrie where you want him. I'm just not sure he's worth it.'

'Oh, he's worth it.'

'Easy for you to say. You don't have to . . .'

'I'm sorry. Let me make it up to you.'

'You are the most vain, most impossible man I have ever met.'

'I know. And you love me for it.'

Whitehall Life

*What's the job of a minister, really? To be in revolt against the
bloody government.*

The Master

He had just turned off Whitehall, and was a few yards
from the door of the department. Normally Davie looked
about him, but the air was chill today, and all morning he'd
felt deflated and tired. He'd turned the collar of his coat up,
his chin was pressed to his chest and he was barely aware of
anyone around him. So the whack of a thick, meaty hand on
his shoulder startled him. He looked up. The secretary of state,
his new boss, a socialist of the old school, was standing staring
at him. He'd clearly just said something, but Davie hadn't
caught it. He shrugged.

'Oh dear, Mr Petrie, we don't seem ourselves this morning.'
The man, whom David had written off long before as a soggy
mass of uncomprehending ambition, leaned in towards him.
His breath, very unusually these days, smelled of tobacco.
'We've seen through you, Mr Petrie. You, old son, are not up
to it. Your posh friends have done everything they can to pump

you up, but the air keeps leaking out, doesn't it?' The secretary of state took his hand off Davie's coat, stepped back and looked in the direction of Big Ben.

'Grand, isn't it? What a place we work in. How lucky we are. But you know, it's harder than it looks. An excellent digestive system, and an ability to sleep like a baby, then a truly wily mind . . . And even all of those aren't enough to make a good minister. You were a local hero, I'm sure. The Nationalists certainly hate you. You've been picked up by the right, by the old lot, and they've done their best. But matey, take it from one who knows. You are not quite good enough. My advice is to get out while you still can. Get back to your mountains and glens, or whatever they are, and build some more houses. Then at least when you retire, you'll feel you've done some good.'

He didn't like to admit it even to himself, but for his first few months as a minister Davie felt out of his depth. Almost literally: the building that housed the department had been built in the 1970s, and ignored ever since. Long, low-ceilinged rooms with striplights and insufficient window space meant that even the ministerial offices were gloomy and crepuscular. It was like living underwater in a dirty lagoon. Apart from the ministers, the department was staffed by sullen young graduates who had struggled and borrowed their way to get into government service, hoping for the Treasury. They resented being shoved here, where they already knew they had failed in life. In the Treasury they would have worn ties, or smart skirts and blouses; here they wore ear studs and corduroy trousers.

Inside the building, he was never alone. The government

had taken on new powers over urban development, as over many other things. Arguments about the demolition of 1960s car parks, or the rerouting of traffic through housing estates, or the siting of new out-of-town supermarkets – which ought, he couldn't help thinking, to have been dealt with by the local authorities – ended up on Davie's desk. His office had three doors: one, at least, was always open, and he was sometimes approached from different directions at the same time. He grew to loathe the sight of his private secretary – a Wykehamist with tousled fair hair, en route to the Treasury – arriving, smirking, with yet another fat folder.

Nor did he have any control over his own diary. He was just allocated meetings: meetings with backbenchers, meetings with groups of mayors, meetings with the trade press and the national press, and meetings with junior Treasury ministers (who seemed to be able to take all the real decisions that he'd hoped to take himself). Another man might have been flattered; Davie was shrewd enough to see that he was simply being given the meetings the other ministers in the department recoiled from. But there was no one to complain to; the secretary of state had not wanted him there in the first place.

Away from the stifling department, there were the Commons committee meetings, the regular question-and-answer sessions in the chamber, and the mandatory lunches, provincial tours and party events. Davie had always thought of himself as a physically strong man, but after a few months of being a junior minister, he felt as if he were on the ropes. He sagged in chairs, and lolled in the backs of cars. He found himself puffing in the street. He hardly had time to see Ella after his official car dropped him off at his flat. Utter exhaustion overtook him; sitting with yet another red box, half-watching the late-night news, sometimes he remembered his regular telephone call to Mary and the boys. Sometimes he forgot. And occasionally he just couldn't be bothered.

During all those first few weeks and months, there was no word from the Master, or Murdoch White, or Sir Leslie Khan. It seemed that he was on his own. How was he doing? He knew he hadn't screwed up badly yet; and his private secretary said he took decisions faster than his predecessor, which was apparently a good thing. He learned to throw himself into his paperwork, reading so fast he barely took anything in, while looking out for the wavy line in pencil that indicated where a decision might have to be taken. It was as if he had been gently ushered onto a running machine that was going just a little faster than he could manage. Nothing he said or did seemed to be noticed anywhere else.

If he had ever been in any kind of race with Caroline Phillips, he knew he was now falling far behind. She'd become a popular sofa guest on television discussion programmes, and recently she seemed to be making waves with some big idea on corporate responsibility that Davie couldn't bring himself to try to understand. Being an adequate junior minister was, he realised, just another way of failing.

Then, to rescue him, came a great crisis. The government was wallowing, as the economy faltered and the prime minister failed to come up with a plan. Ahead of the budget the polling was terrible, and the troops were mutinous. In the end it was the chancellor of the exchequer who came up with the big idea – a massive expansion of house-building, including entire new towns, to put an end to the growing agony of the housing crisis. The chancellor spoke well. He sounded visionary. The commentators compared him to Attlee and Harold Macmillan. Some said that he might, after all, be a plausible replacement for the PM. And then, like a sprinting rugby player, the chancellor passed the greasy ball in a blur to Davie's department; it would be their job, not his, to decide where all these new homes, roads and shopping malls would actually have to go. The hospital pass.

And so, one cold, bright morning there was a departmental meeting, with the secretary of state and all the ministers present, plus a dozen of the leading civil servants in the department, for a 'strategic review'. In politics, the Master had said, strategic reviews are never strategic: they are always tactical and panicky. Nor are they *reviews*: they deal mostly with what has never been properly viewed in the first place.

The country needed hundreds of thousands of new houses built; and everywhere there were vigorous local campaigns against 'horrid little boxes'. Grandee journalists banded together to defend Oxfordshire. Actors and actresses spoke movingly of the delights of unspoiled East Anglia. Shropshire wasn't bloody having it. Rutland was revolting. Clearly, the smack of firm government was needed. Some parts of the country were going to have to be upset, their objections ignored. Obviously, this being a Labour government, the idea was to find as many safe Conservative and Liberal Democrat seats to build over as possible. But it couldn't be too obvious. Some Labour areas were going to have to be offended too, otherwise the accusation of partisanship would be so serious that the crusade for housing would fail before it started. Even the useless young civil servants who would never make it to the Treasury understood that much.

The secretary of state was like a great slab of pudding – grey, unappetising, apparently passive. But he was as sly as he could be direct. He was tough, and he'd been fixing meetings since he was a teenager. He called on Davie, as the urban planning man, to open a meeting with some clear proposals. Davie, unforewarned, had absolutely nothing to say. He had wondered about suggesting a major new development in Barker, purely to irritate Caroline Phillips, but he couldn't quite bring himself to do it. His performance was terrible. Even his smirking private secretary looked upset.

At the end of the meeting the secretary of state said, 'Well, I think we've made a little bit of progress. Not much, however, because as we have all seen, our new colleague in urban development was rather lost for words. Mr Petrie, I am genuinely surprised and upset; we had heard so much about your extraordinary prowess. Perhaps, after all, you're merely mortal like the rest of us. At any rate, I want to convene again at the same time next week; and by then, Mr Petrie, we are all hoping for some answers from you. Good morning.'

Davie slunk back towards his office. For once, all three of its doors were closed. When he walked in, he found no less a person than Sir Leslie Khan sitting at his desk, his highly polished crocodile shoes crossed on top of a scramble of paperwork. He was fingering his beard.

'Ah, young Mr Petrie. I thought I'd pop by. Used to work

here myself, a million years ago. Came in to congratulate you. The big meeting. Everyone's talking about it. A great chance for you, Mr Petrie. Went well? Oh. No, it didn't go well, did it? I can tell by the slump of your shoulders, and your rather convincing impression of a small dog that has just been beaten. Hmm?'

'It was a fucking disaster. They're setting me up. I'm sorry, Leslie – Sir Leslie – but I didn't see it coming. I have to come up with a list of places for major new developments. Anywhere I propose there's going to be a riot of protest, and I'm going to be held responsible. I know I'm not an educated man, Sir Leslie, but I can see what's happening – they're throwing me to the wolves.'

Leslie Khan's face tightened, and he rose to his feet. 'Never, *ever*, say that. We have plans for you. But never, ever, say that, or you will never see me, or any of us, again.'

'Say what? Leslie – I mean Sir Leslie – it's the bloody truth.'

'*Never* say "I'm not an educated man." Nobody wants to hear that sort of whining. If you aren't educated, it's your own fault. And if you aren't educated, you aren't going to be able to lead this country at the highest level. You either start to educate yourself, or you pretend to be educated. But you never, *ever*, say you aren't educated. Do you promise me?'

Davie, stunned by the force of the attack, simply nodded.

'Good. Well, let's get on with it then. What are the basic requirements? A quarter of a million new homes. On cheap land. Without causing a riot by the people who live there already. And somewhere close to jobs. Somewhere people will actually want to live.'

'Aye. Broadly right. So it's completely impossible. We could stick them up in the Highlands wi' the midges and the Nats, but hardly anyone would ever move there. We could stick them in Kent, but there's not enough of Kent left. We've used Kent up. And so on and so forth. The land in most of southern England is so expensive we simply couldn't buy enough of it. As I said, I'm being shafted.'

'So you have a wonderful opportunity to confound your critics. Think laterally, Mr Petrie. Close your eyes, and think sideways. Think about the weather.'

'What?'

'Where is there plenty of land, whose owners would be delighted to sell cheaply, and where your new city would be in striking distance of the Midlands, and even of London?'

'Wales?'

'Don't be ridiculous. Nobody wants to live in Wales.'

'Well . . . I have no idea.'

'As I said, think about the weather. Winter after winter of lashing rain. Those chocolate-coloured floods. Those ruined farmers. Those ridiculous photo opportunities in newly-bought Wellington boots . . .'

'You mean Somerset? The levels?'

'I do.'

'But with respect, Sir Leslie, that's completely mad. It's a floodplain. It's the one place we just can't build on. We've said it ourselves – this department has said – no more building on floodplains. It's too dangerous, and no one's ever done it on this scale, and as for the insurance . . .'

To Davie's disappointment, Khan appeared to have no

quickfire response. He just shrugged his shoulders, twiddled his beard and changed the subject. 'You need a bit of a break. There is a big urban-renewal conference about to start. Friends of mine . . . I've got your ticket already, and the department will pick up the bill.'

Davie shook his head. 'I've got no time for jaunts . . .'

'I'm disappointed. I've just said you have to start to educate yourself, Mr Petrie. Well, here's an opportunity. And a little bird tells me that young Miss Ella James is available, should you need an adviser out there.'

That was more like it. Davie looked up and asked, 'Out where?'

'Venice.'

The Education of David Petrie

The good politician is international. I've had all my best ideas in airports.

The Master

Davie met Ella at the British Airways lounge in Terminal Five. He was carrying a bulging plastic bag full of books. From the outside, Ella looked much as normal – poised, sipping a bloody Mary, a little bored. But everyone has a limit, and Ella had reached hers. Petrie, never the most observant of men, noticed nothing. He gestured proudly at his bag of books, and began to pull them out one by one: John Julius Norwich, Jan Morris, Francesco da Mosto, Thomas Mann . . .

'Oh, bloody great,' said Ella. 'Not only a sodding conference on town planning, but you're going to have your nose in a sodding book the whole time.'

'I've never been to Venice,' replied Davie modestly, 'so I thought I'd better learn a little about it first. Someone told me to educate myself. It was either these, or more office bumf.'

Unnervingly, Ella made no attempt to keep her voice down.

'Well, I've been to Venice loads, and it smells of shit, and the food is shit, and all the hotels have bedrooms the size of iPads.'

'So I guess you're here purely for the pleasure of my famously exciting company?'

'Oh, for God's sake, Your Royal Highness the Autodidact. Let's drop the pretence, shall we? I'm here because the Master told me to be here – to come along and hold your hand and wipe your bottom.'

'Really? *He* told you to come?'

'I said let's drop it, OK? You know and I know, and I know that you know, that I work for the Master, and for nobody else. For some reason I don't understand, he still seems to think you might have what it takes for greatness. You are among the chosen, his children, one of the last ones standing. But the more I see of you, David Petrie, the more I disagree. You're a drone. A speck. You're at the back of the chorus. That's what I've told him. See? I love it when you flinch. Oh, you think sad eyes will work? Labrador eyes. Little hurt face. Aaah . . . Well, think again, lover. I've only ever tolerated you because the Master wants your loyalty. Step out of line, and there are pictures of us together that will blow your world apart. Did *I* do that? Did *you* do that? They're really quite disgusting. I can hardly believe them myself. Mary and the little kiddies will never speak to you again.'

Davie felt as if she'd just reached into his chest and squeezed. He felt very cold. Then he felt very hot. He wanted to shout. He wanted to cry. But he was a grown-up, and he spoke evenly. 'So all this time it was just a game to you? You've never felt . . .?'

'Nothing. I've never felt anything. Not for you. Not for anyone else, come to that, except for the Master. For God's sake, don't look at me like that. We can carry on fucking, if you like. Although you might consider flossing, and a mouth-wash . . .'

Davie looked around the lounge, which was beginning to empty. Something was going on inside him: a rumble. He wasn't going to collapse after all. 'We're going to miss the flight. You can borrow a book if you like.'

Less than two hours later, the Serene Republic, like a child's drawing of a fat fish, was visible, glittering on the lagoon, as the jet banked for landing. Davie and Ella had sat in silence throughout the flight, he reading his books, she leafing through magazines. After picking up their cases, he began to lead the way towards a sign reading 'Water Bus'.

'No,' said Ella. 'If we're going to do this, we're going to do it properly. We need a water taxi, our own boat. They've given us a hotel on the Grand Canal, at least, so we can make it go straight in and turn left. It's the only way to arrive.'

Murdoch White had once told Davie that the secret of professional success was to be 'multi-track' – to be able to think of several different things, passionately and intensively, at the same time. During the flight, Davie had been both studying the history of Venice and nursing a boiling sense of rage and injustice directed towards Ella. Now, more than ever, she seemed a stranger. He wasn't going to miss this trip for the world, but she was dead to him. Davie was a handsome man, with a strong jaw and a muscular, well-made face. In repose it had a certain jutting brutality. But from his earliest years he had had actorly qualities too; now he smiled at Ella, his eyes almost disappearing in a crinkle of lines.

'Let's not fight. Let's not spoil this. I don't know what you're really up to, but since were on the same side, I'm going to ignore your little lecture at Heathrow. Bad time of the month, perhaps.'

'Whatever you want. I'm not going to say it again; nobody should need to be warned twice. But, just so we're clear, it isn't a bad time of the month.'

'Well if it isn't now, it soon will be. Ella, sweet-pea, be my guide.'

What did he mean by that? Ella turned on her heel and led the way into the bright sunlight. Five minutes' walk ahead of them, the water rocked and glittered. After negotiating briefly in Italian with the pilot of one of the water taxis, Ella demanded €120 from Davie.

Standing in the open at the back of the boat, bouncing when it hit the bow waves of others returning to the airport, they passed tiny, derelict islands before, through the haze, the cupolas and spires of Venice itself appeared. Soft blues and tiny golden streaks against a violet sky. The Serene Republic herself. Davie felt all his hurt start to blow away in the salty breeze. He stiffened a little as the boat appeared to be heading straight for a line of buildings. Would they crash?

Ella laughed and put a hand on his arm. 'It's all right. Just wait.'

And indeed, the pilot headed straight into the concealed opening of a tiny canal, whose orange-painted and leprous buildings were festooned with drying underwear. Arched stone bridges and narrow alleys apparently leading nowhere were crammed with tourists. Twice, their boat had to slow down and pull to one side to make way for barges carrying concrete mixers and plastic-wrapped furniture, as well as sweaty, beefy workmen. Just like the lads at home, Davie thought.

'Now. Close your eyes,' said Ella, as if she had entirely forgotten their conversation in the airport. She placed her smooth, nervy fingers over his face.

'And . . . open!'

Davie was initially blinded by the scorching light, and dis-orientated by the crowded movement of boats and blue shadows. And then he fell in love. He fell out of love with Ella and in love with Venice. Giant, peach-coloured or pink palaces were all around him. On either side of the canal there were balconies, elaborately hooped windows, marble columns and bucking gondolas. Each building seemed more fantastical and exuberant than the last. A stained white fairytale bridge rose up before them. They passed underneath it, and turned another corner; to Davie the Grand Canal seemed infinitely more impressive than the Grand Canyon could possibly be. A nimble wooden bridge came into view, but their water taxi turned right before it, and came to a halt alongside an elegant little palace studded with medieval statues.

'Damn,' said Ella. 'The best was yet to come. Never mind. This is us – the Palazzo Stern.'

Inside, there were more statues, and ancient-looking stone columns and old mosaics. Davie couldn't make out whether it was a real palace, or some kind of large private house owned by a mad collector. They were shown to a modestly sized room whose windows looked directly onto the canal. Still reeling from all he'd seen, Davie pulled out a wodge of glossy paper he'd been given at the department the night before. It contained a couple of passes, and pages of details about the conference. His heart sank a little. 'I suppose we'd better go and register. We're not here to have fun – which is lucky, considering.'

'Don't be sulky. We need to get ourselves to the other end of Castello, where the pavilion is. I guess it will be the "Biennale" stop.'

'Bloody hell, you know your stuff. Who *are* you, Ella? You always dodge the question whenever I ask. Trustafarian?'

'Something like that. We'll take a vaporetto. It's just like catching the bus. Line 2, I think.'

And so they passed by the Salute, and St Mark's Square, with the Doge's Palace looking like a strawberry confection sculpted out of cream and drunken dreams, and the two giant columns. On one, Davie recognised the Lion of Venice. On the other, an armoured thug appeared to have just defeated an enormous croissant.

'A dragon,' laughed Ella. 'St George.'

The conference was heralded by a huge plastic banner on a low-slung building among some trees further down the island. 'Urbanity 22', it read. There were metal barriers and clusters of police carrying machine guns standing around. In a gusty wind, men dressed in smart dark suits struggled to hold umbrellas over the heads of crouching, chic women. Tourists were pointing at famous faces. There were ministers and other representatives from many countries taking part, including what Ella called 'my Americans'. After they'd registered, she disappeared off to meet them. Davie was due to attend a round-table seminar on the City of London, and to speak briefly at dinner – but neither was until the following day. On the spur of the moment, he decided to chuck the conference, leave Ella behind, and head off on his own.

'I'm not bloody missing this,' he thought to himself. If Ella was worried, so much the better.

For the next four or five hours, Davie wandered through the maze of tiny alleys and canalside dead-ends, marvelling at the liquid beauty of the place even as he struggled to make sense of his map, and signs which appeared to point to the same destination in opposite directions. Periodically he stopped to rest his aching feet, order a coffee and read a bit more about the city. He might have been a late starter, but he was a fast and attentive reader, and bit by bit his views of Venice began to change. Ella would forever see the city through the memories of love affairs and extravagant purchases; Davie saw an entirely different place. Behind its façades and glittering stonework, this was a city of corrupt merchants, slave traders and bankers. Venice had been famous for her torturers and dungeons, her greed and her assassins, before she was famous for the nobility of her architecture. The very foundations of the place, driven into the mud of the lagoon, were smeared with blood. After the ages of cruelty and the ghetto, Venice had been a city of adultery and disease. Her real inhabitants were the giant rats scuttling along deserted alleys.

Even as the scales dropped from his eyes, the builder in

Davie was fascinated by the technical solutions to the problems of building a city on over a hundred islands in a lagoon – the deep wooden piles, with the stonework and brickwork placed on top; the soundly paved embankments around which the water moved so easily. An education. So *that* was why he was here. Clever Khan. So much beauty, and such devotion to a God of love: the churches, the paintings – and all of it based on the rape of rival cities, and murderous local politics. Men with daggers driven through their eyes. Bodies dumped in canals. Cheating merchants, terrifying prisons, torture, corrupt bankers. They had been efficient bastards here, all right. And then he would set off again, in another direction, vaguely aiming at something else one of the guidebooks had assured him was not to be missed, but missing it anyway, for how could you hit anything first time off in this bewildering maze?

His mind returned to Ella's venomous tirade at Heathrow. So she despised him. So she was only obeying orders. The Master, it seemed, hadn't quite given up on him after all; but now, thanks to that betraying little bitch, there were incriminating pictures. To keep him in his place. Or, as Bunty would have put it, 'to have him by the short and hairies'.

In the dark, cramped little alleys, it seemed to Davie that the world was pressing in on him from all directions. Ella's curved mouth, which he had once found erotic, now seemed merely part of another Venetian mask, hanging with empty eyes and painted cheeks. He had absolutely no idea who she was. She must think him a pathetic fool. But Leslie Khan was quite right. If he wanted to be a player on the stage – not this stage, not Venice, but a big stage nevertheless – then it was time to act. Davie began to turn down the corners of pages in his guidebooks, and make little notes to himself. Perhaps a kind of madness was taking him over. Detached, almost amused, he watched the dark Venetian shadows as they swarmed and flickered.

Because of the power of the Bad Sex Awards, what happened between Davie and Ella that night must remain private. The following morning, to Ella's surprise and annoyance, Davie failed to turn up at the conference. He arrived after lunch for the round-table, at which he performed in a lacklustre fashion, and then disappeared again.

'You know I'm not your biggest fan,' Ella told him at the dinner that evening, 'but even I'm surprised that you're so lazy. Just bunking off – that's not like you.'

'I wasn't bunking off. I've been working.'

He didn't say any more about his perambulations, but concentrated on his meal – plates of tiny, deep-fried crabs and other gritty seafood. 'Yuck,' said Ella. 'I told you the food here was foul.' Davie, however, enjoyed it all – the sardines smothered in onion, and cuttlefish cooked in its own ink, rich and black and oily. Peasant food – the Venetian versions of stovies, cockles and black pudding, however handsomely they dressed it up.

After the dinner he spoke perfectly well, but Ella thought his mind was elsewhere. He talked to her about paintings. Had she seen the Carpaccios in the Dalmatian church? He'd never realised before that Renaissance painters could be witty, even downright funny – those monks running away from the lion like a flock of scattering birds . . . Ella closed her ears, but she was impressed despite herself. Perhaps the man was learning after all.

On the third day, their last in Venice, Davie surprised her again.

'I want to take a boat trip. Torcello. And then Burano, perhaps?'

'I don't get it, Petrie. Torcello's got a famous old basilica and a couple of expensive restaurants but nothing else. And so far as I remember, Burano's just a luridly painted fishing village.'

'Indulge me, Ella, this one last time. I think I can learn something over there. Prove something to myself.'

And so, missing the final plenary session of the conference, the two of them walked through the snaking alleyways of Castello to the Fondamente Nova opposite the Isle of the Dead, with its castle-like walls and black fingers of cypress. From there, they took the Number 1 2 boat. Davie was carrying a rucksack Ella hadn't noticed before. As they were clambering off the boat, she tried to lift it.

'Christ, that's heavy. What have you got in there?'

'Oh, books and stuff.'

'You are completely mad. What books?'

'*Death in Venice.*'

'Well, that's short at least.'

On Torcello, they trudged in the heat to the basilica, paid their five euros, and stood, awestruck, before the huge mosaic of the Last Judgement. Davie found himself talking about his own Catholic upbringing, and how scared he'd been of the fires of hell. Pointing out the skulls with the worms writhing through them, and the damned in the flames – Muslims, scarlet women, dirty old men – he said, 'It still makes me shiver.'

Ella surprised him by putting her hand in his, and squeezing it. He looked at her; she smiled very slightly.

'You're a funny one,' she said.

'You bet I am.' He wanted no intimacy.

They crossed back the short distance to the fishing island of Burano. Walking past the canals lined with houses painted lime green, bright orange, shocking pink and cherry red, they finally came to a scrubby beach on which a few small, decrepit fishing boats were tethered. The lagoon was a blur of grey light, the sky an oppressive glare.

'You see, I've got an idea from all of this,' said Davie, showing her one of his books. 'Do me a favour, and go and take some pictures of the houses. The brightest you can find. Just half a dozen. I know you're good at pictures.'

After she had gone, he wandered among the boats, kicking them until he found a grubby, unloved-looking little craft which he could move unaided.

It was noon, very hot, and there was nobody around. Davie found a discarded white plastic chair and set it up on the shingle, where it sank slightly among the scrunching stones. He was sitting there when Ella returned, dangling her camera. He got up, and gestured at the chair.

'I've got a wee surprise for you, Ella. Just take the weight off your legs, and look ahead of you. See that line of trees and buildings way in the distance? That's the Lido. That's where the wicked Lord Byron galloped his horses, and where Thomas Mann wrote *Death in Venice*. Half an hour on the oars and we could be there. Amazing, eh?'

Those bloody books, Ella thought to herself. It was as if he'd gorged on them too quickly, and was vomiting them out again. Real politicians didn't read books. The Master struggled to get through a Dick Francis.

As he was talking, Davie was quietly unzipping his rucksack. He pulled out a roll of duct tape he'd found in a small general store not far from St Mark's Square. With a throwaway knife, he cut a few inches off it. He still had a workman's strength. Then, moving at lightning speed, he grabbed Ella under the chin, hauled her backwards and taped her mouth shut. That felt good. Ella, taken completely by surprise, didn't have time to say a word. Tumbling backwards out of the chair, she fell heavily on the beach. Davie was on top of her almost immediately, his knee sharp and heavy in the small of her back. Calmly, deliberately, he hit her heavily across the side of the head, then taped her hands and feet together.

'Sorry, Ella. Bit of a surprise? It shouldn't be.'

Soon, she was grunting and twisting furiously. There was blood on the stones. Unhurriedly, Davie reached back into his bag and pulled out a length of plastic rope, which he used to bind her arms and legs more tightly. He looked around. Not a soul. Good. Those pitiless saints of Venice must be looking down on him. Heaving Ella onto his shoulder, he stumbled towards the small boat and threw her into it. Then he went back, still not rushing, for his rucksack, threw that in as well, and pushed the boat down to the lagoon. The warm, salty green seawater reached up beyond his knees before the boat was afloat, but Davie barely paused. A minute later, he was rowing gently away from the island. Nobody shouted. Nobody seemed to have seen him. Fortune favours the bold. Ella lay looking at him in complete astonishment, a thin trickle of blood running from her ear.

After a few minutes' rowing, a gentle eddy carried them further out. In the middle distance, Davie saw their vaporetto chugging gently back towards Venice.

Davie pulled in the oars and leaned towards Ella. 'Sodomy. That's what it was.'

Ella's eyes widened.

'No, don't get me wrong. But you really should read these books. You learn all sorts. You see, Ella, in the Venetian navy there was a real problem with sodomy. Do you know what they did with the buggers? I can see from your eyes that you don't. Well, what they did was, they got a great big block of Istrian stone – that's the white stone you see all around you in Venice – and they tied up the offender, and they put a bag over his head, and they tied him to the block of stone, and – yes, you've guessed it – they dropped him into the lagoon.

'You were very rude about the seafood here. You said it was gritty, and tiny, and not worth eating. That was unfair. It's only tiny because it doesn't have much to eat itself. It's cold and empty down there. So we're going to do our bit, aren't we? Now then, I'm afraid I lied to you, Ella, just like you lied to me. It isn't a lot of books in my wee bag. It's just a big lump of stone. Istrian stone. I picked it up in one of the builders' yards. And here's the rope. Lucky I'm good at knots, eh? But do we have a bag? Oh yes, of course we do. I've been humping it around all day.'

The rucksack was jammed over Ella's head – Davie felt that it was hardly his hands doing the jamming – and then he looped the rope tightly around the neat block of stone, before tying the other end around Ella's neck.

'Death in Venice, Ella. Books are wonderful things . . .' And with his hard-skinned builder's hands, he gently eased her over the side.

Ella kicked and writhed wildly, and for a few horrible moments Davie thought she'd pulled herself free – or worse, that they were in a part of the lagoon that was only a few feet deep. But it was all right. It was fine. One leather-shod foot pumped frantically, and then she vanished out of sight into the thick green depths. He circled the boat around the stream of bubbles until they disappeared. After a while, he rowed gently back to shore. As he dragged the boat up the shingle he noticed with a start that there was an old woman watching him. But she merely shook her head at him as he walked past her. If anybody on the late vaporetto back to the Fondamente Nova noticed his sodden trousers and ruined shoes, they were too polite to say so.

From his hotel room, Davie emailed Leslie Khan.

Thank you for the education. It's done me a power of good. Ready for that meeting now.

P.S. Ella's done a runner. She was with some Americans at the conference. What should I do?

For an hour or so he just sat in his room. Looking out of the window, he was relieved to find that he was able to get as much pleasure from the glorious buildings, now vanishing into the twilight, as he had before the murder. Perhaps people in books made too much of these things.

Just as he was getting really worried, he received a message back – not from Khan, but from the Master himself.

Glad Venice went well. Don't worry about Ella, she always bobs back up. Come back soon!

A Moving Speech

There is nothing as lethal as vision.

The Master

Back at the department, the secretary of state had extended his invitation to a number of outsiders. The second meeting included the chancellor's special adviser and two researchers from Number 10. For no reason that Davie could see, Sir Leslie Khan had managed to get himself there as well.

So many smiling, unfriendly faces. With the possible exception of Sir Leslie, Davie knew that not one person in that room wanted him to succeed. But as he got to his feet, he felt strong.

'Secretary of State. Fellow ministers. Others. Let me start by saying, quite frankly, that I screwed up a week ago. I wasn't thinking genuinely creatively, but thanks in part to Sir Leslie, I have since been able to revise my thoughts. And, ladies and gentlemen, I've got a new proposal to put before you that I hope you'll find interesting. Such is the scale of our housing crisis that we need not just a few modestly sized new towns, but a whole new city. You all have the figures. Where could such a city be built? Particularly as we need cheap land, and we need the locals to welcome what we're planning, not to fight us.

'Over the past years, we've all become accustomed to a more extreme weather system – hotter summers and wilder, wetter winters. No part of the country has been more affected by this than the Somerset levels. They're flooding regularly, year after year. The farmers there are desperate, and house prices are at rock bottom. Villages are emptying as people try to get away. My proposal is that we should build a new city right there.

'It was only a few days ago, when I was in Venice, that I realised what might be done. Like the lagoon there, much of the Somerset levels are below sea level. With excavation and careful planning, there's no reason why we can't create a new network of canals. These would allow the surrounding land to dry up, and would provide a perfect drainage system during the winters. They would give us, in effect, new reclaimed islands. Less land, but more useful land. If the Venetians, seven hundred years ago, could build the foundations for large stone churches and palaces, then we, with our industrial technologies, can certainly do the same here for housing, schools and hospitals. Given the low cost of the land, we can even do it as cheaply as building on less waterlogged ground.

'So I propose a new city, a Venice of the West Country. Our critics say we in the Labour Party have no vision, no big picture of the more sustainable, better-built Britain of the future. They will never be able to say that again. I've taken the liberty of speaking to architects and engineers – Lord Rogers of

Riverside is enthusiastic – and they assure me that this thing can be done. Proposals for feasibility studies, sketches and costings will follow.

'But let me say this. I have a bigger ambition for this new city than that. Why should we not make it beautiful? Why have we put up with so many dreary, utilitarian buildings in our small country for so long? I want to see bright colours, and a certain joy, a wildness even, in the buildings we set up here. Centuries ago, the benighted peasants of the West Country rose up against the British crown, so desperate were their conditions. At the Battle of Sedgemoor they were mown down. Today, many of our fellow citizens are just as desperate as their forefathers. In the new, floating city of Sedgemoor they will have their vindication and their triumph.'

There was a shocked pause. Then the secretary of state began to bang the table – not in irritation, but as applause. Ragged clapping broke out around the room. Sir Leslie Khan appeared to be dabbing his eyes.

The Joy of Routine

In politics, every strength, flexed just a little too much, becomes a weakness.

The Master

Alwyn Grimaldi was a man who believed in routine; and routine had always done well by him. Up early, paperwork dispatched at speed, the long list of necessary phone calls ticked off. As a small boy he had been bullied into the routine of writing thank-you letters after Christmas and birthdays. It had stuck. Polite notes and an ability to remember the names of dull people, plus a pleasant smile, had helped him rise silently, first as a journalist, then a Labour Party researcher, then an adviser, then an MP, then a minister, and finally prime minister.

Routine meant that Alwyn Grimaldi was rarely surprised, and never under-briefed about what to say. He had been expensively educated. For the first two dozen years of his life he had been tutored at home, at school and at university in the long, self-confidently nasal vowels of the English ruling class. Then, as he contemplated public life, he had had almost equally expensive lessons in losing them again. He was taught the glottal stop, and a certain laziness of the tongue which helped him fit in beautifully. He had read the right books at the right time, forgotten them again just as everybody else did, and ditched the 'wrong' opinions with faultless precision.

As early as his late twenties, he looked like a minister, and he sounded like a minister. In opposition and in government, everybody knew he would be promoted, and everybody was right. He accumulated an essential little store of self-deprecating stories, and even his least sincere smile could melt away resistance. He tied his ties in a perfect Windsor knot, and never failed to floss his teeth or to clip his nails.

Thus, it was a matter of general bafflement, not least to Alwyn Grimaldi himself, that he was failing so badly as a prime minister. This was due to something not just beyond his control, but beyond his imagination – to the fact that he had nothing interesting or novel to say about anything, and never had had. The country was bust and people were angry. The British media talked constantly of a political crisis, or a 'fundamental malaise'. What they really meant was that the people were in a right strop. Alwyn Grimaldi's talents for order and politeness, his clothes sense, even his self-deprecation, were failing to calm them down.

What was to be done? In the first place, he stuck by unflappable, reassuring routine. Routine knew what to do. Routine dictated that Alwyn Grimaldi invited a small number of prominent backbenchers and junior ministers for a drink in the White Drawing Room at 10 Downing Street at 6.30 p.m. on the first Wednesday of the month. The main point of this was to make the invitees feel better, and with any luck, warmer towards him. The secondary point was to discover whether any of them had something useful to say to him. His housekeeper chose the guests and, where possible, tried to introduce a theme.

His housekeeper did this because Alwyn Grimaldi had no wife or partner to do it. Other than routine, Alwyn's great political secret had been an almost entire absence of sexual desire. From an early age he had found the concept of bodily intimacy funny, and when not funny, disgusting. For grown men and women to think about one another's body parts, never mind shoes, stockings, lingerie and innumerable other pathetic perversions, made them, in his view, ridiculous marionettes. Having never felt the slightest stirrings of lust, Alwyn Grimaldi calculated that he had between 20 and 50 per cent more time to get on with politics than did his rivals. His secret nation was Celibacy, that calm, temperate country, without gales, without foolishness and mess, where scandal was never whispered. But this did mean that, perhaps, there was something slightly bloodless about Alwyn Grimaldi. And, of course, that he had to rely on his housekeeper, paid for by the taxpayer, to assemble his invitation lists.

We may ask: was this entirely wise? Alwyn Grimaldi's housekeeper was called Eileen Wilkinson. She had looked after the Master and his family during their years in Downing Street and at Chequers, retiring when the Conservatives came back to power. As soon as the Grimaldi government tottered into office, Mrs Wilkinson had presented herself again at Number 10 and offered her services to the new prime minister. Alwyn liked to boast: 'Mrs Wilkinson moved smoothly from the Master to me. She always says that things were much harder for her back then; I don't think she got on with the Master's wife very well. I rely on her absolutely.' Alwyn Grimaldi's confidence in Mrs Wilkinson was based on two things – her utterly banal and expressionless exterior, and her occasional bitchy remarks about life with the Master, to whom, he assumed, nobody could remain loyal. But we must ask again: was this entirely wise?

On this particular MPs' evening, the theme was Women. The Grimaldi government had done moderately well on the Women Question: about a third of its cabinet ministers, and nearly a third of its ministers generally, were female, as were nearly half of the backbench MPs. But very few of 'Grimaldi's girls' ('Alwyn's angels' hadn't flown) were much admired by the public. Like the man himself, they were polite, well turned out, said the right thing, and were smoothly forgettable. His press officer complained when broadcasters confused the names of the female ministers; but he did so only dutifully, for form's sake.

This evening, Mrs Wilkinson had assembled more than two dozen Labour women of different ages, backgrounds and talents. Even as she completed her list in ballpoint pen, however, she had found it hard to visualise those she was inviting. There was, however, one particular woman . . .

Grimaldi had been strongly advised to promote Caroline Phillips by his permanent secretary, who had been a very junior civil servant in the Treasury during the Master's years. He'd heard rumours that Mrs Phillips was highly ambitious.

But if there was one person on the planet unlikely to be susceptible to her famous charm, it would be the prime minister. Everyone in the room understood this, so everyone was watching as she arrived. Would this be 'a moment'?

A gentle but unmistakable glow of bronze-coloured light seemed to enter the drawing room a yard before Caro did. Her glance laughed its way among the pillars, armchairs and gathered MPs like a rebel, liberated beam of sunlight. Rival ministers, sour-faced backbenchers and even Alwyn Grimaldi's housekeeper found delighted smiles playing on their faces without knowing quite why. Napes tingled. Fingers rubbed excitedly on fingers. The room, which had been slightly chilly, warmed up nicely.

Alwyn Grimaldi, feeling the warmth running down his back, turned around. In front of him he saw an unremarkable-looking woman in a smart cream suit, whose eyes seemed to him to possess the candid gaze of a wild animal – a lioness, perhaps. As she looked at him he seemed to see not her, but himself through her eyes: a neat, light, stooping man with a smile of water. He felt very slightly sick, or excited. He couldn't tell which. Routine was being disturbed. He extended his damp palm. She smiled.

'Prime Minister, what a pleasure. How kind. I've never been upstairs.'

'Mrs Phillips, the pleasure is all mine. We should have had you round long ago. There are so many things I'd like to talk to you about.'

On their way out, as the drinks party ended an hour and a half later, Doreen Clarkson, the Northern Ireland secretary, said to Phoebe Marks, chair of the public accounts committee, 'I thought it was bloody rude. The two of them just stood there in the corner of the room yacketing away, as if none of the rest of us were there at all.'

'If it were another man,' said Phoebe, 'I'd have said he was a little smitten.'

'Well it's not that, at least,' replied Doreen. 'Though he did flush, I noticed. It's almost as if there's some blood in his veins after all. Still, rude.'

'Terribly.'

Alwyn Grimaldi and Caroline Phillips had not in fact been flirting. After a lifetime of subtle evasions, Alwyn was incapable, while Caro, somewhat awestruck to be chatting to a prime minister – even this prime minister – was unaware of any effect she might have had on him. But they had been talking deeply, even intimately, about politics.

Alwyn had started his working life as a political journalist, before hopping briskly over the fence. 'It was all those years of watching so many obvious mistakes, and sordid scandals. There was never any possibility of me joining another party; my late father was a professor of politics, and brought us up to read the *Guardian*. When I was fifteen I was taken to a party to meet Polly Toynbee, as a treat. She was wonderful, though I'm afraid she regards me as a bit of a disappointment these days.'

'Oh, I'm sure she doesn't, Prime Minister. For me, I'm afraid, it was really the New Testament. Do unto others, easier for a camel, and so forth. There has never been a more revolutionary call to arms, nor one so widely ignored. My partner,

Angela, actually went into the Church, but I'm too selfish for that. Or I wanted – I don't know, recognition or something.'

'We all have mixed motives. That's why there are no good novels about the political trade. They bang on and on about the treachery and the double dealing, the vanity and the greed, but they never explain the other side – the real wish to do good, the decision to take less money and more abuse in return for a chance of helping people in the real world.' Alwyn feared that he was beginning to whine. 'Though of course, we're very privileged to be here.'

Caro rescued him. 'Why are we on this planet? We're only here for a very short time, so how should we conduct ourselves? By being kind, and helping others. I've always felt there were only two jobs that made any kind of moral sense. To be a politician, in order to lead people, however uneasily and awkwardly, to better ways of living; or to be a priest.'

The last thing Alwyn had expected was a serious conversation here in Downing Street. He felt excited. 'That's rather good, Caroline. Would you mind if I . . .'

'No, Prime Minister, be my guest. Although, to be strictly honest, I was quoting my partner, who took the other path.'

Alwyn had the retentive memory of a professional politician. 'Angela, yes of course. And now she has a living – how very Church of England to call it a living, rather than a calling – up in Barker? Well, do you know, I'd love to meet her. I have a feeling, Caroline, that you and I can work rather closely together. I have some really quite worrying things on my mind, and . . . Why don't the two of you come and join me one weekend at Chequers, so we can all get to know one another better?'

'Prime Minister. How very kind. But Angela is unbearable on Saturdays. She takes her sermons very seriously. Writes them all out in longhand herself.'

'You could come on your own.'

'Or we could join you for Sunday lunch, after the service. The drive down from Barker can't be more than an hour.'

Alwyn found himself feeling slightly disappointed.

In the Country

The only time I really felt like a member of the ruling class was during those weekends at Chequers.

The Master

Prime minister after prime minister had found the remodelled Tudor country house at the foot of the Chiltern Hills in Buckinghamshire a place of indispensable solace and retreat. Margaret Thatcher, hardly a sentimentalist, had fallen in love with Chequers. John Major found it essential; his wife loved its rose gardens, lawns and ancient rooms so much that she wrote a book about them. Later, Tony Blair leafed through its extensive library, had quiet conversations with Princess Diana while walking in its grounds, organised football matches on the back lawn – Prince William had had to play – and resolved to go to war against Saddam Hussein in the grandeur of its Long Gallery. Some people confused Blair with the Master; certainly, the Master had enjoyed Chequers every bit as much.

Alwyn Grimaldi, who was more conscious of the Italian origins of his family than he ever let on in public, rejoiced that the original twelfth-century house had been owned by one Elias de Scaccario – which made 'Grimaldi' seem almost homely. He had no family to play football with. Romping was alien to his nature. But he much enjoyed the scents of the rose garden, which was visible from his upstairs study. In the almost ridiculously spacious Great Parlour, with its fine wainscoting and oil paintings, he had gathered his cabinet on several occasions as they tried to discover that elusive but essential quality they were missing – a purpose. They had tried in vain, but Alwyn had found the trying invigorating. Now he hoped that this mysteriously charismatic woman, in partnership with a mysterious vicar, would help him out.

All too often, Alwyn found the underlying theme of Chequers to be discouraging. He was a thoughtful man, and the large collection of Oliver Cromwell memorabilia, including the lord protector's death mask, and the immaculately bound, untouched yards of memoirs by previous premiers, suggested to him the only ways in which his own career was destined to conclude, and perhaps sooner rather than later: either in death or in resignation and unread, remaindered self-justification. Death scared him very much. It had been glibly said that politics was show business for ugly people. Really, Alwyn thought, it was tragedy for the modern man – a giant, pitiless stage on which no one normal survived.

And there was now a new source of pressure. Here, at Chequers, Alwyn had recently been on the receiving end of no fewer than four telephone calls from the president of the United States. Their theme was no surprise to him; the subject had been raised at weekly meetings of the Joint Intelligence Committee for weeks now. Washington's Department of

Homeland Security and the CIA were pressing for the signing of a secret memorandum which would pass authorisation for surveillance of all British citizens, on their own turf, to the United States. GCHQ would become what the president called 'the properly reliable and loyal collaborator' of American intelligence. Al Qaeda, the president said, was a single, flexible enemy with a single ideology and command structure, operating around the world; to combat Islamist terrorism, it was necessary that the West become the same.

The president had been calm, persuasive and friendly. There hadn't been the merest hint of the whiff of the ghost of a suggestion of a threat. And yet Alwyn understood perfectly well that he had no choice. Britain, now that she was outside the softly stifling embrace of the EU, found herself very short of friends – the Grimaldi government could not be choosers.

Glancing around the lovely old room, birdsong in his ears and the scent of freshly cut grass in his nostrils, Alwyn asked himself what Churchill would have done. He knew the answer. Then he asked himself what the Master would have advised. Alwyn would have been considerably alarmed had he received the news from Sir Anthony Bevins about what the Master was currently up to; but the Bevins memorandum had gone from the FCO straight to the prime minister's private office, and his private secretary was another member of the staff at Number 10 who remained loyal to the Master. It was the Master himself who used to say that in politics, where one most looks for help, there lies the worst of the danger.

*

Caro and Angela had been arguing all the way down from Barker, and nearly lost their way shortly before the Chequers gates. Had it been a good idea to bring the boys? Caro, although in general a too-tolerant and appeasing figure in their lives, thought not. She hadn't mentioned Nick and Ben to the prime minister; he would have made no arrangements. And what would they do? Chequers would be like a musty old National Trust house, crammed with things that might be knocked over. Angela, however, was unmoved. The prime minister had become an almost ridiculous figure in the country, a limp and bloodless intellectual nobody wanted. He had invited Caro and her not to be kind or flattering, but because he wanted their help. That in itself was flattering enough, but if the price was to put on a few fish fingers and allow the boys to kick a football around outside, he'd find it a price well worth paying. Nick and Ben hadn't been listening from the back seat; they had their ear-buds well jammed in.

Mrs Wilkinson, who hated children, was tremendously welcoming as the visitors tramped across the gravel and into the house. She would put on some pasta with cheese sauce, she said; the boys wouldn't necessarily enjoy what she'd got ready for lunch. Sitting around an oval oak table, the adults were served beetroot soup, followed by home-made steak pie with beetroot salad.

A Sermon in Barker

In politics, there are hardly any good ideas. One comes along perhaps every decade: so be sure you notice it.

The Master

Angela had found that she loved Barker. Barker was ugly. Its town hall had been built in the 1950s, when there wasn't enough money around for beauty. A clumsy gyratory system had carved its way through medieval streets; in the High Street, now pedestrianised, there wasn't a single local shop left – all chains, just like everywhere else. But Barker was alive. Things were still made here; in its narrow avenues and red-brick crescents, people left home every morning for factories and regional headquarters; not everyone had given up hope. The town was small enough for her to be swiftly recognised. Her sermons became shorter and more urgent. She took to wearing jeans and trainers with her black shirt and dog collar. Nick and Ben made friends with sharp-eyed, assertive Asian boys, who teased her at home about the wine, yet seemed to have a natural politeness their English contemporaries did not. She ordered in Chinese and curry, Thai and chips.

Caro was with her every weekend, and now that she was in government she had the use of a limousine and driver. She'd sweep up outside the house bursting with bundles of paper and all the latest gossip. Sometimes she brought a young man from the office to work with her for a few hours. He always seemed to be the same young man, yet his name kept changing; Angela assumed there was a type. Anyway, life in Barker was both faster and more interesting than it had been in Pebbleton. Angela was so happy that she was managing to drink quite a bit less; she kept the wine – mostly – for the weekends. Above all, she found that she noticed more, and thought more deeply.

The constituency people, who would drop into the house, seemed unpretentious and friendly. Nobody in Barker made a lot of money. There was a couple on the outskirts of town who had won several million pounds in the lottery, and there was a scattering of converted farmhouses in the nearby countryside where City workers, exhausted by the week, would come for a rest. Yet so far as Angela could tell, the town was devoid of jealousy: the lottery couple were said to have blown most of their money on cars, which they then pranged; and nobody envied the draining existence of the rich commuters, who would occasionally be seen tottering, white-faced, into the town's few delicatessens or wine merchants.

If happiness means not having to crane your neck upwards at people earning more, then Barker was a happy town. The people who came to church, the people in local politics, were hard-working but relaxed, as if England still really existed. Here, to be a head teacher, a surveyor or the works manager of a light-engineering company was to have reached the top of the social tree. Caroline, as the MP, and Angela, as a vicar, were considered part of the social elite. That would never have been the case in London or any of the big cities, or even in Scotland. And it made Angela think. And when Angela thought, things changed.

Miraculously, one soft, warm Thursday evening, Caroline was back from London early. The boys were downstairs on the Xbox. Caro and Angela were curled on the sofa in Angela's study upstairs. And Angela, having thought, now spoke.

'What do people want? That's the question you lot at Westminster never really ask. Because you *think* you know what they want – more money, more . . . stuff, better medicines, longer holidays.' She gently pushed herself away from Caroline and stood up. She needed to use her arms.

'But from what I can see around here, they're not made happier by money. I know lots of happy people. And I'm beginning to see what makes them happy. Ill, well, young, old, they come and talk to me. Teachers, women working in shops, traffic wardens, engineers, you name it. And I listen. And Caro darling, what makes people happy is very simple. It's to be respected. I don't just mean status, in the sense of titles, or handles; they want a certain look to come into their neighbours' eyes when they pass them in the street. They want to be known and admired for being – I don't know – *good*, I suppose. That's the fundamental need that the Church has always understood and that politics, particularly perhaps you so-called socialists, has never got.'

This was, for Angela, quite a short speech, and initially Caro was disappointed. She drained her glass. 'It's lovely to have a philosopher in the family,' she said. 'But I've come up here with two heavy boxes full of practical and immediate decisions that have to be taken. Which measure of inflation should be used to uprate the minimum wage; whether we should bring our gangmaster regulations into line with those of the European Union. And complaints from both branches of the local Muslim community about favouritism being shown to the other. Plus, a long, whining letter from the prime minister complaining about government drift and hinting strongly that he's about to give me the Home Office. So, with the best will in the world, I'm not absolutely sure where your lecture on "respect" is taking us. It'll make a fine sermon, I see that . . .'

Angela, having upended the last of the bottle into their glasses – a good half-inch more for her than for Caroline, Caro noted – interrupted. 'Well, let's start with that letter from the PM. He's quite right. Nobody has the faintest idea what the Labour Party really stands for these days. What's it all about, sweetheart? You haven't got the revenues to build a proper, modern welfare state, and even if you did, the state's failed so often. You stand for equality, except that you're too scared of the rich and powerful to really squeeze them. Probably rightly, because in the modern world, they'd just bugger off somewhere else. You want to rein in big business, but you don't know how. So consider this.

'Think of it as the Barker Bulletin. To persuade the people who really do have power, the leaders of industry and business, to do your work for you, you have to offer them something radically different. If you could get all the biggest companies to pay a living wage and to offer serious, well-funded trainee-ships, and not to base themselves overseas, but to pay a fair amount of tax, how much of your real agenda would you be able to accomplish?'

Caroline considered. 'Almost all of it. It would make us serious, certainly. But I've met the glossy, bumptious men and women who run the big companies, and it's no good, darling, it's no good. They'd give us *some* of what we want, but only in return for tax breaks that would undermine and cripple us.'

'Which is exactly where my little sermon comes in. You're offering them the wrong thing. You're being too narrow. You still control the state – that is, you control the fount of honours. You control how people are seen, whether or not they're respected. Just imagine if you divided all the major companies into two groups – those that did, broadly speaking, the right thing, and those that didn't. The companies that played fair and paid fair would be designated – I don't know, call them "National Merit Companies" or something. Only their bosses would be eligible for honours. They'd get respect. Real respect. Only they would be appointed to commissions and inquiries into the future of their industries. Only they would be invited onto the prime minister's plane when he's making his next trade visit to China or Brazil. Only their companies would be legally allowed to fund political parties. They'd get, in short, political and public respect, and they'd get it for the right reasons. Because they were the leaders of business and industry who paid people properly, trained the next generation, and paid their taxes. They'd be the genuinely admired knights of industry, looked up to and respected by their fellow citizens. The rest, the ones who didn't play ball, would just be grubby little profit-mongers.'

Caroline laughed and applauded. 'You are so gorgeously naïve, Angela. You're still Pep on the edge of the playing field, with your eyes burning bright, dreaming your dreams. In the horrid real world, none of that would work. We'd be laughed out of court.'

Angela kissed her, without anger, on the forehead. 'You couldn't be more wrong. All you people down there in that buzzy, self-important world of politics have lost sight of how the rest of us think. Give it a go. Though, speaking of being laughed out of court, you'd need the support of the king. Do you know the king?'

'Not yet, darling, but it can't be long. Let me think about this. Do you mind if I talk to the Master?'

Angela, who had already spoken to the Master's wife, shrugged and shook her head. She was thinking about pouring herself another glass of wine. It didn't look as if there would be any sex tonight, so she did.

What Happened to the Idea?

*The state, as we used to understand it, is over. It's very important,
however, that the voters never notice.*

The Master

When the Master was in town, he had his haunts, or
perches, in the most obscure places. He dropped in for the
big news, force of habit. The home secretary, a baby-faced
former researcher, had resigned, and Caroline Phillips had been
appointed as his replacement. The Master had not expected
Grimaldi to work so fast, and wondered why he had.

Once upon a time he would have arranged a tryst with Ella
while he was in London, but Ella had vanished. The Master's
tentacles spread everywhere, but even he had been unable to
track her down. He strongly suspected that she had run off
with one of the Washington players who'd been in Venice —
she'd have been impressed by the raw power at their fingertips.
Sometimes he wondered whether David Petrie had had something to do with it. But Petrie still had a bit of the air of a
bumpkin. Ella had called him a second-rater. At any rate, the
Master thought, it was time to replace Ella. There would be

plenty of candidates, but he needed someone very discreet, someone with almost as much to lose as he did.

The obvious someone had called him even before he had called her. Caroline Phillips arrived five minutes early for their meeting in the Academicians' room at the Royal Academy. The Master, who had slipped in discreetly by a back door, directly from an exhibition of Damien Hirst's late works, was ten minutes early, however. Was it a trick of his, or simply a tic? Even he could never decide. The room was almost empty; an elderly architect was going through some sheets of drawings with a young woman. The broadcaster Jon Snow goggled and waved at him, but, his curiosity whetted, had to leave, frustrated. The Master hoped he'd have left the building before Caroline arrived.

'Did you see Snow?' he asked as she click-clacketed across the wooden floor.

'No.' It had been windy, with some sleet – Caro didn't yet speak fluent politics. But she got straight down to business. 'I've had a sort of idea. It's quite a big idea, but it's very simple. Perhaps too simple.'

The Master, who had never believed in complexity of thought, only of organisation, leaned back and listened intently. When Caroline had finished, he thoughtfully rubbed his upper lip, almost as though he were smoothing an invisible moustache. Finally, he delivered his verdict. 'I like it. I like its simplicity. It's actually very New Labour – socialist ends, better wages, better investment, but without socialist means. No, it's very good, even if we might have to exempt a very few very important companies from the list of those who fail to meet the criteria.'

'No, we can't do that. No exemptions. Start to let people off the hook, and the whole thing collapses. That's the point. Sorry.'

'Caroline, are you standing up to me? Not what I'm used to.'

'I'm sorry, Master. But there can be no exemptions. Even for your friends.'

'Cheeky. But I'm still impressed by the idea. And I like the fact that you didn't back down. You are slowly strengthening into leadership material, my dear. Now, I should warn you that time is getting short. I fear our Mr Grimaldi may soon decide to step down. He's not a well man. Say nothing to anybody at this stage, I'm just tipping you off. I'm coming round to the idea, by the way, of backing you when the time comes. It's come down to just you or Mr Petrie. You have the reach into the south of England and London, which Mr Petrie, fine man though he is, doesn't. But he's got the big picture . . . Venice, and so forth. One thing, however. There should be honesty between us. Was this idea of yours entirely your own?'

'Yes, of course. I wanted to bring it to you first.'

'I had the strong impression that it was Angela's. She discussed it with my wife two days ago. So you prove yourself a liar. But that's not necessarily a bad thing in general. Just make a mental note, would you, not to lie to me again? I have my little tentacles everywhere, you know.'

His mobile started to vibrate. 'An old friend. Would you

forgive me? Mrs Wilkinson!' The Master nodded goodbye to Caro, and left for his rendezvous with his former housekeeper.

Following Angela's advice, Caro had already told the prime minister about her idea. She didn't want the Master pretending he'd come up with it himself; and Grimaldi was too weak to do the dirty on her. But he'd left a spate of increasingly urgent-sounding messages on her BlackBerry, asking her to 'drop round' as soon as possible. So after leaving the Royal Academy she hurried down St James's Street, past the old brick palace, and straight across the park. Entering Downing Street through the back gate – a privilege of her new position – she was sitting in the prime minister's study fifteen minutes later.

Grimaldi was standing in front of a mirror, adjusting his smart blue tie; but his customary cream suit, she thought, like the man himself, had no gravitas.

'Thank God you're here, Caro. I was beginning to think you weren't going to make it. Now, I hope you don't think I'm being previous, but an idea like this – well, we have to strike while the iron is hot. It goes nowhere without the enthusiastic support of the king. I've taken the liberty of calling his private secretary, and he's interested enough to have invited us to lunch at Windsor.'

'That's very encouraging. When?'

'Now. I couldn't very well tip you off with a text message. The car's waiting.'

'I'm hot, and I've got a ladder, and my shoes are scuffed. Also, apart from the day of my appointment, I've never met the man.'

What Happened to the Idea?

'None of that matters. He doesn't notice clothes, he likes ideas. And he very much likes my new idea – I'm sorry, Home Secretary: *our* new idea.'

'I have an uneasy feeling it will soon become *his* new idea.'

'Nothing wrong with letting the monarch think that. Authorship, as you know, is all in the briefing.'

As they settled into the back seat of the prime ministerial Daimler, Caroline still felt unsettled, suspicious and prickly. Alwyn was talking about an entirely new start for Labour, and he felt that this idea, this 'partnership with the real world', could relaunch his premiership. Would it not be a good idea to announce that no government contracts – 'and we're talking billions of pounds every year, Home Secretary' – would go to any firm that was not a 'National Chartered Company'? And, pushing further forward, 'Could we not raise with the king the idea of, over time, completely remodelling the House of Lords so that it was made up, entirely and solely, of leaders of business and industry whose companies had agreed to what I'm going to call the "Five-Point Plan" – fair wages, honestly paid taxes, basic environmental standards and . . . Caro, help me out here, I can't remember the last two.'

'Traineeships, and supporting democratic political parties, of whatever stripe, so that we get away from the sordid business of fund-raising. I'm sorry, I don't mean to be petty, Prime Minister, but I do believe that this was *my* idea.'

Alwyn didn't answer. He stared out of the window as the car, preceded by two police motorcycle outriders, turned past Buckingham Palace and headed towards the Embankment, from where the driver would zigzag his way west until he was on the motorway towards Windsor Castle.

Caro felt oddly upset. This was just politics, after all. And yet, without lovely Angela and her optimistic lateral thinking, which had come out of her commitment to Barker, none of this would be happening. It felt surreal.

She wasn't going to let the prime minister remain silent for the rest of the journey. 'By the way, PM, how are you feeling? In yourself, I mean?'

That caught Grimaldi's attention. One of the few things he had in common with the Master was that, although he had always been unusually fit, he was a lifelong hypochondriac. They exchanged notes on polyps, blood pressure and funny turns. And as it happened, he wasn't feeling quite himself that morning, and hadn't for a few days. 'What do you mean, Home Secretary? Have you heard something? If you have, you have a duty to let me know who's been gossiping.'

'No, nothing at all,' lied Caroline. 'I just thought you were looking a little pale.'

The prime minister tugged at his throat and fell silent again. As they reached the M4, Caroline tried again. 'I don't know the king, of course, but I really think his decision to close Buckingham Palace down for royal purposes and retreat to Windsor is the height of selfishness. It simply means we have to spend far more time stuck in cars with each other. I don't want to sound like a raving lefty, Prime Minister, but whose time is more valuable?'

A safe topic at last, Alwyn thought. 'It wasn't my favourite decision either, though it's saved the public purse a lot of money and given the government, as well as big business, a wonderful new venue for conferences in London – even the Chinese like the idea of inviting their clients to Buckingham Palace. But there's a broader point, Caroline. We in Labour are on the same side as the monarchy, and certainly as this king. He's essentially conservative. He's uneasy about us being outside the European Union, and he has his family's natural suspicion of the Americans. The Windsors are the last people in the country who have never entirely forgotten 1776. He wants a Britain that's cautious, kindly, and where those with money and power do a little bit – not too much, but a little bit – to help those with neither. In all those ways he's much more a natural supporter of ours than of the other lot. So long as we don't go mad and republican, Labour is also on the conservative and monarchical side, and at our best we always have been – Clem, Harold, Jim. Even, in their way, Tony and the Master.

'That's why he loves this idea. It doesn't work without the crown, and royal patronage. He'll be standing alongside his ministers in a common project to spread a little more civilis-ation in our time. That's how he'll see it. He'll like it as much as he likes the idea of building a new Venice in the West Country. People don't always give him credit for it, but at heart our king is actually something of a man of vision.

'Now, when it comes to authorship . . . a few home truths, Home Secretary. Although we have a parliamentary system, it's evolved into an elective prime ministership. That's why we talk of the Thatcher revolution, the Cameron coalition, and so on. It follows that any big ideas which determine the course of a government are inescapably associated in the public mind with the person of the prime minister. Who happens, as it happens, as it were, to be – me. Historians, I'm sure, will track the origins of this idea down, and pay due credit to yourself. But the first thing we must do together is to ensure that the king doesn't take all the credit for himself. We have to be shoulder to shoulder as politicians, and ensure that the Labour government – *my* Labour government – gets that credit. Do you follow?'

Caroline was almost too irritated to reply. She noticed that the driver's shoulders were shaking. She suspected he was laughing, and struggling not to show it. 'I follow, Prime Minister,' she said. ('But not *you*, not for much longer, you little weasel,' she thought.)

For all his intellectual monarchism, Alwyn Grimaldi loathed Windsor – a crouching, cringeing little town, tugging its forelock throughout the streets that crept around the castle walls, a town of twinkly tea shops and tatty souvenirs and witless flag-waving, whose only other industry was the peculiar crenellated school that provided the Conservative Party with its leaders, and Hollywood with its villains.

They passed through the castle gate in a blur of ancient stonework, red uniforms and saluting policemen. They pulled up in the main courtyard, to find that the king had done them the honour of coming out to wait for them at the top of a flight of stone stairs.

'Goodness. He must be really keen. This is going to be fun, Home Secretary,' said the prime minister.

What Happened to the Idea?

The king gazed down at the pair of them – the slightly flushed woman and the thin, smirking man in a white suit whom he was obliged to call his first minister.

'Little weasel,' he muttered to himself.

How to Bring Down a
Prime Minister

*During my time in Number 10, the person I most missed was a
good, reliable poisoner.*

The Master

At more or less the same time that the home secretary
and the prime minister were being ushered into a private
dining room for lunch, back in London, Murdoch White's son,
a laboratory technician at the Hospital for Tropical Diseases
in Bloomsbury, was munching a sandwich in the street as
he waited for Mrs Wilkinson. All an observer would have
noticed was a pale, nervous young man in jeans greeting an
elderly lady in a headscarf, before passing her something
tightly wrapped in a plastic bag. His mother, or aunt? A
little domestic shopping? It was a touching little urban
vignette – but the future of the United Kingdom was
contained in that plastic bag.

Eileen Wilkinson unwrapped it gingerly back in Downing
Street, having first put on a pair of latex gloves. This was wise,
because the fluid in the glass bottle inside the bag had been
infected by Banquo White with Coxsackie B virus. Mrs

Wilkinson got methodically to work. With some careful sluicing and smearing, she transmitted the virus to the china cup Alwyn Grimaldi used for his breakfast milk.

No serious crime was being committed. Coxsackie B virus is not fatal, or even particularly serious. It causes Bornholm disease, characterised by diarrhoea and a sharp pain on one side of the chest. Known as 'the Devil's grip' or 'the grasp of the phantom', its effects generally last no longer than a week.

Alwyn Grimaldi, a creature of habit and a man of milky decency, had no obvious vices for an enemy to exploit. He could not be blackmailed. He was, in his way, a man of dogged persistence and some courage. To start with, without Eileen Wilkinson's observant presence, the Master and his circle would never have known that he suffered so acutely from hypochondria.

Hypochondria? So easy to mock. What the prime minister really suffered from was a terror of early death. It wasn't a fussy obsession with liver spots or winter coughs; it was a genuine, well-founded awareness of oblivion. Grimaldi's father had died early, of a stroke; his mother of breast cancer. To the prime minister, Caroline Phillips's gently probing question in the car on the way to Windsor had been like the sudden extinction of the sun behind a dark cloud. Despite his terrors, Grimaldi had fought on; his determination to stifle his night fears took considerable courage. In recent months, as the American pressure for a new security and defence agreement had weighed ever more heavily upon him, he had become more dogged, not less.

Alwyn Grimaldi might even have shaken off the Devil's

grip, which would get its fingers into him later that evening; but Mrs Wilkinson was a dogged and well-connected woman. The Master's wife remained a friend, and was close to Fara Clara Jenkinson, who had unwittingly provided the final solution. For, bizarre though it may seem, what finished off the premiership of Alwyn Grimaldi was a humble but inexplicably fashionable vegetable. As Fara Clara had once mentioned to Sadie in passing, if you eat sufficient beetroot quickly enough, the symptom of what appears to be severe rectal bleeding becomes all too apparent.

Beetroot had therefore featured heavily in the prime minister's diet in the days leading up to his meeting with the king, and beyond that, when he was virally infected. The combination of weakness, pain in his chest and apparent haemorrhage exhausted Alwyn's resources. Lying in bed early one morning, soaked in sweat, the Devil's grip around his chest and blood on the sheets, he telephoned his private Harley Street doctor. This doctor had once faced a GMC inquiry, which he had survived – he had never forgotten the handwritten note of support that arrived from Downing Street during the Master's era.

No physical examination was required that day; what was happening was all too obvious, and the doctor's tone of voice confirmed everything Alwyn needed to know. He ended the conversation, then dialled again, this time his private secretary, who put him through to Windsor Castle. His Majesty was properly concerned and sympathetic, just as his mother had been when Harold Macmillan had found himself in a similar fix. There was no need for an undignified rush. A full consultation in Harley Street would be required; and then, as soon as it could be arranged, the cabinet would have to be informed. Alwyn Grimaldi would remain as leader of the party until the forthcoming party conference in Stoke. He'd put in place the formal mechanisms for a change of leadership, and would remain as prime minister until his successor emerged from the vote of party members and MPs.

The prime minister felt intense relief. Mortally ill though he was, he managed to shower, dress, and eat a poached egg on brown toast for breakfast. Mortally ill though he was, he felt curiously vigorous as he planned the day ahead. It was like the flush of energy that often follows a bereavement. There were so many things to do, so many people to tell; but Alwyn felt something akin to gratitude. The great burden was being taken away, and he could at last acknowledge privately to himself that he'd never known what to do with it in the first place. Even his new plan for relaunching the government wasn't really his plan. It was fraught with difficulties ahead – the jealousy of competing companies, the inevitable accusations of favouritism, and the revelation of scandals involving the favoured, chosen ones. Well, let Mrs Caroline Phillips – he supposed it would be her – deal with all of that. He would watch from his hospital bed.

The Choice

We are all Americans now; the only distinction is between those
of us who know it and those who haven't noticed yet.

The Master

A metallic clunk. A whine. A thump and a groan. Sir
Leslie Khan had tracked down the Master, finally catching him,
as so often these days, on the treadmill. The Master was not
pleased. Much of him was in rivulets down his chest and legs.

'Can't stop. Can't talk. Just increased my speed . . .'

'Very good. You don't need to talk. I've just heard that
Grimaldi's resigning. Ill-health. Completely out of the blue.'

'Really? Just like Wilson. How *extraordinary*.' The last word
was panted.

'Indeed. But Master mine, it's too early. We're not ready.
We don't even know who it's to be.'

'I'm ready. Phew! I'm going to turn this thing off. Never
mix work and pleasure; not unless you want a stroke.' The
machine whinged and coughed to silence. The Master's face
was puce with effort. As he rubbed himself down with a small
towel, Sir Leslie took a pace back; the Master was superhuman,

but even he sweated. Sir Leslie discreetly sniffed his own wrist, well doused with a Vetiver scent from Paris.

'So, you're ready, are you? You know which of them it's to be? Have you heard about Ella? Have you heard back from our American friends about Petrie?'

The Master, unembarrassed, pulled off his singlet. A heart-rate monitor was around his chest. His torso was that of a far younger man, although liberally planted with sprightly grey hairs. He picked up a bottle of Evian water and poured it over his head.

'Leslie, there are times when even we have to let fate take its course. Yes, our old friend the ambassador, who was there in Venice with the Americans, tells me he's made exhaustive enquiries. Nobody, but nobody, had anything to do with Ella. The only person she was seen with there was our Mr Petrie. Hard as I find it to believe, I think he may have got rid of her, perhaps bribed her to disappear. Well, she had her claws into him, and as I know, that is a very . . . intense . . . experience.'

'Her father's been in touch with the Foreign Office. He thinks she may have been killed.'

'Oh, pooh. Pooh. But I bet you one thing. If that's so, and if it was Petrie, we will never know. Leslie, we picked our candidates well. He was Murdoch White's, and Murdoch would have spotted a fool long ago.'

'So it's possible?'

'Anything is possible. Multi-coloured rain is possible. Surrey declaring independence is possible. A readable novel by Justin Can'twrite is *possible*. It's all a question of likelihood.'

'So just let's be clear. You're telling me that one of our

prime candidates for Number 10 might be a murderer? The killer of your former . . .'

'That's enough of that, Leslie. As I said, business and pleasure. If Petrie's desperate, so much the better. Don't you remember my first and unbreakable law of democratic politics?'

'Bad people doing good things?'

'Bad people doing good things – the best hope left for civilisation. Now, David Petrie is without doubt, in some conventional ways, a bad man. Perhaps it's something to do with his upbringing. I neither know nor care. But if he's solid with the Americans and solid with business, and can hold the party together – and I think he probably can – then anything that's happened in the past shouldn't stop us from helping him. And frankly, it helps us too. If he thinks we know what may or may not have gone on out there in Venice, we have another hold on him. Darling Ella helps us in death even more than she helped us in life.'

Sir Leslie scratched vigorously at his beard. He'd always admired the Master's clarity. Along with his boyish good looks, it was one of his most attractive features. 'So we're going with Petrie?'

'I didn't say that, although he's genuinely an option. But we have to think about Caroline Phillips too. She comes up against my rule: we have no evidence that she's a bad person, by which I mean a truly ruthless person. But in some ways she reminds me of myself. She has charisma. She makes people like her and want to help her, and that's a rare and precious gift. Politically, she's a nothing. Her girlfriend's more interesting. But again, that needn't be a problem for us. Quite the reverse. She's popular and suggestible, and I think the public will really go for her. Frankly, Leslie, *I* rather go for her. We can provide the steel, but I'd be a lot happier if I thought she had at least a certain amount of ruthlessness, as well as political reliability.'

'Master, I'm beginning to suspect you have a plan.'

'Well suspected, Leslie. As you know, there's a big security conference, OSCE stuff, in Rome next week. All our friends from across the water will be there, the vice president included. Naturally the home secretary will be going, and I suggest we find a reason for sending Mr Petrie too. Then we can let our friends choose between them. Test them, put them under pressure: Gaza and Palestine, Trident, homeland security, Google, Amazon, health services – the lot.'

'You're saying we should let Washington choose our next prime minister?'

'Certainly not. I am shocked, Sir Leslie – shocked – *shocked* – that you can even suggest such a thing. No, our American friends will merely give their opinion, as ever. We will choose. *I* will choose.'

With that, the Master headed irritably for the shower. He didn't like explaining himself, even to the inner circle of the inner circle. And his morning routine had been interrupted, and therefore ruined. But as ever, the pummelling force of the scalding water on his scalp reinvigorated him. He'd like, he thought, to see the extraordinary Mrs Phillips later on. She couldn't resist him, of course. They were alike in that respect – irresistible to lesser creatures. It was almost like that problem of physics: what happened when two irresistible forces collided? Something for CERN . . .

The Master's eerie youthfulness had been explained by his friends in many different ways. Some thought it was the daily gym sessions, others an utter lack of pensiveness or self-questioning. But really, it was simply that his curiosity had never waned. Stay interested and you stay alive. How, he wondered, would Caroline explain her unfaithfulness with him to the remarkable Angela? Would she even admit it? An interesting question of psychology.

A Flying Pot

Don't drink — it's my only lifestyle advice. Just don't drink. Not if you want to hold power.

The Master

Angela and Caro were having a fight. They were having it in mutters and hisses, because they were having it while they were clearing the small back garden of the Barker house for a bonfire, and there were neighbours a few yards away, also gardening. But the low volume didn't make it any less savage.

Caro, bent low over a bedraggled azalea, which she was murdering, was literally shaking with anger. 'How *could* you? That was just cruel. When did you become so judgemental?'

A year ago, Angela might have made some appreciative remark about Caro's bottom, tightly encased in filthy jeans. But that was a lifetime ago. Now she lifted her head, tasting alcohol in her mouth, and snapped back: 'Judgement's the *job*, you grand bloody minister. Hadn't you noticed?'

Caro stood and turned to look at her with an expression of undisguised dislike. 'Don't take that tone with me.'

Angela, clutching a large, cracked flowerpot, straightened, ignoring her. 'And since, around here at least, the Lord has delegated His work to me, I rather think a bit of plain speaking is the least you should expect. Quint's a *revolting* man. I've looked some of his stuff up, and it's nothing more than toadying drivel. I just gave him a bit of plain speaking. What? Don't look away from me. It's what he needed. So he writes *that*' – she pointed at a scrunched newspaper lying on top of the silage bin. 'So what? It's what he does. How you ever got mixed up with him I'll never understand. You used to be better than that.'

'You – you – pious little prig. That's only a dog collar, you know. This is only Barker. You're not Mother bloody Teresa. Yes, Peter Quint has helped me in the past. He was going to help me in the future. But now you've blown it for me. I've got an enemy for life in one of the most important papers in the country. Thanks, *sweetheart*.'

Angela had never heard the word spoken like that. She flamed. 'You know what I used to like about you? It seems funny now, but from the first day we met at school, I always thought you had a soul. Other people fell in love with your beautiful face, and your charming smile, and all those nonsense things that were just given to you – which, by the way, aren't really you, and they'll go away one day. They will.

'Oh yes, they will. But I saw more. You were rooted. Your feet were firmly on the ground, and you understood that we're put here to make this stinking world a slightly better place. Sometimes I believe in paradise, and sometimes I don't. But

A Flying Pot

I always thought we could make a little paradise on earth if we put our backs into it. And I thought you did too.'

The argument was at a fork; it could fall back, or it could worsen. Caro hedged. 'So why do you think – we should knock that fence down, by the way, the whole thing – why do you think I went into politics in the first place?'

Angela no longer cared. 'Because it's all about you. That's what's changed. It's always about you. You barely have a moment for the boys these days – and by the way, they've noticed. As for me, I'm just an embarrassment. Oh, yes. I told your precious soon-to-be-ex-leader Alwyn Grimaldi what I thought, that day at Chequers. I just said stuff I say all the time; and you squirmed, and tried to act as if you'd only bumped into me the day before. Next thing, it'll be some man. Now you're picking a fight with me – me – about Peter Quint, who's less' – Angela brought her gumboot down on a large snail that had been struggling its way across a paving stone, crunching it into shards and goo – 'than *that.*'

Angela was red-faced. A year ago, Caro might have found that attractive. Now she said, 'You're drunk. In the middle of the afternoon. Just after you've taken a service. You're disgusting.'

As Caro stomped down the side of the house towards her car, slamming the side gate behind her, Angela hurled the flowerpot after her. Missing by some distance, it shattered against the back wall of the house. She howled a word which scholars, working hard, have so far failed to discover in either Testament.

In the next-door garden, Mr Grant raised his eyebrows at

Mrs Grant, who was trimming the edge of the lawn. 'Just like normal married people.'

As she drove back to London, Caro reflected that perhaps Angela's disgraceful behaviour wasn't quite such a disaster after all. If ever she decided to separate herself from her mouthy and increasingly priggish and erratic partner, there was at least one person who could be relied upon to be supportive: Peter Quint would be delighted.

Building a Better World

Serious politicians are remembered by the buildings they leave behind — Canary Wharf, Holyrood, the Dome. Most politicians leave behind no buildings at all, which is of course the point.

The Master

Ever since the murder of Ella, Davie had felt extremely well. There were no night-time writhings, no black moments, no regrets. He felt cleansed, as if he'd been through a scouring, icy shower; and the world looked as if it had been freshly rinsed as well. He spoke to Mary and the boys in exactly the same way as before. He missed Ella not at all. The only cloud on his bright horizon was the distant possibility of a police investigation, and of him being questioned. In retrospect, of course, he and Ella might have been seen together and remembered — on the vaporetto, having a coffee at Burano — who knows? Everybody has a camera in their pocket these days. Perhaps the old woman who shook her head at him had seen something after all.

And yet, on balance, Davie thought not. He'd had a great triumph in the department, and he was still luxuriating in it.

Political success was as instantly warming and reassuring as heroin in the blood vessels. Even Bunty had gone quiet. She made no impertinent comments. She asked no awkward questions. She just seemed pleased to have seen the back of Ella. And she managed Davie's constituency business with calm efficiency, he had to give her that. When Mary and the boys came to London, Bunty showed an almost maternal side. She fixed tickets to musicals, and told the boys where the best burgers were to be had. When he moved into the secretary of state's spacious office she didn't replace the imperturbable private secretary, Moira, he had inherited, but the two women appeared to get on, and they worked well together. So it was no particular surprise when during one of his Monday-morning planning sessions Bunty appeared in his office with a buff envelope and a serious expression.

This was by far Davie's favourite time of the week. With the departmental planning officer, his architectural adviser and the permanent secretary, he was contemplating a beautifully constructed three-dimensional model of the new city he planned to raise in Somerset. Perspex buildings, on tiny Perspex piles, rose above a rippling, coloured landscape which showed the positions of the existing buildings and of the new canals that would end the problem of flooding forever. 3-D printers allowed the department to visualise the entirely new landscape, while simultaneously costing the acquisition of the land and the provision of new rail, road and water links. Davie had insisted that there would be a Grand Canal twisting through the centre of the city, with water frontages more ornate and beautiful than anything that had been built in

England since the Edwardians. Every Monday there were new additions. Private contractors brought in suggestions all week; large computer screens showed visualisations of individual buildings and of the views along the canals or across the piazzas (Davie had banned the use of 'squares').

Sunlight fell across the beautiful model. The permanent secretary had just brought some good news: one of the larger farmers was prepared to sell up at a very decent price, in return for a canalside mansion, which he wanted the king's favourite architect to design for him. Everyone would win – the department, the former farmer, and the flattered monarch.

Bunty tugged at Davie's elbow. 'It's frae Maw. Dinnae fash. It's no' aboot the hoor.' The permanent secretary smiled and raised his eyebrows. Not for the first time, Davie thanked his lucky stars that nobody in the department understood a word of Scots.

Bunty passed him the envelope. 'Go on, buggerlugs, open it then.'

Inside, there was a single coloured photograph. It showed an elderly man wearing a grey jacket and a military cap, crouched down and staring at an architectural model of a town.

'Ken tha' bampot?'

'Of course. It's Linz . . . and *him*.'

'Aye. 'Itler. It's Maw's way of telling you you've lost the heid. Doonfa' . . . awa' wi' the fucking fairies, boss.'

By now everyone else in the room was looking concerned. Flushing, Davie ordered them all out: 'It's a constituency matter that Bunty here has drawn to my attention. Can you just give us a few moments?

'Now, really, Bunty . . .' he began when they were alone.

'Aye, aye, yerra busy man. No' time ferra wee bit girl who didnae go t'the college. But see here, Mr Petrie, my maw's a very bright woman, and she's been keepin' a close interest. You'd be surprised. And she's not the only one. My man suggested I come and have a wee talk with you. Maw likes all the new hooses you're building for working folks down south – just like you built them in Glaikit a' those years. And Maw, and the hale party back home, are dead chuffed wi' how fast you've scampered up the greasy pole – like a damned little monkey, she says. They're no' so pleased wi' how you've treated Mary and the boys, mind – but they don't ken a'thing. Mebbe enough said.

'No, she says you couldnae hae done it wi'oot powerful freens – Murdoch White, and New Labour and a' that crowd. Good for you: politics, Maw says, is aboot poo'r and how to get it. But there's the rub, Mr Petrie. A'body kens – the birds in the trees, Maw, the dumbest auld cooncillors, even daft wee Bunty, even her man – a'body kens that the Maister has eyes only for Caroline Phillips. She's who he wants as wir next prime minister. That's no' great. Maw says Caroline Phillips will do anything – she'll sign up with the Yanks and all the Maister's business freens. She says – begging your pardon, Mr Petrie – that you're no' the brightest bulb in the set, but you're honest and you've got values, and you'll stick up for the rest of us. But meanwhile, there you are in the bunker, staring at little models while the world changes around you. So the message is this: forget about your bloody hooses for a minute or two, and get back to bloody work. You've got a fight on your haunds, whether you want it or not.'

Davie was staggered. Not by Bunty's unaccustomed eloquence – he'd figured out long ago that she was entirely formidable – nor by the message she brought. Ever since Grimaldi had announced his imminent resignation, cabinet gossip had been hot for either Caroline Phillips or him, and he was well aware that he was continuing to act as a departmental minister, not as a man campaigning for the highest office. The truth was, he hoped and believed that the party would go for substance, not for the grand, airy-fairy guff Caroline was spouting – all those fancy companies, all that capering around with captains of industry. It was like 'triangulation', and 'the third way', and 'one nation' – all the trite catchphrases that impressed Westminster commentators and left the rest of the country stony-faced. But perhaps he was wrong. *Private Eye* had just carried a very subtle insinuation that the Master and Caroline Phillips were more than merely tutor and pupil. He didn't quite believe that either.

No, what had staggered him was Bunty's cool insolence in coming in and lecturing him. Did the votes of the Glaikit electorate, his rapid rise through the ranks in Parliament, the flattering profiles in the press, the television appearances and the policy breakthroughs, mean nothing at all? Did she think he was stupid? And worse, if he had no idea what was going on in that girl's head, perhaps he really *was* stupid – perhaps he didn't understand the first thing about what was going on.

At any rate, she was right about one thing: he had to pull himself together. He had to ready himself for the fight.

'Thank you, Bunty. You've been very candid. Just one thing. This man of yours . . .?'

'Aye. An older fellow. And on the other side – for Christ's sake, dinnae tell Maw. But he's got his head screwed on, and like he says, he keeps his ear to the ground.'

'And this older fellow, does he also hear what your mother's been hearing? What does he say about it?'

'He says wha' he always says – "Quite concur."'

To Glaikit – and Back

Make enemies; it's the cardinal rule, because if you don't make enemies, you stand for nothing. And then eventually everyone's an enemy.

The Master

Davie Petrie? Who was David Petrie? It was a question that, rather late in the day, he realised could not be answered in London, but only back in Glaikit, where the ghost of a brutal father, and his very much alive, betrayed family, must be confronted. On his rare trips home he always tried to get a forward-facing window seat in first-class carriage F, on the sunless side, where he could work. As that work piled up, he began to bring along his private secretary, a single man who lodged, uncomplainingly, at the station hotel. Davie had become used to being recognised, and had developed a practised, glassy, unwelcoming response which kept all but the most persistent constituents and busybodies away. So the train had become almost a refuge.

This time, however, there was no private secretary with him. Davie had left his red boxes behind. And such was the turmoil in his mind, he wasn't sure whether he'd ever be returning to London. He'd done more than he could have believed possible when he was first elected. He'd done the most terrible thing – but he'd erected good stone walls around the story of Ella, and locked the door on her, and he'd never gone back. He'd also done some rather wonderful things. He'd promised to build, and build he had. His policy of tax breaks for more ornamented and better-designed modern buildings – the so-called 'beautiful policy' – would result in fine, carved-stone police stations, schools and council offices all across the UK. In future, most of the blurred towns that passed the train's window would bear the Petrie mark. There was talk of a new golden age in architecture. It wasn't ridiculous. Yes, he'd be remembered, and in a good way. How many modern politicians could say the same?

The immediate future, however, seemed darker. He couldn't be sure whether or not he had the Master's blessing. On balance, he thought not. He'd learned a lot, from Murdoch White and others, but it seemed pretty clear that the next chapter was to be a full-on fight to the death with the home secretary, Caroline Phillips. She, according to the commentators – including Peter Quint, who was actually now being a bit nicer to him – had the support of the king and most of the leading English Labour MPs. He had the unions and the north, even if Nationalist Scotland held mostly aloof. This was exactly the kind of battle that had ripped the party apart so many times before. Even assuming he won, what sort of authority would he have?

The crucial test, he knew, would be the security conference in Rome, and trying to get the defence, trade and intelligence deal agreed by the cabinet. Nobody had forgotten that he'd made his first political mark by backing Trident and the American alliance. But alliance was one thing; this was something else. Even the JIC top brass, slaveringly subservient to the Yanks, hadn't been able to disguise the fact that it was a takeover, not a collaboration. And it wasn't as if they'd be handing over the privacy and security of the British people just to Langley or Foggy Bottom. No, the big US internet corporations would be involved as well – so no hope of a silicon economic revival on this little island. It was all terrible; not even an earnest, several-bottle evening with Murdoch White had been able to convince him otherwise. But if he didn't play along, that smarmy Caroline Phillips would.

Davie wasn't a fool; by the time the train pulled into Glaikit, he'd worked out that if either he or Caroline refused to do the deal, they would never become prime minister; and if either of them agreed to it, he or she would go down in history as a traitor to the Labour Party and to Britain. That was the hideous conundrum the Master had handed them. Clearly, they had been set up, and were going to be tested at the conference. It was impossible. The Master, of course, would be watching. Should he even go?

Mary and the boys gave him a warm welcome, entirely unmerited, which brought moisture to his eyes. There was an ordinariness, a cosiness, to the squabbles about the pasta bake, and who wanted to watch which box set, that seemed to him unbearably poignant. Mary, who was being suspiciously nice to him, packed the boys off to bed early – she wanted to sit and have a talk. But Davie said he had constituency work to do. He ignored the hurt look in her eyes as he pulled on his coat and left the house.

There was a keen edge to the air, and the smell of coal smoke brought him back to his childhood as he trudged under the sodium lamps towards the increasingly decrepit council estate where Elspeth Cook would be waiting for him, a pot of scalding, dark-brown tea at her elbow and a copy of the *New Statesman* on the table. Funny how he'd come to rely on 'Granny Stalin' as a moral guide. A lot of that was down to Bunty. How long ago it seemed since he'd trapped her, drooling, behind her desk at the council offices. But who had really trapped whom?

Elspeth opened the door even before he'd chapped it. 'Come on in, then. Sit yourself down and have a cup. I ken why you're here, mebbe. If Bunty's right you've got a lot on your mind.' Rosa bared her teeth as Davie sat down. There was no point in dissembling here. He painstakingly explained the situation. Elspeth famously loathed the Master and his old wars, but she sat and listened patiently. It was as if she knew it all already.

'I'm not one for the drink,' she said, 'but this is a special occasion, Davie – and by the by, under my roof you're just wee Davie Petrie, no' the cabinet minister or future prime minister, or any of that nonsense.' She brought out a bottle of Cream of the Barley and, unasked, added a hefty slug to the two cups of tea.

On the small television in a corner of the room, the news came and went. Tiny fragments and splinters of wars, domestic tragedies and bogus scientific reports, unnoticed by either of them. Even a brief item featuring the face of Caroline Phillips didn't halt the flow of conversation. Almost unconsciously, Elspeth flicked channels. Evan Davies harangued silently for another half-hour, during which Davie's concentration remained fixed intently on Elspeth. For it was quite a story she was telling.

She spoke about his father. Whatever Davie had always believed, all the village knew what a brute he was, and all the village had sympathised with little David and his mother. 'But there was nothing we could do for you puir souls. Your da had them all sewn up – the council, the social services, even the doctors. There was naebody in Glaikit who'd look big Bob Petrie straight in the eye. There were rumours that he had some of the bigger lads from the firm to break a few teeth, even a leg or two, but I never credited that. Bob did it mostly on charisma, and the rest on hard cash. Like a lot of bullies, he was a hell of a man. Handsome till the drink got him, like a big dark bull.'

'Mrs Cook, you almost sound as if you were smitten.'

'Aye, Davie, I hoped we wouldn't get onto that. But yes, forgive me, I had my moments with your da. I wasn't the only one, mind. Feel wretched about it now – your poor mother. But you have to understand that for many years Bob Petrie was Glaikit, and Glaikit was Bob, and the Labour Party was both of them together.'

'But you stayed.'

'In the party? Aye, of course. Where else was there to go, for a widow woman who cared about other folk? The kirk?

The Nats? The bloody Tories? Aye, I stayed Labour. But it's a horrible, corrupt, cynical story round these parts. That's why you mattered so much to us all.'

'But I was just the bad man's son. Around these parts I was Big Black Bob Petrie the second.'

'Naw, Davie. Naebody the second. You aye had something special. We all saw it. A kind of innocence. Said what you meant. Really cared. You never took a bribe in your life. So when we packed you off to Westminster, for a lot of us it was like a new start. This sounds daft, and Bunty would be laughing if she could hear me, but you were Glaikit's second chance, a possibility of redemption.'

Davie wasn't sure whether she was laughing or crying: 'But I got tangled up with the Master. If I get the top job, if I really get to put this town on the map, I have to deliver things to him that I don't want to. And Mrs Cook, I don't want you to get the wrong idea about me. I've done some bad stuff on the way up. I'm no angel.'

'Listen, pet, we all have our suspicions.' Davie grimaced as she topped up his cup with more whisky. 'And we're all on the side of Mary and the boys. That cousin of yours is hanging around a wee bit too much. You want to heal the wounds your father caused, and that job begins at home. You've got a fine family, and if you don't care for them properly, nothing else will work. Don't underestimate Bunty. In some ways she's your biggest fan, but not everything she's told me about your life in London has made this old woman's face light up with joy.'

Like most Catholics, David Petrie hadn't been to confession

once in his adult life; but he imagined that this was what it must feel like. This tough old woman, who'd maintained for so long that old Joe Stalin had known a thing or two, and who'd been so bitter about Kinnock, Blair, Brown and Miliband, was the most unlikely mother-confessor he could imagine. Even so, he felt wretched and relieved at the same time, which he imagined was the outcome the Church was aiming for.

'He was always a bastard to me,' said Davie. 'If there was one thing I always hoped, it was that I'd never be that kind of bastard myself. But perhaps I've just become a different kind of bastard.'

Elspeth sniffed. 'Enough of the self-pity. You want to know what to do? You don't come hirpling away out in the middle of the night to ask some daft old wife's advice. Life's no' a fairy story. You ken fine well what you have to do, David Petrie. But since you seem to want my advice – the prize is within your grasp. Take it, and make us proud. As for the so-called Master, it's time to drop all that shite. If you're a man – and I think you are – you take your own fucking decisions.'

Later that night, before he went to bed, Davie surprised himself by going down on his knees and muttering a promise. The Roman Church, he thought: all roads lead to Rome.

Upstairs, he gently rolled over the comatose Mary, and kissed her on the earlobes and neck before making love. He thought he tasted tears on her cheeks, but that made him more excited, not less.

Back in Barker

People say I made nothing better. That's not true. I was jolly good for gays.

The Master

If there was one unexpected lesson that Caro had learned from her years with Angela, it was that drunkenness didn't make her less worth listening to – far from it. If there had been a coat of arms for their relationship, the motto scrolled on the bottom would have been *In Vino Veritas*. In *Chablis Veritas* in particular.

Angela drunk and angry was a very special experience. Standing with her black eyes blazing, hands on hips, and clearly not caring if the boys could hear her upstairs, she was giving Caro everything she had. They had begun the evening with a romantic meal in the local Italian trattoria, where things had started to go awry – briskly snapped breadsticks, too much eyeing of wine glasses – then they'd moved on to the George and Dragon, where the Dragon had the best of it, and ended up back home after a loud public argument, during which they had tacked along the pavement like a pair of drunken yachts heading into a storm.

'Lesbians have stars,' explained Angela. 'There are five-star lesbians, never looked at a man, brave, bright, glittering, glittering . . .' She waved her arm vaguely towards the door, which at that moment represented the universe. 'And there are four-star lesbians, who won't go with a man, but will go with *any* kind of girl. And there are the three-stars, keep their heads down, smirk at the boss – homebodies, not ashamed, not proud. And there are the two-stars, married all their lives until they get bored at fifty-five, go for the woman next door, quiet life, quiet bed. And then there are the one-star lesbians, the hypocrites, the faithless . . .'

Angela began to cry. But she brushed the tears aside, and her mouth puckered in fury. 'How many stars do you wear on your fucking cap, Caroline Phillips? I had you down as a three-star lesbian. Just like me – no great heroine, but a decent, honest woman, true to herself, true to me. But as of this evening, I officially downgrade you. You're a hypocritical one-star fraud. Are you even, you know, actually gay?'

Caro waited for the outrage to come bubbling up, but it didn't bubble. She knew the Master had been coming on to her, and that she'd felt more intrigued than irritated. And yes, she'd had men, just sometimes, in the years before Angela. And no, it hadn't been revolting, just mildly disappointing. Making love to a man was like making love to an eager, panting domestic animal, desperate for his head to be scratched, and with a silly little sausage he wanted rid of. Making love to Angela felt, by contrast, an entirely adult and grown-up activity. But Caro realised that it was unlikely to be on the cards tonight. Best thing was to knock Angela out until the morning. So she shrugged, and went off for another bottle of life juice from the fridge.

The trouble in the restaurant had started over whether Caroline should go to the security conference in Rome at all. Over the breadsticks and prosciutto she'd told Angela about Alwyn Grimaldi's cynical appropriation of their great idea. ('*Whose* great idea?' Angela had asked.) Angela, though she'd tried for Caro's sake, had never seen Grimaldi as a serious figure; and when his resignation had been announced a few days earlier, she had been straight on the phone to Caro, urging her to run. 'It would be a great thing,' she said, 'to be the first gay partner in Downing Street, with the boys there too. A real moment in history. You know, Caro, I want to be part of that. There's so much we could do together.'

But she couldn't help noticing, as they divided the pasta, that Caro hadn't been quite as enthusiastic as she would once have been. These days she harped on about Angela's drinking, as if it was a real problem – which it wasn't, or hardly ever. When they talked about whether she was up to the job, again and again she'd bring up something the Master had said; and there was something about the way she talked about him that Angela didn't like.

'It's almost as if you're smitten by him.'

'Don't be ridiculous. I'm faithful to one person, and one person only. If you don't know that, you don't know me at all. But . . . he's an extraordinary man.'

'Pah. He's weak, actually. He reminds me of the little boy in the playground who looks around for the biggest boy there and goes and stands next to him, desperate for protection. That's all you need to know about the so-called Master and the Americans, or the Master and the banks. He may have his tricks of the trade, but believe me, Caro, if you get into bed with him, he'll exact a horrible price. You'll never recover. Nor, frankly, will we.'

'Who said anything about bed?'

The argument had spiralled downwards from there, until it ended up in the shouting match.

The following morning, her face swollen and her head thumping, Caro had nevertheless kissed Angela tenderly.

'You'll just have to trust me, sweetheart. I'm going, whatever you say.'

'Going where?' Angela groaned.

'I'm going all the way. But first, I'm going to Rome.'

In the Hotel

The Americans. Stand beside the Americans. If you stand with the Americans, not much can really go wrong.

The Master (but quite a long time ago)

On a hillside studded with umbrella pines overlooking Trastevere, the Hotel Excelsior Splendide lived up, with peacocky Latin swagger, to the cheerful pomposity of its name. The pruned walkways of its gardens were strewn with looted marble fragments from the age of Augustus. Its entrance hall was a half-kilometre square of mosaic marble exuberance, with plush red sofas and waiting staff dressed rather more smartly than the most senior ranks of the Italian armed forces, surrounded by gilded Corinthian columns. In the bedrooms, there were original artworks. Andy Warhol's prints of multi-coloured dollar signs were particularly popular. Benvenuto Cellini had designed the cutlery, and Paolo Veronese had done the wallpaper – or so it appeared. Down in its bowl of dusty tourism and mafia-run shopping, the rest of Rome sometimes raised its eyes to the faraway gelato palace of the hotel and felt a spasm of jealousy.

326

In the Hotel

Most weeks, the Excelsior Splendide was simply there to host international business conferences. Men with high blood pressure and button-down shirts fought over the lobster buffet in the evenings and waddled down to the Imperial Roman bathing pool the next morning, like so many warthogs in thongs. Air-conditioned limousines and oleaginous guides could be hired for spouses or mistresses who wished to shop or view the sights of the Eternally Cynical City. Around the grounds, former taxi drivers and retired policemen posed in short white smocks, with plastic helmets, shields and swords; in the evenings they engaged in listless, slow-motion gladiatorial combat for the entertainment of executives on their way to dinner. It was widely believed that their meaty thighs and weatherbeaten faces were available for hire later. The front desk took care of everything.

But on this particular week, under the shade of the pines and behind the yew hedges, the gladiators were sulky. They were outnumbered and outshone by the magnificent carabinieri of the Tuscania airborne regiment – leaner, younger men, and indeed better-armed. The gladiators, who had their pride after all, suspected the jumped-up policemen of sniggering at their skirts. If so, they kept their laughter mostly to themselves, and adopted poker faces as the guests passed. For the carabinieri were on duty to protect the many dozen American and EU politicians and military top brass who had gathered to debate intelligence issues following the recent bombings. This week it was all very serious, and very grown-up.

The public face of the conference was, naturally, meaningless:

there would be a televised speech by the European security commissioner, and a short statement by the US vice president. Nothing surprising would be said, though what was unremarkable would be said well, and truisms repeated with elegance and force. (What else, after all, are the literature degrees at so many expensive universities on both sides of the Atlantic for?) In the hotel's conference rooms, there would be briefings about Islamist penetration of European cities; vague descriptions of outrageous surveillance strategies, swaddled in a cocoon of euphemism; and an elegant talk from a self-congratulatory professor from Bologna about the history of radicalism in Pakistan and Egypt. But all the real business was conducted quietly in the hotel bedrooms, or the American Bar. Politicians spoke about unspoken deals; shook hands on silences; and ended the careers of people who had been warmly praised in the public sessions. And this serious business had brought to Rome two of the least well-matched Americans the current administration could have sent.

Symon Cantor had risen to the vice presidency via Harvard Law School, a firm of blue-chip New York attorneys, two successful congressional races, and a spell as majority whip. Members of his family had served under Eisenhower and Bush senior. Lean, aquiline and disdainful, Sy Cantor had been the kind of public prosecutor tough enough to take on the mob, and elegantly rich enough to be an honorary member of the yacht clubs without going to the bother of owning a yacht. If, after dressing, he saw a smudge of grease on the tip of one of his loafers, his whole day would be spoiled.

Out West, all of this didn't wash. 'Sy's no cowboy,' the

younger Bush had said. 'He's the kind of guy who gets out of the shower to take a piss.'

Buzz Boyd was a different kind of political animal entirely. The Boyds were haulage contractors and beef men from Wyoming; in his younger days Buzz had narrowly avoided a jail sentence for drunk driving, and had burned down his cousin's mall in a family feud, before he discovered business school, football, love and Jesus, in more or less that order. Not only was he a real Cowboy, having played football for the University of Wyoming – or Yoo Dubya to its friends – but he had married a Cowgirl.

Buzz Boyd's lovely wife Betty had come to UW on a track scholarship. She and Buzz first met on Prexy's Pasture, on the university campus. Alcohol was involved, and Laramie bars. But soon enough, Betty's membership of the Harvest Family Church rubbed off on Buzz. A teetotaller, a proud westerner, and soon a rising executive at Mukwon Energy, Buzz cut his political teeth as an adviser to Sarah Palin, before arriving in Washington as a political consultant to the Tea Party.

Where Sy Cantor was tall and silver as an aspen, Buzz was squat, red and aggressive as a prickly pear. Sy had scored his share of birdies on the Blue Course at Congressional Country Club. Buzz shot birds, as well as birdies. Sy read French novels, in French. Buzz played computer games, in American. Sy Cantor looked like a politician. But Buzz Boyd of Laramie, now head of homeland security for the United States of America, really was one.

In Rome, with his huge footballer's frame sprawled across

a reproduction gilt armchair, Buzz seemed to Sy an eruption, a sweaty boil, in his immaculate hotel suite. As VP, Sy had bagged the best rooms, and a view that spread out towards the Vatican, with St Peter's, like a giant bald guy, in the far distance. He'd have to work with Boyd over the next few days. The president had brushed aside his agonised plea to send somebody else. But Sy hadn't anticipated having Buzz crowding the foreground, actually turning up in the room.

'Mr Boyd, how do you do that?' asked Sy. 'I can't do that. What's the secret?'

'Only pissy people from out east say "Mr Boyd". I'm Buzz, and not ashamed of it. How do I do what, Mr Vice President?'

'Sit there with a smile on your face, yet radiating absolute anger and – I don't know – contempt. The more you smile, the scarier you look. How do you do it?'

'I dunno. Natural talent, I guess. Enjoy your suite, anyway, I've got a pissy little room overlooking the car park. But I guess Rome seems in better shape than I'd expected.'

'Well, Mr Boyd – Buzz – this isn't really Rome, you know. This is just a hotel. All the broken-down stuff out there, all the stuff with the roofs gone – that's ancient Rome. You should take some time out, give it a visit. You might surprise yourself . . .'

'The hotel suits me fine, Mr Vice President. I haven't seen a whole lot of Europe, but what I have seen is enough.'

'Here we go . . .'

'No we don't. I guess there's nothing you like more than hanging around art galleries in Paris, or going to the opera to see a bunch of Italian fags. I accuse you, Mr Vice President.

I accuse you of watching polo and knowing all the names of the British royal family. How do you plead?'

Cantor whinnied – the kind of noise a thoroughbred race-horse would make if it was trying to laugh at a joke it didn't find funny.

'OK. Guilty as charged. But when did it become un-American to understand old Europe?'

'When they gave up on the rest of the world, I guess. We're here to cut some quiet deals. I get it. And if the president wants us to do that, I guess he's got his reasons, and I'm fine with that. But Europe generally? It's just thousands of miles of New York, so far as I'm concerned. A whole *continent* of New York. And the people? Soft, pacifist, work-shy, left-wing atheists who are scared of the future. It's a continent of perverts. My wife originally came from over here, and she knows. They don't make anything, they haven't got any convictions to have the courage of – and they wouldn't, even if they did have. Give me the Russians, the Chinese, even the Indians, any day. This place was the future once. But it isn't any more. I say let's get the job done and get home as fast as we can.'

Sy Cantor yawned. Perhaps the head of homeland security was going to be amusing after all. At least he'd have a good store of anecdotes for when he got back to DC.

'Very eloquent, Buzz. I don't entirely disagree, but let's remember why we're here. Europe is frankly rancid with terrorists – the French jihadis who went to Syria, the Egyptian plotters in Rome, the Pakistani deobandis in Britain. But they've still got intelligence services over here, and we need everything they've got to give us a fighting chance of defending ourselves. Who knows what the Brits will do next – out of the EU, nearly lost Scotland – but their next leader, apparently, will be one of the delegates they've sent to this conference. So, in words a Wyoming boy like you will understand, let's squeeze their balls.'

'Well, I never thought I'd hear some sound common sense from a Jewboy New York lawyer. We live and learn. But set my mind at rest on one subject, Sy – I can call you Sy' – it was not a question. 'What are *you* doing here? Me, I understand. I'm the security guy, along with the CIA. But I don't understand why the president went to all the trouble of sending you over here to size up a couple of possible future leaders of a third-rate power?'

'"Sy" is fine. And that's a fair point. My answer? He didn't put it this way exactly, but the president foresees a much closer relationship with the Brits in the years ahead. Now they're out of the EU, they've got no one to turn to but us. Corporate America is still going through a rough patch. We could do with the City of London humming "Yankee Doodle" a little more enthusiastically. They need to open up their socialised, out-of-date health service to US companies. Plus, Fox, Google and Netflix are just a few of our companies who would love to see the BBC broken up. And there's a lot more after that. Local government contracts, infrastructure work, offshore drilling . . .

'There's not much left of the British, Buzz. This is our moment. It'll be good for them, too – give them a place in the world, and some investment that isn't Chinese or those bastard Qataris. They just have to be led gently by the hand.

As you know, we've been working with that primping show-pony, their so-called Master, for years. Security's the least of it; I think the president wants to see whether our British friends have really delivered the country itself. Think of this, Buzz, as final payback for the White House in 1814.'

Buzz was impressed – if Sy was a Europe-lover, well then, America was in good hands – but still managed to look mildly contemptuous. It was, as he had said, a talent. 'See you at dinner. They'll be there?'

'They'd better be.'

The Happy Accident

The good politician wastes nothing, including misfortune.

The Master

The rain arrived in pencil-sized arrows of water, and within seconds the streets of Barker were half an inch deep. Orange-coloured brick buildings turned purple-brown. Night was falling, and a rumble of thunder echoed through the town. A tall, black-haired woman, water pouring down her back, was running from a supermarket entrance across the car park. She was screaming imprecations; the only thing that jarred about the scene was that she was wearing a clerical dog collar. She stopped. She began to hop on one leg.

Angela had had a squealing, honking, out-of-control, pig of a day. Sanity required that she thought about one thing at a time. But for eight hours, struggling through admin jobs, balancing books and placating parishioners, she had had Caroline on her mind. There was a bad taste in her mouth about the best thing that had ever happened to her. Something was wrong with Caro. She didn't really want her in Downing Street. That much had been clear before Rome. The more she thought about it, the more she realised that something had always been wrong. Caro was a blue-eyed angel with a golden gaze – but angels weren't fully human. Caro had distanced herself from Angela in recent months, and whenever Angela tried to confront her, an infuriatingly bland, self-possessed smile came onto her face. It was as if she was withdrawing into a cloud, a nimbus of her own charisma.

Angela could, most of the time, cope with that. But Caroline seemed finally to have lost touch with their family life together. She didn't do any of the shopping, or pay any of the bills, or more important, ask any normal questions about normal things. An orphan herself, Angela firmly believed that family was made, forged by willpower and love. It was not something you were simply handed. So she had made time to go with Caroline to see her parents, the dull and frosty Phillipses, in their overheated, chilly home, even though Caro never seemed to want to go. And by sheer dint of talking and pressing, she'd made Caro take an interest in the boys' homework, and even got her to recognise their friends. Family had to be worked at, strenuously. In recent weeks she'd come to fear that Caro simply didn't regard it as worth the effort. And if that was true, then surely they'd run out of road.

With these loud thoughts buzzing around her head, Angela had found the small connections that had held this day together beginning to come apart. To start with, her slightly battered, flaking debit card had been refused at the supermarket during the weekly shop. She made the necessary call; but of course she had forgotten her online password: nearly £2,000, for which she'd worked jolly hard, was apparently beyond her reach. Struggling at the checkout to find the notebook in which the password might have been written (but was not), she had dropped her phone. It promptly shattered. The checkout girl looked down and shook her head. She didn't seem upset. The screen was crystalline-mazed. The bloody thing was useless. Then the phone had rung nevertheless. Still shaking with frustration and being stared at by the rest of the supermarket queue, holding the crumbling glass tile to her ear, Angela heard the school secretary say that Nick, her older boy, was being kept behind for bullying and 'vandalism' — whatever that meant.

Leaving her shopping still piled on the belt — a man three back at the queue had shouted 'Shame on you!' — Angela had sprinted across the car park. She was drenched. The heel of one shoe snapped off. Kicking away the other, she had driven home in soaking stockinged feet. At least she would be there when Ben arrived from school. Then she'd go back for Nick. On the way home, she had stopped at the phone company's High Street store, hobbling wet and shoeless in from the pavement. A very calm Sikh man had pointed out that everything was her fault — that most of their customers either bought rubber cases for their phones or simply didn't drop them. Anyway, it would take weeks to replace. It had her contacts list, her diary for the weeks ahead, and a fat stash of photos. Had she backed everything up? Well, they could do that, at least. They'd need the password, of course. Not the online password, the other one. But because the screen was broken, she couldn't get into her phone to get at it.

The man smiled pityingly at her. There was no solution for

that. With a sinking heart, Angela left the phone with him anyway. By the time she had driven home she was shaking, probably with stress as well as cold. She splashed her way up to the front door. No lights on. She was desperate for a pee, and could murder a drink. She stabbed the lock with her key. It broke. The man across the road had a spare. The tarmac had torn her tights to pieces. Little pieces of wet, oily grit stuck to the soles of her feet. The man across the road was out. She really needed to pee. Angela shouldered her way past a laburnum bush, heavy with water, to the back garden, where she found – thank you, Lord – that she'd forgotten to lock the kitchen door. She dried her feet. She had her pee. She found Caroline's slippers. There were two bottles of Chablis in the fridge, screw tops. She unscrewed one. As she poured her second glass, she vaguely wondered what she had forgotten about. The house phone rang. It was Nick. He never normally sounded distressed, but he was plainly in tears. *'Please,* Mum, come as soon as you can.'

Just at that moment, Ben had come barging through the front door. He galumphed towards the stairs – his feet were currently too big for the rest of him to properly control – heading for the Xbox. Angela intercepted him, and kissed him hard on the sweaty crown of his head. There was no more pleasurable scent in the world than Ben's hair. Then she explained that she was off to get Nick, and headed back to the car. She clambered unsteadily in, and turned the key.

During the next few minutes Angela thought in a hard and concentrated way about what might have gone wrong with Nick. He'd had to cope with so much – his parents' divorce, a busy professional mother, several changes of address, the whole coming-out thing. Caroline gave him hugs and kisses, in a perfunctory way, but never her whole attention. In turn, Nick gave little away. Ever since he'd been a toddler his calm, expressionless face had been that of an old man who had seen much of the world, and been impressed by very little of it. His estranged father had called him 'Old Nick'. Angela had come to rely on his impassivity; sometimes it seemed to her as though he were the adult and she the striving, attention-seeking child. She remembered his now-famous fifth birthday party as she turned the car sharp left towards the school driveway.

Nicky had . . . Her thoughts were interrupted by a loud banging sound. She saw a blur in the rain, and something thumped across the windscreen before falling towards the kerb. Jamming on the brakes and turning the engine off, Angela got out of the car. She realised that she was still wearing Caroline's slippers. Something blue and silver was lying in front of her. The bicycle looked as if it had been subjected to major surgery. Its frame was badly bent, one wheel was crooked, and the other was missing altogether. There was a shatter of something silver on the road. It reminded Angela of her phone. The cyclist, on the other hand, seemed fine. She was lying in a comfortable-looking position on the pavement, legs and arms stretched out like a child making sand angels at the beach. She was an elfin girl with closed eyes and red hair.

Angela knew at once that she was dead. A passer-by, no one she recognised from the church, took her by the arm. A few minutes later the police car arrived. By now there was a small crowd. People were gasping and wailing. 'She stinks of drink,' somebody said.

The policewoman was one of Angela's parishioners. She spoke kindly. 'I'm so sorry, vicar, but I'm going to have to ask you to stand to one side and blow into this.' Then she arrested Angela, not quite as kindly.

Twenty minutes later Angela was sitting in a police cell. She'd been told she should call her lawyer. The dead girl hadn't been wearing a helmet, but she'd had lights and a reflective belt. One of the witnesses, who'd been driving behind Angela, had said that she hadn't indicated. To her shock, she found that she didn't dare call Caroline. Had things become that bad between them? Instead, she called Nick. But she found she didn't know what to say to him, so she just told him to go home and look after Ben.

Once upon a time a small suburban police station on the outskirts of Barker, washed by the dark and the rain, would have been a million miles away from the centres of power; but that time had long passed. Just half an hour after Angela had been admitted, the newsdesk of the *Daily Mirror* received a quiet phone call from Peter Quint, and tweeted the story. Among those to whose attention it was brought was the Master in faraway Rome, who was halfway through a workout in the opulent, over-decorated gymnasium of the Hotel Excelsior Splendide. He leaned forward and slowed the treadmill down. Then, still on it, he did a little jig of pleasure.

A Frank Talk

*The top politician who doesn't intend to be prime minister isn't
a top politician.*

The Master (while still young)

David Petrie had not particularly wanted to travel
with Caroline Phillips, but now he was pleased that he had.
The first-class cabin of the Airbus was virtually empty, and
the minute he had put aside his paperwork with a theatrical
groan, so had she. How could he exorcise the memory of that
earlier, ill-starred flight to Italy with Ella? He turned to Caro
with a broken smile, at his most gallant.

'Well, my fair enemy – can I tempt you to a glass of champagne and a little light conversation?'

'Thanks for the fair. And yes, you can. And if we can't talk
across an empty first-class seat, where can we talk? So, my
turn first. You've been against me from our first hours in
Parliament. Why was that?'

'Because I'm in this game to get to the top, to play it as
well as I can. And everyone told me that of all my colleagues,
you were the one who was better than me – the one who

could stop me. Come on, Home Secretary, you may be a very nice woman, but you're a politician, and you know how it is.'

Petrie, who had rejected champagne in favour of a brandy and soda, drained his glass and fell silent. He twisted in his seat so he was looking directly at Caroline. Most people who did this close-up flinched; not from her beauty, but from her questioning candour – those clear blue eyes, those acrobatic eyebrows. But Davie just stared back at her, intent, comfortable.

'But you know what, Mistress Phillips? You can have it. You can have the whole damned lot. OK, so I'm here for the same reason you're here. The Master wants us here, aye? He wants us to meet the vice president. So what do we deduce from that, Home Secretary? I tell you what – we deduce that this is big potatoes. Top tomatoes. It means the president himself's involved. *He knows our names*. He's interested in whatever challenge, whatever deal, awaits us over there. How did that happen? Do you know? I don't. My guess is, three reasons – the Master, the Master, the Master. Many questions, only one answer. But for me, at any rate, I've just realised, it's all becoming a joke. For me, it's too late.'

Caroline replied, 'I wonder, Mr P, if perhaps you're just a little bit drunk. You seem unusually . . . passionate. Not like you. I imagine we've been sent for some kind of test – some test of loyalty or of ruthlessness – and I assume that, as so often before, we're meant to compete with one another. But you understand all of that, Mr Petrie. If you didn't, you wouldn't have said that I can "have it". That's very kind of you, but I'm not sure I want "it" either. I'm here because I'm interested. I just want to know what happens next.'

Petrie smiled again. He leaned forward and touched Caro on the arm. He'd never been less drunk in his life. 'I want to know what happens next, too. Perhaps we can work together after all.'

'The Master wouldn't like it.'

'No, he wouldn't.'

'Interesting thought, though.' And she turned back to the thick file of human incompetence and misery she'd been given to deal with.

As the plane banked into its final descent to Leonardo da Vinci airport, Caro twisted towards Davie and asked him, 'What do you mean when you say it's too late for you? You're as ruthless a politician as I've ever known. You don't just shrug and give up.'

'I'm surrendering. My hands are up – look. The thing is, Caroline, I'm guilty of a failure of love.'

Of all the answers she had expected, this was one that hadn't passed through her mind at all. She didn't even know what it meant. Instead she asked: 'David Petrie, what's your Achilles heel? What's your fatal flaw?' She leaned forward. 'We all have one. Everybody in politics has one thing, hidden inside them, which one day will bring them down. What's yours?'

'The game – I don't love the game enough. I don't love it beyond everything else.'

'That I've seen before. Alan Johnson. Alistair Darling. Personally, Petrie, I think you're being too kind to yourself. I think your flaw is a lot more common than that.'

He smiled and raised his eyebrows.

'I think your flaw is that you're led by your cock. You're a pretty man, but you're a simple one, too.'

Davie was annoyed. 'I'd say that's a simplistic woman's explanation. I might even use the lesbian word. But since we're talking frankly, what about you? What's your secret weakness?'

'My charisma. My charm. Everybody — well, almost everybody — falls for me. It's all they see. But what they don't see is that I don't care.'

'Care for what? The game?'

'Oh no, the game is interesting. It keeps us going. No, I mean I don't care about anybody else, not really. I can fake it so bloody easily, but I find almost everybody *intolerably* boring.'

Davie nodded. The plane trip had been well worth it. 'I think what you mean, Caroline Phillips, is that you are a psychopath. Just what we need in a prime minister.'

The black-suited man waiting for them in the arrivals hall held a placard reading 'HM government ministers'. Two carabinieri motorcyclists were revving their engines just in front of their limousine. Once they were settled inside, the driver handed Davie an envelope. 'Open please, it is for both of you.'

Inside it was a brief, handwritten note from the Master himself. It instructed them, after they'd checked in, to make their way to the Niccolò Machiavelli private dining room, where 'some gentlemen will be waiting for you. Please be with us no later than 8.30 p.m.'

'Mysterious,' said Caro.

'Peremptory,' said Davie.

'Should we?' said Caro.

'We have to,' said Davie.

'Do we?' said Caro.

'He'll be furious,' said Davie.

'And?' said Caro.

'Fair point,' said Davie, and tapped the driver on the shoulder. 'Piazza da Santa Cecilia, Trastevere,' he said. 'Roma Sparita.'

'Not hotel?' asked the driver.

'Not hotel,' said Davie.

The sudden detour was worth it, if only to watch the motorcycle escort heading off in the direction of the hotel, then circling round and chasing them, followed by a bellowed conversation through the window of the car as the bikes and the Mercedes sped along the bank of the Tiber.

'Red?'

'Bianco.'

'The melon?'

'Bruschetta.'

'The fettuccine with truffles is famous.'

'The ravioli.'

'Are you being deliberately perverse?'

'No, just honest. Food is too important to play games about.'

'Well, at last we agree on something.'

'Can I suggest, Mr Petrie . . .'

'Davie.'

'Can I suggest, David, that we agree about something else? Tonight, we turn our phones off. The Master and his friends will ruin our evening if we let them.'

'You're bolder than I'd expected, I admit it.'

But at that moment Caro, whose eyes had been flickering towards her mobile, which was shouldering itself around uneasily on the table and making tiny, mouse-like noises, seized it and stabbed it into life.

'I'm sorry, David, but it's my partner, Angela. Two missed calls. And half a dozen from the Master. And texts. Something's happening. Just give me one second.'

Caro's side of the conversation consisted mainly of gasps, moans and 'Oh my God's. Davie pulled faces intended to express concern and interrogation; Caro waved him away. She smiled – at some level she didn't mean the expressions of shock. Still, by the time the call had ended she had changed colour. Her lively, tanned pink had faded to old candle-wax, and was heading towards grey.

'Angela's had the most terrible accident. She's killed someone. On the road. An accident. Obviously. An accident. But she'd been drinking. Obviously. Oh my God, what a terrible bore. I'm going to have to go home this minute.'

Davie found himself voicing thoughts – clear, fast, direct – that later made him wonder if he'd been a better pupil of the Master's than he'd realised.

'You can't possibly stand by her, Caroline. You can't go home. You're the Home Secretary. Drink driving has become one of those things that are simply indefensible. If you go back now, you'll destroy everything you've worked for. The most sensible thing you can do is give a bland statement, let the law take its course, and do your best to look after the kids.'

'Look after the kids?'

'Well, Angela's going to go to jail, of course. How can we have a Home Secretary who stands by a partner who's in jail for killing someone because she was pissed? For Christ's sake,

Caroline, get a grip. You can be kind to her in private. I expect you'll need to get some kind of live-in help for the children, but you can do your bit too. What you can't do is rush back and stand by your woman. That's just common sense.'

'Is it? It feels like treachery to me. In the plane earlier, you said you couldn't carry on because you're guilty of a failure of love; that the game isn't worth it. I said I didn't care enough. Maybe we were both mistaken. At any rate, duty calls, and for once it calls me back.

'All right. But promise me this at least. Send her a message. Tell her you love her – whatever. But stay here in Rome tonight. Eat with me. At least think this through. And for Christ's sake, Caro, stand by me while we deal with those bloody Americans.'

Caroline said nothing. But she picked up a piece of bruschetta and bit into it. She felt very hungry indeed.

Meanwhile, the bloody Americans were bloody angry. The Niccolò Machiavelli dining room was on the fifth floor of the hotel; it seemed that the Florentine philosopher had a taste for fuchsia velour and modish photographs of urban decay in Detroit and Chicago. Sy Cantor had consumed two peach Bellinis. Buzz Boyd, who didn't drink, had downed about a gallon of Coke Zero, and was belching with irritation. Neither man was used to being kept waiting, and the Master, still pink and smelling of pine shower gel after his session in the gym, was finding it hard to calm them down. Two British ministers were now nearly an hour late, and the police reported that they had told their driver to take them to Trastevere, where they had left him. Neither was answering his texts, an unheard-of rudeness.

A Frank Talk

'Guys, guys! Look, I think I know what's happened. About an hour ago I got a message telling me that the home secretary's partner – you know, guys, she's not one for the guys, I'm sure your guys have told you that – well, she's been arrested in a fatal drink-driving case. Terrible for Caro Phillips. She'll have to cut her loose. But guys, this gives us something to hold over her. It'll make her more malleable, not that she isn't . . .'

Buzz walked over, invaded the Master's personal space as if he were General Patton crossing the Rhine, and placed his broad, faintly pimpled nose right up against the Master's. 'Well, it seems that she's not malleable enough to turn up for dinner. Where are those crazies?'

'Clearly she's going through some kind of personal crisis. Come on, guys, we've all been there. It's part of life. My guess is that David Petrie – you remember, the one who's backed America time and time again – has taken her off to talk some sense into her. My suggestion, guys, is that we give them a bit of time to sort themselves out. They'll be here just as soon as they can be. Meanwhile, there's a lot we can talk about in private. Let's not waste the time.'

Grumpily, the two Americans sat down at the table. As they were being served, the concierge arrived and whispered in the vice president's ear.

Sy flushed. 'No, sir, I most certainly did not "order a gladiator". It was probably that faggy Brit' – he waved his fork at the Master. Normally he would have gestured at Buzz; it would have made a much funnier story. But he was too angry.

The Master, however, had a great talent for ignoring the inconvenient and the unpleasant. 'Guys. Let's talk about the BBC.

I mean, have you heard them on Israel? They're completely bloody unreconstructed. I was talking to Lachlan . . .'

'Really?' broke in Buzz, suddenly interested. 'I thought you and he – you know –'

The Master didn't even blush. 'Oh no, that was long ago. Ridiculous. And completely forgotten. No, Lachlan was saying . . .'

And so the meal continued.

Meanwhile, in Trastevere, another meal had ended. Davie had always been told that Caro was charismatic, that she had an irresistible appeal – something to do with candour, something to do with beauty, and perhaps vulnerability too. Even she had told him she was irresistible. But until that evening, he had never really felt it himself. Over the food and the guarded conversation – neither fully trusted the other, not yet – he felt himself melt until she possessed him. Led by his cock, indeed! Caroline, meanwhile, was surprised by how unconcerned she felt about Angela's awful situation. It was something she understood, but no longer really felt. This Rome was a place of velvet and diamonds, whose very night air was scented with wonderful possibilities. She noted that Petrie was doting on her with a little boy's appeal for recognition, and this warmed and amused her. Yes, yes, led by his cock. And what happened next is their business, not ours.

In the Gallery

God, the Italians really are impossible. Some nice stuff, but impossible people.

The Master

Later, at the hotel, a terse note from the Master had been pushed under the door of Caro's room. She would have been taken aback by its contents, had she noticed it and read it; but she did not. By the bed there was a silver-topped trolley with a bottle of champagne, a bowl of fruit and a stiff cream envelope which contained invitations to various galleries and monuments, with the special compliments of Antonio Manca Graziadei, the Italian minister for culture. Caro was not drunk – living with Angela meant that she was never drunk – but she felt reckless. Above all, she felt an intense curiosity . . .

She woke the following morning with a strong sense of things not being right, of unresolved disasters all around. She remembered Angela, first of all, and then what Davie had told her to do. She wondered what the Master thought. There was an unfamiliar scent in the bed. She remembered about Davie, opened her eyes, half-moaned and half-yawned, and rolled over. If you had to be led by anything . . . But there was no one else in the room. It was already late. She pushed herself out of bed.

A mile and a half away, with the dew still on the grass, the Villa Borghese, one of the most opulent caskets of art and sculpture on the little green planet, had opened its doors early by special arrangement. David Petrie was standing in front of a terrifying figure, pursuing a naked woman. Her hands, stretched upwards, were visibly turning into twigs and leaves. Davie had no intention of reading his guidebook, but he understood that in front of him was a cruel challenge: in those veins, liquid marble blood was running; the lungs of the figures were nothing more than stone, yet they were breathing, and one of them was dying. She was becoming wood, undergoing an agonising metamorphosis. Air became stone, wood petrified too; and then flesh became stone. He remembered Ella as she spiralled downwards through the waters of the lagoon, a lump of marble attached to her neck. Really, who was the psychopath?

'Clever guy.'

Davie turned round. A squat, dark-suited man with light-blue eyes in a fleshy red face was smiling at him.

'Oh, yes. It's . . . quite something.'

'Bernini. The master propagandist of the counter-Reformation; on a different side from you Scots at the time, I think. Are you here to size up the enemy?'

'Uh, well, no. Just a bit of early-morning self-improvement. As it happens, I'm a Roman Catholic myself. Sort of.'

In the Gallery

'No kidding? I guess I should have known that, Mr Petrie. It is Mr Petrie, isn't it?'

'That's me. But how did . . .'

'Sorry, I should have introduced myself. I thought maybe you'd recognise me. Barnaby Jonathan Boyd, director of Homeland Security. Most people call me Buzz.'

'Yes, of course. We're supposed to be meeting, aren't we?'

'Mr Petrie, as you very well know, we were supposed to meet last night. For supper. I guess you were making some kind of point?'

'We had other plans.'

'An interesting use of "we". The Master, as your people call him, had given us to understand that you and Mrs Phillips were deadly rivals. My view, though it seems the White House doesn't share it, was that on paper at least you were our man. We came here to do some business with you. Your country needs a big dose of investment, your government needs some good economic news, and we need your help with some . . . small matters. You understand all of that, Mr Petrie. So how come you and Mrs Phillips are thumbing your noses at us?'

Davie walked slowly around the statue, and then headed off to the next room. He was concentrating on not losing his temper.

'There's lots more I want to see,' he said over his shoulder, 'and not much time. Just because Caroline Phillips is my rival, it doesn't mean she's my enemy. And I think you grossly underestimate how difficult it would be for either of us to sell a much closer American alliance to our party. Labour might have changed, but not that much.'

Buzz appeared to be barely listening. He gestured at another sculpture, this time one of David about to loose his slingshot, his body twisted with effort and his face in a timeless grimace.

'There you go. That's the real thing. Back in the days when Europe could do this kind of stuff – the leading technology of the age – you would have been worth an alliance back then. Us, we've had more than two hundred years of democracy and economic success, but we've never had a Bernini.'

'I must say, Mr Boyd. I'm surprised. I hadn't expected you to be a man of . . . well . . .'

'Culture? I'm not. But Mr Petrie – and here we come to the point of this conversation – my wife is a woman of great learning and discernment. If I'm actually a little less rough than I choose to appear, it's all down to her. She's from your part of the world, you know.'

'You're married to a Scot?'

'She calls herself American these days – doesn't look back any more – but yes. And not just a Scot, Mr Petrie, but an Ayrshire lassie.'

Davie felt something stir inside him. 'Where in Ayrshire?'

'Right question. Little town called Glaikit. Now then. What's your next question, Mr Petrie?'

Davie's throat was suddenly dry. 'What was your wife's name? I mean, what was her name before she got married?'

'Right question again, Mr Petrie. Smedley. Her name was Betty Smedley. She was devoted to her father, Mr Petrie. *Devoted*. He was a teacher. But you know that.' It would be wrong to say that Buzz was poking Davie in the chest. It was more that he was tapping him. Hard taps. Although he was squat, Buzz was a big man. 'Yes, they spoke on the telephone almost every day. He gave Betty her love of literature, art. He gave Betty her curiosity. And her curiosity, Mr Petrie, was what made me fall in love with her. But it fell away, Mr Petrie. It all fell away like a building being demolished when that vile thing happened to her father, and of course to her grandmother too. She sought solace in the Church, and her faith has kept her alive. Over the years I've learned a lot from Betty about what you might call the world of the mind. Through her, I've come to respect Mr Walter Smedley, to understand what a remarkable man he must have been.'

'I think he was a remarkable man. He taught my children. I knew him. Slightly.'

'You knew him. Slightly. Don't get funny with me. I said that what happened to him was vile. Vile is a strong word, Mr Petrie. I don't forget vile.'

Crouched in the shadow of David about to slay Goliath, Davie felt his knees begin to go. At that moment he caught sight of another man in the small gallery, sitting quietly on a guard's chair with his legs folded, watching the two of them closely. The Master. What was he doing there? Didn't matter. The nick of time.

But when the Master unfolded himself and walked towards them, Buzz greeted him with a nod of acknowledgement.

The Master turned to Davie. 'I see you're having that conversation after all. Well, none of us can ever escape the past entirely. On which subject, Ella sends her regards.'

'Ella?'

'You do remember Ella, don't you?'

Now, at last, it was clear to Davie that he had been comprehensively set up — stitched up, ambushed and caught. What a fool. Time slowed down. He found himself standing outside, looking in at himself. If he'd lost control and urinated on the floor of the gallery, he wouldn't have been surprised.

'What do you want?' he asked, dry-mouthed.

Buzz looked at the Master, who replied for both of them. 'What we want is for you to help make Caroline Phillips the next leader of the Labour Party and prime minister of Great Britain. To do that, she has to distance herself from her girlfriend, and in doing that, she needs your wholehearted public support and private encouragement. When she wins, as she will, you will accept office as her foreign secretary. You will broker our new agreements, and you will help her every step of the way.

'Whatever else might happen between you is up to you; though the country loves a cheesy story. She has the charm, the charisma, which you lack. But you have a ruthlessness — as all three of us here know — which she doesn't.'

'Not me? It wasn't going to be me? Not ever?'

'No. Her. Question of character, you understand.'

Davie's first reaction was that none of this seemed nearly as bad as he'd feared. Do what they want. Help her up into a job that could only be done by monsters. His second reaction, however, was that what they were asking was impossible. He'd had it. There was nothing left inside. And anyway, he knew that Caroline was a good person, who would never, ever betray her soulmate.

'I'll try,' he said, 'but I don't think it can be done.'

'It can be done, Mr Petrie,' said Buzz, who looked entirely unsympathetic. 'And you will help to make it happen. Or I will personally tear off your testicles and choke you with them.'

'Goodness me,' said the Master, 'the conference starts in an hour. We're going to miss breakfast. Was that really necessary, Buzz? Shall we take a car back together? We can do the Caravaggios another time.'

A Clever Plan

The complicated plan rarely works; in politics, as in machinery, the fewer moving parts, in general, the better.

The Master

Davie found his room, stumbled into the shower, shaved and dried himself. He couldn't remember feeling this rough since he was a teenager, discovering shots. On the untouched bed someone had laid out his grey woollen suit, a fresh white shirt and a claret tie. He dressed, doused himself with Acqua di Parma, and headed downstairs for breakfast. He'd noticed before that all his sharpest thoughts came in the shower, as if something as simple as a hail of hot water on the cranium really did stimulate the brain.

Right now his mind was revolving around a single thought: Caro would save him. She wouldn't cut her partner loose. She'd stay loyal to this Angela. Cheers all round; the first gay PM. Though she'd more or less confessed to him that she was a psychopath, that was something the world never needed to know. There would be public outrage if Caroline dumped her partner. Her reputation would be shredded, surely? She had no need to do the US deal – no skeletons in that closet – and with Angela at her side, she'd have proved her independence from the Master. She just had to do the right thing. She had to stay strong.

For his part, he'd plead with her to cut Angela off, just as the Master had demanded. Caro would assume that he was doing it for the narrowest, sleaziest personal reasons – led by his cock – and she'd refuse. They'd fall out. Her disappointment and her contempt for him would be part of his justified punishment; he'd have tried to do what he was told, so he didn't need to worry about blackmail. He certainly wouldn't serve as foreign secretary; certainly wouldn't broker any deal. And because she wouldn't do what *they* asked, and nor would he, their whole plan would fail. If she would only stand firm, Britain would get, in Caroline Phillips, a new leader untainted by either the Master or the American deal.

As he headed downstairs to the breakfast area, shouldering past a dishevelled gladiator, he felt his mind race. He'd be absolutely open with Caro – tell her that she was the chosen one, explain what she'd have to do, give her his support, and tell her he was resigning from Parliament. She had a good tactical sense. She'd understand what was going on. She'd realise that this was the most important moment of her life. She'd brush his sleazy pleading about Angela aside. And she'd make the right decision; by refusing to disown her lover, she would save herself; by saving herself, she would save him. He'd get his honourable exit. The Master, having had two candidates, would be left with none.

She just had to do the right thing.

Feeling considerably brighter and sharper, Davie enquired of the restaurant manager where Mrs Phillips was sitting.

'She not here,' he shrugged.

She'd have taken breakfast up in her room, perhaps. She was due to speak. She'd be rehearsing her speech, or struggling with some paperwork. Of course she wouldn't have come down for breakfast; she, at least, was a professional.

He banged three times on her door. No answer. Beginning to feel flustered, he went back downstairs to the reception desk, and asked the concierge to phone her room. Again, a shrug, and when he rang there was no answer. Pulling rank, and explaining that it was a matter of political importance, he persuaded one of the hotel managers to return upstairs with him and open Caroline's door.

She just had to do the right thing.

In his head, spinning with dark dreams, Davie already knew what they'd find – the rumpled bed, the empty glasses scattered on the floor, and that beautiful, mature but almost flawless body lying naked, face-down, and lifeless.

But he was wrong. The room was lifeless, certainly – it had been cleaned, and the bed had been made. There were no cases, papers, clothes or any other sign of Caroline Phillips. Even her scent had vanished. She had disappeared.

Showtime

God, but I hate the House of Commons.

You know who

Caro flashed her pass and strode through the security barriers at Portcullis House. As she click-clacked towards the Despatch Box, the little coffee bar that serves the building's atrium, her colleagues put down their cups and stared at her. There were enemies here, as well as worshippers. At the little tables under the expensively rented fig trees, parliamentary officials, MPs and journalists circled, gossiped and conducted business. More political work, more real deal-making, goes on in the Portcullis atrium than in the lobby of the House of Commons – or in the chamber itself. Now it seemed that everyone was waiting for something, and was looking at Caro.

She immediately picked out the tall, portly figure of Quentin Royle, with his heavy black glasses and his slicked-back custardy hair; the hero of the hard left, who had in the past been fancied by many as a future leader of the party. Since her first days in the House he had regarded her with naked contempt.

'Going to let the rest of us in on the secret, Miss Caroline?'

'All in good time, Quentin. If I'm lucky enough to catch the speaker's eye, all will be revealed. No private briefings, I'm afraid.'

Royle had an ability to smile without a twitch of good humour or warmth. 'A word of advice, Miss Caroline. You've got a perfectly ordinary arse. The sun doesn't shine out of it, whatever you may think. You're not bloody unbeatable, you know. Today's *Evening Standard*, I'm very sorry to say, calls you a cheat and a hypocrite. "The home secretary shacked up with a jailbird." That's what it says. You may come to rue the fact that you never bothered to make any solid friends in this party.'

Caro felt the blood rush into her face and her heart begin to race. She mustn't show any weakness. She mustn't rush away, or stoop to abuse; almost certainly there would be journalists listening, or worse still, colleagues.

'Quentin, dear – I've always thought "Quentin" was a strange name for the people's hero, by the way, never mind "Royle" – you're beginning to sound like a grubby little gossip. And the *Standard* isn't out for hours yet.'

'Come on, Missy, don't –'

'Which means that if any nasty words like that are indeed in it, they must have come from a certain Mr Quentin Royle, and nobody else.'

'Don't you dare impugn . . .'

'*Impugn*? Oo la la. Careful, Quentin, or I might be tempted to complain to the chief whip about the tediously predictable misogynistic behaviour of some of my so-called brothers in the party. And Quentin, you might want to take a stiff brush to your shoulders, by the way.'

Quentin struggled for a response. 'Got a bit of toffee on your nose, Caroline?' was the best he could manage. She smiled, bowed slightly and walked towards the lifts with her head held high. That hadn't been so bad. A nearby backbencher who had been listening in gave her a surreptitious thumbs-up. But the truth was that Quentin Royle was wrong. Wrong about Angela, and wrong about Caro.

Mr Speaker, who had reverted to the grey wig, court trousers and silk stockings of tradition, drew himself up to his full five feet of self-certain splendour.

'Order, order! Personal statement, the home secretary. I call – Members must contain themselves, order! – the Right Honourable Member for Barker.'

Caro, still wearing the blue silk trouser-suit she'd bought for Rome, stood up. She'd never felt more comfortable in this strange, fusty little amphitheatre. It was crowded, and as usual her enemies were sitting behind her, on her own side of the House. Facing her, the shadow home secretary, with his ratlike teeth and claw hands, was hunched, ready to leap. And yet she felt that around the chamber there was more curiosity than hostility; and perhaps, even now, more friendliness than curiosity.

'Mr Speaker. As the House knows, I was meant to be in Rome this afternoon, at an international conference of great importance for the security and long-term prosperity of the British people. Before I say any more, I would like to place on record my profound apologies to all of my colleagues from Europe and North America for my sudden withdrawal. That conference was important. It still is important. But Mr Speaker, nothing is more important to me than my own honour, and the respect in which I hold this House. It therefore seemed paramount to me to lay before this honourable chamber certain facts, some of which have been well rehearsed in the media, and certain decisions which I have taken.'

From the Labour, Conservative, Liberal Democrat and Ukip benches there came the same mixed symphony of sympathetic mutterings, grunts of bewilderment and 'Get on with it' groans. A Conservative Member rose to interrupt. Caroline waved him away.

'As the House knows, my partner – indeed, my wife – the Reverend Angela Boswell, was arrested yesterday afternoon following a fatal road accident, and has subsequently been charged with the serious offence of driving with a blood alcohol level three times the legal limit. As home secretary, I cannot turn a blind eye to such an incident. Angela Boswell has been a loyal and close partner to me for many years. I believe she has also been a good and loyal servant of the Church of England, as her parishioners would confirm. But I have to say to the House that Angela Boswell has been battling with alcoholism for some time. I have done my utmost to support and help her to deal with this difficult problem. But it is with the utmost regret that I say, as home secretary, that she has brought her current problems entirely upon herself.

'Under the circumstances, I feel I ought to make it clear to the House that we have now separated entirely. The

Reverend Mrs Boswell will have her day in court, and I wish her every good fortune in the future. But I must also say that I hope and expect that the full force of the law will be exercised in this case, and no undue leniency granted because of the identity of the defendant. This was a terrible and serious crime, and deserves the sentence – including, should the court so decide, the custodial sentence – that would be applied in the normal way. That, too, I support.'

There was a desperate scrambling in the press gallery overhead, as journalists rushed to report the story. Down in the chamber, the music was entirely sympathetic. But Caroline had not finished.

'I have not finished. Mr Speaker, the whole House has expressed its gratitude to the prime minister for the remarkable service he has done his party and the country. But we are all aware that, for good and honourable reasons, the Member for Dunton has decided to step aside. Today, having dealt with my own painful personal issue, I would like to make it clear that I intend to stand for the leadership of my party, and if I have the good fortune to be successful, I hope to be invited to be the next prime minister of this country.' There were roars and whoops from the Labour benches, theatrical groans and dismissive wavings of order papers from the opposition side. The Conservative leader, Sir Boris Johnson, shook his balding head and jabbed his thumb downwards.

A Stranger in Barker

Go into politics, and the only people you are certain to hurt are your kids.

The Master

Nicky was smiling. Yet again, he hadn't gone to school. He stared through the heavy rain at the Toyota Prius gliding away from the house. It had been the second visit from social services, and the second clear home win to Nicholas Boswell. He wasn't quite seventeen, but he knew he came across as older. It wasn't so much his incipient moustache as his heavy, stolid, expressionless face and his calm voice. Ben had left for school on time as usual, but there was no legal obligation for Nicky to attend, and the fierce little woman from the council had found it hard to suggest that he wasn't a responsible adult. The house was clean, he'd cooked breakfast and cleared it away. Since his mother had been gone, there were no empty bottles lying around. The council woman had said she was going to come back with a colleague for a second opinion, but Nicky had the feeling that the fight had gone out of her.

He could manage fine. The only problem would be money;

Angela quickly ran through what she got from the Church every month, and although he had discovered her debit card and knew her pin, the £2,000 that had been in her account had already almost gone. He'd phoned Caroline several times, but she hadn't picked up. Probably she didn't have his number on her mobile, so she didn't know who was ringing. And she had a big political thing on. Still, he wanted to see her. And not just for the money.

Really, he thought, his mother ought to be out on bail. They should have just banned her from driving until the case came up. But the paparazzi had been hanging around the house for days. They'd rung the doorbell again and again. When Angela had closed the curtains, they'd knocked on the windows. They'd got into the back garden by climbing the neighbours' fence, and had started taking pictures of the kitchen. Angela, inevitably, had had a few, and had stormed out and grabbed some guy's camera and smashed it. Then the police turned up – they'd ignored all Angela's pleas to help keep the hacks at bay, but the minute a Nikon got cracked they were all over the house like insects. Angela, in her clerical collar, had gone out and slapped a six-and-a-half-foot-high constable. It was just, as she said, an open-handed slap, not a punch, but they arrested her anyway. The pictures had been great.

Nicky couldn't make head or tail of it all, but one thing he did know was that Mum clearly wasn't coming back any time soon. At least the photographers had gone away. He and Ben were under age, so there was no money to be made from shots of them.

He dug his hands into his pockets and flexed his legs. Things were going all right, given the circs. Ben was moody and kept telling him to eff off; but Ben was fourteen, and although he was big for his age, he hadn't yet reached puberty. It was understandable if he had things on his mind.

Nicky saw an alien car enter the close. By 'alien' he meant that it couldn't possibly have come from around here. An old Land Rover, covered in rust patches and splatters of bright red soil, it was the kind of car that would normally have accommodated half a dozen wet and overexcited dogs; but there were no farmers and no landowners around Barker. The driver accelerated past their house, screeched to a halt and then reversed back, dangerously. Out of the car stepped a tall, plain woman with an enormous bosom. This, Nicky thought, must be the other woman from the council. She looked a lot more formidable than her predecessor. The bell rang angrily, and he nipped downstairs to open the door.

'Benjamin? No, you must be Nicholas. My name is Elizabeth. But you can call me Lady Broderick.'

'Yes, I'm Nicky. Are you from the council?'

'No, Nicky, I'm not from the council. In fact I've come to help you escape from the council. You can't stay here. Not with what's happened to your poor mother and that ghastly girlfriend of hers. I was very fond of the vicar, and I always thought I'd try to help her out if I could. Now, can you get everything you'll need into a single suitcase?'

'I . . . No, I can't. Where you taking me? And what about Ben? I'm not going anywhere without him.'

Lady Broderick marched into the house. 'You're going to do what you are told, young man. Angela was always hopeless.

We'll pick Ben up at school. I want you to pack a suitcase for yourself – just the essentials, clothes, gumboots, books, that kind of thing – and one for Ben as well. You can do that, can't you?'

'Yes, I suppose. But why?'

'Because you're coming back to Pebbleton with me. Warm rooms, plenty of space to play outside, good old-fashioned cooking – not me, Cook. And you know the schools already. And then we'll see what happens to your mummy, but at least she's not going to have to worry about you pair for a while.'

Nicky opened his mouth, and then closed it again. He had been about to protest that he liked it in Barker, and that he and Ben could manage, and that Caro would help, and that he didn't want to go back to Pebbleton. But then he realised that none of it was true. Caro wasn't going to help. Ben had got hold of her a couple of days before, and she'd apparently said to him, 'Ben, I am not your mother.' Nicky had pushed this out of his mind, and tried not to dwell on it. But if Caro cared about them, she would have been here by now. And he remembered how much Angela had always told them she liked Lady Broderick. He did want to go. He turned to go upstairs and begin packing, but then paused.

'All right. But I have two conditions. I'm not going to go to school any more. And I'm going to call you Elizabeth.'

'You're a very cheeky young man. No, to the school – you bloody well will go. But yes, if you insist, to Elizabeth.'

Two hours later the battered Land Rover, which did indeed smell strongly of wet labrador, was charging south-west across country towards Devon.

The Triumph of the Fourth Estate

If the hacks are as one, then it's horseshit.

The Master

The media coverage of Caroline's speech was almost unanimous: she had acted bravely, and shown herself to be not just another member of the cynical and out-of-touch political establishment. The *Guardian*'s political editor, Jonathan Freedland, wrote that 'Mrs Phillips has not tried any special pleading or expected the country to treat her differently just because she happens to be gay. Her personal courage reminds one of . . . Well, it doesn't remind one of anybody else. And that, surely, is the point.'

The Times leader writer felt that 'If Mrs Phillips' partner is found guilty of the crime of which she is accused, she will have caused just as much hurt and destruction to another family as if she had walked out with a gun and shot a cyclist down. As for Mrs Phillips herself, she seems to be a modern, forward-looking enthusiast for Britain's relationship with America, and we welcome her candidacy for the leadership of her party, and the country. Certainly she cannot do worse than her woeful predecessor.'

The Triumph of the Fourth Estate

The *Sun*'s headline read: 'Sexy Caroline: I'm Free!'

Only the *Daily Mail* did not join in the general enthusiasm. Its front page asked the question: 'Is She Really Gay?' In an opinion piece, the very elderly Sir Stephen Glover referred to widespread rumours that 'Mrs Phillips' much-advertised Sapphic enthusiasm is just a clever marketing ploy. The names of various possible boyfriends have been circulating at Westminster for some time. If she does indeed win her party's leadership, and then brings a boyfriend with her into Downing Street, she will have proved herself just another cynical female con-artist.'

Still, for the moment there was a general groundswell of warmth and affection for Caro that couldn't be misunderstood.

Soon afterwards, Alwyn Grimaldi called a special conference of the Labour Party at Stoke-on-Trent, where, with clear majorities from the parliamentary party and the socialist clubs, plus the support of the public-sector trade unions, Caroline Phillips trounced her only serious rival, Gloria de Piero. To widespread surprise, David Petrie chose not to stand, but instead called on his supporters to back Mrs Phillips, whom he described as 'a loyal comrade who understands the reality of power and has developed policies that will enable a modernised Labour Party to achieve its ends'. There were rumours that the new leader intended to appoint him foreign secretary.

A Minor Failure of Empathy

We have the finest jails in the Western world.
                    Caroline Phillips, home secretary

Angela stared at the green-painted walls of her cell,
a Good News Bible in her hands, a small, dusty transistor
radio stuttering beside her, and failed to digest the news about
Caro's elevation. She was allowed a small television as well as
the radio, and she watched and listened obsessively. None of
it made the slightest sense. Caro was a good person. Angela
realised now that she had been moving away, turning off the
lights, for weeks. But she could never have foreseen that
speech. Not that scale of betrayal. Caro might not be very
high on the empathy scale, but she had always been a good
person. Ever since they had met at school she had been
Angela's rock. Far more than just her lover, she had been her
best friend, her confidante, her pal in the great adventure of
life, her other mother – her better mother. Never cruel,
never a liar.

It was inconceivable to Angela, even in the darkest hours
of her longest wakeful nights, that Caroline could believe what

she had told the House of Commons. Angela had humiliated herself by repeatedly texting. She had called and left countless voice messages, all too conscious that she was unable to avoid a broken, whingeing tone. She was sorry, sorry, sorry. She just wanted to talk, talk, talk. She didn't want to put any pressure, pressure, pressure on dear, dear, dear Caro. And yet, hour after hour, day after day, not a single message came back. Nothing. Nothing. Nothing.

Angela shuddered and curled into a ball, feeling as if there was a pulsating tumour inside her. It was so hot in the cell during the daytime that she had to strip to her underwear; and it was so cold at night that she found herself rapping on the door, begging for more blankets. A prison-service psychiatrist visited her, but what she said had made no sense. Her lawyer came, and after Angela had insisted that she would plead guilty, left again. There was no news about the trial date.

By now, Angela was quite sure that she was going mad. At last she knelt on the floor and prayed. She wanted to know what she had done in the past that had led her to this disaster. Had she always been this way, weak and pathetic, even as she performed like a clown in public? Sometimes she felt that God was answering her – a wrathful God with furrowed brows, a list of her misdemeanours in His hand. Caro had *always* been a good person. Angela would kill herself if she didn't hear something soon. Day after day, there was Caro on the television, smiling that same bewitching smile, staring out at her, looking through her, talking, talking, talking.

A week into her incarceration, Angela had a visit from Lady Broderick. She described Caro as a heartless bitch, and said that she had taken charge of the boys. Angela was helplessly grateful for that, at least. Nothing made any sense at all.

Nicky, meanwhile, found living in Pebbleton Hall a much easier and more pleasant experience than he'd expected. The old lady turned up for breakfast and supper, but most of the time the house was run by servants who apparently didn't have names, but job descriptions – Cook, Gardener, Help. It was a cold life, but an easy one, and Nicky discovered, not that he was sly – he'd always known that – but that he enjoyed his slyness. On the surface he remained polite, well scrubbed and hard-working. In his real life, he searched out and found new consolations – ketamine, skunk and legal highs, freely available after school. Once or twice he slipped upstairs after toast and cornflakes for a mug of vodka and milk. There was always enough money lying around in Lady Broderick's desk for him to keep topped up with vodka. Surfing the web, he discovered a wasteland of sexual cruelty. And so, crookedly, he began to grow up.

Lady Broderick seemed to think that she'd saved him, taken him to a little green Devonian Eden. Nicky slithered delightedly through it, a snake gorging on forbidden knowledge. He saw very little of Ben, who had been bullied during his first few days back at their old school, but had hit back with his fists and feet, and was already rising through the ranks as a promising young bully himself.

Only once, during a *Newsnight* interview, had Caro been challenged about what had happened to the children in her previous relationship. Not missing a beat, she had replied that they were 'being looked after by good friends, and very happy'. Luckily, she wasn't asked if she ever saw them. Some journalists tugged away at the story; but nobody had heard of old Lady Broderick, and Angela was of course unavoidably detained elsewhere. So two young lives quietly curdled, further examples of the inevitable collateral damage of parliamentary politics.

Making Good

Land. That's the thing. Everything else drifts away — shares,
bonds, bits of paper, digital scoring of all kinds. Even houses go
out of fashion, fall down. But land. The old guys understood
that.

The Master (getting above himself)

Callum Petrie was an outside kind of boy. After foot-
ball practice he'd head up to the brae, ramble through the
plantings — spruce and larch, mostly — and fill his pockets
with brambles, and rub dock leaves on his shins for the nettle
stings. He'd found a badger sett, and the corpses of birds killed
by a hawk, and once the dried-up body of a sheep that had
lost its way. The wool was as fluffy and fresh as if it were still
alive. Mostly, he let his mind run far away, to impossible places
and forgotten stories. He was William Wallace, hiding from
the English. He was a wounded clansman, with the redcoats
on his tail. He was a ridiculed inventor, with flying tanks and
jet-pack soldiers. Following the stories inside his head, he'd
break into a run, slipping and panting along old banks of earth
on the edge of the forest until his legs ached, then diving

374

behind roots and bushes. Callum was fourteen, old enough, he realised, to know better. Sometimes he felt ashamed of his long 'jaunts', as his mother called them, but life without them would be impossible – airless, headachy, dreich.

So his first reaction when he saw the tall, unfamiliar figure of his father, climbing up the brae, hunched against the wind, with his hands in his pockets, was a feeling of shame. He shouldn't be wasting his time daydreaming up here. He should be doing something useful. Dad would want to know what was up. His second reaction was annoyance, for beside his father he could see the tall, gawky, figure of his younger brother, Fergus. Fergus was an inside kind of boy. He listened to his music. He had even given up football. He had no right to be here, led by Dad up to Callum's private domain. It was an intrusion.

Davie spotted him standing by the side of the woods – his scarlet and black football strip stood out clearly.

'Hey, boy. Out here for the birds?'

'No, Dad. I was just walking about.'

'Well, there's peewits a' around. Golden plovers, too. And I swear I could hear some grouse back on the brae.'

Both of the boys thought Davie sounded different. Normally he didn't talk to them much; they'd got the idea they were in the way, and Mary didn't disabuse them. They were fond of their father, in a general, abstract way. But, as Fergus put it, he never made an effort. He didn't know their friends, or even which subjects they were doing for Highers. To ferret Fergus out of his room, and then drag him up here to find Callum, was unheard of, and made both of them slightly uneasy.

'Sit down, lads. I've got some toffees in my pockets. Look out there – grand view, isn't it?'

And it was. From the top of the brae you couldn't see Glaikit at all. There were only undulating blue hills, darkly marked with woodland. The spidery remnants of a couple of Ayrshire's old pits, closed since the strike, could just be made out. But as the sunlight fell slowly on the bings, they seemed ancient and mysterious, not modern and mundane.

'Do you know your history, boys? Do they teach you in that school what a great land this is? Do you ken that Robbie Burns himself cut land over there, to the right, with his plough, before he daundered off to Edinburgh, leaving lasses in half the farm houses for miles around greeting for him? And see that wee house peeking up beyond the kirk spire? It's not so wee at all. That's where Jimmy Boswell, the greatest journalist of all, grew up, scared witless of his father. Hey, lads – you've never been scared of me, I hope, have you?'

The answer was no. You couldn't be scared of a vacancy. Fergus sat motionless, his knees drawn up to his chin, wondering what the old guy was up to, with nothing to say. But Callum found the words tumbling out.

'Aye, they taught us about Burns. The school took us to Mauchline. We learnt "To a Mouse". I havenae heard o' the other fellow. But Da, this was William Wallace country, too. He was burning and killing all over, but only the English. And there were moss troopers.'

Davie was impressed. 'You know a bit of your history, then, Callum. Is this your playground, then, this bit wood?'

His son assented.

'So you know there's an old track coming round the other side of the hill, up through the woods?'

Callum pointed. 'It ends there, just on the other side of the gate.'

'Well, see here – all this flat bit of ground, the grassy bit, between yon fence and the start of the heather? Well, boys, it's ours.'

Callum was mildly offended. 'Da, it's mine mostly. Fergus prefers indoors. I've been coming here for years.'

Davie shook his head. 'No, I don't mean like that. I mean it really *is* ours. I've bought it.'

Fergus raised his head. 'That's daft. Who'd want a useless bit of lumpy grass? Just the sheep.'

'It's not useless, Fergus. Come on – you've just been admiring the view. Imagine looking out at this every evening, with the rustle of the woods, and the deer and the birds at your back.'

Callum couldn't keep a quaver out of his voice. 'You mean you're going to build a house up here? Where it's all quiet, and wild, and unspoiled? There's going to be cement mixers, and lorries, and pipes, and all that?'

Davie felt a little disappointed by Callum's reaction, but also quietly impressed. Once he'd have been angry. No longer. Mostly what he felt these days was tired. He didn't feel guilty, particularly. Ella had been a bad, bad woman, and she would have come to a bad, bad end sooner or later. When he'd had power he'd done some good things. Good man, bad man? The strength of politics, the Master had once said, was that it got bad people – ambitious people, angry people, damaged people

— doing good things. Davie hadn't understood that at the time. He wasn't sure he did now. But what he did know was that the best rules were the simple, old ones. You look after the ones you love.

The first thing he'd done when he came back to the town was to go and see 'Granny Stalin'. Bunty was with her. The old lady had surprised him by saying she agreed with his decision to stand down from Parliament. 'You're a builder. The family were aye builders. You're no' enough of a snake for that place down there. Mind, we still need our own folk to keep their eyes peeled for us.' It was clear who she meant. Over the next few weeks, Davie would put his shoulder to the wheel of Bunty's campaign.

He thought she'd probably win, actually. But she was up against a powerful opponent. Tony Moretti had never bothered with the Labour Party — he'd moved directly from the Scottish Socialists to the SNP. He badgered Davie to go for a drink with him, and although he had no intention of deflecting himself, Davie went along out of curiosity. Moretti had grown heavier, and seemed more substantial. He was perfectly friendly, but he hadn't lost an ounce of his radicalism. 'See here, Mr Petrie, it's a' very simple. We are going to build a better, fairer Scotland. I don't need to tell you about the corruption of the Westminster elite. You've been there, done it, been in it yourself, and had the good sense to get out again.'

Davie had replied with the best arguments he had — the sheer impossibility of a small country like Scotland standing up to the great forces of international business; the failure of solidarity if working-class Scots turned their backs on their brothers and sisters across the north of England; the decades when the SNP were little more than tartan Tories. But Moretti just smiled, slightly patronisingly. Moretti or Bunty? It would certainly be a fascinating fight.

There was one final thing to do. With the familiar scent of coal smoke in his nostrils, one evening Davie walked down the hill towards the railway track, in the direction of Walter Smedley's house. If he found it, he thought, he'd probably kneel in the dirt in front of it and ask for forgiveness. This, after all, was his original sin. But after half an hour of searching, he realised that the Smedley bungalow must have long disappeared. There was a new housing estate covering what had been the southern edge of the town – and built by his firm, too.

If the boys weren't ready, he decided, then he was in no hurry. 'You know me, lads, I need a project. I'm not staying down south any more. Your mother needs me here. Maybe one day you'll think you do too. No pressure, mind. Let's get down the brae and see her, shall we?'

And Davie reached out a hand to Fergus, and hoiked him up. Callum walked down the hill beside them, and just as they reached the hedge that led to the playing fields he leaned into Davie, so his father's hand rested on his head.

Final Reckonings

*It's a dull truism that politics makes good people do bad things;
the truth is that it works far better when we get bad people
doing good things.*

The Master

With Buckingham Palace effectively sold off, the king
had transferred some of his official duties to St James's Palace.
Even for him, Windsor was sometimes inconvenient. So it was
in the gloomy red state rooms there that Caroline Phillips,
fresh from her triumph at Stoke, was invited to kiss hands.
The ancient ceremony never actually happened; the king was
too interested in having a conversation with his new prime
minister. He'd been impressed with her policies towards business and the environment – particularly after Alwyn Grimaldi,
who he couldn't stand. He liked the idea of being the first
monarch ever to have a lesbian leading his government – let
them call him an old fogey after that! On the other hand,
there was a certain steeliness about her that he felt uneasy
with. That was the thing about democracy: one always had to
deal with people one didn't really *know*.

It being mid-afternoon, he had ordered a light repast of organic ginger biscuits, hand-woven on his own estate; honey-cakes made with the honey of a rare, almost extinct bee; and a bottle of English hock, produced on the sunlit uplands of Wiltshire.

Caroline arrived on time, curtsied low, and took a biscuit. She did rather light up the room, the king felt.

'Well, congratulations, Mrs Phillips. You seem to have won almost all of our filthy press round to your side. May I ask, do you think you can form a stable administration?'

'Your Royal Highness, thank you. Yes, we should have a pretty secure majority for at least a year or two. The cabinet is – between us, sir – too tired and too divided to cause any problems, and the greybeards of the party are behind me. So I think we'll cope . . .'

'. . . without the need for a general election. That is excellent news. We'll get the ceremonial business over in a jiffy, but I really want to talk to you about your plans for the country. Are you determined to return us to the bosom of Brussels?'

'Sir, I am, but it won't happen for many years. It will take endless negotiations, and the consumption of copious quantities of humble pie, with grovel sauce, to get us there. Of course, that's what politicians are for, sir, isn't it? In the meantime, the priority is to repair our relations with the United States. We can get capital from China, but we need American knowhow, freer access to their markets and so on, just to keep our chin above the water. We need to come to some new agreements pretty quickly.'

'So everybody keeps telling me. The ambassador, your old mentor, his friends . . .'

'Sir, it is absolutely not true that the Master was any kind of guide or mentor to me. The man is frankly a liability – and to you too, sir. But he's probably right about that.'

'Nothing comes from nothing, Prime Minister. What do the Americans want? What do we bring to the table?'

'The security stuff, obviously. The *Guardian* will make a stink, and there'll be trouble from a few crusty old military types in the Lords, but we'll get it through without too much difficulty. They want access to the NHS. And they'd like some tough action against the BBC, to make it easier for their media companies to make a bit of decent money over here.'

'To be frank, Prime Minister, to be very frank, I'm not at all keen on the sound of this. The BBC can be a pain in the neck, but at least it's *our* pain in our neck. And wholesale privatisation of the National Health Service would, I promise you, destroy both your party and your premiership.'

Caroline flushed, and put down her glass of wine, which was anyway warm and sickly. She was about to interrupt when the king abruptly stood up, jammed his hands into his pockets, walked towards a window and then turned around.

'I remind you, Prime Minister, of my rights – to be consulted, to be sure, and also to encourage, where that is warranted. But also to warn. You must not take this ill, but many of your predecessors have flinched from facing difficult choices of this kind – both in this very room and, before that, across the park.'

'Sir, I understand. But I assure you that I will move

cautiously. The BBC has become a problem for all the rest of the media. I propose to throttle it, very gently and very slowly, but to death. As for the NHS, again, we will move very gently. Pilot schemes, efficiency programmes, new rules on tendering. Very few of your subjects, with respect, will concentrate on any of that for very long.'

King Charles grunted. He had an excellent grunt. He'd been working on it for years. 'My family has, of course, had its ups and downs with the Americans. For more than a century, however, we have regarded them as our most reliable and trustworthy friends. But, Prime Minister, there's a big differ-ence between that and being, as it were, a wholly owned subsidiary.'

'If that were even a remote possibility, sir, I wouldn't be sitting here having this conversation. I promise you that I intend to be my own woman.'

But even as her own woman, Caro would need help. After the Palace she called Peter Quint. He had been as obliging in his article as he'd suggested. But she did not offer him an interview. She offered him the post of prime minister's press secretary. Quint, who had been a little less self-important since his interview with Angela, accepted.

Later that day, giving her first round of interviews as prime minister, Caro got Peter to have a word in the ear of the BBC's political editor. It would be of mutual benefit, suggested Quint, if he asked her about the Master. Good story. So he did, of course. On air, Caroline replied that the Master had done great service to his country, long in the past, and that he retained the affection of many of the British people; but he had no influence over the current Labour Party, and he would have none over her or her government. 'Let me make it quite plain. There will be no private meetings with, or behind-the-stairs influence from, that source. We will do everything above board. He had elements of greatness, but he has squandered too many years consorting with wealthy private individuals and serving the interests of overseas companies. He's a spent force who is no longer actively involved in the political life of this country – and he himself is very well aware of that fact.'

It was brutal. Even on this day of all days, it led the news.

The Master had had a superb new state-of-the-art running machine installed in the country house he'd bought north of London. It wasn't Chequers, but it wasn't too shabby. It had a tower, Victorian battlements and a tennis court. He had added a cinema, a heated indoor pool and cottages in the grounds for his grandchildren. There was no library; he wasn't big on books. The gym was his special pride, gleaming with oiled and sparkling equipment. The running machine came not only with multiple speeds and elevations, and a screen showing 'Great Runs of the World' – through forests, along mountain tracks and down the miraculously emptied streets of famous cities – but it also had an 'On-Board Coach' whose disembodied voice crackled out of speakers. The Master was close to his record time for a 10-k, just leaving San Francisco under the Golden Gate Bridge, with sparkling turquoise water to one side of him and the shadows of redwoods to the other. He was gasping.

'Way to go! Keep those thighs pumping!' said Coach's recorded voice.

The Master accelerated.

'Yeah! Good job! Who's the man?' Coach wanted to know.

'I'm the man,' puffed the Master.

'Damn right! Don't quit on me now,' said Coach.

'Nnnnnn . . .' said the Master.

'Who's the man?'

'I'm the man.'

But then, without warning, half a kilometre before the finishing line – which featured a row of graphically enhanced women jumping up and down, whooping and calling his name – the Master found himself slowing down. The machine was rapidly decelerating.

Coach was furious. 'Don't quit on me now! Don't you dare give up now! You a man or you a chicken?'

The Master was too exhausted to give a coherent reply, though he felt suitably rebuked. But it wasn't his fault. His wife was standing behind him, having turned the machine off.

'Sadie! I was about to beat my record. Didn't you hear Coach?' he panted.

'You really are overdoing it. Those aren't buttocks any more, they're a pair of gooseberries. I'm here on more serious business, however. Have you seen the news? Have you heard what that ghastly Phillips woman has been saying about you?'

He hadn't. As he vigorously rubbed himself down, Sadie filled him in, omitting no hurtful detail. He clicked onto News 24, and there it all was. The commentators had taken the new prime minister's words as signalling that it was open season on him, and they were all piling in – all those half-forgotten scandals, all those decomposing disappointments, freshly stirred up. The pouchy faces of his disgruntled enemies were being interviewed again and again, in a never-ending purgatorial loop of denunciation. It was Dante. It was foul.

'It's foul,' said Sadie.

The Master turned and looked her full in the face. 'No it's not. It's hurtful, yes. She's going to be a monster. But as soon as she threw her vicar to the wolves, I knew that one day she would deny me too. And in a way, it's really rather wonderful.'

'Wonderful?' spat Sadie. 'She's a cold-hearted bitch. Caroline Phillips is a bad woman!'

'Exactly. Bad people doing good things. She's just what this country needs. Of all of them, you see, my dear, she was the only one who *really* listened.'

Postscript

Mary said it was the pressure: it was only after he'd finished the job that the physical effect of those years in Westminster came home to roost for David Petrie. At any rate, while he'd been mucking in on the foundations for the new house, he'd had a mild heart attack. The cottage hospital, small as it was, had saved his life. He'd taken things a bit easier since then. The firm could almost look after itself; the new Scottish government had accelerated house-building, and in Ayrshire, Petrie Homes had a better reputation than anyone. Using the new legislation he'd brought in himself, the company was also now expanding into the construction of beautiful, traditionally-designed public buildings. Bunty, who'd lost to Tony Moretti in the by-election (the PM had been furious), was working for Davie as general manager, and doing a fine job.

One November morning, with a bright blue sky and sharp, vivid, almost horizontal light producing incandescent colours on the larches he'd planted around the new house, Davie was outside, cutting back some rose bushes. He'd just waved goodbye to Callum – a big bugger these days, but a constant delight – when he noticed a small black figure coming towards him on the new road that wound up to the house. A woman, judging by the halo of dark, crinkly-looking hair, but a tall one. He'd never seen her before in his life.

Angela had served nine months in prison. She'd found she almost enjoyed it; she worked with the prison chaplain, of course, and discovered a real talent for teaching reading and writing to her fellow unfortunates. Now she was out, and sober, the Church of England had shown true forgiveness and understanding. The possibility of being the first ever female bishop in the West Country was dangling before her.

But Angela didn't believe in loose ends. She'd tried very hard to understand Caroline, and she'd followed her closely, not with particularly hostile eyes, as she grappled with the almost impossible job of being prime minister. Lady Broderick had helped engineer her return to Pebbleton. The boys were both being ghastly, and were staying up at the big house, refusing to move to the vicarage. But the church was full, and the village, if anything, friendlier than it had been before.

'I'm sorry to turn up unannounced, Mr Petrie,' she announced. 'I think you're looking better than you used to on the telly, by the way.'

He straightened up, and stretched out a cautious hand.

'We have a mutual friend. Or we used to. I'm Angela. I felt I had to come up here to talk to you. There's so much I don't understand.'

'You won't get much help from me, I'm afraid. I don't understand it either.'

As he said this, David tried to imagine Caroline. He found he couldn't picture her. There was a bright, glazed oval, a sense of warmth, excitement — but no features at all. What colour were her eyes? What was the real shape of her nose, her mouth? Davie concentrated. He could see the Prime Minister's face clearly in a newspaper picture. But he couldn't remember her as a person, at all. Was this the truth about political success? There was always a gap between the human being and the political mask — so much was obvious, so much was well known. But then, for a successful politician the face and the mask must fuse; the flesh must grow into the caricature, so the politician is never off-guard. Eventually, there is no space between the human being and the public figure; the takeover is complete. There can never be a lapse, or a flaw, or 'the real story'. But what would you need to do to yourself to achieve that? How far would you have to go? And once you'd got there, what would you be capable of?

'I'm sorry to say,' he said, 'I think your ex-girlfriend was always a bit of a psychopath.'

'But I think you loved her. We have that in common, don't we?'

'I did. We do.' Davie lowered his voice. Mary was inside, probably watching television. Probably. 'But I always had this problem. If she'd stuck by you, if she'd been the person I hoped, I'd have wanted her — but then, of course I couldn't have had her, by definition. But because she didn't, and wasn't that person, I found I didn't want her after all . . . ken, being —'

'A psychopath? I can't disagree. Poor you. But so far she's making rather a good fist of being prime minister, isn't she?'

'She is.'

'And do you think you need to be a psychopath to be a successful politician?'

'I think it helps.'

'But you're not a psychopath.' Angela looked around her. 'You seem to me to be a happy man, in a happy place.'

'I'm not a psychopath – now. I was. But I got out in time. Others don't.'

As they'd been talking, a small, slight, golden-headed girl, no more than eight or nine years old, had appeared, and was standing beside Angela.

That was curious. Davie was sure she hadn't been there before. He remembered church times. She was a wee angel. She reminded him, somehow, of Caroline. It was very odd.

He looked straight at the vicar. 'I was going to try to persuade her to stick with you, you know. I think she truly loved you. I think you were the only person she'd ever felt anything for in her whole life. I'm truly sorry about what happened.'

Angela smiled. 'Thank you. But I've got the boys back, and I'll sort them out one day. And I haven't really lost Caroline.' She gestured at the angelic-looking little girl.

Davie leaned down and said quietly, 'Hullo, little one. Where've you come from? And what's your name?'

Angela answered for them both. 'She won't say anything. Not to you. She's called Caroline, actually. She used to hang around the other one. Now she's been deserted.'

The small girl smiled, and Davie felt himself blaze with an inexplicable sense of joy.

Many years later, on a cold, dry December morning, across a lake, beyond the willows and the gorse, in one of the wild grey ziggurats of the University of East Anglia, a seminar was held. The department of politics had invited her three bio-graphers, four professors of politics from other universities, and a dozen political writers from the major websites. The proceedings were being recorded, and published in real time on the UEA democracy site.

The smell of coffee and fresh baking wafting through the overly warm room made some of the students in the audience restless. But it was a lively morning. The final session attempted to answer directly the question: had Caroline Phillips been the most successful prime minister since the Second World War? All the wearily familiar cases were made for Clement Attlee, Harold Wilson, Margaret Thatcher, and the Master. All had, in their way, found new solutions to old problems. It was the rangy Professor Emily Catherine from Cambridge who had summed up their conclusion: in returning the UK – still as one political entity, just about – to the reformed EU and a global leadership role, and providing ten years during which private companies took a much greater share of the burden of educating and supporting working people, Caroline Phillips had proved herself a modest modern Titan. By this stage, intrusive and irrelevant questions about her private life were barely discussed. She'd been much more important than that.

Afterwards, enjoying a perfectly adequate early lunch, the academics and journalists chewed over their discussions. The man from the *Times-Mail* site felt that they'd failed to confront the hardest question of all: had she been a good person doing bad things, or a bad person doing good things? The sages there agreed that there was no chance of answering such a question.